I would like to thank Cory SerVaas and Patrick Perry for early encouragement, Billy Fitzpatrick and David Bernardi for critical editorial comments, David, Jeff, and Debra Zipes and Marilynn Wallace for helpful suggestions, and my wife Joan, my best friend and roommate, who, more than any other, helped make this book what it is.

The Black Widows

Doug Zipes

iUniverse, Inc.
New York   Bloomington

The Black Widows

This is a work of fiction. All of the characters, names, incidents, organizations, and dialogue in this novel are either the products of the author's imagination or are used fictitiously.

iUniverse books may be ordered through booksellers or by contacting:

iUniverse
1663 Liberty Drive
Bloomington, IN 47403
www.iuniverse.com
1-800-Authors (1-800-288-4677)

ISBN: 978-1-4401-8555-7 (sc)
ISBN: 978-1-4401-8553-3 (dj)
ISBN: 978-1-4401-8554-0 (ebk)

Printed in the United States of America

iUniverse rev. date: 1/28/2010

Prologue

Wahad, code name for "the first," slipped into the building and past the guard sleeping in front of the bank of four gray elevator doors. The guard's thick, hairy arms rested on the front desk, cradling his head of white hair. His loud breathing could be heard through the crook of his bent elbow. Despite the weeks of careful and vigorous training, Wahad's heart raced. The first kill was always the toughest.

The guard shifted position and coughed. Wahad tensed. The Black Widows' instructions did not include killing him, but being seen going in or out of the building was not an option. Wahad reached deep into a large pocket of the black army trousers and took out the stainless steel Bard Parker scalpel, the #10 razor-sharp surgical steel blade already in place for the operation later. The guard raised his head from the desk, eyes blinking rapidly to adjust to the light. Wahad pounced, grabbing the guard's hair and yanking back his head. With a quick slash it was all over. Messy but finished.

The black carpet muted Wahad's footsteps to the stairs around the corner from the elevators. The elevator would have been easier and quicker, but a computer system tracked each elevator trip, and an unauthorized ride this late at night would be linked to the killing. Sooner or later the cops would figure it out, but the longer discovery was delayed, the greater chance the mission had to succeed.

Wahad took the stairs two at a time and exited at the twelfth floor, barely breathing hard. After checking the empty hallway, Wahad pulled on a black hood from the knapsack and hugged the wall, melting into the shadows. Eyes searched through tiny slits in the hood for the security camera the BWs said would be concealed in the wall lights. As the camera made its thirty-second circular sweep, there was plenty of time to cover the probing lens with masking tape.

Wahad unfolded the floor plan and walked quickly to the corner office, the only one with light spilling from the window in the top half of the door. Inside, Karen Driver hunched over her computer, her back to the door. The black figure crouched, sitting back on the Nike heels, set the black knapsack onto the rug, and took out the .38 handgun. After screwing the specially-designed silencer onto the end of the barrel, Wahad stood, body slightly angled, knees flexed, and tried the door handle.

Karen stopped typing at the rattling and Wahad ducked out of sight before she swiveled around. She rose and went to the door, opened it, and peered outside.

"Anybody there?" she called, peeking into the dark hall. Seeing no one, she shrugged and returned to the computer. Wahad moved back into position and aimed at Karen through the window rather than risk opening the door again. Charging into the room would certainly make her spin around and likely force a chest shot, which was unacceptable. She *had* to die by a head shot, clean.

Right arm extended, Wahad gripped the gun handle with forefinger alongside the trigger guard and left hand supporting the gun's base, exactly as taught. The phone rang, and Karen leaned far left to reach the receiver. The angle now made the head shot risky, because the bullet could ricochet off line if it did not hit the window straight on.

"Yes, Kenneth, I'm still working," Wahad heard through the thin door. "Pretty soon. Another twenty minutes or so." She paused. "Yes, it's late, but I have to finish this last tax return and e-mail it tonight." She paused again. "I know it's a bummer, but we need the overtime. We did promise them the new Play Station ... I miss them too. Did they eat all their dinner? Okay, I'll stop for Chinese on the way home. Hot and sour soup, pot stickers, and chicken chow mein, as usual? We'll have a quiet dinner together once they're asleep. Love you too."

She phoned in the Chinese order and turned to her computer.

The conversation lingered in Wahad's mind. *A waiting family ...*

Wahad fended off the sentiment, slipped a finger through the trigger guard, aimed, and slowly squeezed. A fraction of a second after the soft pop, Karen slumped forward. Wahad smashed the window with the gun butt before returning it to the knapsack, and then entered the unlocked office. The Bard Parker blade flashed in the yellow office light a moment before it plunged through her soft skin.

And so it began.

Nine hundred ninety-nine to go.

Chapter One

As I walked down the hall toward the victim's office, a young blond-haired woman in police blues bolted through the door, hands over her mouth. Her face showed wild-eyed panic, a look I had seen before. Frantically, she glanced up and down the corridor, stepped to the left, changed her mind, and went right. Then she stopped, twisted her face to the wall, collapsed to her knees, and erupted. Vomit splashed off the baseboard, onto the rug and her clean uniform. I could hear her groan between retches, both hands grabbing her stomach.

Harry Scarpia, my partner for the last two years, poked his head out the door. He saw her and grimaced.

"They don't make 'em tough like they used to," he said, as he held the office door open for me.

"She just start?"

He nodded as I walked in. "June's graduating class. Salutatorian, she told me. Aced her homicide finals, but this is her first real one. She came in with the usual hotshot attitude: 'I'll solve this one real quickly.' But after one look at the corpse, she turned white as chalk and was out the door looking for a bathroom. I was afraid she might keel over and hit her head, so I followed her out."

"You're all heart, Harry. At least she moved fast enough not to mess up the crime scene. Transfer her to a desk till she gets her sea legs." I started to walk out of the office.

"Where're you going?" Harry asked.

"Make sure she's okay. Poor kid, it's a helluva way to start. The crime scene can wait a few minutes." Harry made a face at me as I went back into the hallway. I shook my head at him. "No, Harry, we always look after our own."

1

I saw her sitting on the floor, her back against the wall and her chin resting on her chest, eyes closed. She was pale as a corpse and sweating like hell. I wasn't sure she was conscious, so I felt her radial pulse: fast and thready.

"You okay?" I asked.

"No. I feel like shit," she said, not moving. "My stomach's flipping and I want to vomit again, but there's nothing left. My head's spinning and I feel like blacking out."

"Typical vasovagal reaction," I said, my medical background surfacing. "First of all, you need to be lying down, not sitting." I took her shoulders and gently moved her from the wall, resting her head on the floor. The floor was hard, so I took out my handkerchief, folded it, and made a tiny pillow for her. "I'll be right back. Stay here."

"I couldn't move if I wanted to."

I found the men's room and brought back a handful of paper towels soaked in cold water. I knelt down next to her, wiped the vomit from her face with one of the towels, and put the others on her forehead and neck.

Her face was pinking up. "You going to live?"

"Questionable. Thanks."

"Cops stick together. What's your name?"

"Patricia O'Malley."

"Well, Patricia O'Malley, I'm Zach Dayan."

"I know who you are, Detective."

"Good. Let's see if you can stand." I helped her up on wobbly legs. "I'll walk you to the lady's room. You can get some more wet towels and clean up. If you get faint again, lie down and prop your heels up on the wall. Once you feel normal, come back." She nodded and groped along, one hand on the wall for support, the other on me.

I walked into the office. Harry was waiting for me, scowling with impatience.

As I stood over the body of Karen Driver, I shook my head. I couldn't blame Patricia. It reminded me of some of the suicide bombings I'd seen when I was still on the Israel Defense Force. Her chest was torn to shreds, as if it had taken a direct hit from a cluster bomb or a grenade. As I stared, my legs felt unsteady, and I had to lean against the wall. I wasn't close to losing it like Patricia, but the eyes-dilated, mouth-open panic look I had seen on her face triggered memories of Yom Kippur years ago. I wouldn't let myself go there. I felt sorry for her, though; the stress of your first murder is pretty rough.

"I shouldn't have recruited her," Harry said. "She's such a wimp."

"Like you knew how she was going to react to her first stiff. Cut her some slack, Harry."

"If you were in the office when we interviewed, you could've screened her instead of me. Maybe you wouldn't have taken her. You're not the first guy to get divorced, you know."

I grunted something and stared at him. He was right. The divorce was affecting my work, and Harry had taken up the slack by interviewing the new recruits. But how the hell do you split with your wife of fifteen years, and your two kids, and stay normal? Maybe I wouldn't have to carry candy in my pockets anymore. Or, more likely, maybe I'd have to double the amount to make sure they kept on loving me.

"Sorry I spoiled your breakfast," he said.

He had called my cell phone during my usual breakfast at Le Bistro. I was starting to taste the scrambled eggs and sausage all over again, and they were not that good the first time.

The smell hit me first. You never get used to this kind of brutality. Or at least *I* don't. Not when you're actually at the scene and after what I had lived through in Israel. Pictures are easy. The smell is not. Some guys hold their breath as long as they can, but that doesn't help me. For me, the smell makes it so much more personal. I can't help thinking that these molecules—or whatever the hell causes the smell—were once part of this person in front of me, and now I'm inhaling them, taking a piece of her inside me. That's hard to accept, even after investigating hundreds, maybe thousands of murders in my ten years in homicide. I probably got a small town living in me after dealing with this stuff so long. The first few minutes are the worst; all I can do is tough it out, focus on the facts, and push on.

"Harry, tape off the hallways starting from the elevators so no gawkers from the other offices disturb the evidence." Preserving the integrity of the crime scene was most important, since defense attorneys generally attacked the *way* we collected evidence, not the evidence itself. "I got to tell you everything?"

3

His mouth got tight, but all he said was, "Sure, Zach." I heard him give the orders to the uniforms standing around.

We were pretty different, Harry and I, and not only in appearance. Harry was dark complexioned with a thick mustache and a five o'clock shadow, even though it was ten in the morning. He said it came from his Italian father and Spanish mother. My dark mustache matched his, but I had a beard showing flecks of gray—lots of flecks. Harry was careful and calculating, even anal, while I led with my gut. He filled out all the police forms on time, in triplicate, and his desk was spotless. Mine always looked like New Orleans after Hurricane Katrina.

He was tall, wiry, and trim, with curly short dark hair, and ran five miles four times a week, always in training for the next New York marathon, where he placed pretty well. I was the same height, six feet or so, but well muscled. In fact, I was the heavyweight division weightlifting champ in college. More than once after a beer or two, Harry tried to beat me in arm wrestling. I'd let him start with my hand halfway down, but I'd pin his wrist in seconds, drunk or sober. The bad thing was I added pounds in a blink if I missed a session pumping iron or looked sideways at a jelly doughnut.

I turned to the police photographer, who was staring at the body with his Nikon hanging from his neck. His bottom jaw was hanging as well. Maybe he had the same feeling about the smell that I did. Cops don't talk about these things. Makes us look soft. "Alex, I want lots of pictures from every angle. You know best, but use lots of different camera exposures, lenses, and shading, whatever you need to see what I don't." I hoped the camera would pick up something the naked eye missed. There could never be too many photos of the crime scene. He clicked away with his digital camera.

"I can't remember someone cut up this bad. You, Harry?"

Harry shook his head. "Not like this."

"Must be a dozen or more cuts across her chest." She had a clean shot to the back of her head that must've killed her instantly, but the perp repeatedly slashed the front of her chest. Slabs of skin hung like clothes on a line. I thought of my mother drying our shirts in the backyard in Jerusalem when I was a kid.

"The killer used something very sharp, judging by the thinness of the cuts," I said. "Maybe box cutters or a razor blade." Both bra straps were severed and the bra cups yanked down. Interesting, her blue plaid skirt was untouched—the hem was below her knees.

"Want me to cover her chest?" Harry must have seen the look on my face.

"Better not," I said. Locard wouldn't approve.

Chapter Two

I took a deep breath and crouched close, balancing my two hundred and twenty pounds on the balls of my feet. Lucky for her—if you can say that about a corpse—there was no frontal exit wound to mess up her pretty face. She had full lips, still faintly colored by rose lipstick. Her brown eyes were open and filmed. They stared back at me like the mineral-filled pools at Yellowstone, opalescent and dead, but still reflective.

I took plastic white gloves from my jacket pocket, snapped them on, and rolled her head to the side so I could look at the entry site. In the back I saw the bullet hole, matted down by her wavy salt-and-pepper hair. Relatively small caliber or, more likely, a silencer to quash the noise. That would explain why the bullet didn't exit or shatter the skull. The silencer had slowed it down. My legs started to cramp, and I stood and flexed each one to restart the circulation. I peeled the gloves off inside out so no blood would drip on the carpet, popped them into a Ziploc baggie, and looked around the office. Nothing seemed out of order.

The office door opened and Patricia walked in, looking sheepish. She had gotten some color back, but still looked pasty. Her light complexion added to her sickly appearance. I'd read someplace blond people were more likely to faint seeing blood than brunettes. She fit the image.

"Is there anything I can do?" she asked Harry.

"Ask him," he said, bobbing his head at me.

She walked over, taking a wide detour around the body, and looked up at me. "Thanks."

"No problem."

"Seeing her, it hit me. I knew I was losing it, and I didn't want to do it in here. I'm better now. Can I help?" Her tongue worked around her lips as her eyes darted about the room.

She held her hand out and I shook it. Her grip was firm. "Happens sometimes," I said. "Put it aside."

She was pretty, not in a model sort of way—she was way too thin for that, maybe ninety pounds soaking wet—with blonde hair and blue eyes. Although I guess a lot of models are that skinny today. About five foot one. I didn't know how she passed the physical to get her shield. Maybe she knew martial arts or something.

"Thanks. Tell me what I can do."

"Come with me. Don't say a word, and be ready to tell me what you think, but only when I ask."

I walked over to the desk. It had the usual office stuff—pencils, paper clips, and a computer.

"That'll go to the FBI lab," I told her, pointing at the Dell. "They're specialists in squeezing every morsel from a hard drive. Everybody thinks when you delete something from a computer it disappears, but the Bureau guys have ways to find material people think is gone."

"Where do you start?" Patricia asked.

"At a murder scene, the first thing I do is recreate how it happened, based on the evidence. That's what Locard did."

"Who?"

"Locard. He was known as the Sherlock Holmes of France, a forensic scientist who died maybe forty years ago. Locard's Exchange Principle was that every contact left trace evidence. It was there; it was just up to us to find it and use it."

I leaned back, propped a foot against the wall, and took in the entire scene. I tried to project myself into the murder, to become the murderer, to get into his head. She appeared to do the same, even propping her foot back like mine.

After a few minutes, I turned to Patricia. "So, what do you think?"

Her color had returned, and she lit up when I asked for her opinion. Maybe eagerness would make up for what she lacked in size.

"There are three obvious facts. First, there's blood on the keyboard. Then, the body on the floor, and finally the broken door window. So the vic must have been sitting at her desk with her back to the door and slumped forward, propelled by the bullet through her head. The drag marks on the rug," she pointed, "fit with the killer pulling her to the floor and then slashing her chest open."

"How do you know she wasn't slashed sitting at her desk?"

"Arterial blood splatters in pretty specific ways, according to the laws of hydrodynamics. That's been studied lots of times." She looked at me.

My eyebrows must have risen, because she added quickly, "As I'm sure you very well know." She continued. "She had to have bled on the carpet because pools of blood have mingled with the beige nap. So, at that time, her head was dead but her heart was not, still pumping away when she got slashed."

"Good. But why?"

"She has a silver Seiko watch, not top of the line but still expensive enough, and it's still on her wrist,"—again she pointed—"and the guys had told me they found fifty-five dollars in her purse. Clearly not a robbery."

"Okay, but what about the broken window? That doesn't fit."

"Why not?" she asked.

"Because if the bullet is still in her head, it must mean it didn't have the weight and speed to exit."

"So?"

"So not enough velocity to shatter the window."

Patricia looked puzzled for a moment. But then a smile creased her face as she walked to the door, bent and retrieved several large glass splinters. She held one up and looked at me through the intact bullet hole.

"This what you're looking for?"

"Very good. The killer must've smashed the glass after shooting Driver so we wouldn't be able to analyze the hole. I bet he looked for the slug, too. Good thing he wasn't a brain surgeon." Patricia gave the piece of glass to Harry, who slid it into a large padded envelope for crime lab analysis later.

"What about the casing?" she asked me.

"The killer either picked it up or used a revolver."

She continued to look for a casing but came up empty.

"So that was the 'how.' Now for the 'who' and 'why.' Sex?" I asked.

She shook her head. "I don't think so, not with the hem of her skirt down around her knees. Yet her breasts were slashed. Personal hatred?"

"I doubt it." I thought Driver didn't look the type to arouse such anger in another person. Not with that pretty, delicate face.

"Maybe he was a psycho who somehow had gotten into the building looking for any victim and just lost it when he found one," Patricia said.

"Harry, what do you think?" I asked.

"A random killing? Lord knows we've had enough of them," Harry said.

I shook my head. "This is too well planned. Hell, he had to kill the security guard and bring two weapons."

"But the single shot killed her," Patricia said. "Why the butchering? And why shoot through a window ten feet away and risk the bullet deflecting instead of entering the office and killing her up close? Or killing her with the knife, like he did the guard? It was late at night, so no one would have heard her cry out. Doesn't compute."

My gut told me she was right, and that there might be more murders. But this wasn't your typical serial killer.

"Run it through BSU?" Harry asked.

"I thought about that," I said. The Behavioral Sciences Unit of the FBI in Washington profiled serial killers. "Problem is, they'll give me a picture that'd fit thousands of people. Serial killers are your neighbors, business associates, even priests. Psychos, but not insane—just no conscience. And they'll tell me it couldn't be a woman, because women are rarely serial killers, and even when one knocked off a bunch of husbands she used poison or something like that. Not a gun."

"Still, it may be a good job for me to pursue?" Patricia asked, her voice hopeful.

I looked at Harry. He gave a slight head nod. "Okay."

"I'm on my way," she said, gathering her things and leaving the office a bit too eagerly.

"She going to make it?" I asked Harry as the door closed.

"She's as eager as any I've seen. Bright as hell on paper. But wimpy, as you saw."

"Give her a chance, she'll come around," I said. "A good head makes up for a lot. I liked the way she pieced the evidence together."

"I'll keep her at a desk for a while," Harry said.

I took out my Meerschaum pipe. I always reasoned better with that thing in my mouth. I fingered the hand-carved lion's head. It used to be white, but now was deep amber from many years of heat and smoke. Miriam had bought me that pipe to celebrate our first wedding anniversary, when we barely had food money. I always carried Flying Dutchman pipe tobacco in a brown leather pouch that was now pretty worn and cracked. Slowly I filled the bowl. I followed the same ritual ever since I switched from cigarettes to a pipe more than fifteen years ago: I packed the tobacco down tight at the bottom and sides and more loosely in the middle and top for easy drawing. Then the sweet tobacco aroma would permeate the air. Now, living in my own apartment, I could even smoke indoors. The pipe stem knew my mouth and settled easily against my teeth. I had worn grooves in the hard yellow plastic, and it slid into place. I hated the smooth contour of a new pipe stem, which I had to replace about every three or four months because my teeth drilled a hole through it. The guy in the pipe store knew me pretty well by now. It was like breaking in a new pair of shoes, and I constantly shifted the stem from side to side in my mouth, chewing and grinding until it fit my teeth like a key in a lock.

The stale tobacco residue from my after-breakfast smoke tasted bitter. But it was a good bitter. I let the cold fluid roll around my mouth. I once watched a wine tasting show on TV, and I could imitate the wine experts as they tongued samples. But I didn't spit mine out. I was as hooked as the crack addicts I arrested.

"Harry." He was now at the computer, lifting prints before taking it to the FBI lab. "What else you got?"

He put down his fingerprint kit and carefully walked around the body to where I was standing. Clad in double-layered booties, he tiptoed around the pools of blood, barely looking at the corpse.

Harry wore the best of Italy, always with a white Zegna shirt, Brioni tie, and Gucci shoes that you could see your face in. Miriam used to tease me that I could stand in as the poster boy for Goodwill, complete with tiny burn holes in my jacket from pipe cinders. Then she'd make nice, or try to, by kissing me and saying, "But a real good-looking one with beautiful browns," and she'd kiss each eyelid. She tried to jazz me up once with a monogrammed handkerchief for my birthday, but it didn't take, even though I still carried the handkerchief with me.

I liked to think my body contoured my clothes, while Harry's hand-tailored suits shaped his. I guess maybe I was a little jealous of his nice threads, since most of my salary went toward alimony and child support.

"Not much, Zach," Harry said, removing his gloves to consult a small black spiral notebook pulled from his pants pocket. "Karen Driver, 44, certified public accountant, apparently happily married to a minister, with three kids, two girls and a boy. She was working after hours, getting some tax statements ready for her clients, according to her husband. Probably alone, on this floor at least. All co-workers had left an hour or more before, so no chance of spotting the killer.

"She made her last call from her phone to China Ruby at eight forty-one, ordering takeout dinner for two, to be picked up in twenty minutes. So she was getting ready to leave. It takes about ten minutes to get to the Chinese restaurant from here."

"Bummer she didn't leave earlier. And why be killed tonight and not one of the other nights? Why was this one different?" After I said that, I remembered one of the four questions Jews asked each other on Passover: *Why is this night different from all other nights? We escaped the Angel of Death* was the reply.

"Don't know," Harry said.

"Prints?"

"Not from the perp. Her prints are smeared on the doorknob, so he probably wore gloves and turned the knob after she did."

"Vacuum the office?"

"Crime scene guys already did."

"And the guard in the lobby?"

"Apparently asleep before he got his throat cut."

"Was he on the other nights?"

"No. The usual guard was but got a sore throat, and this guy replaced him at the last minute."

Before I could ask him the obvious question, Harry said, "I checked it out. The usual guard actually had a script for amoxicillin from his doctor, so he really was sick."

That was a good follow up. But it started me thinking. It was incredible how fate, or luck or whatever you believed, could turn your life on a dime. A single event triggered an avalanche of consequences. One man's strep throat allowed that man to live while another man died. Like missing a plane because you get stuck in traffic and then the plane crashes. And the guy who thought he was lucky to get your plane seat is now toast.

"What about the video?"

"We're checking the film from the surveillance camera on this floor, though the perp taped the lens so I doubt we'll get anything useful. Tape was generic. No video in the lobby."

"She have a rap sheet?"

"Not even a speeding ticket."

Harry turned a page. "Mortgage, but no other debts. Didn't gamble but was a heavy smoker. Two packs a day. Tried to quit lots of times but couldn't. Nicotine chewing gum in her purse and a nicotine patch, along with an unfilled prescription for Wellbutrin. Took frequent short breaks to go outside the building and have a drag. Had some heart problems according to her husband, but we haven't been able to track down her doctor yet. Two bottles of heart meds in her purse—digitalis and Lasix. That's it." The way Harry closed his notebook and shrugged his shoulders told me he was passing the buck. That was okay. It went with the job of being head of homicide and covering about a murder a day. Life in the Big Apple was not for the fainthearted.

"That's bullshit," I said. "Nobody gets shot and filleted like this if that's all there is to it. She was dead when he slashed her and sure as hell wasn't resisting. Not likely we'll find anything useful under her fingernails, but bag her hands anyway just in case."

"I agree," Harry said. "This morning I spent three hours with all the workers on this floor and got nada. The woman has never been out of the country, voted Democratic, and contributed annually to the Methodist church, United Way, and the local police. Paid her dues on time to the American Institute of Certified Public Accountants. Even sang in the church choir. There was no reason for her to get whacked, certainly not like this."

"You're sure you've got the vices covered? No boyfriend or co-worker she pissed off?"

Harry shook his head.

"Husband?"

"Says he was home with the kids waiting for her to bring in Chinese for dinner. Checked with the restaurant and she did order. Something about him, though."

"Like what?"

"I don't know. My vibes. Maybe not sad enough?"

"What did you find when you searched the house?"

Harry's mouth turned down and he shook his head. "Nothing. He had a set of steak knives I took in for testing. To shave he uses one of those triple-bladed razors, which couldn't have made those cuts. I went through his clothes closet and his laundry. No blood on anything. Nothing else."

"But you still had vibes?"

He nodded yes.

"I'll check it out. Who's doing the autopsy?"

"New York City medical examiner has jurisdiction. Dr. John Hunter."

I grimaced. "Driver's our answer, the way she was killed. The chest slashing's the clue. And the autopsy's got to be done right. I want a forensic pathology expert. Somebody from the Armed Services Institute of Pathology in Washington." That was the closest I could come up with someone of Locard's caliber.

"From where?"

"You heard me. ASIP. My hunch is there's more to this than a simple killing. When's the last time we had a murder like this? It's too vicious; some local medical examiner won't be able to handle it."

"You just reminded me of one."

"Which one?"

"Donahue."

"That's just it. Think, for Christ's sake. The Donahue case was a vicious killing *because* the husband had a purpose in mind, to prevent anyone from ID'ing the body." A deacon at a church killed his wife and cut off her fingers and head so she couldn't be identified. Then he put them in the garbage for trash removal.

"So whoever did the chest slashing here had a purpose in mind. But why slash her after she's already dead? We answer that and we solve the case. I know a lady pathologist at the ASIP. Specializes in the heart. JJ's her name. I've used her a couple of times in the past before you joined. An Indian doctor," I said.

"I'll do what I can. Hunter's got first dibs and I know he won't want a Washington gunslinger brought in on this."

"Tough. Just tell him not to mess up the body too bad before a real pro gets to her."

Harry's eyebrow arched. "Yeah, sure I will. He'll be pleased as hell to hear that. He'll probably bulls-eye me with a damn scalpel."

"Then learn how to duck."

"You plan on being there?"

"Somebody has to watch that guy."

Chapter Three

And that would be me. Most people didn't know I actually went through the first two years of medical school, so I knew what to look for more than the average detective.

St. George's, University of London, was where I went. And I thought about it afterward, every day of my life.

London was a great adventure for a twenty-two-year-old, on my own for the first time since graduating Hebrew University in Jerusalem, where I lived at home to save money. I wanted to travel. My father wanted me to become a doctor. We struck a bargain: I would go to medical school outside Israel and he would pay for it. After graduation, I would return to Israel and go into practice, perhaps with him.

The first year, and most of the second, we spent focused on classroom fundamentals like anatomy, biochemistry, and pharmacology. Then, toward the end of the second year, we had the chance to put all that knowledge to use, seeing patients under the watchful eye of an experienced clinician.

Medical rounds started at 7:00 a.m. sharp. The professor was a grizzled old guy known for his ruthless treatment of medical students and interns, especially those not prepared. He had an encyclopedic knowledge of medicine and was an effective teacher, though brutal. His attitude was that you needed an emotional incentive to learn, and he gave us one—fear. If one of us screwed up during the night, when we presented the patient to him the next morning, he would say, "What this patient needs is a doctor," and you were branded with a scarlet letter for the rest of the year, if not for the rest of medical school.

We turned summersaults to please him and spent hours preparing our cases. Still, he was so intimidating you could almost hear our sphincters snap shut when he walked into the room.

During ward rounds, the professor would examine each patient, comment on the unusual physical findings, and then we in turn would listen to the lungs and heart and observe whatever was of interest.

A twenty-seven-year-old mother of two boys, ages two and five, changed my life forever.

She was tiny and debilitated from a heart problem, a particularly aggressive form of rheumatic heart disease that had narrowed her mitral valve to the point where she needed surgery. She was still beautiful, with blonde hair and blue eyes, but in a fragile way. A heart catheterization was planned later that morning to determine the extent of the damage prior to open heart surgery. "Routine," her doctor said.

She was the first female patient I had ever examined. I was struck by how casually the professor opened the front of her gown to listen to her heart, exposing her breasts without even an attempt at modesty. I looked away and stared at her nightstand, where there was a picture of her holding one son on her lap, the other standing next to her on one side and her husband on the other, his hand on her shoulder. She was even more beautiful then, more robust, with an angelic look on her face. A lovely family.

I can still hear his gruff voice. "Zachery, did you hear what I said about mitral stenosis?"

"Yes, sir," I lied.

"Fine. Then tell me what to listen for." I could hardly concentrate with the woman lying exposed on the bed.

Fortunately, the intern had warned me about the diagnosis and I had read the chapter on mitral stenosis and the abnormal heart sounds and murmurs it produced. I told him what they were. He only grunted, perhaps disappointed at not being able to skewer another medical student. "Then, listen," he said, pointing to her chest.

I plugged the ear pieces of the stethoscope into my ears and bent my head toward her chest. Her young breasts rose and fell inches from my face, and I could see the whitish stretch marks from her previous pregnancies fanning out like spokes from her nipples. I wondered if her husband gently traced them with his fingers when they made love. I know I would have. When I finished listening, my forehead was beaded with moisture and my hands were trembling. I smiled a silent thank you at her. She smiled back.

"You're welcome. I hope I helped you learn a little," she said.

I assured her she had and fumbled to close the front of her gown.

"Leave it open," the professor said, "so the others can listen."

Later that morning, the girl went for her catheterization and came back several hours later complaining of chest pain. The nurse paged me to see her.

"My heart hurts," she said, "and I can't catch my breath."

I listened to her lungs and heart as before, this time really focusing. I recognized the fast, irregular rhythm of atrial fibrillation she must have developed from the cath. I quickly ran an EKG, which proved I had made the right diagnosis. She needed my help right away. Her narrowed valve couldn't handle a heart rate of one hundred sixty per minute for very long.

"Give her a beta blocker IV to slow her heart rate and then start quinidine orally," my professor said when I called him on the phone. "I'm tied up right now, so write the orders for the nurses. If the quinidine doesn't work, we'll have to cardiovert her electrically." He gave me the doses he wanted and I did what he asked.

An hour later, I was gulping down a fast-food lunch when I heard the code over the loudspeaker system. I went running to her room. She had suffered a cardiac arrest, and at least six doctors surrounded her bed trying to resuscitate her. One was giving her oxygen through an Ambu bag, and another was pumping on her chest. Someone else was running an EKG, another was giving IV medications, and several were conferring in hushed tones.

My professor came charging up, breathing hard. "What in God's name happened?" he asked when he saw me.

"I don't know, sir. I heard the code and just got here."

"Anaphylactic shock," said one of the senior attendings who had been seeing a patient in the next room and was first on the scene. "Apparently her blood pressure dropped to zero and then she went into cardiac arrest. We defibrillated her pretty quickly, but I'm afraid having no blood pressure for even that short a time, coupled with her mitral stenosis, may have been too much for her. Her pupils are fixed and dilated, and she is non-responsive. I think she's brain dead. It doesn't look like we're going to get her back."

"My God, she's only a kid," said the professor.

The attending shrugged. "Allergic reaction is hard to predict sometimes."

The professor stormed out to the nurses' station with me trailing behind. I could barely see through my tears. "Give me her chart," he demanded.

A nurse handed it to him, and a moment later he stared hard at me, his eyes lasering holes through mine. His tone was quiet, ominous.

"You took a history from her when she was admitted, did you not?" he asked, more an accusation than a question.

I was barely able to nod.

"Did you pay any attention to what she told you?"

"Yes, sir," I said. "I wrote it down in my evaluation."

"Yes, so you did. Read what you wrote. Over here." He pointed to the second page of my write up and thrust it in my face.

My heart stopped. "*Allergic to penicillin and quinidine.*" I had totally forgotten what I had written, what she had told me in plain English when she was admitted, what she had then trusted me *not* to give her.

"You killed her! You bloody well killed her!"

I felt numb. It didn't matter that he had given me the order to start quinidine. I was responsible. I should have remembered and stopped him when he ordered the medication. The picture of her with her family flashed through my mind, and the image of her so trusting, so open, helping us learn, helping *me* learn. *Allergic to quinidine* pounded in my head. Guilt, a hot coal in the pit of my stomach, grew until it felt like my gut was on fire. I had to cling to the wall or collapse.

"In my forty years caring for patients, there have been many I haven't been able to help, but I've never harmed a patient," he said. "Not once, do you hear me? '*Primum non nocere,*' above all, *do no harm*, remember? Hippocrates? The oath you took? She needed a doctor she could trust, and you weren't there for her. Find another profession, Mr. Dayan, because you're finished here."

I don't remember leaving the hospital, and I can't remember exactly where I went or what I did in those first weeks after that. It's all a blur. I know I attended her funeral, but I couldn't muster the courage to talk with her husband or kids. I stood in the back, ashamed, hiding behind a pillar in the church, wanting to apologize but frozen in time and place. There was talk of a lawsuit, but the hospital quietly settled with the widower. I was formally chastised by the school's disciplinary committee and asked to resign, which I did. I didn't tell my folks and kept my phone calls with them short.

Alcohol eased some of my pain.

Chapter Four

Kenneth Driver answered the door at my first ring. He was a good-looking guy, mid-to-late forties, I'd guess, with a thick head of black hair and solid build. Probably pumped iron at some point. His macho looks made it hard to picture him in clerical garb.

After I introduced myself and flashed my badge, he let out a gasp. His frown made it clear he was not happy to see me. But he let me in and we sat in his small living room. As I settled in the chair, my jacket opened and I could see his eyes travel to my holstered gun. The tough facade dissolved, and it didn't take a Locard to see him fight back tears.

"Twelve years next week," he said, shaking his head. "We were going to get a sitter for the kids and rent a hotel room in town, no smoking for me but with a balcony so she could."

"Was she a big smoker?"

"Yes, until she had a heart attack couple of years ago. Then cut back to half a pack. She tried to quit lots of times but couldn't."

He buried his face in his hands and I could hear him willing himself to breathe slowly in and out, but his chest seemed to have a mind of its own, and he was sucking air as if he had just run up a flight of stairs.

"I see a shrink for hyperventilation and he tells me, 'Slow your breathing down when you're upset or anxious.' And for that he charges me a hundred and fifty bucks an hour. My wife told me the same thing for free."

I watched his hands open and close as his fingers gripped his sides, fighting the quickening respirations. I had never formally studied kinesics, the interpretation of non-verbal behavior like facial expressions, gestures, and breathing, but even an amateur could read what *his* body was saying. It wasn't just sadness. It was panic.

I asked some simple questions about his ministry to calm him down—how long he'd been a minister, how many congregants, stuff like that—and got simple answers. I needed to bond with him. He stopped hugging his chest and his breathing slowed a little as I connected.

"I know it's tough to talk about, but I need you to tell me about your wife."

"Like what?"

"Like where she went, what she did, who she knew."

He fidgeted and then sat on his hands.

"She was a good person. Didn't do anything unusual. Worked hard, took good care of the kids and me."

"You two get along okay?"

"Yes, absolutely." His response was a bit too quick, I thought. He didn't look like a killer, but I remembered the Donahue case. Maybe he sensed my feeling. "Well, we fought on occasion."

"Over what?"

"Usual stuff. In-laws, money, the TV remote." He smiled saying that.

"Did you argue a lot?"

He shook his head. His breathing was picking up, his hands restless.

"Did you know all her friends?"

A nod and his hands came up, kind of pushing me away. *Don't go there* his body was saying.

"No one she saw without you? Someone who might have done this?"

He shifted in his chair and now his eyes darted around the room. The corners filled up and he squeezed the base of his nose with his fingers. What the hell had I said?

"Something you want to tell me, Mr. Driver?"

He shook his head.

"If you need to unload, now'd be a good time."

He sat motionless. I suddenly realized what his body language was telling me.

"Someone *you* saw without *her*?"

21

After a long pause he reached for a tissue from the box on the table.

"It's my fault," he said.

"Why?"

"Francine said she would find a way to get even when I broke it off."

"Who's Francine?"

"Francine Walters. A friend. Lives in the city."

"You have an address?"

"Corner of Sixty-fourth and Lexington. An old brownstone apartment building. Look, am I under suspicion?"

"Should you be?"

"I didn't kill her. But …"

"But what?" I watched him wringing his hands. He sat without saying anything. "But what?"

"I haven't been exactly faithful." The color drained from his face.

"Want to tell me about it?"

"Not really."

"Your decision, but I remind you husbands are often prime suspects in a murder like this."

His eyes widened and he went silent. Then he seemed to make up his mind and his breathing slowed.

"She's quite seductive. Even at church when she leaned over in the first pew to kneel and pray, I couldn't keep my eyes on my prayer book. I once read a description in a paperback that was me all the way. *'His eyes clung to her like a hot iron on a wet shirt.'* Did mine ever."

He stopped, staring in the distance.

"Go on."

The prompt made his eyes drift back as if they regretted leaving the image, and he crossed his legs. I think the guy got a hard-on just thinking about her.

"But I wasn't going to leave Karen and the kids for anything. Francine was only a little fling. Lots of one-nighters and once a weekend at the Sleepy Hollow Inn in Tarrytown, when Karen took the kids to visit her mother in Charlotte."

"Why not her place?"

"Frankie liked adventure."

I made a note to check with the hotel. I knew it well. Right near a great golf course in Westchester that I used to play about once a year when the owners wanted to suck ass with the NYPD. There were a lot of members who lived in the city and appreciated not getting nailed for parking violations.

"You ever do something like this before?"

He paused and looked at the rug. "Once, after we got married. We had a fight and I went walking out alone to cool off. A prostitute solicited me, and we had an hour fling. But that's the only time, ever. I swear. "

"How'd you meet her?"

"At a Pilates class my church sponsored. We held a fitness night for singles. You know how these young kids are into exercising. I figured it would bring them into the church. Ecumenical exercise. Next thing I know, she's attending my sermons and sitting in the first pew."

He smiled.

"Something funny?"

"I was just remembering. She came in looking like some Hollywood actress, low-cut blouse sort of thing and a gold bellybutton ring."

"I guess that would cause a stir in church."

Driver nodded. "During the next Pilates workout, she suggested I meet her in a hotel bar for a drink after the class ended. So we did. We had a few drinks, and the next thing I know we're in bed in a room upstairs."

"And then?"

"We met after classes pretty routinely until the sixteen-week course ended. Then we had that weekend I told you about. At that time, Francine asked me to leave Karen, but I wouldn't. I couldn't. We joked about pulling a 'same time next year' fling, but I was having second thoughts. I've counseled enough people on the best thing to do in this situation, so I decided to take my own advice and call it quits. She got very upset and made all kinds of threats and stomped out. That's the last I've seen her."

"Do you think she could've done it?"

Driver shrugged. "She has a short fuse and gets angry really quickly. She had some sort of upsetting home life she wouldn't discuss and often exploded over some trivial thing, often about the church or religion. The next minute she would be as nice as could be."

He stopped talking, but the sentence hung there unfinished.

"And?"

"She carries a gun."

"What?"

"She showed it to me. Said she was 'packing' and was not ever going to be a victim. Not in New York City or any other place. She even gave it a name. Called it Boom Boom."

Pretty remarkable, I thought, in New York's post-9/11 consciousness, with security detection in almost every building.

"You didn't tell my partner Harry Scarpia any of this."

He shook his head.

"Why not?"

"It's obvious. If this got out it would ruin my ministry."

"And?"

"And he might think I killed Karen, or maybe that I planned it with Francine."

"Then why tell me?"

"I don't know. The way you're sitting here talking to me, you seem like someone I could trust. Your partner stomped around and said things as if he was already convinced I killed her."

"How do *I* know you didn't?"

"I was home waiting for her."

"Doing what?"

"I'll show you."

He led me to one of the bedrooms. Two little girls were sitting on the rug listlessly holding their dolls. "That's what," he said, pointing. "Taking care of them. Karen was going to bring in Chinese for us."

The older one ran over and tugged on his arm. Tears rolled from her brown eyes and her nose dripped. She looked like her mom.

Driver pulled out his handkerchief. "Blow." She blew once and then pushed his hand away. She hugged him around the waist and buried her face in his shirt, her chest jerking with each sob. Driver wrapped both arms around her, hugging her close. The younger one came over and stared up at him. He squatted and held them both.

I reached into my pocket and pulled out two Harry London Butterscotch candies. I held out my hand and silently each little girl took one.

A boy of about ten or eleven came in and stood in the doorway. "I hate God!" he shouted and slammed his fist on the door. He glared at his father, hands on hips, chin jutting. He had his father's features, but his eyes were sparking. "You always say God can do anything and watches over us. Then why did He let this happen to Mommy? She never did anything wrong. Not to anybody. Why punish her?"

Driver cringed. He had no answer and looked vacantly at his son, slowly shaking his head and shrugging. I left as he pulled his two daughters tight to him and rocked slowly back and forth, mouth open, starting to gasp like a hooked fish out of water.

Harry was wrong. Driver didn't kill his wife.

Chapter Five

I drove back to headquarters, my mind replaying the picture of Driver with his arms around his little girls. The sad scene spoke of the family intimacy he had squandered before her murder. How many times had that same scenario played out in history? Husbands or wives driven by foolish urges that ruined the really important things they had. And then they were left with a lifetime of regrets.

I was a good example. It was easy to say, "My wife and family come first," and I would tell the young guys who came on the force exactly that. But I didn't follow my own advice. Even after Miriam and I were counseled by the rabbi, and he told me, "I've never been at the bed of a dying man who said he wished he'd spent more time at the office," I couldn't stop saying yes to "cop things." I skipped a lot of birthday parties, and you don't get second chances at those.

After the divorce, I still saw my kids on alternate weekends and Wednesdays, but I missed the simple things I took for granted as a father living at home. Their soft arms around my neck when I carried them to bed, sleepy heads with silky hair nestled into my neck. Their pleas for one more story before they'd go to sleep. Seeing the world through their eyes, like the one time I could get away for a week and took them to Disneyworld, watching how they were a little scared and then enraptured by Mickey and Goofy. They tasted their first Harry London candies on that trip, and I had carried them in my pockets ever since. I guess, overall, I missed the intimacy of a family life, where I could love them, protect them, and care for them.

I had it, but I blew it. Well, maybe not just me. Miriam helped, I think, by wanting out of her present life. She no longer took the kids to Sunday school or Friday night services—stuff like that. Secretly, I think she was going back to church. But I was the major factor. The final straw came when Miriam really needed me and I was not there for her and our daughter.

Rachel, our older child, was always a bit sickly. Got short of breath, easily fatigued, and couldn't keep up with the other kids in her class. Our pediatrician, an old-timer named Finnegan, examined Rachel and said she was fine. All she needed was more sleep, he said.

One day in school, Rachel had a blackout spell while chasing a friend on the playground. She lost consciousness for a couple of minutes, but by the time the school nurse arrived, she was fine. The nurse called Miriam to bring her to the doctor, and Miriam called me. But I was on a stakeout with no backup. There was no way I could leave right then without putting Harry at great risk. Plus, frankly, it didn't seem that serious to me.

"She's okay," I told Miriam. "Just bring her to Finnegan and I'll meet you there as soon as headquarters sends a replacement." Miriam became hysterical, yelling that I wouldn't even help my own child, that Harry was more important, before she slammed down the phone.

On the way to Finnegan's office, Rachel had another blackout, and this time she stopped breathing. The hospital was less than half a mile away, but instead of stomping the pedal to the floor, Miriam lost it. She jammed on her brakes, pulled off to the side of the road, and flagged the next passing car, screaming her daughter was going to die. Fortunately, it happened to be some nurse who knew CPR. She called 911 on her cell phone, started resuscitating Rachel, and by the time the EMTs came, Rachel was fine again.

They took her to the hospital, where she was examined by a pediatric cardiologist. Turned out she had congenital complete heart block, something to do with Miriam's antibodies attacking the baby's heart and screwing up the electrical wiring. So Rachel was born with a heart rate that couldn't go much faster than forty or fifty, and sometimes that wasn't enough to pump blood to her brain, and she would black out. The heart doctor said it probably had been going on for a while and we never noticed it. She needed a pacemaker. That was a pretty simple thing. The pacemaker itself was not much bigger than a fat silver dollar, and after they put it in, she was perfect—but our marriage wasn't.

I still loved Miriam, and I would do all I could to help her, but the marriage was no longer working. I think she wanted to become Erika again.

****

The day I left medical school I met Erika at the Golden Stag, a pub near my flat. I had no place to go and too much to think about, so I began drinking. I considered suicide and decided I'd do it with booze.

The Golden Stag was at least a hundred years old, with lots of dark, shiny mahogany, and it smelled of countless glasses of ale, drunk and spilled. The owners were a kind, elderly couple. The wife cooked and the husband tended bar, while Erika von Hummel served the few tables. She was a pretty lady, about my age, a few inches shorter, with dark Middle Eastern features but the facial structure of a Westerner. She had understanding eyes, soft and deep brown. Gentle. She later told me she needed the job to pay her way through art school. The owners gave her flexible working hours and even lent her tuition money, knowing they might never get it back.

In my more sober moments, I watched her work the tables. She seemed to have a gift with people, quieting an unruly drunk or laughing happily with a group, sharing their birthday celebration. There was an old upright piano in the back of the pub, and when things were slow, Erika sometimes played. I didn't know much about music, but whatever she played sounded pretty great to me. Occasionally, the people at the bar started to sing something, like "Danny Boy," and she would accompany them.

Early one Saturday afternoon, two men burst into the pub wearing stocking masks and waving guns.

"Nobody move or I'll shoot," one of them shouted. Judging by his slow movements and shaky voice, he seemed to be an older man. The other guy hung in the background, casually standing near the door, his gun put away.

"You," the old guy pointed his gun at Erika, "open the cash register."

Erika was busy with a customer and didn't move fast enough for him, so he aimed the gun at the ceiling and let off a round. It sounded like thunder in the small room, and we all jumped. Erika went to the cash register, scooped out a handful of bills, and gave them to him. He pocketed the money, waved his gun at all of us, and said, "Don't anybody move until we're gone." The two of them left and Erika went on serving the customers, none of whom seemed too upset. My eyes were glued to her face and I was amazed at how composed she seemed.

I was pretty drunk, and I thought maybe I had been hallucinating. I remember yelling, "Isn't anyone going to call the police?"

The guy at the table next to me leaned over with an amused look on his face and asked, "How long you been coming here?"

"Couple of weeks."

"Then you don't know Sir Thomas Middlethorpe?"

I shook my head.

"His father was a baron or something. Sir Thomas is a harmless old nut, pretty wealthy, lives on a big estate outside Brighton. Must be at least eighty. Fancies himself Willie Sutton."

"Who's that?"

"Guy robbed about a hundred banks in the States during the Great Depression. Said he robbed banks 'because that's where the money is.' That became Sutton's Law: go where the money is. No banks close by, so Sir Thomas robs the pub."

"And the gun?"

"Like Willie, it only shoots blanks," Erika said, her voice a little shaky despite appearing unruffled. "This time he pointed it at the ceiling. It gets pretty dicey when he points it at me and it goes off with that loud bang. But I stand my ground now. First time, though, I fainted dead away. No one warned me."

"How can he get away with it?"

"Been doing it for years, once every several months. Cops locked him up the first few times and made him see a shrink, but now he's only a nuisance and nobody bothers. He's supposed to be on medication. The guy at the door—I guess you'd call him Sir Thomas's manservant—will return with the money in an hour or so, along with a big payment for the owner. That's why it doesn't get reported anymore," she said, her voice now steady. "He's a nice old codger, means no harm." She smiled at the husband and wife behind the bar. "And those two have been so grand to me. They need the money he gives them for the charade. I put up with it for them."

"You're a good person," I said.

Erika left to tend a customer and I went back to my ale.

After helping fuel my drunken state for another week or so, early one evening Erika sat down next to me.

"Enough," she said, pushing my glass aside. "Want to talk?"

I shook my head no.

"Lost your love?"

"No. I mean, yes."

"To another guy?"

"No."

"Then, what?"

Crazy, but in my head I think I actually loved that patient. How could you not, when someone so vulnerable puts total faith in you? It's like holding a helpless baby animal in your hands, a motherless lion cub for instance, protecting it from other wild things in the jungle, and bottle-nursing it. It crept into your heart, and then you dropped it and it died. And you'd never be the same.

I tried to explain but I started to cry, little sobs first, then an avalanche. She sat there and held my hand until I stopped, crying a little herself. Fortunately, it was still early and the pub was mostly empty.

"Now do you want to talk?" she asked after we both dried up. And so I told her everything. When I finished, she said, "Let's start by getting you something solid to eat."

She brought me some sort of pot pie and I wolfed it down. It was the first solid food I'd had in two weeks. It didn't stay down long, but I ate a second one several hours later and that one was okay. We talked until the evening crowd began to come in and she had to go back to the tables. She brought me dinner and a glass of orange juice. I remained until closing, and then walked her home.

"Can I see you again?"

"I was hoping you'd ask," she said.

Chapter Six

I dreaded telling my father about both medical school and Erika. He was angrier about her than my leaving medical school. I didn't tell him the real reason I left, only that I wasn't cut out to be a doctor, which he really knew from the beginning but hadn't wanted to admit.

"Are you crazy? Are you totally out of your mind? A German girl you want to take out when there are hundreds of nice Jewish girls here in Jerusalem waiting for you." We argued on the phone for an hour or more, and he made me promise I would stop seeing her.

But we began dating and I fell in love. Erika's roommate had just moved out, and when she suggested I move in with her, I didn't think twice. I was as happy as I had ever been, even though I had no school and no job. Erika was so patient and understanding. She was working at the pub at night and weekends and going to school during the day, so breakfast became shrink sessions for me.

"Yes, you should have remembered she was allergic to that medicine, but people make mistakes. We all do. You can't hit 'replay' and rewind your life to do it over. But what you can do is to learn from what happened and become a bigger person for it. I don't remember who said something like 'that which doesn't kill you makes you stronger,' but it's true. What you need to do now is tell her husband what happened and that you're sorry. You won't have peace until you do. And after that, move on."

Erika was right, of course.

I called him and we met following dinner the next night. He was a factory worker, a big guy about my size who lived in a small flat in east London with his two sons. We sat in his living room and he offered me a beer. I hadn't had a drop of alcohol since I had met Erika, and I politely refused. He gulped from the bottle and then had another.

"Your professor told me all about it. You did a dumb thing that cost me the mother of my two boys. You apologize now, but what good does that do me? I got big expenses sending the boys to daycare so I can go to work. Plus, we have to eat out a lot, because I can't cook."

I was about to write him a check, even though I knew he had gotten money from the hospital, when a young women clad only in lace undies walked sleepily out of the bedroom, rubbing her eyes. When she stopped rubbing, she took one look at me and darted back into the room, slamming the door.

"My wife's sister," he stammered. "She's helping out with the kids. My wife was sickly for a long time before she died, and Connie moved in … only to help, mind you."

"I understand." I stood. "Once again, I'm so sorry for my mistake. I wish you and your boys," I tipped my head at the bedroom door, "and your wife's sister all the best."

That wasn't exactly how I had expected the meeting would come out, but even so, it did provide closure, and gradually the nightmare began to recede.

****

I worked odd jobs for a while to help with the rent and groceries, and Erika and I talked about our future. But I knew I was only postponing the inevitable confrontation with my father.

I returned to Israel for the High Holy Days that September, and I told my parents that Erika and I had decided to get married. Predictably, my father had a fit and my mother had to quiet him down with a brandy.

"Your whole life you are throwing away! And for what, a *shiksa*? Do you know what you are doing to me? I'll tell you. You are killing me! I'm seventy-five years old and you are going to bring me *goyim* grandchildren?"

"Dad, she promised to convert. The children will be brought up Jewish."

"What she promises doesn't matter. Jewish law says the children take the mother's religion. And the rabbis of Israel decreed if she was not born Jewish, she is not Jewish. Period. And never can be."

"I'm sorry, but that's not the way I see it. I love her and we *are* going to get married."

"And medical school and the money I've spent?"

"I learned some things ... so it wasn't entirely wasted."

"What did you learn? Wait, I'll tell you. You learned to marry a *shiksa*. Where will you live?"

"I want to come home to Israel."

"You'll have to serve in the army for three years."

"I know."

"And the marriage?"

"In Jerusalem. At the Wall."

"An orthodox rabbi will not marry you."

"Then, it'll have to be a conservative one."

My parents came to the wedding, but they didn't speak to me, Erika, or my new in-laws. They never did talk to Erika's parents, who both died several years later.

Erika converted to Judaism and changed her first name to Miriam moments before we said, "I do."

We honeymooned at Eilat for a week before I started my army stint. Shortly after we moved into our tiny apartment, my mother invited us for a Friday-night dinner, an attempt at reconciliation. After we said prayers for Shabbat and over the bread and wine, I tried to prompt the discussions my dad and I used to have about Bush, Arafat, anybody. No use. My father wouldn't even look at me. To him I was dead.

In retrospect, I'm not particularly proud of the way I acted. Not that I got married, but that I groveled for his affection afterward. He kept pushing me away, and I kept coming back, like an abused puppy whimpering for affection. Easy for me to say now, at age thirty-nine, but tough to accomplish when you're in your early twenties. After all, he *was* my father, and I loved him. But even a needy pup whipped enough eventually leaves.

Years later, when Miriam and I returned to Israel after the birth of both children to celebrate the High Holy Days with my family, my father spoke to me for the first time. And even then only after my mother's urging. "So," she told him, "you'll die an old man and never say another word to your only son and your only grandchildren who have come from America to visit you. This will pass. Forgive him. He's your blood."

But it was too late. The puppy had grown up.

In my third year, the army trained me for military police work, and I liked it a lot. I found out later that my old friend Jake Hertzog had set it up. I should have figured he had plans for me. When we were kids, he was always thinking one step ahead of the rest of us.

Before discharge, he came by to see me. "How'd you enjoy the last year?"

"It was great, Jake. I really liked chasing down the bad guys."

He smiled. "I can relate. I liked field work, too. Now I'm just a strategist sitting behind a desk. What're your plans?"

"I don't really know. Maybe law school, though the thought of sitting in a classroom after these three years turns me off."

"What about staying with the police work? Ever consider that?"

"Actually, I have. It would be a way of helping people and that's something I want to do … it's something I *have to* do."

Jake flashed an understanding smile. "I was counting on that. Payback time?" He was the only one except Miriam I had told about medical school.

"Something like that." I looked at him closely. His smile got broader.

"I know that glint in your eyes. You've got something up your sleeve," I said.

"Actually, I do. The army has got me doing some interesting things I can't really talk about in detail. But as part of that new activity, it seems we've got lots of signals telling us our local terrorists are not so local any more. They are going international, and I'm worried about them setting up cells in foreign countries, blending in with the people and plotting big surprises for the Western world."

"A modern day 'Charm School'?"

"Precisely. It would be nice for me to have a friend in the U.S., for example, working for the New York City Police Department. You and I would talk periodically about what was happening and maybe help each other out. NYPD would like that also."

A week later, the chief of the New York Police Department called me.

"Zach, your boss talked with me a few days ago. I won't beat around the bush. He and I exchange people periodically. Jake likes to have a pair of eyes and ears in New York and I like to learn how you guys deal with terrorists. He said you'd make a great cop, and he'd pay your salary and expenses, at least for the first year. Then, we'll see. Interested in moving?"

The timing was right. My relationship with my father was in the toilet, and I'd had it. Miriam was all for living in the Big Apple. I took the job and we moved to New York City two weeks later.

Chapter Seven

In Chappaqua, a hamlet of fifteen thousand people forty miles north of New York City, two widows kept house. One was portly, a bit disheveled, and walked about in a faded house dress, looking like an elderly grandmother ready to mop her kitchen floor. The other stood tall, with a cultured bearing, and spoke with a faint British inflection from her college days in London, when her parents were still wealthy landowners. *Before 1967.*

Both wore gray hair pulled back into a bun, the short one with uncontrolled wisps flying about like dandelion fuzz and the tall one coiffed into tightly sculpted, obedient curls, framing her still handsome face. They shopped together, cooked together, and walked about in American clothes wearing sensible shoes, attracting little attention. Ruth Abramowitz and Sarah Silverman met for the first time in New York a decade previously, almost like an arranged marriage.

They operated a small secondhand book store attached to their three-bedroom ranch, where comings and goings went unnoticed. The store seemed to cater to a local Pace University clientele. Students, in singles and groups, ambled in, and those with a purchase in mind searched for their book, leaving soon after they found it. Others browsed at odd hours, usually early in the morning or late at night. They would stop to chat with both women, who often as not brewed a pot of tea. Then, the two ladies with their students crowded around a small table and engaged in an hour or more of subdued conversation. Sometimes the women would display pamphlets extracted from a locked drawer. The students would then leave, usually without buying a book, but with a determined gait and a look of purpose.

Both women grudgingly admitted to infirmities from past events, now aggravated by their age. The tall one walked with a limp, her left hip never completely healed after tripping on the curb outside their former New York condo. Her long, shapely fingers, once trained to play Mozart sonatas, now gracefully gripped the handle of a cane expertly fabricated by a master craftsman at the Istanbul Institute of Gunsmithing. The shorter one constantly flexed arthritis-gnarled hands severely deformed by frostbite when she hid for a week on a winter mountain trail.

At 10:00 a.m., Mrs. Abramowitz hung a "Be Back Soon" sign in the front window of the bookstore, locked the door, and walked to the curb with Mrs. Silverman. The weather had turned rainy and both ladies felt its effects. Mrs. Abramowitz limped, leaning heavily on her cane, while Mrs. Silverman massaged her swollen knuckles. They climbed into a three-year-old black Buick four-door sedan, bought secondhand at a local dealer in Chappaqua when they moved into town. Mrs. Abramowitz drove, staying below the thirty-mile-an-hour speed limit. It took about ten minutes to arrive at the town's center and park the car.

The ladies shopped on Tuesday and Friday mornings at the neighborhood Safeway grocery store. They enjoyed American food and television. One night they rented *The Godfather* and heard Don Corleone say, "Keep your friends close but your enemies closer." They liked that. *A lot.*

They attended the Jewish High Holy Day services, Rosh Hashanah and Yom Kippur, each year at Temple Emanuel. Sarah liked the rabbis, a husband and wife team who made the religious experience enjoyable for her. Ruth thought being a Jew was too casual. She was upset at the religious services last fall, when the rabbi started his sermon with a joke, something about how Canada geese were creating a problem on the temple lawn, but he would solve it by making them members of the congregation. That way, they would only show up twice a year for the High Holy Days. She really didn't understand what was funny, but the congregation laughed appreciatively, even a little guiltily.

At the checkout counter they spoke with the clerk—MY NAME IS *JIMMY*, his shiny name tag said—a pleasant high school dropout who had been their friend since they moved to Chappaqua. His white apron had a new button: EMPLOYEE OF THE MONTH.

"Hello, Mrs. Abramowitz and Mrs. Silverman. How are you both today?"

The women smiled. "Doing well, Jimmy," said Sarah. "And congratulations," she said, pointing at his chest. "That's wonderful."

"Thanks. Gets me an extra dollar an hour for this month. Plus my own parking space, which I rent out for ten bucks a day. So the award's worth almost five hundred bucks."

"Fantastic. And how is Eloise?"

Jimmy's daughter Eloise had severe asthmatic attacks and had to be rushed to the emergency room for inhalers and intravenous medications as often as once a month. After Jimmy told them about his daughter's near-death experience, the women had made a one-hundred dollar contribution in Eloise's name to the local chapter of the American Lung Association and had dropped off hot soups and casseroles, with Sarah Silverman babysitting so Jimmy's wife could go to work.

"Fine for the moment. Thanks for asking. The lung specialist at Mt. Kisco General Hospital started her on a new drug that seems to be helping. Singulair, I think it's called. Name reminds me of the telephone company. But it costs a mint. I'm hoping Medicaid will pay for it. Either that or I'll have to go to the bank for a loan. Or I'll have to be the employee of the month for the rest of my life!"

"Jimmy, you know for help you can always come to us," said Sarah. "We have enough to live on and can certainly spare for good causes some more money. Let us know what you need."

"You two are so sweet. I don't know what we'd do without your help." He packed their groceries and helped carry them to the car.

****

That evening Ruth prepared the salad as Sarah cooked spaghetti marinara with meatballs. They ate in the small dining room at a round table covered by a red checkered tablecloth. A blue Colonial lamp with an eagle on its black wooden base sat in the middle. Using a knife's edge, Ruth pressed the bird's beak and a concealed drawer opened at the base. "The phone number," she said to Sarah, folding a piece of paper and slipping it into the drawer.

Sarah nodded. "Have some more baklava," she said, offering Ruth a plate of the honey-soaked pastries. "Not that good, but okay for Chappaqua. When we go home in nine more weeks, we'll celebrate with some *real* baklava."

Chapter Eight

On my way to work the following morning my cell phone went off.

"Zach, it's me, Harry. I thought you'd like to know Hunter's about to start the autopsy. In case you want to be there."

"Of course I want to be there. You coming?"

"Hell, no. Last time I puked my guts out and damn near fainted. The smell was on my clothes for days. Never again, partner, never again."

"Chicken shit."

"Maybe so, but I know my limitations."

Harry and I weren't exactly Holmes and Watson, but we did pair pretty well and made up for each other's limitations. When he joined the force he sought me out to partner with, and he became the best partner I'd ever had, always reliable in a jam. Even though we had our differences, we covered each other's back more than once. Dark alleys didn't frighten him.

Literally.

About a year ago, we were called late at night to a murder in Brooklyn Heights, where several members of the Latino Lords had killed a seventeen-year-old foot soldier in the Gangsta Zulus, an African American gang, by hacking him to death with machetes. Apparently the Gangsta's kid had gotten drunk and wandered onto foreign turf on his way home, where he got too friendly with a young Hispanic girl. Being on the wrong block can get you killed. The Gangstas wanted revenge, and seven of them had cornered four Lords in an empty lot off Henry Street.

The guys were lined up opposite each other preparing for the fight when I flipped on lights and sirens. They all scattered as we drove up.

We had a mug shot of the Latino Lords' chief, and I saw him duck into an alley. I was first out of the car while it was still screeching to a stop and ran after him. Not a smart idea. His three buddies were waiting near the end of the alley, which had been bricked off. I stood between them and the only escape. They walked slowly toward me, waving machetes and knives. I had my gun drawn and pointed it at the first guy coming.

"NYPD! You're under arrest for murder! Stop right there and get down on the ground!"

"Fuck you, cop. We're gonna make chopped meat outta you, like the Gangsta kid."

The chief lunged at me with his machete raised overhead. I had no choice and shot him in the chest when he was a couple of feet away. He went down, with only the sound of the machete clattering to the pavement. I whirled to face the second attacker, ducking under the swipe of his blade, but the guy must have known martial arts, because he spun around and with a perfectly aimed kick, knocked the gun flying from my hand. I leaped at him, hoping our entangled bodies would prevent, or at least slow down, the machete thrusts of the others. Wrong. From the corner of my eye I saw the glint of a blade poised above my head, and I put one arm up to ward off the blow. I had a fleeting vision of my hand being chopped off when I heard a gunshot and saw the guy spin backward. Harry came charging down the alley sounding like a whole brigade, gun blasts echoing and bullets pinging off the sides of the building. The one guy still standing dropped his machete and put his hands up.

Harry pressed his gun to the head of the guy on top of me. "Off, if you want to live." He wanted to live.

Harry had guts but the detective role didn't come naturally to him, and sometimes I had to push a bit to get him thinking. He was great at following orders but not too creative, and was quick to dump a dead end in my lap and move on to an easier case. That was another way we differed. I didn't give up, probably one of my strongest traits. I could spend a week on the *New York Times* crossword puzzle—Saturday was the hardest—and no cheating until I finished it. When I still lived in Jerusalem, a single chess match with my father lasted days. The loser had to wash dishes until he won the next match. I had dishpan hands for a lot of years growing up.

Chapter Nine

The spider-webbed basement reeked of antiseptic, formaldehyde, and death. Bare bulbs in the ceiling cast shadowy light as I looked through the door into the windowless office of the Chief Medical Examiner, John Hunter, MD. I watched him dog-ear the page corner of a spy novel, sigh, and push himself up from his battered wooden desk to answer my knock. He grunted as he mobilized his three-hundred pounds.

"So, you're back." Good thing his job wasn't an elected position or he'd be out of work. "I heard you said I wasn't qualified to do this fucking autopsy. Like you would really know."

I didn't answer, and he didn't say another word. I followed him as he crossed a narrow gray cinderblock corridor to a room labeled "Autopsy Suite," a grandiose name for a dimly-lit collection of tired rooms. He pulled a stainless steel container labeled "Karen Driver" from a refrigerated storage bin. A cold blast washed over me and I shivered.

"Temperature's thirty-eight degrees Fahrenheit. Maintain it near freezing to slow bacterial growth triggering body decomposition, yet warm enough to autopsy non-frozen tissue," he said. "But you know that, don't you? Or at least you should."

Hunter knew I had some medical training, but he didn't know how much. Regardless, that didn't stop him from preaching to me each time I had to view an autopsy.

He used an overhead pulley to remove the body from the slab and slide it onto the autopsy table. The gears squealed in noisy protest. "Goddamn this machine. I keep telling maintenance to oil the equipment. Four years old and it's already falling apart."

He studied X-rays and photos of the body. I could see the metallic image of the bullet in the brain.

After donning gown, mask, and gloves, Hunter looked like a surgeon in an operating room. I watched him suck in his huge gut, partly camouflaged by the green gown, and stand tall, actually preening. Scalpel poised in one hand, brows knit and eyes focused in serious concentration, he waited theatrically, letting the tension build. I must admit, his performance and the authority of death in the room commanded total attention.

"I now begin surgery on the dead," he announced dramatically. "Equally difficult, if not more so, than surgery on the living, as it involves operating on the *entire* body. No practicing surgeon can do that. I will start with brain surgery. Any questions before I begin?"

I had none since I was busy fighting down a queasy stomach. Harry had the right idea about not coming.

But the shroud-draped body mesmerized me. With a flourish, like a magician revealing the reappearance of his beautiful assistant, Hunter stripped off the white sheet. Despite all the times I have watched an autopsy, I still gasped as he exposed the pallid nude corpse. Her dead eyes were open, staring vacantly at the ceiling. Hunter glanced at me and I could see him smile through the mask. As usual, the bastard was enjoying the show—or my discomfort.

Driver was totally naked except for baggies still protecting her hands. Hunter said, "I'll remove those later when I take palm and fingerprints and check for debris beneath her fingernails. From the police report, I don't expect to find anything, but you guys could be wrong. In my experience, it is always possible to find a bit of the murderer's skin, hair, or clothing." Locard again.

Then he did something that amazed me. He took an antiquated stethoscope from a drawer and placed it over the tatters of her left breast, listening for a heartbeat. My jaw dropped. "In medical school they warned us pathology students about some case, somewhere, sometime, of someone waking up in the morgue just before the first knife slash, so I listen for a heart beat exactly as a cardiologist would."

"Ever hear anything?"

"Not yet. But you never know." Driver's skin was doughy, and a circular indentation remained after he removed the head of the stethoscope.

I shook my head. This guy was even weirder than I remembered. If ever anyone looked dead, Karen sure did.

Hunter's right foot hit a floor pedal that activated a dictating machine, and I listened to him describe Karen's external appearance into the microphone suspended on a wire over the body. "They just cleaned this mike," he said. "It gets glommed with blood showers and body detritus that periodically mute its function." He continued dictating. "The body is a Caucasian female looking her stated age of forty-four years. Multiple slashes across her anterior chest have greatly disfigured the normal anatomy. From the neck up and from the waist down, her external physiognomy appears normal."

He spread her legs and peered intently. "Due to the lack of any bleeding or other signs of trauma, there does not appear to be forcible entry of any orifice," he dictated.

His foot hit the light switch, shrouding the room in darkness. He shined the ultraviolet ray of a Woods Light at her vagina and anus, but nothing fluoresced. "Looking for semen," he explained.

"I know," I said. "We did the same thing on the office rug and also came up empty."

He grunted an acknowledgement. "Maybe so, but that's why they bring 'em here, 'cause you aren't doctors," he said, squinting at me.

After turning the room lights back on he opened a rape kit, swabbed and scraped her skin carefully, and put the samples in bottles for later analysis. "I won't do a wet prep, since I doubt we'd find any viable sperm. Waste of my time and the city's money."

He rolled the body onto its side. "Her back, buttocks, and legs all appear normal. There is a bullet hole in the occiput with no obvious exit site." He read from her chart. "Police at the crime scene measured her temperature with an ear thermometer. Eighty-two degrees Fahrenheit, close to my ten-hour estimate, given that body temperature falls one to two degrees per hour after death at room temperature.

"No tats." He turned to me. "I really didn't expect tattoos on such a person, but you can't tell by looks. Women like to get tattooed in lots of places, on the back of the upper shoulder, hip, breast, mid-back, or ankle. And more recently, bracelet tattoos over the biceps. I did an autopsy last week on a homeless woman with a snake tattoo coiled on her left breast. The snake's fangs were biting her nipple. Your buddies found the tattoo artist who did it and were able to ID the corpse."

His foot hit the pedal. "Livor mortis present on the posterior half of the body, its extent consistent with estimated time of death, which matches her being found on her back."

He looked at me. "The homeless lady I told you about had livor mortis in the lower half of her body because blood pooled there after she was killed in a sitting position. But she had been found lying face down, so she had to have been moved at least two hours after death."

Hunter picked up a scalpel, and I braced for what came next. He cut a horseshoe incision into her scalp, careful to stay within the hairline. Then he peeled the scalp off her skull like an orange rind, from back to front, leaving an anterior flap intact that shielded her eyes like the brim of a baseball cap. I almost lost it. I had to grip the edge of a sink to keep from going out. When I took my hand away it was covered with a dark, sticky something that looked like blood. I looked for a piece of paper but wiped it on my pants.

Hunter said, "As an American history buff, I always wondered how Indians scalped their victims. Did they drive their knives down to the skull or only shear off a superficial layer with hair on it? I've researched that and can't find the answer. You know any museums that collect scalps?"

I shook my head. *Who gives a shit?* But I didn't say anything.

He donned thick plastic goggles and pulled his mask in place. Then he took a Stryker saw, flicked on the power, and began to carve a large oval through the skull. Flying bone chips and blood particles pinged off the microphone. I moved back—way back—out of the line of fire.

Hunter fanned the small plume of smoke drifting from the whirring blade, carrying the smell of burning flesh. He turned on a water faucet, and I could see blood and tiny body pieces seep through perforated holes of the tabletop into a catch basin beneath.

When the oval was finished the saw whined to silence, and there was stillness in the autopsy room that intensified after the abrasive sound died. Hunter inserted into the cut groove a small tool with a wedge on one end. It had a crossways wooden handle on the other, which he twisted and popped off the top of Karen's skull like flipping the crown from a hardboiled egg. It made a sucking sound as if resisting the separation from its rightful place. He jerked his head away muttering, "Oh, shit."

"Oh, shit," I echoed seconds later when the distinct stench of old blood assaulted my nostrils. Thinking of all the autopsies Hunter must have done, I figured he had a whole city of people inside him.

Hunter removed his goggles and peered inside the cranium, dictating the ravages left by the bullet. I peered over his shoulder. The brain was a hemorrhagic mass. He shook his head from side to side, setting his jowls jiggling. He "tsk, tsk"ed loudly and started to expound on the type and extent of tissue damage caused by bullets of various calibers fired from different ranges.

I held up a hand to silence him. "I know all that."

He shot me another squinty-eyed look and went back to her head. Using gloved fingers, he pried the brain from the skull's interior, cut the vessels and nerves and whatever else was holding the brain in place, and lifted out the entire mass, plopping it onto an overhead scale suspended alongside the microphone. It reminded me of weighing vegetables at the supermarket. He read and dictated the weight of 1684 grams, several hundred over normal because of the bleeding, he told me, and set the brain in a white rectangular Tupperware container. He then secured the bony skull cap back in place and stitched the scalp into position, hiding his sutures in the hairline. Hunter stepped back from the stainless steel table to admire his work and smiled. He obviously took pride in his sewing, and with some good reason, I guessed. No one could tell Karen Driver had lost her brain. "A neurosurgeon could not have done it better," he said.

"You going to section that?" I asked, tipping my head at the brain.

"There's no hurry. At the end after I finish the autopsy."

Hunter picked up the scalpel and began a Y incision, slicing through the skin at each shoulder and thrusting the scalpel down until it met bone. He joined both shoulder incisions at the breastbone and completed the stem of the Y. From past autopsies, I knew at this point the skin peeled back easily, uncovering the underlying sternum and ribs. But Karen's skin was in tatters, and he fumbled exposing the chest.

Finally done, Hunter picked up the Stryker again, but the electric cord had become tangled and the saw jerked from his fingers. It fell with a clatter on the tile floor, and the plastic handle shattered.

"Shit!" he yelled. "That's the only saw I have." He rummaged in a cabinet drawer and took out a pair of shears, like rusty hedge clippers. Hunter wedged the blades around the first rib and cut. The crunch of metal on bone gave me chills as he continued cutting through the ribs on each side of the sternum. When he finished, he lifted off the breast bone, as if removing a knight's armored chest plate, and opened the pericardium to reveal the heart, and alongside, the lungs.

"The lungs are collapsed but appear normal. The heart is slightly enlarged and shows an anterior whitish scar consistent with an old myocardial infarction. No acute changes seen. No stab wounds have perforated the chest wall." He looked at me. "Now that's unusual. Pay attention to that, Detective. The frenzied attack was all superficial. No penetrating chest wounds at all. Why not?"

"Good point, but I don't know why."

After removing the heart and lungs, Hunter weighed each in the grocery scale and placed them aside in separate Tupperware containers, red for the heart and green for the lungs.

I was about to ask the same question, but he anticipated it. "I will section the heart at the end, when I cut up the brain," he said in a suffering tone of voice.

He extended the incision into the abdomen, cutting to the left of the umbilicus and down to the pelvis. Odors freed from their confinement once again made me gag, this time from a fecal miasma. "Got to be extra careful with the scalpel in here," he said, almost as a warning to himself. "Pathologists nick their fingers about once in every seven autopsies, especially in the abdomen where we can't see too well."

"You know, you forgot to get a blood sample for a tox screen," I said.

"What?"

I repeated the statement.

"You don't think she OD'd on anything, do you?"

"Not that we know of, but that's why we wanted a tox screen."

"I'll stick her bladder and get one from her urine."

"Not enough. Should have a sample from her blood *and* urine, since one could have drug and the other not, depending on when she took it."

He stared at me with an angry look. "Well, we won't this time, now will we?"

Hunter stuffed all the organs except the heart and brain into a plastic bag and placed the bag in the abdominal cavity. "Always reminds me of my ex-wife's first turkey dinner. She cooked it with the organ bag still in the bird. Tasted like shit."

Last, he fit the sternum back in place like a jigsaw piece and closed the skin incisions with a ropey black suture, taking big bites with the needle. There was no hiding these thick stitches, and when he was finished, Karen Driver had black seams that outlined a giant Y from her shoulders to her pelvis, quilting her skin together like laces of a football. "A pretty dress will cover it all," he said.

Finished, Hunter activated the squeaking pulley to load Karen onto the slab and slipped her back into the refrigerator. "Here're the two organs you want to look at, the brain for the bullet and the heart because of the scar likely caused by an old heart attack."

I watched him use a very sharp, flat knife to bread-loaf the brain on a wooden cutting board at half inch intervals from front to back. On the seventh slice, I heard the blade clink against something hard, and Hunter reached in with a pair of forceps and extracted a bullet, partially flattened to a nickel shape, with irregular borders. After photographing the bullet and the brain sections, he carefully slid the bullet into a cellophane envelope, sealed the top, labeled it with Driver's name, the date and time, and the bullet's position in the brain, and handed it to me. "This what you want?"

I said thanks and pocketed it.

The heart weighed in at four hundred ninety-two grams, more than fifty percent larger than normal for someone her size, he said. The lady certainly had heart disease. With sharp, small curved scissors, he sliced into the coronary arteries like opening strands of spaghetti lengthwise. One was occluded. "I knew she had a previous heart attack," he said. "Probably related to her smoking. She was lucky, though. This obstruction's called the 'widow maker' because it produces sudden death."

Too bad, I thought. She had escaped that one only to suffer a different kind.

After glancing at the clock, he hurriedly suspended the heart by a suture in a large porcelain jar with the brain settled at the bottom, where they would stew together in formaldehyde until I solved the case. But predictably, Hunter had failed to explain the chest slashings, and until he did, those organs might marinate a long time.

Chapter Ten

Francine Walters yawned, opened the door to her sixth-floor apartment, and bent down to retrieve the *New York Times*. The sixteen-year-old who delivered the paper precisely at 7:00 a.m. before Frankie went to work was always late for the rest of his paper route because he lingered around the corner in the hall each morning to catch a glimpse of her bending over. And she obliged, ever so slowly.

She stood in her doorway in bra and panties, because she was freshly showered and still warm and because the old fart married to the hairy shrew in the apartment across the hall had a hard-on for her. She spent several minutes flipping through the paper before closing the door. She pictured him staring at her through the tiny round security hole in his apartment door, breathing hard, with a hand on his crotch. She finger-combed her short spiky blonde hair, still damp, and then ran her fingers along the perimeter of her bra to ease the pull. Her skin still felt stretched after the surgery almost a year ago, but she loved the full C cup and so did all the men who did a double take seeing a full upper deck on such a slim chassis. The downside was that their conversations were often directed at her chest.

Afraid the old guy would have a stroke if she stood there too long, she closed the apartment door and retreated to the kitchen area of her one-room studio. She poured her second cup of morning coffee and settled down in the sunlight to read the rest of the paper. She hummed along with Nora Jones singing "Sunrise" in the background.

Not really concentrating, she flipped pages, glancing at headlines until she came to the New York Report section of the *Times*. There she read about Karen Driver's murder. Frankie's eyes raced through the article and her heart beat rapidly until she finished the last sentence.

No clues, she realized. The cops didn't have any idea who did it or why. She read the article again, more carefully, and only then did her breathing slow down.

The phone startled her.

"Frankie, it's me."

She recognized his voice. "I can barely hear you."

"I can't talk loud. The kids are in the next room. Do you—"

"I read it in the *Times*."

"The cops have been here. First a guy named Scarpia and then a Dayan."

"So? What did you tell them?"

"I told Dayan about us."

"What about us?"

"Frankie, stop the games. Did you..." He waited.

"Did I what?"

"You know."

"No, ask me." She sat back, feet on the table, and wondered if he would.

The line went quiet. "You didn't do it, did you?" Driver said.

She played with the phone line, twisting it around her finger. "So, you're a free man now. We can do Sleepy Hollow Inn guilt free."

"For God's sake, Frankie. My wife's been murdered."

"How convenient."

"Frankie, you know how I feel about you, it's just that—"

"Just what?"

"Well . . ."

"So, all your 'I love you' stuff was when you had an erection and now it's gone?"

"Frankie, I have to think of my ministry ... my kids ... I can't take the chance."

"*You* can't take the chance. What about me? Don't you think I've taken a chance?"

"Yes, but—"

She cut him off. "But, but, but. Do you want to marry me or am I only an afternoon fuck?"

She heard his breathing quicken as she hung up.

She sat there and stared at the phone for a moment, thinking about Karen. The fact that three children had lost a mother upset her most. Kenneth, despite his hyperventilation, would survive.

She pushed aside the *Times* and turned to *Al Raii*. As usual, the daily Arabic political newspaper covering Jordan and the other Arab countries was mailed late from Amman. She could get the copy on the Web, but she didn't like reading off a computer screen. Reading between the lines of the flowing Arabic script kept her up with the intrigue in the Middle East, but she wanted it delivered on time. She'd have to write the editor again.

Frankie topped off her coffee with a cholesterol-light cherry yogurt and put the dishes in the sink. Quickly she changed into her elastic athletic bra, which flattened her chest as much as the implants could be compressed. The male joggers probably enjoyed her bouncing breasts, but she didn't like the heavy tug from the silicone. In fact, she was still adjusting to her new silhouette, and her boobs often got in the way, like when they scraped the side of the mountain when she went rock climbing.

She pulled on black running pants and matching shirt, thick white athletic socks, and laced up her red and gray running shoes. She snapped her jogging pack in place and slid the belt around so it sat over her belly. She made sure the snub-nosed Colt Cobra .38 special was loaded. One thing was damn sure: she wasn't going to be the next Central Park jogger victim, broad daylight or not. Frankie took the steps two at a time to the lobby, bid the doorman a brief good morning, and turned west to the park for her four-mile morning run.

Chapter Eleven

I leaned back at my desk and plopped my feet on the corner alongside the computer. Molly had just dropped off the autopsy report. At least Hunter was prompt. After my second reading I came away with nothing new. Karen Driver had had a heart attack at some point, but her husband had told me that. I regretted letting Hunter do the autopsy, because there had to be more, and he missed it. The only thing helpful was the slug in her brain, which was now undergoing ballistics testing. The trip through her skull had defaced the gun markings, but I thought there was enough for ballistics to study. The weight of the bullet suggested a .38 caliber. Boom Boom immediately came to mind.

I picked up the phone on the first ring. "Dayan here."

"Zach, Henry Gallagher from ballistics."

"I was thinking about you. Anything?"

"We checked the bullet's fingerprints against all handguns sold in New York State and have no match."

"Oh, really," I said, frowning. "Wouldn't expect any, for Christ's sake, even if the gun was bought new in New York." Several years ago some smart-ass politicians passed a law requiring all new guns sold in New York to register bore markings at the time of the sale so that any future bullets found in a crime could be traced back to the original gun and owner. I told them from the very beginning the idea was flawed, because you can't compare bore friction markings on the bullet *now* to a gun sold years before. They change over time because of wear and tear in the gun barrel, like tire treads changing after twenty thousand miles.

"Zach, you're preaching to the choir."

"And besides, any perp could've altered the bullet markings by scratching the bore of the barrel with a file or even with a dab of toothpaste on the bullet. I'll bet you didn't check for that."

"Actually we did. Routine. No toothpaste residue."

"You're smarter than I gave you credit for."

"Don't knock yourself out with compliments. Maybe we'll hit a match with DRUGFIRE."

Now that *did* make sense. A DRUGFIRE match, comparing bullets found at different shootings to see if they came from the same gun, had led to the capture of the Virginia snipers, Malvo and Muhammad. Maybe we'd score here if the gun had been used in another killing. "When did you enter it? Anything yet?"

"No, I uploaded the ballistics fingerprint half hour ago. We're still searching," Gallagher said.

"Okay. Keep me posted." I thanked him and went back to the report.

I reread the section where Hunter emphasized that all the chest slashes were superficial. So what? The lady was already dead and the killer didn't need to stab her in the heart or lungs to finish the job. But maybe Hunter was on to something and his head wasn't a box of rocks after all.

Lots of negatives. No evidence of sexual assault, which fit with the skirt being in place. No rape or sodomy, which probably ruled out a sex psycho but certainly didn't exclude some guy who hated women. No skin or hair under her fingernails, no foreign fibers or fingerprints, and the tape from the security camera was blank.

The slashings made no sense, but they had to be the key. As expected, Hunter resisted an outside expert reviewing his autopsy findings. "I'm as good as anybody in the field, and I'll be goddamned if I need my autopsy results supervised!" he had yelled at me when I told him I wanted to call in an expert from ASIP. I needed a bigger stick to make him comply, so I went to the captain for help. He promised to talk with the mayor's office if necessary to get JJ in to review the autopsy. There had to be more clues than Hunter had found.

Molly had also dropped off the pictures of the crime scene. I fingered the thick manila envelope and took out the pile of glossies shot by the crime scene photographer. This guy was good; he shot them at varying aperture and timing settings, just like I'd asked. My office is kind of dark, not quite as bad as Hunter's though, and I had to pull a desk lamp over to see. I held each of the forty-three prints under it but still didn't see anything I didn't know already. Not even bloody footprints, so the murderer had to have been pretty careful to avoid all that blood from the chest cuts. He—maybe she—was pretty sharp. I was about to give up when the last shot caught my attention. It was a picture of the body from an angle that showed a barely visible, roundish bloodstain on the rug, the size of a small pager to the left side of Driver's head. We had all missed it, probably because of the lighting. I tilted the photo under the desk lamp, trying to catch the light. Maybe it was a partial palm or heel print.

I needed a closer look and rummaged around my desk for my magnifying glass. Missing as usual.

I hit the intercom.

"Molly dear, when are you going to get bifocals and stop taking my damn magnifying glass?"

My office door banged open. "You know, Detective, if you just asked nicely and didn't accuse a person, we'd get along much better. Didn't your mother teach you better manners?"

Molly glowered at me from the doorway, hands on hips, wearing her usual "don't bullshit me" look. She was short, just under five feet, I guessed, and wore a long-sleeved brown dress buttoned to the neck and hanging almost to her laced brown Oxford shoes. Not a bend or curve softened her stiff figure, and with her brown face, she reminded me of the chocolate cookies my mother used to bake. Those had an M&M smile, and so did Molly, but you had to work to get it. "Molly, there's no earthly way we could get along any better than we do now."

She strode to my desk, back straight, but I saw the crack of a smile play in the corners of her mouth. I moved my chair out of her way. It took her five seconds to find the glass buried beneath a stack of reports I had already looked through.

She rolled her eyes. "What is it with men they can't find anything unless it jumps out and bites them?"

"Probably genetics. A right brain/left brain thing?"

"The problem is you *look* but you don't *see*." She pointed her finger at me. "You'd think a detective, of all people, would be able to find something missing."

She'd been my secretary since I made detective and on the front desk fifteen years prior to that. More precinct lore was stored beneath her gray, tightly-coiled hair than in the hard drive of the office computers. And it was a lot more secure from hackers. During my divorce, she supplied the steady hand that helped both Miriam and me steer through the dark waters.

"That's why I have you, Molly dear."

"It's a good thing, too," she said. She placed a yellow legal pad and a newly sharpened pencil in front of me. "You might want these so you can do your doodle thing with those silly stick figures."

Along with my pipe, the other thing that helped me concentrate was doodling. I was no competition for the famous doodlers like Caruso or Reagan, but drawing, even stick figures, helped me concentrate.

I picked up the picture again and studied it through the thick glass. In addition to the round bloodstain, I saw a wisp of a thin, bloody, snake-like thread coming off it. Maybe a foot long, I estimated.

I drew the position of the body with the little round bloodstain and the tail trailing off. I thought about what could have made those marks. Maybe the killer dropped something from his pocket into one of the pools of blood. Or did he set something down and then pick it up? I drew the killer standing over the body dropping a pager. But that would have bounced on the rug without leaving a neat round circle with a tail. I drew him setting a round container down in a blood pool and then dragging it away. That didn't work, because the drag line would have been wide at the beginning and then get fainter and thinner as the blood wiped off. I studied the picture again. An enlargement would help. I would ask the photo shop to do that. Maybe show it to Hunter to see if he had any ideas. Better yet, send it to JJ at the ASIP.

Chapter Twelve

Harry came in without knocking, flopped down in one of the two worn brown Leatherette chairs in front of my desk, and stretched a carefully creased pant leg over the arm of the chair. The charcoal Armani suit perfectly hid the Ruger Vaquero .357 Magnum revolver I knew he carried in a black leather holster beneath his left arm. He told me he often wore that Italian line because the clothes draped loosely and concealed his weapon. Zegna and Brioni jackets were too form fitting when he was packing the Magnum. He saved those for when he holstered a smaller handgun. I thought that was kind of amazing. A cop tailoring his clothes to fit the gun he was packing!

Harry was twenty-eight years old and had been on the force seven years. As far as I knew, he lived alone and didn't talk about girlfriends or family. More than one cop had remarked about his suits, and finally Internal Affairs got involved but found no evidence of anything illegal. In fact, he was a good guy, and in his spare time he volunteered as a coach for the Special Olympics. On the wall of his office hung a framed picture of him and a child with Down syndrome, both sporting big smiles and holding a first-place blue ribbon.

I watched Harry's eyes scan my office, which was on the second floor of One Police Plaza on Park Row in lower Manhattan, across the street from City Hall. It's a small room, but big enough for a few things on the wall and a recessed built-in bookshelf behind locked glass doors that told the story of my career. It spanned most of one wall and held an assortment of weapons—knives, handguns, several rifles, a pair of brass knuckles, and two disarmed hand grenades.

"See anything you like?" I asked.

He grinned. "Sure." He pointed at my Detective First Grade certificate hanging on the wall. "I'll take that one." Harry knew I had been a uniformed cop for only two years before I qualified for the detective exam. What he didn't know was that Jake, my Israeli buddy, had set it all up.

That started me remembering.

*****

It was Yom Kippur, thirteen or fourteen years ago. Arafat still commanded the PLO, but he was sick and determined to show the world he still had balls. So they set off a car bomb in the Mahaneh Yehuda market in West Jerusalem, blowing up both Jewish and Palestinian shoppers.

Jake called me. He was four or five years older than me and like an older brother growing up. Back then he was a tank commander, and he looked like one—lean and muscular, browned from days in the desert, with blond hair bleached almost white by the sun.

"Zach, the bombing fits what informants have told us. Arafat's got a terrorist cell in Nablus, maybe making the bombs."

"Sounds like that's our next move," I said.

The following day, Jake got a group of eight men together and, using two Merkava Mark IV tanks as protection, we rolled into Nablus. The town seemed peaceful, but there were groups of young men standing around watching our every move. We climbed down from the tanks in a residential area west of town. It was a neighborhood where our informants had spotted a lot of activity.

In front of one small white wooden house, two boys were playing some sort of a game with little silver balls. They were shouting good-naturedly at each other, having a fun time throwing the metal balls into a circle they had drawn in the brown dirt. The objective seemed to be to hit the opponent's balls out of the circle while keeping your own in. Neither boy paid us any attention.

But something about the balls intrigued me. I beckoned to several of my group and we walked over. It was then that the boys first saw us and bolted, one through the front door of the white house and the other down the street.

"This may be it," I told the men. "Fan out and cover the windows and back door. Hymie, come with me. We're going in the front way."

The door the boy had darted through was now locked, but I broke it down with a single shoulder crunch. Inside, an old man and a middle-aged woman were sitting around a table trying to look is if they were eating. A pitcher of water sat in a liquid pool spilled on the table, the water still lapping over the edge from having just been placed there. Empty plates were in front of both of them, but no glasses or silverware.

The old man stood. "What do you want with us? Get out of my house." He waved his left hand at me. The thumb and first two fingers were missing. We were in the right place. Something was about to happen. I could feel it coming. I looked at Hymie and we both fingered our M16s.

I scanned the room. "Where's the rest of your family?" I asked.

"Out, working."

There was a closed door off to the right of the table. "What's in the next room?"

"It's my bedroom."

"Where's the boy who just ran into the house?"

"Nobody came in here."

"Then you must be blind." I walked toward the door, pointing my rifle.

"Get away from there," the man screamed.

The door flew open and two men stormed out, guns drawn. Hymie and I opened fire, hitting both men multiple times, but not before they got off several rounds. One caught Hymie in the throat, and he went down coughing up a geyser of red foam. I got hit in the chest, and the force of the slug drove me backward into the wall, knocking the wind out of me. The Kevlar vest stopped the bullet from tearing a hole in my lung, and I staggered unsteadily to my feet.

The older of the two men, a bearded guy who could have been the other's father, went down on one knee, bleeding badly from a chest hit. Somehow he managed to stand and drive his body into me. He threw both his arms around my neck, but I was able to get the barrel of the M16 into his side and pull the trigger. His body parts flew against the wall as the stream of 5.56 mm slugs almost cut him in half. The other man, clean shaven and maybe twenty or so, was trying to stem a bleeding gut with one hand while scattering wild shots with the other.

My M16 ran out of ammo, and I had no time to reload. I swung the gun barrel at his head and the "thwack" sounded like hitting a pumpkin with a baseball bat. He crumpled without a sound, and from blood spurting through the crack in his skull, I knew he wasn't ever going to move again.

By that time, my men had come flying into the house. The old man sitting at the table pulled a gun from his waistband, but before he could move, two guys shot him at point-blank range. The woman, now hysterical, was screaming that I had killed her husband and son. She came snarling at me with long fingers, trying to claw my face with her nails. My guys restrained her and took her outside.

There was blood all over the floor and walls, even reaching the ceiling. We worked on Hymie for several minutes, but it was futile.

In the second room, as I expected, was a cache of bomb-making materiel. Three wooden boxes were filled with the little metal ball bearings the boys had been playing with outside. They would be packed into the bombs to become projectile missiles on explosion.

"Good job, Zach," Jake said, bringing up the rear.

"Stupid of them to let the kids play with those balls out in the open."

Jake grimaced. "We've now eliminated one more bomb-maker. We got maybe a hundred or two to go. But it's a start, Zach—it's a start."

I turned to leave when I spotted a quick movement near the window, but then I got distracted, and when I looked again, the street was deserted.

*****

"And definitely the Legion of Honor award." Harry's voice brought me back to the present.

"Good luck on that, my friend. You'd have to kill to get that one from me." It was for outstanding bravery in the line of battle, and I was real proud of it. Four or five years ago, we had a shootout on the lower West side with some bad guys doing a drug deal that went sour. I saved a teenager caught in crossfire. Turned out his parents were Palestinians and had recently moved to the United States from Nablus, where his father had been mayor, to escape the violence of the Middle

East. Naturally, the papers made a big deal out of that. They moved back to Nablus pretty quick afterward.

I picked up the pile of photos and flipped them to him. "Have a look." While he did, I toyed with a pipe on my desk, cleaning the bowl with a pearl-handled penknife. After several minutes I said, "So what do you think?"

Harry shrugged. "Nothing we didn't see at the crime scene."

"I missed it first time also. Look closely at the last one."

Harry's eyes momentarily flared and his eyebrows bunched.

"See something?"

"I thought I did, but now I'm not sure."

"Right the first time." I went over to him, put a hand on his shoulder, and pointed to the round stain on the last picture. I handed him the magnifying glass. "Now what do you think?"

Harry shifted uncomfortably in his chair. "I have no idea what it is. You?"

"Nope. But it sure as hell is something."

He shrugged.

"Let's go."

"Where?"

"You and I are going to visit a very interesting young lady, according to what Driver told me. Maybe she can explain what it is."

Chapter Thirteen

Francine Walters answered the door dressed in a pale pink exercise jumpsuit with a white stripe down the sleeves and pants. She wore pink Nike running shoes. Little diamonds of sweat sparkled on her upper lip and forehead. Big baby blues and blonde hair. It was easy to see how Driver lost it. I might myself.

"Doing Pilates in the apartment," she said by way of greeting. "I'm Frankie Walters. Who the hell are you two?"

We flashed IDs. "We'd like to talk to you about Karen Driver's murder."

I studied her face, watching for any sign of anxiety as she hesitated. I figured she was calculating her answer. A "No, I want to talk with my lawyer first" would heighten suspicion, bringing us back with a warrant.

"Sure. No problem. Come in."

We entered the one-room studio apartment, looked around briefly, and sat down on a small sofa. I didn't see a bed, so I figured the sofa doubled as a roll-out. A square brass coffee table with a glass top had been moved against one wall, and a rubber Pilates mat was laid out on the floor in the middle of the room. Sunlight streamed in from a small kitchen directly opposite the couch, and a small TV was showing three girls and a guy exercising. She switched it off.

"Can I get you guys coffee or anything?"

"No thanks. We only want to talk to you informally about Karen Driver's murder."

Frankie pulled up a yellow wicker kitchen chair in front of the sofa and sat on it backward, her arms draped over the chair back. Perspiration showed through the jumpsuit as maroon half-circles under her arms and beneath her breasts. Harry held his head straight forward, but his eyes were on her chest. She snatched a white terrycloth towel from the floor alongside the mat and settled it across her shoulders and neck, draping the ends over her breasts.

"What do you want to know?" Before I could answer she added, "The lady's husband and I were fucking."

If that was meant to shock me, it succeeded. I fumbled around in my pocket to find my ringed notebook. Finally, with pencil and pad poised, I said, "We know that. Driver told us. Go on."

"And did he also tell you he was breaking off the relationship and I got pissed?"

"He did."

"Probably just as well. I got tired messing with a minister. Too stiff." She smiled.

"Something's funny?" I asked.

"Yeah. Actually not stiff enough." She giggled. "Couple of times he forgot to take his Viagra and ..." She shrugged with arms akimbo.

I bit my lip to stifle a grin and concentrated on writing in my notebook. I could see Harry squirming on the couch. Even dirty jokes in the precinct made him uncomfortable.

"Where were you last night? About 7:30 or eight."

"Movie."

"What did you see?"

"I forget the title. Something with Tom Cruise. A rerun at one of those theaters that show old movies—the ones you wanted to see but missed."

"*Collateral* or *The Last Samurai*?" said Harry.

"That's it. *Samurai*. Thanks." She smiled at him and he blushed.

"Ticket stub?"

"Nope. Threw it away."

"How did it end?"

"He died."

"Who?"

"Both of them."

"Were you with anyone? Can anybody corroborate your story?"

"No. I go out alone lots of times. It's a nice walk from here to Times Square. Part of my exercise plan."

"There are some dark stretches at night."

"I'm not scared."

"How come?"

"Boom Boom."

"Driver told me. A .38?"

"Colt Cobra .38 special. Double-action snub-nosed revolver. Same as Jack Ruby used to kill Lee Harvey Oswald."

"Impressive. I assume you have a license to carry a concealed weapon?"

She brushed away the question with the back of her hand. "You don't think I'd be dumb enough to tell you about it if it wasn't legal?"

"Can I see your license?"

She rose, removed her purse from a drawer in the kitchen, and dumped the contents on the kitchen table. It took her a minute to plow through her stuff, find her wallet, and take out the license. While she did, I watched Harry get up and wander the small living area, nosing around, opening and closing drawers without apparent purpose. Probably a good idea. Never know what you might find. And without a search warrant, he had to be casual; any objections from her and we'd have to leave.

Frankie glanced up to watch Harry's roaming. "Looking for my underwear drawer? I have some cute see-throughs and lacy thongs. They're in the second drawer to your left. Bras are on your right."

That brought Harry, red-faced, back to the couch. He sat down as Frankie grinned at him and handed me the license. I wrote down the number.

"And the gun?"

Before she got up she asked Harry, "Strolling again?"

His eyebrows rose, but he said nothing.

Frankie retrieved a pink and white jogging pack that coordinated with her outfit. She handed it to me but I shook her off. "Please open the pack and hand me the gun."

I removed a handkerchief from my pocket and took the gun from her, handle first.

"When did you fire it last?"

"A week ago."

"Where?"

"Joe's Guns. It's a shooting club off Times Square. Near the movie."

"Have you cleaned it since?"

"Outer's Nitro Solvent and Gun Oil. Standard stuff. Do it after each shoot."

I wrote down the serial number of the gun and handed it back to her.

"Did you ever meet Karen Driver?"

She shook her head. "No. I saw her from a distance at church and once when Ken and I were leaving a hotel after a lunchtime quickie. Close call. But that's it."

I took out the photo. "Recognize her?"

"Oh, my God!" She gasped. "Yes, that's her. But her chest . . ."

"Do you see this round stain?"

She looked closely.

"What is it?" I asked.

"I have no idea."

I stared hard at her. Her face was ashen, eyes riveted on the glossy. She was either a good actress or pretty shook up. "Driver said you wanted him to leave his wife."

"Leave her. Not kill her."

"Do you think he did?"

She shrugged.

"Why did you start with him in the first place? An attractive young woman like you must have lots of opportunities."

"I like the religious types. Ministers, priests. Though I haven't tried nuns yet. Maybe next time." She cocked her head, looking at me. "Or rabbis."

"Why?"

Her eyes flashed. She had her color back.

"You ever see *The Blue Angel* with Marlene Dietrich? She had that poor Professor Rath cackling like a rooster at the end. Power like that is intoxicating. Driver didn't cackle, but I made him sit up and beg. Priests are the best for that, especially when I tell them it's over."

"Why?"

"Simple. I have two weapons—a gun, which I haven't had to use yet, and sex. Either stops men—all men, no matter their age or what they do—dead in their tracks." She looked from me to Harry, who was wide eyed. "Trust me. The best way—no, the *only* way—to a man's heart isn't through his stomach. Haven't met an exception yet," she said, looking directly at Harry.

"Were you going to end it with Driver?"

"Maybe eventually. He beat me to it."

"And that made you angry."

"It did."

"Enough to kill Karen?"

"I told you I was at the movies."

Usually I can read people, but I didn't know what to make of her. I looked up from my notebook and stared into her eyes. She stared right back, unflinching. The contest lasted several seconds, and then she wiped her face and neck with the towel and tossed it into the kitchen, aiming at a chair but missing. It fell to the floor and she made no move to retrieve it.

"What else do you want to know?" she asked. "I don't have all day to spend with you, as fun as it might be." She winked at Harry, and he cracked a tiny smile.

"Would you mind if I took your handgun for ballistics testing?"

"You're damned right I would. I don't leave the apartment without Boom Boom, so unless you have whatever papers you need to take him from me, he stays here."

"Okay. But keep the gun available in case we want to test it."

"No problem. But give me warning, because to be honest, I will splurge and buy another one—maybe a .45 this time. Like the American Express commercial, I don't leave home without it. At least not in this city. I'm sure you guys don't either, do you?"

I was one of the last cops to still carry a .38. The Smith and Wesson Model 10 was the firearm I started with and the one I still relied on. The young guys called me a dinosaur, because they all packed standard-issue 9 mm semiautomatics. I had one in an ankle holster, but I worried that the semiautomatics might jam, while the revolver always had another round ready in the chamber to fire.

I figured that was enough for a first visit. I stood up and walked to the door. Harry quickly followed but walked to the kitchen. He picked up the towel, folded it, and put it on a kitchen chair. Frankie didn't move, arms still draped over the back of the chair. She turned her head to look up at us.

"That's it? I didn't mean to scare you off. No grueling questioning, water dripping on my forehead, strip searches? I was looking forward to that. Or maybe a full-body pat-down?" she said, leaning forward, her lips parted slightly.

She looked at Harry. "I'm disappointed."

"Thanks. You've been most helpful. If we want to talk further—and it's likely we will—we can try those things then," I said.

She rose and her eyes softened as she looked at Harry. "You hardly mumbled a thing." She tilted her head at the towel. "Thanks."

Harry glanced at me. "Detective Dayan asked all the questions I would have."

"Maybe. Next time come back without him and do your own thing. Cops are almost as good as priests." She smiled again at him and this time he returned it.

Back in the car I watched Harry study the road in front, concentrating on the New York traffic. "Got a little thing for Frankie, do you, Harry?"

His grip tightened on the steering wheel and he looked at me. "Not me. I've got a hunch this lady may well be our man."

Chapter Fourteen

Frankie sat with Boom Boom on her lap long after the cops left, analyzing the encounter. *Am I a serious suspect?* she wondered. She turned Boom Boom over in her hands, its familiar heft and feel calming her.

She had loved guns ever since she was little, plinking at cans in the backyard with her father's old Mossberg .22. At Princeton, she started shooting again and became a first team free pistol NRA Collegiate All-American selection. A scout for the FBI approached her during her final match, feeling her out about her interest in joining. She was flattered, even though she knew she was a natural candidate given her shooting expertise and her major in Middle Eastern studies.

A week after graduation she tried out for the FBI job. Even now the memory haunted her. That goddamn Fire Arms Training System program had been her nemesis. She sailed through everything else. The three scenes in particular were seared in her brain. The morning began with a three-hour lecture on the FBI's Use of Deadly Force Policy. Her FBI instructor—she forgot the prick's name but could visualize him as the square-jawed crime-buster star of every TV program—gave her a real Glock .223 handgun, converted to shoot a laser beam. He positioned her fifteen feet in front of a large white screen and said, "You and your fellow agent, who is standing behind you," involuntarily she looked over her shoulder, but of course no one was there, "will face a series of sixteen scenarios I will project as a video on the screen. These are from actual encounters scripted and acted by professionals and filmed by the FBI to simulate the real event and test prospective agent's ability to think and react quickly. Use what you learned this morning as you carry out the instructions I give you before each episode. Got it?"

"Yes."

"You will be the SAC—special agent in charge—and will have to determine how to stop the bad guy and whether to use deadly force according to the rules you learned this morning."

It struck her as silly how the SAC instructor referred to the perpetrator as the "bad guy." She expected something more descriptive, like "bank robber," "killer," or "rapist," something other than the "bad guy." This *was* the FBI, for Christ's sake.

The SAC continued. "Like I said, the handgun you're holding is, or was, real. Instead of a bullet, it now shoots a laser beam that registers on the screen, so when I replay the video you can see where your bullet hit—that is, if you decide to use deadly force."

He looked at her to see if she understood. "Talk to the screen as if the people there are in a real crime scene. I'll work the video controls and manipulate the scene to respond—or not to respond—to your commands. This is a test to see how potential recruits perform under simulated real-life dangerous conditions—whether to shoot and whom."

He moved a small desk in front of her. "You can crouch down behind that to simulate protection if you feel you need to."

She stood in front of the desk facing the screen, her heart pounding at about 150 beats a minute. "I won't need it."

The SAC squinted at her. "Your call. Ready?"

"Yes."

Frankie took the shooter's stance, body turned slightly sideways to minimize her silhouette, knees bent a little to move quickly, right hand on the gun, arm extended, and trigger finger alongside the barrel. Her left hand, shaking slightly, cupped the heel of her right hand to support the base of the gun.

The first scene was straightforward. A masked robber burst into a bank with gun drawn. The teller hit a silent alarm summoning the FBI to the scene. As the bad guy was collecting his loot from a teller, Frankie, feeling awkward saying it, yelled at the screen, "FBI. Drop the gun." When the robber didn't and turned toward her getting ready to shoot, she quickly aimed and squeezed the trigger, dropping him to the floor instantly.

"Very good." The SAC looked at his stopwatch. "You responded one point one seconds after he turned on you." The replay showed that her laser shot had caught the robber square in the middle of the chest. "You could've been a little faster, but not bad. How does that feel?" His tone improved a notch.

"Fantastic. This thing," she waved the gun, "*really* makes you feel powerful. He went down like a ton of bricks."

And so it went well for the next several scenarios. She made appropriate decisions with lightning speed, who to shoot and when. Her aim was dead-on and her reaction time dropped to less than a second. Then the incredible adrenaline rush slowly ebbed, her heart rate fell, and she started to relax. Never let down your guard, never be complacent, the SAC had warned her. Response times measured in milliseconds determined whether you walked away or got carried out in a body bag.

The SAC said, "In this next sequence, you are entering an apartment where a suspected drug dealer lives. You are to arrest him. Clear?"

An expectant smile tugged at the corners of her mouth. Her eyes narrowed. She flexed her knees, gripping the gun with both hands. "Roll it."

The scene opened in the sparsely furnished living room of an apartment. A sofa along one wall and two chairs on either side of a folding bridge table in the middle were the only pieces of furniture. She looked into the distant bedroom. "FBI. Come out with your hands up!" she shouted. Her voice was strong, commanding.

A very tall, muscular, bare-chested African American emerged from deep in the shadows of the bedroom, connected by a doorway to the living room where she stood. He raised his hands high over his head in response to her order. He walked slowly across the bedroom rug toward her. "Stop and drop," she yelled, "to the floor, now!" Her finger was ready to slip into the trigger guard of the gun.

He kept walking toward her, but his hands were high and she saw no weapon. He appeared non-threatening and even had a slight smile on his face. Her trigger finger twitched, but the morning's lecture flashed through her mind and she knew she couldn't use deadly force yet.

"Stop!" she yelled again, her eyes dilating as he approached. *Too late!* When he passed through the doorway from the bedroom to the living room, his right hand jerked upward in a flash, grabbed a revolver concealed in the door jamb over his head, and shot her before she could even get her finger to move.

"You're dead," the SAC instructor said. He checked his watch. "Over two seconds, way too slow. You were correct in withholding your fire initially, but when he kept walking, you should have known something was up and been prepared to react when he grabbed for the gun."

"Maybe I could have wounded him before that?"

The SAC wrinkled his brow. "Bullshit. That's for Hollywood. You shoot to kill. Period. No further discussion. Someone threatens you with imminent harm, off him."

Frankie promised herself to shoot first in this next one. *Ready, fire, aim* was how she would play it. Her heart rate rose.

"Okay. In this scene there's been a murder a block away. Witnesses saw the suspect run into a first floor apartment, which may be his home. You and your partner have been ordered to capture him. Clear?"

"Start the fucking video."

The screen showed a dirty room with a white man standing in the middle holding a handgun.

Frankie ducked behind the desk, pointed her Glock at the screen, ready to shoot him if he so much as twitched his gun arm. "FBI! Drop the gun and put your hands up!"

The man did as told.

"Now, kick the gun toward me and get down on the floor on your stomach."

He complied.

As Frankie walked in front of the desk directly facing the man, she heard a noise and saw a movement from the right side of the screen. A boy, about ten or twelve, slowly walked into the room. He looked spaced out, and his arm hung at his side holding a revolver pointed straight down at the floor.

She didn't know what to do. He was so little and seemed to be in a sort of trance.

"Stop," she said to the boy in a soft voice. He kept walking toward the man on the floor. "Stop and drop the gun," she said louder. The boy continued walking, staring at the man. "You stop or I'll shoot," she shouted, thinking, *How can I shoot a little kid like this?*

Without warning the boy raised the gun toward her and pulled the trigger. She was dead.

Frankie heard the SAC groan. He strode over and stared into her face. "What the hell did we spend three hours talking about this morning? Act! Don't react when there is *probable cause to believe that the subject poses an imminent danger of death or serious physical injury to the agent*," he recited verbatim. "The kid was a clear and dangerous threat to you. For Christ's sake, he had a gun in his hands, and he disobeyed your order to drop it. If that isn't a reason to apply deadly force, I don't know what is. You're as dead from his gun as you would have been from the guy you got on the ground." He stopped for a moment, shaking his head. "You're a good shot, Francine, but your judgment sucks—twice now."

He waited to see if his tirade had sunk in. She tipped her head. "Okay. You're down two. Three strikes and you're gone. Don't blow this one," the SAC said. "Ready?"

Frankie didn't trust her voice and only shook her head up and down.

"In this scene you are to arrest a potential terrorist who has been spotted by an informer eating lunch at a Chinese restaurant."

The scene was a small restaurant with only two customers. Obligatory orange paper lanterns hung from the ceiling, radiating a yellowish hue. A swarthy-looking man with a black beard—the presumed terrorist—and a woman were seated at a small table against the far wall, facing each other. Frankie shouted the familiar refrain and pointed her handgun. "FBI! Hands up!"

The couple looked at her, startled, and the woman jumped, spilling her tea on the white tablecloth. A Bonnie and Clyde glance passed between them as they raised their hands over their heads.

"Now, stand slowly and keep your hands up where I can see them."

They did as commanded and the woman inched around the front of the small table to stand at the man's side. Frankie kept the gun pointed at him and stared without blinking. She was not going to be caught again. This time her finger was already on the trigger and her eyes took in his hands as well as his face.

The woman now moved next to the man, but Frankie ignored her. *He* was the terrorist and he was the one she trained the gun on. Suddenly he moved slightly, appearing to turn his back on the woman. Before Frankie could respond, the woman reached into the small of his back, pulled a gun hidden in his belt, and shot her.

"You'd better hope you're a cat because you're dead again," the SAC said, derision dripping in his voice. "When you're arresting someone you need to watch *all* hands at all times. You watched *his*, but you didn't see *her* hands slowly drop, reach into his belt, and draw the gun. You were only looking at him. Women can kill as well as men."

Frankie was shaking with fury as she stood there with the laser gun at her side. She felt like screaming at the SAC, "It was you who told me *he* was the terrorist, you bastard," but the SAC was right. She should have been watching the woman also. *Never presume anything* was another part of the exercise drilled into her this morning. *Be proactive, not reactive.*

"You'd better keep your day job, 'cause you sure as hell aren't going to make it in the FBI."

"You know what?" she said, slamming the gun on the table with a crash. "After taking all this shit from you today, I don't want to! If that's what the FBI is all about, you can take this job and shove it up your deadly policy fucking FBI ass! And we'll find out if you act or react!" She stalked out.

The next day she bought Boom Boom.

Chapter Fifteen

Wahad asked the man on the computer screen, "Do you think it is too soon to hire workers to start on the lab?"

Seated in the hidden back room of the bookstore, Wahad scanned the activity through the one-way glass. There were two large rooms spilling over with books crammed together on shelves, tables, and the floor. Three overstuffed easy chairs, the brown leather cracked and stained by countless coffee spills, and a two-seater couch were comfortably arranged around a coffee table. Bright reading lamps arched over the backs of each chair and flanked the couch. A sideboard held a coffeemaker, tea service, and a plate of homemade chocolate chip cookies that Sarah baked each morning while Ruth worked the computer. A large new bookcase had been built into the back wall of the second room. Pressure on the upper right corner swung it open like a door to reveal an eight-by-ten-foot room where Ruth and Wahad had spent their day studying the master list to pick candidates, map routes, arrange for collection and storage of the drop-offs, and plot new assignments. Wahad now sat at a desk in front of an Apple computer screen, video-conferencing with a male colleague. Ruth sat alongside.

"Is the site secured yet?" Wahad asked.

"Not until you give the order. But remember, we will have to import a lot of skilled people and expensive equipment. Our contact seems to think we should get started now."

"Yes, I'd agree," Wahad said. "Once we finish the collections we'll need to go right into production without losing a day. We have two weeks from that time. So now would be a good time to lay the foundation."

"The final date is definite?" the man in the screen asked. Even on the screen he appeared large, with broad shoulders, a big square face, and a carved flint arrowhead for a nose, all framed by thick black hair.

"Fairly definite. Enough so that we can plan for it. But knowing how these things go, it could be delayed by a day or two. Not enough to change our plans much at this time. Certainly as the date approaches, our source will be able to tell us the precise day and location. The latter won't change but the date might," Wahad said.

"Very good. I will give the order in your name. We will communicate again in two days as usual?"

"Yes," said Wahad, "give me an update then." Ruth reached over and clicked off the screen.

"There are so many things to remember," Ruth said, as she returned to her list of names.

"But think of what we will accomplish," Wahad said.

"I dream about it. I want the biggest impact possible," Sarah said, joining them.

"We all do. When we are done, there will be singing and laughter in the streets of Gaza and young people like you, Wahad, will come from every country to join our crusade," said Ruth.

"And the regimes in Cairo, Riyadh, Amman, and Islamabad supported by the West will come crashing down like straw houses. Islam will be again pure. *Inshallah,*" said Wahad.

Wahad stood behind Ruth as she went back to the computer, marveling at her transition from a London schoolgirl to now. Ruth had told her story many times.

As Zahira Abdullah from Nablus, she attended the Bedford College for Women, founded in 1849. It was the perfect place for a privileged daughter, selected after much discussion by her parents, who worried about her living alone so far from home. Their worries were unnecessary. Wearing a white hijab, she entered a mosque through the women's door, prayed separately five times a day, ate with other girls, and never even held hands with a boy. She knew of the terrible things Allah inflicted on girls who strayed.

After graduation she returned to Palestine to become the virginal bride of Zahira Najar. Two years later, she became pregnant with her first boy, followed four years later by another son. But the 1967 war terminated her privileged life. The Six Day War between Israel and its Arab neighbors of Syria, Egypt, and Jordan, gave Israel the West Bank and East Jerusalem, the Gaza Strip, the Sinai Peninsula, and the Golan Heights. Her parents and new family were stripped of large land holdings and forced to become farmers and tenders of the very olive groves they had once owned.

Zahira's husband, never educated in a skill, joined the Palestine Liberation Organization right after the war. He fought in the first Intifada from 1987 to 1993, and led the bombing of the Mahaneh Yehuda market in 1997.

And Sarah, Wahad thought. *An even more courageous tale.*

Sarah told him how her first life had ended in Kabul, Afghanistan's capital, in December 1979. Nadia Nematullah was living with her husband and their three small children in his parents' house when deafening Soviet explosions lit up the night sky. She remembered it beginning precisely at 7:30 in the evening, as she was serving the leg of lamb to her father-in-law. The noise drowned out his complaints that the meat was overcooked and when would she learn he liked more potatoes and gravy. They ran outside to see Soviet troops storming the palace and the Russian Airborne in the initial phase of the invasion, white parachutes silhouetted in the black sky, floating lazily to the ground.

"They will be after the Pashtuns next," her husband said, flexing his muscular worker's hands into large fists. "We have to flee." He was a tall, bony man, with an ebony mustache and matching heavy eyebrows. He had married her despite almost no dowry, a fact her father-in-law drove home daily. "Your mother and I will stay," her father-in-law said.

"Where will we go?" Nadia asked, fright clouding her eyes.

"The mujahedeen will protect us," her husband replied.

So they packed what little food and clothing they had and fled east to Khost, a tiny town in a mountainous region controlled by the Pashtun. There, on the Afghan-Pakistan border, Nadia's husband became a commander. But they were no match for modern arms when the Soviets assaulted the Eastern provinces. Pashtun resistance crumbled as bombs flew once again. The Soviets overran Khost, killing anyone they found. Nadia's family was wiped out. She was dragged from her home, gang raped, and left to die. But she survived and escaped shivering into the snow-covered mountains of neighboring Pakistan, mourning her children and husband.

As the war progressed, she and other women were accepted in fighting roles. Women terrorists, particularly suicide bombers, became lauded by word of mouth, and their stories of martyrdom, told and retold, achieved folklore status. Brides were said to no longer request a dowry, but an M16 assault rifle. The press labeled them *The Black Widows,* female killers seeking revenge for the loss of their menfolk.

Nadia was among the heroines.

When the Soviet occupation of Afghanistan ended in 1989, Nadia moved back to Kabul. But now the Taliban, one of the mujahedeen groups formed to fight the Soviets, took control. She had to live with her in-laws, who had somehow survived, and could not go out unescorted or work outside the home. She and her father-in-law fought constantly. He was bitter feeding another mouth.

Anger gripped her heart, and she would sit in her room for days, strangled by how unfair life had treated her. She was now forty-three years old and looked fifty-three; the Soviets had taken her family, the Taliban her freedom, and her in-laws her self-respect. *Revenge!* That's what she wanted. She had little to live for and decided to become a suicide bomber. She wanted to be strapped with a bomb and sent out to kill the enemy, *any enemy.* Then she would join her husband and children in Paradise.

Nadia asked Taliban leaders for permission to work in an al-Qaeda terrorist camp sanctioned by them. At the camp, a flint-nosed man approached her about starting a terrorist cell with another woman in New York.

"The Americans are to blame for all of this," he said, waving his hand over the ragged group. "They must be killed."

"How soon can I leave?" had been her response.

The computer screen sprang back to life and the voice jarred Wahad into the present.

"Confirming, order transmitted as you requested. Process activated."

And now, Wahad thought, smiling, *the events that will help overthrow the Western World begin to unfold.*

Chapter Sixteen

"The husband was away at some church meeting. When he returned about 10:00 p.m., he found his wife dead in the bedroom. More than dead. Slaughtered. I read about Driver's murder and immediately had the dispatcher call you. Sorry to get you out of bed, but I figured you'd want in on this."

The call came at three-thirty in the morning and woke me from a sound sleep. I reached across the bed to answer.

"Hello." It came out in a sleep-washed growl. I had been up late the night before going through human anatomy books trying, without success, to find something that looked like the round bloody image in the photo. I rubbed my eyes with my free hand and leaned back against the headboard with the receiver against my ear. The phone cord tightened, pulling the phone base to the floor with a rug-muted crash.

"Detective Dayan? This is the police dispatcher from Hazardville, Connecticut. Sorry to wake you, but I was told to call immediately. There's been a murder here. I was instructed to tell you it had an MO like your Driver murder."

I left a message on Miriam's recorder apologizing that I wouldn't be able to pick the kids up later today, and two and a half hours later I was sitting in the police station of a small New England town talking with Police Chief Dorothy Symanski. I was exhausted from the drive and from lack of sleep, but I remained focused on what she was saying, busily taking notes.

I sat in front of the chief's desk, holding a hot cup of strong black coffee. The omnipresent box of donuts on the desk was tempting, and I hoped they were only as old as yesterday. I grabbed one and checked for green mold before taking a tentative bite. Stale but edible. I scanned the office, which was about the same size as mine but tastefully decorated in pastels with yellow and blue chintz curtains. The decor was obviously picked for a female occupant. Even the chair I sat in had those little white doilies on the arms, to keep them clean, I supposed. No guns and knives behind glass cases, but red and yellow roses that bloomed in a planter on the windowsill. A small bathroom with pink walls opened off to the side. Probably had a hair dryer and a round lighted magnifying mirror. I worried about how much crime passed through this office and how well they could handle a murder investigation.

Symanski looked about fifty, with a head of wavy gray hair and gray-green eyes, muscular arms, and a generous midriff. She had a large mouth with full, unpainted lips and a shadow of a mustache. Polish, I guessed from her name. She wore her wide, no-nonsense Sam Browne utility belt with the assorted cop's tools dangling from various hooks and a big Glock G20 10 mm in a holster. Nothing meshed with chintz curtains and flowers; she was more like some tough cop in a detective movie. I only hoped she was as good as she looked. I wiped white powdered sugar from my mouth. "What do you know about the Hansons?"

"John Hanson's a pillar of the community. Christian Science Practitioner, he calls himself, always talking about that Mary Baker Eddy and her book about science and health and the scriptures. His wife, Melinda, is … *was* a bit of a gossip, but helped him with his work. Also did a lot of volunteering at the local preschool with infants and toddlers. Changed diapers and gave baths. She was good with the little ones. No children of her own. He held meetings at the church once a week or so, usually on Tuesday nights. So it was not unusual for him to be out of the house. According to him, when he came home he suspected nothing. The door was unlocked but he always left it that way. The dark house was a bit unusual, because Melinda usually read late at night or until he got home. They slept apart." Symanski said this with a shrug, and I glanced at her left hand and saw the gold wedding band shine in the morning sun that pushed through the curtains.

"Anyway, he went upstairs and into her room to say goodnight. He turned on the light and found her in bed. Her chest was flayed apart and blood was everywhere. He said he passed out from fright and called us when he came to. He didn't know how long he was out, but we were there three and one-half minutes after the call, the same time as the ambulance. She'd been dead about two hours. Actually she was shot in the head, but he didn't notice the bullet hole. All he saw was her chest, which is understandable, I suppose."

"Any clues?" I asked.

She shook her head. "Very experienced killer. No prints—finger or shoe—and nothing touched in the house. This wasn't a robbery."

"Neither was mine."

The chief grunted. "I know. Two identical murders in different cities scare me."

"Me too, Chief. Copycat murderer or serial killer. Any ideas about motive? We've got none for ours."

"Nope. We questioned the neighbors, but they didn't see or hear anything. The Hansons were quiet people. Rarely went out at night except for church business, like I said. No enemies we know of. Her husband was no help."

"Did you talk with him?"

"No. My assistant did."

Not good. That's why I personally interviewed Driver.

"Family?"

"None, although an adopted daughter lived with them for some years until she went away to college. At least I think they adopted her and a little brother, but I don't know for sure. The brother died as a baby. The children's parents, both doctors, were killed in an auto accident, and she lived with her grandparents for a couple of years until the old folks died. Then the Hansons raised her as a very young girl. Haven't seen her around for a long time, come to think of it. I don't even know what's become of her after she went away to college."

"What was her name?"

Symanski thought a moment, shrugged, and then shouted, "Shorty, get in here."

A gnome of a man entered. Eighty at least, all wrinkled and bent over, he looked as if he'd been left to bake in the sun too long. Shorty wore a gray sweatshirt that said Indianapolis Colts World Champions 2007 with a big white horseshoe and was about three sizes too big for him. The hood on the back reached halfway to his butt, and the bottom of the sweatshirt was almost at his knees. It looked like he slept in it. But his eyes were bright, Paul Newman blue, quick and alert.

Symanski said, "Shorty's been here forever. He'll know." She repeated my question to him.

"Well, her parents' name was Walters. I used to do some yard work for them. Father was a doctor, liked to hunt a lot. Taught the daughter. Real nice kid, though a bit wild. Didn't mind her new parents, as I remember. Or her teachers, for that matter. She liked guns a lot, from her father I guess, but the Hansons wouldn't let her shoot. Won some contests before they made her stop. I watched her grow up till she left for college. Princeton, it was. She had a funny first name. Almost like a man. Let me think for a minute."

I refilled my coffee and stared into the dark bottom of the cup as the chief closed her eyes and leaned back in her chair remembering. It couldn't be, I thought, twirling the cup to fragment my image reflected from the black, still surface. Too coincidental.

"Frankie," said Shorty. "That's what they called her. Real name Francine."

The chief's eyes popped open and her chair jerked upright as she connected with the name. "That's it. She ever come back after college?"

"Haven't ever seen her after she went away," said Shorty, waiting to see if his chief wanted anything more. She waved her hand and he disappeared back into the front office.

Frankie had suddenly jumped to prime-suspect status. The first thing I needed to do was enter the markings of that .38 she wouldn't give me into the computer. The stuff she fed me now sounded like bullshit. I should have taken the gun when I was there. I felt sucker punched.

"Find the slug?" I asked, bringing us back to the murder.

Symanski shook her head. "We found nothing."

"Too bad. We've got the one from Driver's murder to compare. Autopsy?"

"Yes, as we speak."

"Is he any good?"

"Who?"

"The medical examiner."

Symanski shrugged her shoulders. "Name's Billroth. This is the first murder since I've been chief, so I don't know what kind of experience he's had. But we did use a medical examiner and not a coroner."

"Good. Better an MD than a political hack doing the autopsy. Can we go to the morgue? I assume that's where the autopsy is being done."

****

"Shot in the face, probably from the doorway leading to the bedroom," Billroth said, "with the bullet entering her left eye socket and emerging from the back of her head." Hanson was laid out on a stainless steel table, a clone of the one Hunter used. She had a loose drape over her pubic area, in deference to the female captain I guessed, but was otherwise totally naked. Her pendulous breasts were in tatters and her ribs showed through.

The medical examiner lifted Hanson's head and pointed to the hole. The hemorrhagic eye socket was gruesomely obvious. "Someone was a good shot, though probably not that far away. Then her chest was knifed repeatedly with something very sharp."

I donned gloves and studied the corpse. The similarity to Driver's murder was striking. I turned to the chief. "Did you happen to note any blood stains near the body, sort of a roundish stain about the size of a small pager?" I asked. "Maybe on the sheet or blanket?"

Symanski shook her head. "No, why? I don't remember reading anything about that from the papers."

"Wasn't in the papers," I said. "Something I found afterward from the photos and kept it quiet." I stared at Symanski. "You did take photos of the scene?"

"Of course," she said, an angry look on her face. "We may be a small town police force, Detective, but we're not stupid. We have lots of digitals. I haven't seen the prints yet, but it might help if you tell me what I'm looking for." She added, sarcasm dripping, "Or should I try to read your mind?"

I ignored her tone. I probably had it coming, but this place had small town written all over it, and I think she was being defensive. I described the round bloodstain with the short tail.

"I'll certainly look for it. What's it mean?"

"I wish I knew, but my gut tells me it's important." After a pause I continued, "And you carefully searched for the bullet?"

She folded her muscular arms and took a wide stance.

"Like I told you before," she said, "we turned that bedroom upside down. No bullet and no casing—probably because it was a revolver. The slug plowed through the pillow behind her and into the headboard of the bed. There's a fresh gouge where the killer dug it out."

He was smart. This had to be the same guy. "Is the gouge sharply cut, as if he used the same instrument he slashed her with? Is there blood in the wood?"

"No to the sharp cuts, yes to the blood. We haven't gotten the tests back yet, but I'd bet it's her blood."

So he had to have brought three tools, gun, knife, and a gouger. This guy was prepared. "Describe the bedroom."

"Nothing special. Blue shag rug, usual bedroom furniture. Kind of a blonde color. Light blue walls. Couple of pictures. Nothing disturbed."

"You worked the rug carefully?"

She gave me an irritated sigh. "Look, Detective, my guys have already been there and done that. Vacuumed and also swept it with a metal detector and found nothing. You want to get on your hands and knees and check it yourself, please be my guest."

My rapport with Symanski was dissolving. "Chief, I'm only trying to be helpful. Believe me, I want this solved as much as you do."

Maybe I did have a problem with a woman cop trying to be a detective in a small town with its first murder, but I really was trying to be helpful. To start with, she should have interviewed the husband personally. And then the rug needed a more thorough search. Down on my hands and knees was exactly what I had in mind.

"You know, at first the cops didn't find the bullet when Marlon Brando's kid killed his half-sister's boyfriend, because it got lost in the thick shag rug. They found it later, when they combed the rug carefully."

"Like I said, be my guest."

I chewed on my Meerschaum.

"No smoking," Symanski said, jabbing a finger at the sign.

"I'm not, only chewing." I pointed the pipe stem at her.

Another idea struck me and I looked at the pathologist. He had finished the autopsy and was sliding Hanson back into the refrigerator.

"She have any heart disease? An old heart attack maybe?"

The doctor shook his head. "No. A perfectly normal heart, at least from what I've seen so far. I'll study the microscopic slides of the samples I took, but I'll be surprised if she has any heart damage. It looked like there was some liver damage, fibrosis consistent with excess alcohol."

"Any signs of sexual assault?"

"None."

I watched the man wash and dry his hands. "Doctor Billroth, I don't want you to take this the wrong way, but would you mind if I had an outside expert review your autopsy findings?"

Billroth threw the towel into the sink and backhanded my question as if returning a tennis serve. "No problem. May I ask why? Do you think I missed something?"

I smiled to lessen the apparent insult, but Billroth didn't seem to care. "I'm not suggesting you did. I just think it would be good for one doctor to compare both victims if we're trying to pin it on the same guy."

"Sounds like a good idea to me. Who were you thinking of?"

"There's an expert cardiac pathologist at the ASIP who I have worked with—"

"Jayanti Joshi," Billroth interrupted. "I trained with her. Superb teacher. One of the best, if not *the* best. Her friends call her JJ. I tried that in my first month of training and she almost put me on her autopsy table. First and last time I ever tried that!"

We both laughed. This guy was Hunter's opposite. Lots of ego strength. "When was your training?"

He frowned. "More years ago than I care to remember. She's taught a lot of us over the past twenty years or more. We're good friends now. When I see her at meetings I still call her Dr. Joshi. Even a little genuflect might be appropriate in the presence of the queen. Come to think of it, I think she did get knighted—or the female equivalent of that—some years ago in England. Whatever, I'd be happy to have her review my findings. I actually would enjoy her critique of my work, see if I lived up to her expectations."

"Glad you don't mind. She's an old friend. I'll call her when I get back to my office. Chief Symanski, can we visit the Hansons' house? I'd like to see the bedroom myself."

"Going to work the shag rug?"

"That and more. I want to talk with the husband."

"I told you, my guy already did that."

"I know. But a second interview might not hurt."

Chapter Seventeen

Symanski drove to a middle-class section of town. She parked her police car at the curb in front of a small two-level brown shingled home with a tiny, well-kept garden. Yellow police tape was strung from the mailbox at the end of the driveway to the front door. The house sat connected to a modestly-sized church called The First Church of Christ, Scientist. A sign on the lawn in front of the church announced the 10:00 a.m. Sunday lecture, "Understanding Science and Health and Treatment through Prayer," John A. Hanson, Christian Science Practitioner.

"You're sure he's home?"

"Yes. The tape's for the town's busybodies. They were pestering the hell out of him. We have Melinda's bedroom closed off, which is fine since John sleeps in his own bedroom, as I told you. He should be inside waiting for us. I called ahead."

She reached for the car door handle, but I put a restraining hand on her arm and held her eyes for a moment. "Look, Chief, I don't want you taking this wrong, but I'm pretty good at conducting one-on-one interviews. I'm sure you are too," I added, seeing her frown. "But would you mind if I interviewed Hanson alone? I don't want him distracted."

She sat and stared at me, her face reddening. "First, take your goddamn hand off my arm." I released her. "Distracted? I've been called a lot of things, but never a distraction. Have you lost your goddamn mind? You do remember whose town this is, who has jurisdiction, and who called whom, *out of courtesy*, to find this perp before there's another murder? No, I goddamn well will not let you interview him alone. I'm getting tired of your big city attitude. In fact, if you want to sit your own goddamn ass in the car and wait for *me* while I do this alone, that would be just fine."

With that, she got out, slammed the car door shut, and stomped toward Hanson's front door.

"Thanks for your understanding," I mumbled to her empty seat. I got out and chased after her.

Symanski rang the bell several times before John Hanson answered. The old man stood in the doorway wearing a bewildered look. His stained white shirt and dark spotted pants were badly in need of cleaning and pressing. Black suspenders kept them from falling off his skinny hips. A white clerical collar hung askew from the top of his shirt. His thin gray comb-over, long on the right, hung down almost touching his neck. Red eyes made his features seem even more gaunt than usual. The smell of alcohol hung on his breath and surrounded his head like a stalled cloud.

"Mr. Hanson, I am Dorothy Symanski, Chief of Police. I talked to you on the phone earlier today. This is Detective Dayan from the New York Police Department," she said, gesturing to me. Her voice was soft, kindly. This was not the same lady tearing into me moments before. Maybe she *was* good at interviewing.

Puzzled, Hanson jerked his head from her to me.

"We'd like to come in and talk with you," I said. My voice came out kind of loud. Symanski glared at me and recaptured the momentum.

"Do you mind if we ask you some questions about your wife?" she said, entering the small foyer by cutting me off and moving toward Hanson. With a hand in the small of his back, she gently steered him into the living room and sat him down on the couch. She sat next to him as I drew up a chair. The room was gloomy, with drawn shades and the only light coming from a small lamp.

"She's with the good Lord now," were Hanson's first words.

"Yes, I'm so sorry," Symanski said, patting his forearm. He looked at her through tear-soaked eyes. "I know you talked with someone from my office earlier today, and I know how stressful it must be to repeat it all, but we're here to find out everything we can so we capture whoever did this horrible thing. Would you tell us again exactly what you found?" Her voice continued to be soft, reassuring.

Hanson began, slowly at first, and then more rapidly in a booze-lubricated voice, describing the unspeakable tragedy he found when he came home. There was urgency in his slurred rendition, a need to share the horror, perhaps to lighten the load. When he finished, he buried his face in his hands.

We sat silently, waiting for him to compose himself.

After a while, he said, "She did it, you know. I'm sure of it."

"Who?" Symanski and I asked simultaneously.

"Frankie, that's who."

"How do you know?" the chief asked.

"She hated us. Always did. We were never good enough. Always complained when we spent any of the money her parents left her, even though we did it for her. She was never happy. Especially with Melinda."

Hanson reached for the vodka bottle but Symanski covered his hand with hers. "Can you wait and talk with us first?"

He put the bottle down with a shaking hand. "When she came here last week I knew she was up to no good. I said that to Melinda, but she said to give her another chance because—"

Symanski jerked upright. No soft voice this time. "Wait a minute. She visited you last week? Frankie?" Both of us, now united by surprise, looked at each other wide eyed.

Hanson nodded. "Melinda still loved her, and she thought Frankie felt the same." He shook his head in amazement. "If only I had known."

"Why was she here?"

"Said she wanted to get her high school yearbook she had left in her room. Her friends were having a ten-year reunion and she wanted to read what they had written about each other and to look at the high school pictures. I told Melinda not to let her in, but she did anyway. Melinda's more forgiving than I am, at least when it came to Frankie. When Frankie got what she wanted and came downstairs again, Melinda tried to be friendly and give her a hug and kiss. But Frankie pushed her away and left the house. Didn't even say thank you."

"Did you say anything to her?"

"I told her to get out and never come back."

"Can you tell us a little more about when she lived here, when you raised her?" I asked.

Hanson sat back and stared at his hands folded in his lap. His eyes were unfocused, and he seemed to have trouble concentrating. He shook his head, trying to clear the cobwebs. "Took her and her brother in when she was nine or ten. He was a lot younger. They had no relatives. We got nothing in return except the pleasure that comes from doing good deeds." He gave a little nod at Symanski to emphasize that point. "I've included this theme in a number of lectures over the years."

"Then what happened?" Symanski's voice was soft again.

"At first it was fine. Melinda washed their clothes, cooked, and was a real mother to them. I would help with her homework and stuff like that. Then the brother got sick and died, and Frankie blamed Melinda for that. My wife! Can you imagine? Melinda! She'd never hurt a fly." He looked from Symanski to me, his face reddening and his lips pressed white.

"What did you do?" Symanski asked, her voice continuing to be gentle but persuasive. She was good, moving in quickly to capture the private details pouring out with the alcohol vapors.

"Do? Why nothing of course. It was all lies." He stared at her as if she was crazy to even ask. "I told her to quit making up these terrible stories."

He paused, collecting his thoughts, a pained expression on his face. "She stole things, too," he said, vigorously shaking his head up and down.

Neither of us responded. I was waiting to see if more revelations were coming. Finally Symanski broke the silence. "What things?"

"Money, for one thing. When she wanted to buy something that we thought unnecessary or too expensive, she would take money from Melinda's purse or my wallet. She said it was her inheritance and she was entitled to it."

"Did she take anything else?" I asked.

"She stole Melinda's pearls, a necklace and matching earrings. She said they were really her mother's and belonged to her."

"And were they?"

"Well maybe they were, but she was too young to wear them at the time. Still, she took them without asking. I prayed for her after that. We had long talks about right and wrong, and being a good Christian, but she didn't change. She said you got sick or you didn't, nothing to do with God. And once she even told me religion was … bullshit." He choked on the last word and his eyes welled up.

"Mr. Hanson, can we see your wife's bedroom please?" I looked over at Symanski, and she raised an eyebrow in agreement.

Looking defeated, the old man rose and led us upstairs. The yellow tape across the door identified Melinda's bedroom. It was at the end of a short hallway. Three other rooms had closed doors. I guessed they were his and Frankie's bedrooms and the one for the little boy who had died.

"Does he always drink like this?"

Symanski shrugged, pulled down the adhesive, and opened the door. I followed her in as Hanson quietly retreated downstairs. I could hear the tinkling of glass and a long sigh. "This room has been undisturbed since the crime lab people worked it over," Symanski said.

The room was small, just fitting a queen-sized bed, a dresser, and two chairs. A tiny window looked out into the street. The walls were beige. There were two open doors; one with a full-length mirror on it led to a closet, the other to the bathroom.

Blood, turned brownish red, stained the white sheet on the bed. Geysers painted the headboard in graceful colored arcs. I studied the gouge in the wood. "He sure was thorough."

But were you or your people, I wondered, looking at Symanski. Although the room had been dusted for prints and vacuumed for any other evidence, I couldn't shake the image of a small town police force overlooking obvious clues.

"You said you went over the rug with a metal detector?" I asked Symanski.

"Yes."

"Suppose there was something not metal?"

"I told you, the rug was also vacuumed. And we filtered what the vacuum picked up."

"Okay, but suppose something was too heavy to be picked up or was tangled in the nap. I still think it would be worthwhile to comb this rug by hand."

I could see Symanski was pissed, but she didn't argue my logic.

"I'm really trying to be helpful, Chief."

"Okay, Big City Cop, you take that half," she pointed to the far side of the room, "and I'll take this half." She dropped to her knees and began to finger comb the shag before she even completed the sentence. I looked at her for a moment and walked to the corner of the room. With a grunt, I went down and did the same.

Twenty-five silent minutes later she called out, her voice excited. "Found something."

I stood and hustled to her side. I pulled a ballpoint pen from my pocket, handed it to her, and she teased out an earring buried in the nap of the shag rug. It was a rose crystal clustered inside three green leaves.

"Swarovski," she said, identifying the brand. "See here," she pointed with her finger, not touching the earring hanging from the pen, "this is called a French wire; it loops through the ear. But this earring has a stiff plastic filament instead. That's why the metal detector didn't pick it up. Some women have a reaction to metal in their ear and wear this kind of earring."

"Whose is the big question."

"Let's ask the reverend."

Symanski led the way downstairs. Hanson was busy refilling his glass as she held out the earring dangling on the tip of the pen.

He squinted at it and shook his head. "Not Melinda's. I know all her jewelry, since I bought most of it, and this isn't hers."

"Do you remember if Frankie was wearing any jewelry?" Symanski asked.

"Melinda's pearls."

"Any other female visitors who might have been in her room and dropped an earring, either before or after she died?"

"None."

I repeated the question, this time engaging his eyes. "You're sure?"

The minister caught the implication even through his alcoholic fog. He sat up straighter and glowered at me. The effort caused the liquor to slosh over the rim of his glass and onto his pants, which made him angrier. "What do you think I am? Or Melinda? Get out of my house. Now! Both of you!"

In the car, Symanski stared at me. "You know, your one-on-one interviewing skills were really quite impressive. Reminded me of a high school debating team."

"It was a question that had to be asked."

"'Pretty good at conducting interviews'—is that what you told me? Didn't want distractions? You practically accused him of screwing around, and in his wife's bedroom! Or maybe you thought his wife had a girlfriend that lost the earring? Jesus Christ! Where the hell was your goddamn head? He's sure not going to talk to me about this again."

"He could have been cuckolded by some husband who then shot Melinda. You never know until you ask."

"Oh, cuckold is it? Big city word. How about some guy just fucked his wife? That's how we'd say it in Hazardville."

It took about five miles for both of us to cool off. "Look, I'd like to bring that earring back to New York with me for analysis."

"I'm sure you would, but you're not going to." She glanced at me as she drove to the police station where I had left my car. "That piece of evidence stays here,"—she patted the envelope in her pocket—"until we've had a chance to go over it. Then I *might* send it to you."

"I was the one who suggested we comb the rug."

"I'll note that in my report. But the goddamn earring stays here, at least for now."

"When do you think you might send it so we can run a DNA analysis?"

"Couple of days, maybe. I can take a picture of it now and you can have that. You can claim bragging rights with it."

We rode the rest of the way in silence.

Chapter Eighteen

I drove back to the city a good deal slower than when I left eight hours earlier, taking time to appreciate the serene beauty of southwest Connecticut. The graceful wooded hills and late sunny afternoon helped calm my nerves. I lit the Meerschaum and recapped what I knew so far. The process did not make me happy. Two women killed by a head shot, both mutilated in the same way, one with heart disease and the other with cirrhosis. I was missing the link and hadn't learned anything new except for the earring. Symanski practically threw the picture of the earring at me as I left. But maybe, just maybe, the earring was the first concrete clue. However, a woman killer didn't fit my gut.

A thought struck me. Both vics had been married to ministers. Was that the connection? Someone with a vendetta against the church who wanted revenge? Was Hanson right about Frankie? Lots of questions but no answers. So, my next move would have to be a sit-down talk with her.

A *sit-down talk*.

I thought about the sit-down talks I used to have with my dad when I still lived at home while going to the university. We had one of the larger flats near the center of Jerusalem, with a kitchen-dining room, three bedrooms, and a small living room. My father, a cardiologist from Hadassah Medical Center, dominated the dinner conversation with tirades about how hard life was in Israel, and about how whatever position the U.S. president took on the Palestinian "situation" made it even harder. Interesting that he complained so much about life in Israel but would never leave, while I, who was mostly silent during his tirades, couldn't wait to go.

I recalled one conversation in particular.

"Zachary, Bush is such a stupid man," he said, rubbing his chest as he got worked up. "Doesn't he see he aids the terrorists by talking with that crazy fool Arafat? We'll have more bombings, not less." The old man took a nitroglycerin and sipped a glass of red wine. My mother, twenty years younger, smoothed back his gray hair, still as thick as when she married him, and told him to calm down, it would all work out.

"This too shall pass," was her remedy for all calamities.

"And how will that happen?" my father asked, head shaking and hands slicing the air in exasperation. "Bush needs to leave us alone to solve our own problems and not put restrictions on what we can do. If we weren't so dependent on American money ..." He let the sentence dangle, the ending obvious.

"We may be dependent, but look how successful we've become," I answered. "We Jews have been around for more than five thousand years, and where are the other ancient civilizations? The Phoenicians, the Assyrians, the Essenes, and countless other groups? All gone."

"Yes, but I warn you, Zachary, one of our strengths all these years has been what we've railed so hard against, our dispersion around the world, the so-called Diaspora. You can't kill off all the Jews if we are not in one place. So countries like Spain that threw us out in 1492 in the end did us a favor and helped prevent Hitler from achieving his final solution."

"That may be true, but we have our own home for five and a half million Jews and a strong army to protect them, a thriving economy, and science and medicine competitive with the best in the world."

He nodded, agreeing. "But listen carefully," he said, taking a bag of chocolate candies from his pocket and giving me one, "to always remind us of the sweetness of the family," he would say. He kept them in his jacket pocket so they wouldn't melt. But sometimes they did in the hot weather and got all mushy. I was always careful taking off the wrapper. If I ever got pieces of the silver wrapping near the fillings in my mouth, it was like tasting electricity.

"The State of Israel is both a curse and a blessing. A single nuclear bomb from one of our Arab neighbors could destroy all of it, and much of Judaism as well. Never forget that, my son. I know you want to leave, that you have the wanderlust of all young people, but whatever you do and wherever you are, never forget that you, all of us, have a sacred mission to protect Israel and Judaism. Promise me you will do that."

We actually formally shook hands to seal that promise. I was just twenty years old. I was honored my father had such faith in me, and I vowed to live up to the agreement.

When George W. Bush became the forty-third president, the old man's rhetoric softened as he approved of the new U.S. position, waging a battle very similar to ours. Still, he fumed through dinner. It helped his digestion, he said.

After the main course finished, I usually left the table, knowing how the evening would unfold, with my father drinking his second glass of red wine, my mother coaxing him to bed, and she sitting alone finishing her evening's tea before doing the dishes and tidying up. I watched the latest news on CNN in the living room and then met a group of friends at an outdoor cafe, carefully picked as it was tucked away from crowds and the main street.

We had an interesting relationship, my father and I. It was clearly a loving one—that is, until I got married—but there was also a bit of competition. When he first taught me to play chess, he would let me make some moves on him, capture some pieces, but never enough to win.

"Zachary, chess is like life," he said. "Anything you do, you do to win, and you don't ever give up. Even when I'm playing chess with my only son, whom I love dearly, I play to win." He then quoted the famous Vince Lombardi line that winning isn't everything, it's the *only* thing. Our chess matches went on for years, a shekel a game. I never had to pay up, but we did keep score that way. As I got better, his gifts to me on the chess board became less frequent and finally stopped. Then came the big day when I beat him fairly. I carefully planned an endgame strategy, and *it worked! Checkmate.* I was no more than eleven or twelve years old and never savored a victory as much, before or since. I screamed into the kitchen to tell my mother and she came running into the living room, probably expecting to find someone had been murdered. Then she and I danced in circles until she ran out of breath and had to sit down. I tore outside to tell my best friend, Jacob Hertzog, and of course the neighbors, since my father was the unofficial neighborhood champ. He was happy for me but didn't like losing. The games were never the same after that. And then, of course, they stopped entirely after I married Miriam.

He died in 2003, a year before Arafat, and never got to see the changes that followed. He never again spoke of the mission he made me promise to carry out, but I reaffirmed it at his funeral in a silent promise to him.

Driving rain lashed the car in horizontal sheets, and I slowed to forty-five as the gloom blacked out the road.

The slick road demanded all my attention, and I didn't notice the car creep up until I felt the thud of its front bumper hitting my rear. "You fucking imbecile," I yelled. I braked and then accelerated to disengage him. The car behind accelerated also and rammed me again. I heard metal screech. This was no accident.

Someone was trying to run me off the road!

My Honda lurched forward, picking up speed. I stomped the brakes, but the car wouldn't slow. I looked in the rearview mirror, but the tinted glass and headlight glare off the wet road obscured the driver's face. I couldn't even make out whether it was a man or a woman. Whatever was pushing me was huge, wide. Maybe a Hummer.

It forced me to sixty-, seventy-miles-per-hour, and I fought the wheel to keep from jack-knifing off the slippery, curving surface. Our bumpers continued to grind. I leaned on my horn and flashed the brights at cars in the oncoming direction without effect. I swerved back and forth between lanes, but the car dogged my every move. Then, when I did manage to slow, it pulled alongside my left rear door. I strained my neck trying to see who it was but couldn't. The driver cut right, hitting my left rear wheel and spinning me sideways. I jerked the steering wheel to the right and fought to keep the car on the road. The car's rear whiplashed from side to side. My tires spun up gravel from the edge of the road, and stones pinged the car like bullets. Then I heard the sickening thump of a blown tire, and the back end dragged left.

I glanced at the speedometer: eighty! The powerful car behind me overwhelmed my foot and emergency brakes and the flat tire. I could smell the brakes burning and hear metal whining when the tire shredded and the car spun on the rim. I downshifted, grinding the gears, but the car wouldn't slow. I thought about turning off the engine, but I'd lose power steering and the headlights. It would be suicide.

With my left hand wrestling the wheel, I fumbled with the police radio in the dash and turned it to an all frequency channel.

"Mayday! Mayday! This is an emergency, whoever's listening. I am Detective Zach Dayan from New York City Police Department, shield number 457, driving south on I-95, thirty or forty minutes north of New York City. I am being forced off the road by a car behind me. My partner is Harry Scarpia—"

I was coming to the top of a hill when I felt a massive heave as the big car backed off for a second and then crashed my rear. The airbag inflated with a loud bang, exploding in my face as my car surged forward into the oncoming curve.

With my free hand, I pushed the big balloon out of my face and felt the car crest the hill and shoot airborne. The steering wheel spun uselessly. I glanced down for a split second and saw the big car fight the road, tires spitting up gravel from the shoulder, then straighten out at the last minute and speed by. I braced myself for the plunge into one of those graceful wooded hills at 104 miles-per-hour.

Chapter Nineteen

The dispatcher at police headquarters in Hartford, Connecticut, heard Zach's mayday call. He radioed the state police cruiser patrolling nearest the stretch on I-95, where he thought the detective might be. He also dispatched the police helicopter on a search-and-rescue mission and called for an ambulance and fire rescue backup, fearing the worst. Finally, he radioed Harry.

The spotter in the helicopter found the wreckage in minutes and alerted the ground people. The state police trooper in the cruiser arrived on the scene eight minutes after the crash, followed a minute and a half later by the ambulance. The trooper shut down traffic in both directions so the helicopter could land on the center grass strip.

Zach's car had hit a forty-year-old maple tree, whose thick trunk almost bisected the auto. The vehicle was still upright, but Zach was unmoving, pinned behind the steering wheel, which had ruptured the front air bag and collapsed into his chest. A small fire, flames sparkling bright in the dark night, was gaining foothold deep beneath the car's crumpled front end.

The trooper emptied his fire extinguisher on the fire, dousing it for a moment, but the flames caught again, leaping even higher.

A cop from the helicopter ran up.

"Christ! Get him out quick! That fire's going to explode the gas tank any minute," he shouted.

"The car doors are twisted into goddamn metal knots. Won't budge."

"I've got a Haligan crowbar in my trunk," said the trooper. "Maybe we can spring the door hinges."

He ran to the cruiser and came back with the crowbar, jammed one end of the tubular steel into the edge of the door frame near the left front window, and they both leaned against the free end.

Grunting and sweating, they bent the corner of the door away from the frame but couldn't move the hinges.

"Try the other door edge. Or the passenger door."

"Negative for both. This side's too bent around the frame, and a tree limb's sticking through the passenger side."

"What the hell are we going to do now? That fire's going to spread, and if there's even fumes in the gas tank, this guy is history and us too!"

"Can we drag him out the front window?"

The trooper flipped the Haligan around and crashed through the front window with the pointed tang end. He beat a big hole in the glass and tried to climb in. The heat from the fire warmed his face, and he could see the flames growing larger, closing in on Zach's feet. For a moment he got stuck in the window, unable to go forward or back. Finally, after thrashing his feet and the other cop tugging, he freed himself and retreated.

"No way. The front of the car has collapsed around him with the steering wheel leaning on his chest. The only way is to get the door off or maybe the roof."

"We don't have tools for either. Besides, the guy's not moving. He looks dead."

"I hear a siren. Better be more help."

The fire rescue vehicle arrived with a loud screech of brakes, followed by Harry in a wailing squad car. Harry sprinted to the Honda, running alongside the fire captain.

"Who're you?" the captain asked between breaths.

"His partner. I got the call and got here fast as I could."

The captain quickly surveyed the car. "Get the hydraulic spreader," he shouted.

An assistant ran to the truck for the Jaws of Life. He rammed the tips of two thick metal arms into the opening the Haligan had made. Like spreading legs, the piston-powered blades ripped apart the top door hinge with a groan and then did the same to the others. Three pairs of hands grabbed the door edge and pried it back. Grudgingly, with the flames growing more insistent, the door gave way with a loud creak.

"No time for extrication equipment! Put on the cervical collar and hope he has no spine injury!" the captain said.

They fit Zach with the collar and tried to pull him out, but the steering wheel pinned him in his seat.

"Give me the cutter," Harry said. He sheared the steering wheel, cut the seat belt, and they slid Zach out onto a long spine board, immobilizing him with Velcro bands.

"She's ready to blow!" Fire fighters spraying the car dropped their hoses and bolted for cover.

The others fled with the stretcher and crouched behind the fire truck seconds before the car exploded with a deafening roar. Flames lit the night sky in brilliant reds and oranges, and the smell of burning rubber replaced the sweet perfume of the country night. Sleeping birds rocketed from the trees, looking like flying dark clouds against the moonlight.

"Christ, he looks dead," Harry yelled over the noise of the crackling flames, his voice high pitched.

The emergency medical tech, hands quivering from the drama of the night, examined Zach. "He's definitely alive," the tech said. "Blood pressure's low, and he may have ruptured his spleen and be hemorrhaging internally. Or maybe a head bleed. Blood pressure could crash further any moment. After I start an IV, we'll helicopter him to Windsor Locks."

"Is that the best around?"

"Hartford's bigger, but they're on diversion."

"What the hell's that?"

"Not taking emergencies. Full. Big bus accident."

"Then go to Windsor Locks. I'll go with him," Harry said.

They loaded Zach into the helicopter, and Harry joined his partner, holding his head steady in case of a spine injury.

*****

Eight minutes later, the helicopter touched down on an open field next to the Windsor Locks Regional Hospital. Two techs raced to meet it and helped Harry offload Zach's stretcher. They rushed him into the first cubicle of the small emergency area and quickly hooked him up with an electrocardiograph monitor and a finger probe to check oxygenation. A nurse took vital signs.

"Are you a trauma doctor?" Harry asked the young man in white who approached Zach. "Please say you are. My partner needs help."

The man shook his head. "I'm Dr. John Henry, an internist. We don't have trauma specialists, because we're only twenty-five beds. But we can have a specialist here in seven minutes if it's an emergency. Mostly, though, we don't need them. Too expensive to bring one in for every trauma case."

"This is an emergency! Can't you see that? Can you get a specialist here?" Harry asked.

"Blood pressure ninety-eight over sixty, sinus tachy at one ten," the nurse said. "BP's a bit low, but he seems pretty stable."

The doctor looked at Harry. "Don't think we'll need one," he said. "I can handle it."

He began a brief physical exam, checking carefully for head or internal injuries. Harry stood by wringing his hands, helpless to do anything for his partner. He had already called Miriam, who was leaving for the hospital as soon as she could drop the kids off with a neighbor.

"You sure you can handle this?"

John Henry glowered at Harry. "Why don't you back off and let me do my job?"

"Pupils small, round, and reactive to light," the doctor dictated to the nurse, who wrote his words into a chart. The doctor drove his index knuckle hard into Zach's sternum. The big man did not move. "No response to pain." He looked carefully at the site where his finger had been. "Big sternal bruise with extensive subcutaneous bleeding. Steering wheel probably. Maybe fractured some ribs or even contused his heart."

He raised Zach's arm a few inches off the bed and let it go. It dropped like lead. He got the same response with the other limbs.

"What's all that mean?" Harry asked, brow creased in a frown. He didn't like what he was seeing.

"Could be a cerebral hemorrhage, but his eyes respond normally. Makes it less likely. Still, we'll need a head CT to rule it out."

"Can you get one now?"

The doctor didn't answer, but listened with his stethoscope to Zach's lungs and heart. "Spontaneous respirations, good breath sounds bilaterally. So no lung perforation or pneumothorax. Heart sounds normal. Sinus tachy, to be expected under the circumstances." He felt Zach's belly. "Soft, no guarding." He listened. "Normal bowel sounds, so spleen's probably not ruptured."

"All that's good?" Harry asked, a hopeful note in his voice.

The doctor straightened up. "It is."

He addressed the nurse. "Draw a chem 7, type and cross match for five units of whole blood just in case, and give a liter of normal saline, with a keep open of more saline. Also, get routine toxicology on blood and urine. Then send him to radiology for a total body CT scan. There's no obvious broken bones or internal hemorrhaging, but let's check to be sure. No need to panic, but I'm a little worried about the low BP and mental status."

Harry started to trail Zach's stretcher to radiology.

The doctor put a hand on his arm. "You'll only be in the way," he said. "They'll call us if anything changes. Have a cup of coffee and wait here. Cool it."

Fifteen minutes later came the dreaded page.

"Code blue radiology! Code blue radiology!"

"Oh shit," the doctor said, bolting from an emergency cubicle and leaving an elderly woman with a stomach ache. He motioned to Harry and they both raced to the radiology department.

"He may be herniating his brain stem," the doctor said while running. Harry was close on his heels.

"What the hell does that mean?"

"Death."

Radiology was in the basement of the building where the heavy equipment sat on the building's foundation and the lead walls confined X-ray leakage.

"What's happened?" the doctor yelled between gasps as he entered the CT room.

The radiology technician was white faced, paralyzed. "He's unconscious!"

"I know that, damn it. He was before!" the doctor shouted.

"No, you don't understand. He regained consciousness a few minutes ago—he even asked where he was—and suddenly lost it again."

"What're his vitals?"

"I don't know."

"Well don't stand there like a damn idiot. Get me a blood pressure cuff! Where's the oxygen? Why isn't he on a monitor? Do something for Christ's sake! Don't just freeze!"

The tech ran for the blood pressure cuff and the doctor quickly checked it.

"Forty over twenty! Pulse one hundred forty. That's why he's unconscious! He must've regained consciousness from the head trauma and now he's unconscious because of hypotension. Something bad's happened to bottom out his blood pressure."

"Goddamn it, I'm calling for backup," Harry said, sprinting from the room. "I should've done it first thing." He dialed the precinct, told them what was going on, and instructed them to find an emergency specialist in the area and get him here as quickly as possible.

"Did you finish the CTs?" Harry heard the doctor ask as he reentered the room.

"Yes."

"What did they show?"

"Everything's normal, except his cardiac silhouette looked a little big. I think there was a small effusion. And several cracked ribs."

Harry asked, "What's that mean?"

"I don't know," John Henry said. "Possibly pericardial tamponade."

"What's that?"

"Fluid fills the sac around the heart and prevents it from contracting."

"Well, is it or isn't it?"

"I don't know. I'm not a cardiologist."

"Well, call one, for Christ's sake."

The doctor turned to the technician. "Do a cardiac echo immediately! And page Dr. Derek Williams, on call for cardiology. Tell him we have an emergency cardiac tamponade and I need him to tap the pericardium now. Immediately!"

"I can't do both. Which do you want first?"

"You do the echo, I'll page Williams."

He had his answer in forty-five seconds: pericardial tamponade.

"Shit. Of all places to have a medical emergency, radiology is not one of them," he said. "Open the IV wide. Let it pour in. Get some isoproterenol to add to it. You do have some down here, don't you?"

"No," came the anguished reply.

The doctor rechecked the blood pressure. Twenty over zero! "I can't wait for Derek Williams. With his BP this low, in seven minutes this guy'll be dead! Even in five! Do you have a pericardiotomy set up and a pericardiocentesis needle?"

"Yes, Dr. Williams routinely does elective pericardiocenteses here in radiology."

"Well this is no elective. Get me the set up now!"

Harry could only look on, pacing up and down, rubbing sweaty hands on his pants leg.

In thirty seconds, John Henry swabbed Zach's chest with betadine, making it look like Worcestershire sauce spilled on his skin. He pulled on rubber gloves and took the pericardiocentesis needle out of the tray. It was six inches of lethal-looking round stainless steel with a razor sharp point. He connected the flange at the base of the needle to a plastic syringe. Not bothering with local anesthesia, he palpated Zach's lower sternum, felt the xyphoid notch, and plunged the needle into the chest. Dry tap. He drove the needle in again, nothing.

"What's his blood pressure?" he asked the tech.

"Zero. Nothing. No pulse palpable!"

By now the tech had Zach hooked to the EKG monitor and the heart rhythm began to deteriorate with malignant runs of extra ventricular beats that were increasing in frequency.

"We're seconds from full cardiac arrest and irreversible brain damage." His forehead beaded with sweat. "Where the hell is Derek Williams?"

"Maybe he's not available?" Harry asked. "I've got help coming, but I don't know how soon they'll get here."

"Whenever it is, it won't be soon enough. We've got seconds left."

The EKG machine began beeping a shrill, urgent sound that started slowly but was going faster and faster.

"Do you have a crash cart here with an external defibrillator?" the doctor asked the tech.

"Yes, I'll get it." She walked quickly toward the door.

"Run, for Christ's sake, don't walk! Where's your head?"

She bolted through the doorway. John Henry stabbed the needle in a third time, directly at Zach's heart.

"Dear God, be right this time," he mumbled.

Pay dirt! Bloody fluid rapidly filled the syringe. He emptied it and aspirated again. Four times he repeated the maneuver, until the aspiration went dry. He looked at the monitor.

"Normal sinus rhythm, stable as you please," he said. He rechecked the blood pressure. "One twenty over eighty, also stable as you please." Elation lit up his eyes and he grinned.

"He's going to be okay?" asked Harry, a hopeful look on his face.

At that moment, Derek Williams burst into the room followed by the tech pushing the crash cart.

Derek's run slowed to a walk as he assessed the situation. "Looks like you did fine, John. Didn't need me after all."

"I sure could have used you several minutes ago, but I think all's okay now."

Harry helped them move Zach to the Cardiac Care Unit to be monitored closely. He wasn't going to be separated from him again.

Chapter Twenty

An hour later I was sitting up in bed, sipping water through a bent straw. I was thirsty and made slurpy noises as I drained the glass.

"Not too fast or you'll get sick," Harry said.

"And how would you know, Doctor?"

"They always say that on TV."

I groaned.

"How bad is it?" Harry asked.

"Aside from my chest hurting, a splitting headache, and other assorted pains, I'm doing great. Not much worse than arresting a couple of Friday night drunks."

"You take the pain meds?"

I shook my head.

"Tough guy?"

"No, messes up my thinking."

"I called Miriam as soon as I found out and told her you were okay. She had to find someone to watch the kids, but I'm sure she'll be here any moment."

"Thanks for doing that."

"So what happened?"

I told Harry as much as I remembered.

"That's about what I heard, probably fifteen minutes or so after that asshole ran you off the road. I put out an APB for a large car near and south of that section of I-95—that was all we had to go on. I had all the exits blocked, even those going north in case he turned around, but we got nothing. Pretty thin information to go on—basically just the description that it was a large car."

He paused and seemed to study me. "Why you?"

I shook my head slowly, considering his question. I had been wrestling with it since I regained consciousness. *Why me?*

"I'm not sure, Harry, but it's got to be this murder investigation; all of a sudden it's turned personal."

"You're convinced the two are related?" he asked. "I mean, not just a nut job on the road? Maybe someone you cut off. Road rage sort of thing?"

"Hardly. I was minding my own business—driving pretty slowly, as a matter of fact—when I got zinged."

"Maybe you were blocking the road and he was in a hurry?"

"C'mon, Harry. Cut the bullshit. He—or she—deliberately ran me off the road."

"Should I post a cop outside your room in case someone tries again?"

"Honestly, I don't know what to think. Two similar murders, the last one Frankie's adoptive mother. They got to be related. Check and see if Frankie owns a car that fits the—"

Before I could finish, Miriam burst through the door, ran to my bed, and threw her arms around me. Through her sobs I heard Harry say good-bye and saw him slip out of the room.

She had her head buried into my neck. "I almost lost you. I can't believe I almost lost you."

I stroked her hair. "But you didn't."

"Oh, Zach."

"I'm glad you're here. Hey, you're dripping tears on my bandage."

She tried to smile, dried her eyes, and sat next to me on the edge of the bed, looking at my face. We held hands as she studied my bandages. I was wearing a white gauze turban and beige elastic binders that held padded dressings in place over my ribs.

"You could be a sheik or something."

I laughed but grimaced when it shot pains through my chest.

Miriam's face looked worried. "Are you okay, I mean, really okay?" She ran her fingers lightly over the bandages.

"I'll be fine as soon as they take out this drain in my heart."

She dropped her hand and jumped up off the bed. "My God! It's in your heart?"

"Not to worry. You can't do any damage." I patted the side of the bed for her to sit down again. "In the sac around my heart. I was lucky. They said I'll be fine and out of here in a couple of days."

Her brow furrowed, but then her face relaxed. She hugged me again, gently, and was silent for a moment. I could hear her breathing. Then she said, "Zach, what's happened to us? How did we get here?"

"Not now, Mim. We can't get into that now. My being a cop—"

"No, that was a big part of it, but it was more. Your parents never forgave me for marrying you, for not being Jewish."

"Not true. You were a wonderful daughter-in-law. It's just that—"

"Zach, be realistic. I am German, and that's how your father saw me from when I met him until he died. He also blamed me for your not finishing med school."

"Mim, let's not go there again. It serves no purpose. Especially now." I waved a hand around the hospital room, but she wasn't hearing me.

"I feel guilty, about our marriage, about you, about Rachel's heart problem—"

"That's ridiculous and you know it. You're feeling the shock of my car wreck."

She held my hand, kissing the fingers. "Zach, I've failed at everything—wife, mother ... daughter-in-law." She began to cry again.

Damn, I hated scenes like this. So I held her as she cried, stroking her hair, not knowing what else to do.

Finally she stopped, and we talked about possibly getting together again. She said she knew lots of couples who got remarried after a divorce. I supposed it might work, although I didn't expect either of us to change, but we talked about it, and she felt better.

"What about that Charlie guy?"

"I only saw him once or twice. There's no one, Zach. I feel like I have no anchor anymore. A stiff wind and I could almost blow away."

"Where to? Kansas?" It was a poor attempt at a joke.

"Maybe back to London."

****

Incredibly, forty-eight hours after almost dying, I was discharged from the hospital with nothing more than a taped chest to help my three cracked ribs heal and a Band-Aid covering a tiny dark round scab over the site of the needle puncture in my chest. They gave me pain pills, but I tossed them in the can on the way out.

Chapter Twenty-One

Wahad stopped the car in front of the house, double-checked the address once more, and patted the extra large coat pockets and knapsack to make certain all the tools were there.

After backing the black car deep into the dense shadows of the giant pin oaks in the quiet residential neighborhood of Tenafly, New Jersey, Wahad sat still for ten minutes and watched, eyes and ears alert for any movement nearby. Under the beam of a small penlight, Avery Zimmerman looked healthy. The three-year-old picture showed him on active duty as a Navy SEAL, standing with a group of his buddies outside a bar in Times Square, New York. His arm was draped across the shoulders of one of the other men, looking as if he was propping him up, perhaps from too many beers. Heart failure made him take early retirement. Still, Zimmerman was big, and Wahad hoped he was sleeping.

Wahad opened the door, got out, pressed back against the side of the car, and stood for a moment adjusting to the surroundings. The house was completely dark. The night was overcast, and the moon tried in vain to shine through thick clouds chasing each other across the sky. A light breeze rippled the leaves of the trees overhead. In the distance, a dog barked. Wahad waited another moment to be sure. But all remained silent and still, with only dark shadows from the drifting clouds flitting across the face of the white stucco house.

Confident the situation was in order, Wahad closed the car door softly and moved to the garage entrance, staying within the gloom cast by the trees. At the side of the house the security alarm was easily disarmed. The Black Widows were right again. Their talent to get

111

the necessary information was accurate and timely. Wahad would be pleased to bring them a present this time.

The garage door was unlocked, as Wahad knew it would be. The red and gray Nike running shoes made no noise as Wahad walked up three steps from the garage to the kitchen, entered a short hallway, and flicked on the pen light for an instant. Bearings set, Wahad knew exactly where the master bedroom was from the BWs' map of the house's interior. Wahad moved very slowly, left hand gently caressing the wall as a guide, pupils dilated in the pitch-black house. Wahad's fingers bumped a picture on the wall. That wasn't supposed to be there! The picture rocked back and forth on its hook, and Wahad groped with the other hand to steady it before it crashed. Wahad's breathing accelerated, heart racing until the swinging frame settled.

The entrance to the bedroom was two feet away and the door was open. Wahad heard a rustling of bedcovers as Avery Zimmerman turned in bed, perhaps disturbed by the slight grating sound when the picture wobbled.

Wahad slipped on the night goggles to scan the room. Had they been on before, the picture on the wall would have been avoided, but Wahad was concerned about Zimmerman waking and suddenly turning on a light.

Wahad removed the goggles and let them dangle from the neck cord. Just in time. Zimmerman rolled over, flicked on the light next to the bed, and stood. Wahad froze, black hood, jacket, and pants blending in with the shadows. Slowly Wahad slipped the .45 revolver from the deep side pocket of the jacket. It was bulkier than the slim .38.

Zimmerman stretched, yawned, and walked around the foot of the bed. Wahad knew from the floor plan that he was headed to the bathroom. A light came on. Moments later, the toilet flushed, the bathroom light extinguished, and Zimmerman re-emerged into the bedroom. But instead of returning to bed, he hesitated directly opposite where Wahad stood and squinted into the darkened hallway. Wahad tensed, knees flexed.

Zimmerman was silhouetted perfectly by backlight, and it was clear something disturbed him—a sound, a premonition, or maybe the glint from the gun. Wahad slowly raised the .45 and took aim as Zimmerman lunged. The bullet missed its head mark and plowed into the wall over the bed. Zimmerman flailed blindly in the dark hall, eyes still adjusted to the light in the bathroom. His arms brushed Wahad's shoulder as he cried out and charged forward. Zimmerman got his big hands around Wahad's neck, and Wahad fought to breathe. But the action left Zimmerman gasping for breath. His weakened heart couldn't support the fight and his grip slackened. Wahad fired into the big form, keeping the shot low to avoid his chest. A scream of pain confirmed a gut hit as Zimmerman went down, those big hands now clutching his belly.

Wahad was on him in an instant, pinning him down with a knee in his chest. Not trusting another gunshot into the writhing form, Wahad dropped the gun and snapped out the scalpel, its sharp edge glittery from the bedroom light. With one hand, Wahad grabbed a handful of Zimmerman's hair as the other hand swiped the blade, severing Zimmerman's windpipe and abruptly finishing the battle. Zimmerman's arms flailed a moment longer and a gurgle signaled an end to his struggles on earth.

Wahad ripped open Zimmerman's pajama top, quickly felt the skin, and began surgery.

Chapter Twenty-Two

"What have you found out?" I asked Harry.

I was finally back at work and not happy. I had spent six long days at home, made even worse after Harry called me about Zimmerman's murder. I prowled from one room to the next, restless in my little apartment, trying to fit pieces of the murders together. I even had the janitor hang a blackboard on my living room wall so I could doodle my thoughts. The Meerschaum had practically burned a hole in my tongue, and the apartment reeked of Flying Dutchman.

Miriam came by with the kids every day, cooked and cleaned, and even re-bandaged my chest. She cried a little when she did that, lingering over the last bit of tape. The kids ransacked my candy reserves, and I had to get online to order more.

After almost a week, I was able to badger the doctor into releasing me to return to work as long as I promised not to pump iron for the next month. My cracked ribs needed time to knit. I guess the Cybex machine and weights would cool until then.

Now back at work, I had three brutal murders to solve. Four, considering the sleeping guard.

"Nothing more than I told you before," Harry said.

He was in his usual place in the chair in front of my desk. His double-breasted gray Brioni suit was set off by a four-pointed white silk handkerchief in his front pocket and a pale purple silk Zegna tie. I guess he wasn't packing the .357 Magnum today. But I couldn't believe what I was seeing.

"We've got four unsolved murders on our hands, I was almost killed by a crazy, and you're looking like the cover of *GQ*. What have you been doing while I was home? Shopping at Milano Men?"

"Trying to solve the murders. I re-drove your route looking for clues. And spoke with Chief Symanski."

"And?"

"We think the killer figured Symanski's office would call you about Hanson's murder because of the similar MO and he or she just waited in Hazardville for you to show up."

"And followed me when I went to the police station and then to the morgue?"

"Yes."

"So the next question is, why Melinda Hanson?"

"Symanski told me about the earring. Maybe Francine Walters pulled a two-fer?"

"Kill her adoptive mother and then me? After that, Zimmerman? Possible."

"Symanski said you didn't find any slug in the bedroom."

"Only the earring. The murderer dug the bullet out of the headboard of the bed. What'd you find at Zimmerman's?"

"Same chest slashing with two differences. The fight and a bigger caliber gun. The casing's from a .45 semiautomatic. Took out a big piece of his stomach. The perp dug one slug out of the wall and another from the floor. Probably changed guns to make it harder to trace."

"The neck cut fit the guard at Driver's murder?" I asked.

"We're checking, but probably. Same sharp instrument as the chest slashings."

"I think it's time for another visit to Frankie. Take a look at her earrings," I said. Holding my chest, I rose from the desk, but I couldn't prevent the grunt of pain escaping my lips.

Chapter Twenty-Three

"Not you two again," Frankie said. "Isn't it a little early for S and M?"

"Miss Walters, may we come in?" I asked.

She looked us over in the dim hallway light. "No Taser?"

I shook my head, but no smile. I was in no mood for games.

"I don't have much time for you guys today. Sorry. Job interview."

She was wearing a tailored blue suit with a creamy satin blouse and a double strand of white pearls and matching pearl teardrop earrings. Eyeglasses with blue frames and slate blue mascara highlighted her blue eyes.

Harry had that *hot iron on a wet shirt* look. She winked at him and cupped her hands for a stage whisper. "Remember? Second drawer on the left."

Harry turned scarlet. She laughed.

"Where's the job interview?" I asked.

"The New York Athletic Club on Sixth Avenue and Central Park South. They're hiring an associate director. But they told me there's a long list of applicants."

"Think you'll get it?"

"I hear they've got lots of new Arab members. Since I speak Arabic, I should have an edge."

"Where'd you learn Arabic?"

"Majored in Middle Eastern studies at Princeton."

"You know about Melinda Hanson?" I asked.

"Chief Symanski called me a few days ago. She said you were hurt in a car accident on the way home. You okay now?"

"I am, thanks." I studied her face. "You don't seem too upset about her death."

Frankie snorted. "Upset? Should I be?"

"Isn't it true she and her husband raised you?"

She scowled. "If you call it that."

"Care to explain?"

Our voices echoed in the hallway. The apartment door opposite to Frankie's opened and a woman poked her head out. Frankie made a face at her and twiddled "bye" with her two fingers. The woman glared and slammed her door. "That's the hairy shrew."

"Who?"

"Married to the old fart. Never mind. Just a neighbor. C'mon in and I'll make us some coffee."

We sat down at the small round kitchen table with a rustic pine top. I kept my back to the sun and watched Harry watching Frankie. She turned to the stove and busied herself making the coffee. Harry followed every movement. "What do you want to know?" she said over her shoulder. I stared at her pearl necklace and earrings.

"Why don't we start with why you're not upset your adoptive mother—or whatever she was—is dead? Murdered."

"Because I don't give two shits about her or her husband." Frankie slammed the coffee pot on the stove.

Then I saw a transformation. Her shoulders hunched and she began to cry silently, hands braced on the sink and chin on her chest. After several moments, she stopped and drew a big breath.

"As you can tell, that's not true. Or, at least not entirely true." She turned around and dabbed her eyes with a dish cloth. Her mascara had run blue streaks down her cheeks. "Goddamn it. I am *so* fucked up about them. About her." She poured the coffee and sat down.

"Want to tell me about it?"

"Not really, but I guess I have to." She paused to collect herself. "They took my brother and me in as orphans, adopted us, and raised us from when I was ten until I left for Princeton. So I guess I loved them ... I *did* love them ... but we had a lot of shit going on that made life with them hard for me. For them too, I guess."

"Like what?"

"My brother died of a ruptured appendix, and I felt she was responsible."

I waited for her to continue, but she didn't. "That's it, the whole story?"

She barely moved her head.

I didn't believe it. "When did you see her last?"

"When I left for freshman year at Princeton. Let's see, I have my ten-year high school reunion coming up, so that must have been about six years ago."

"Haven't seen her since?"

Frankie ran her fingers through her hair, freeing up bobs of blonde thistles. "Yes, as a matter of fact," she said slowly, "I saw her last week."

Harry's eyebrows raised. "Why?"

"I went back to get my high school yearbook I had left in my room years ago. You have a problem with that?"

"Actually, I do. You say you loved them, but you don't contact either for six years, and then suddenly pay a visit? A yearbook seems a pretty thin reason to go calling on someone after so long a time. You could have asked her to mail it to you."

She didn't answer.

"Why didn't you volunteer that information?" I asked.

"Which?"

"Your most recent visit."

"I just did."

"Before."

"Why should I? Just forgot. It was such a quick visit."

"Did you fight with her when you left?"

Frankie was silent. She poured coffee into three white and blue striped ceramic mugs and sat down, ignoring the question. "You think I did it? That I killed her?"

I put two sugars in my coffee and stirred the black liquid before I answered. "I had been fixed on the perp being a man, but—"

"Aha," Frankie interrupted. "You do say perp. FBI guys don't."

"What do you mean? Have they been talking with you?"

She hesitated and thought a moment. "I once knew someone there. And if they *were* here, what's it to you?"

"This isn't their jurisdiction. I'd like to know why they were interested."

She left my statement unanswered.

"Miss Walters ... may I call you Frankie? The 'miss' part is getting awkward."

"Whatever suits you," she said, sipping her coffee. She tipped her head at us. "You guys got first names?"

I pointed my spoon at Harry. "Harry, and I'm Zach. I also need to tell you, while this is not a formal interrogation, anything you say can and will be used against you in a court of law."

"No problem. I'm not about to tell you anything important since I didn't do it. Although I've dreamed about her dying a gazillion times."

"You want to elaborate on that?"

Frankie paused again and looked off into the distance for several moments. Then she squeezed her eyes shut, and when she opened them, tears welled up again in the corners. Irritably she brushed them aside. Harry handed her his Brioni handkerchief. In an instant it was streaked with blue mascara, and he grimaced.

"Sorry," she said to Harry, dabbing at her eyes. "I thought I was over all this shit years ago."

Harry put up his hand as she attempted to return the handkerchief. "No problem. Keep it."

Her smile was sad as she took a deep breath. "My parents were killed in a car crash when I was eight years old."

She shifted in her chair, chewing on a fingernail. Then she shook her head, as if trying to dislodge the memories.

"What?" I asked.

"It's hard to talk about. I saw a shrink for a lot of years until I realized you can't outrun your childhood, no matter how hard you try. You carry that smelly baggage all your life. If you're lucky, you reduce it to a carry-on."

"Tell me what happened."

"After our parents died, Tommy and I went to live with our grandparents in Hazardville. It's a small town south of Springfield, Connecticut. When they died two years later, John and Melinda Hanson volunteered to take us in. He was the town's Christian Science Practitioner and she was the town gossip."

"Nice of them."

"So it seemed. An act of Christian charity, John told the church. He forgot to add that we had a multimillion dollar trust fund from our parents' life insurance policy."

"He had access to that?"

"Specific provisions in the policy said in the event of our parents' death, whoever was taking care of us could use the money for our support."

"Do you think they stole from you?"

"Let's say they were generous in paying for what they 'needed' to take care of us, like redoing their house. Anyway, the First Church of Christ, Scientist, was John's life. He was always spouting from Mary Baker Eddy's book *Science and Health with Key to the Scriptures*, about the evils of sin and how a belief in God cured all physical ills."

"But they took good care of you both?"

"Depends how you define 'good.' They adopted us and fed us. That was about it."

"Were you a family?"

"We all ate dinner together. After dinner John drank vodka, because he thought it left his breath odorless, and Melinda sipped gin, but she was always ahead since she started before lunch.

"John helped us with our homework before his postprandial vodka high hit, while Melinda ..." She stopped and stifled a big sob, unable to go on.

We just sat there, waiting until she got hold of herself.

After a while, Frankie gave a sort of apologetic smile, shrugged, and continued.

"Melinda furthered John's efforts to convey God's infinite goodness by disciplining us. Right after we arrived, she told Tom and me how our lives would be from then on. 'You will pray daily, there will be no dentists or doctors, because if you are good you will not get sick, and you will never, ever steal, smoke, drink alcohol, swear, or lie.'

"So, when we were disobedient, her punishments were swift and severe."

"Like what?" I asked.

"Bed without dinner for simple stuff, like scuffing new shoes or tearing a hole in a pair of jeans. We'd be grounded after school for a month if we disobeyed her and shut in a clothes closet for hours—private prayer, she called it—if we were caught lying. Of course, Melinda was judge, jury, and enforcer."

"Sounds tough. How old were you?"

"I was ten and Tommy was five when we first went to live with them."

"What happened next?"

That brought more tears and she dabbed at her eyes. Harry had a peculiar look on his face that I couldn't quite figure out. It was a cross between pity and anger. Whichever, his eyes never left her face.

"'Aches and pains are not real,' Melinda told us, 'only illusions caused by improper behavior and treated by prayer and renewal of true belief.' So, a year later—Tommy was six—when he came home from school on a Friday with a note from his teacher saying he had been reprimanded for refusing to sit at his desk and insisting on going to the bathroom, she had a fit. Next to disobeying her, doing something bad in public was the worst."

"'Why didn't you behave and listen to your teacher?' Melinda shouted at him.

"Tommy told her he had a tummy ache, but the teacher didn't believe him. And that he had to go to the bathroom to do number two, but nothing came out.

"Melinda lost it and slapped him across the face. 'The tummy ache is because you were bad. You have to be punished and pray to God for forgiveness,' she said.

"She accused him of lying, dragged him to the closet, and told him to pray in there. Tommy was kicking and screaming, but Melinda pushed him in, closed the door, and locked it. I fought her for the key, but she locked me in my own room for the night."

Frankie was crying openly now, trying to talk between sobs.

"When morning came, Melinda first let me out of my bedroom, then unlocked the closet door. Tommy tumbled out onto the floor, pale as death and babbling incoherently. His hands were wrapped in his pants, where he had been clutching his stomach.

"'Pray for your brother,' she commanded. 'You see how bad he has been.'

"'He's sick. He needs a doctor,' I screamed.

"'Nonsense. There are no physical ills, only mental. Pray for him and he will get better.'

"She wouldn't listen to me. She picked Tommy up and carried him to his room. He was screaming and clutching his stomach as she put him on the bed. Then she grabbed me by the back of my neck and made me get down on my knees alongside the bed and pray with her. Then she pushed me out of the room and locked Tommy in."

Frankie's hands were shaking as she blew her nose. She stopped for a moment to catch her breath.

"I was out of my head. Even as an eleven-year-old, I knew there was something terribly wrong with Tommy. So I ran to my room and got the Mossberg 0.22 rifle I kept under the bed. I had hidden it when Melinda sold off my father's collection. I inserted a loaded clip and found Melinda in the living room. I told her to call the doctor or I would shoot her. My hands were shaking so much I could barely point the gun."

I guess my eyes must've gotten big, because Frankie looked at me and smiled a bit. "Would you have shot her?" I asked.

"I don't know. I was pretty riled up. Anyway, she yelled at me to put the gun down, and I remember her starting to walk toward me to take the gun. I pulled back the bolt and chambered a round. That stopped Melinda dead in her tracks, and she turned and dialed the doctor.

"I held Tommy in my arms until the doctor arrived. He was burning with fever. Gradually, his cries became little whimpers, and finally stopped altogether. By the time the doctor arrived, he was dead of a ruptured appendix."

"Oh my God," was all I could say. Frankie's crying had stopped and she had become cemetery quiet.

In a monotone voice she said, "I screamed at Melinda that she had killed him, that she was a murderer, but the doctor said he just died; there was nothing that could have saved him. I called him a liar, and he gave me an injection that made me fall asleep.

"Tommy was buried the next day, and that night I ran away. I couldn't live in that house a minute longer. I blamed myself as much as I did Melinda. Anyway, I didn't get very far before somebody called the police about a little girl walking along the highway carrying a rifle and pulling a suitcase on wheels. Not your usual scene, I guess."

Harry and I smiled at the image and at what the cops must have thought.

"What happened when you came home?" I asked.

"Melinda surprised the hell out of me by being warm and sympathetic when the cops brought me back. I found out later the doctor had warned her I could testify to child neglect charges in the case of Tommy's death. So, in a flash, she became a loving adoptive mother and we settled into a sort of uneasy truce. I went to Princeton University on the money my parents left and never saw them again until last week."

"Is that why you do the Blue Angel thing with ministers and priests?"

A tiny nod. "My way of playing Marlene Dietrich."

She brewed another pot of coffee and we sat silent, each deep in our own thoughts. I was replaying my life with Miriam, with all its lost opportunities.

Frankie broke the silence. "I hadn't seen John and Melinda in a long time, and I was curious how they looked and what had happened to them since I left. After all, they were a part of my life for many years. I wanted to thank them for all they had had done for me, and maybe apologize for how I had acted at the end."

"How was that?"

"I got into my car to go to Princeton and didn't even say good-bye, never mind a thank you. So, I guess that was the real reason I wanted to visit. I needed closure on the whole episode about pulling a gun on her, about Tommy's death. I also did want to get my yearbook. That part was true. So I went to their house last week. Melinda wanted to hug me, but seeing her made all the old feelings come flooding back—the feelings of guilt, mine, hers—and I couldn't handle it. I got angry all over again. So I pushed her away and left. John was standing right there the whole time. The total visit lasted less than ten minutes."

"Have you seen them since?"

"No."

"Ever steal from them?"

She shook her head and fingered the necklace. "These were mine to begin with, left to me by my mother. Like I told you, the money they were spending on themselves was my inheritance. And, except for my

.22 rifle, they sold my father's entire gun collection, which was worth a lot of money, and they kept it all. So no, I never did steal from them. Not by my standards, anyway."

"Why did you wear the pearls when you visited?"

"How do you know I did?"

"Hanson said so."

She compressed her lips. "To rub their noses in it."

"Do you have other pairs of earrings?"

"Of course, but I usually wear these. Why?"

I took out my notebook. In the pages was the enlarged photo of the earring Symanski gave me. "Do you have a pair like these?" I handed her the picture.

She took it from me and studied it a long time before answering. "Yes, I wear them when the metal earrings irritate my lobes," she said in a small voice. "Why?"

"Would you get the pair for me to look at, please?"

Frankie walked confidently to her dresser at the end of the room and opened a rectangular red velvet box sitting on top. Debussy's "Claire De Lune" echoed across the room. She quickly found one rose earring and then rummaged for its mate. Her movements became increasingly agitated, until she finally dumped the contents of the jewelry case on the dresser top. The case slid off the dresser, fell to the floor, and the music abruptly stopped.

"Oh shit, not again," she said. "I just had the damn thing fixed two days ago for fifty bucks."

I watched her pushing necklaces, pins, and earrings in circles on the dresser top until she finally gave up and walked back, holding only one earring. Her hands were shaking.

"Only one?" I asked.

She nodded.

"Any idea where the other one is?"

She seemed to regain her composure. "If I did, don't you think I would have told you? I have no idea where it is, but I have a feeling you do."

"Ms. Walters—Frankie—I think the mate to the earring you are holding in your hand was found in the shag rug in Melinda's bedroom after her murder. You said you wore your pearl earrings when you visited them. Do you remember if you had those rose earrings with you, maybe in your purse when you saw them, and if you went into Melinda's bedroom during that visit?"

"No." She appeared frightened. "I didn't wear them and didn't carry them. I wore these pearls," she touched her earlobes, "like I told you, to piss them off. And I didn't go into her bedroom, just my own."

Harry had been sitting quietly all this time. When he finally spoke, he had a pained expression on his face, and his voice was as gentle as I had ever heard it. "Frankie, think hard. Did you lend your earrings to someone who maybe returned only one? Could someone have come into your apartment and taken one? Or maybe you dropped one in the street somewhere. This is pretty serious stuff, Frankie. It can put you at the crime scene."

She finger-combed her hair again. "I don't even like the fucking pair. Ugly roses with green leaves. I haven't worn them in ages. But they're pretty common non-metal earrings. I got them at Macy's. Maybe it was coincidental and the one you found is not the match," she said, holding, up the earring.

"And equally coincidental you lost only one? Maybe," I said. "Lots of strange things happen. The earring we found is being analyzed. Will you provide us with a DNA sample ... we can get that with a swab from inside your cheek or blood from a finger stick ... and fingerprints? And the earring you're holding please."

She handed me the earring. I wrapped it in my handkerchief and put it into my pocket.

"I also want your .38 ... er, Boom Boom. Now. When did you last fire it?"

"A week or so ago."

"Before the murder?"

"Yes."

"Joe's Guns?"

"Yes."

"Receipt?"

"No, but Joe will tell you I was there."

"We'll check. Did you clean it afterward?"

She nodded again as she got up and went to the closet, got out her backpack, removed the gun, and handed it to me.

I took a large Baggie from my inner jacket pocket. "Please put it in here."

"When do I get it back?"

"After we do a ballistics check. What kind of car do you own?"

"None. Too expensive to park in the city. I rent Hertz or Avis if I need one."

"And did you rent a car four nights ago? Drive to Connecticut and then New Jersey?"

"I was here four nights ago."

"Can anyone corroborate that?"

"No, I was alone."

"Frankie, I'll be honest with you. You have a motive for two murders with the same MO, and we have evidence that puts you at the scene in one of them. I've got no choice—"

"Wait. I was home, but I was on the phone for close to two hours with a girlfriend who lives in L.A. The phone records will show the time the call was placed from this phone." She pointed to the yellow phone on the kitchen wall.

"Pretty thin. You could have had someone else make the call."

"That's bullshit, Detective. Give me a break. Call my friend. She'll tell you."

I wavered, thinking. I could always come back and arrest her if she was lying. "Okay. Ordinarily, I would arrest a suspect under these circumstances, but I am going to trust you. Don't even think about leaving town, and if you remember anything else that might help, call me or Harry. Understand?"

I gave her my card and stood. Harry followed.

She didn't get up or look at us. "You guys can let yourselves out."

****

I turned to Harry as we drove back to the precinct. "What do you think?"

"I want to see the ballistics on this .38,"—Harry patted the package on the seat between us—"before I make any judgments." He looked at me. "You?"

"Her story actually smells true, but how do we explain the earring? Unless, of course, it's not hers. But I doubt that. Too coincidental. And if Frankie did kill Melinda, why the hell did she wait ten years after leaving their house? And why make it look like Driver's murder?"

"To put the blame on whoever killed Driver," he said.

"I suppose. But what about Zimmerman? Why kill him, if she did?"

"I'll check the phone records and the girlfriend," Harry said.

I looked at him. "But the thing is, could she be doing all that cutting? That's the key to the murders, isn't it? *All that cutting.*"

Chapter Twenty-four

Harry sat at his kitchen table with yesterday's *New York Times* spread out to protect the black walnut top. His fingers automatically and precisely dissembled the Ruger Vaquero .357 Magnum revolver, standing aside and then oiling its many pieces, and propping the six 158-grain soft point bullets upright like miniature missiles. Most cops loaded the 125-grain bullet, but he preferred the heavier load because he used it to hunt game as well. He recalled two summers ago in Montana when he killed a small buck with a single heart shot. Surprised the hell out of the hunting guide. They gutted the animal where it fell and ate venison steaks that night around a campfire. Harry liked keeping the powerful handgun cleaned and oiled, and the mechanical process of tearing down and reassembling the gun relaxed him, as woodworking might the weekend carpenter. With his eyes closed he fingered the parts, interlocking them like jigsaw puzzle pieces. He reattached the short four-and-five-eighths-inch barrel, buffed the polished stainless steel finish, which looked like chrome, and spun the cylinder to hear its satisfying oiled clicks. He tested the three-and-one-quarter-pound trigger pull on an empty chamber. Exactly the right tension.

But shooting deer, or even saving Zach's butt from the Latino Lords, didn't make him a good cop. The whole office knew he had failed his detective exams twice, and for the past two years he had partnered with Zach, who could make anybody look good. He had to find a suspect for the recent murders so the case could be closed. And that had to be Frankie. But her story got to him. He knew about growing up without a father.

Finally finished, he slowly loaded the chambers, but he knew he was only procrastinating before making the call. For Christ's sake, he told himself, she was just another murder suspect, and he had questioned many. But Frankie was different. He had a difficult time approaching women like her.

But she had said for him to come back without Zach. He remembered her exact words: *Next time come back without him and do your own thing.* And he was only following through like a good cop, to do his own thing.

"Frankie? It's me, Harry. Harry Scarpia." He hesitated, groping. The silence dragged on. "Calling to see if you needed another handkerchief."

Chapter Twenty-Five

I took the early morning Delta shuttle to DC. Twenty minutes later, a cab dropped me at the offices of the Armed Services Institute of Pathology. The ASIP, considered the Supreme Court of the dead and sometimes the living, provided clinical services, research, and education in the field of pathology. I hoped JJ would help me understand the chest slashings.

She rose from her desk when she saw me enter the long gray hallway leading to her office, and she walked quickly to greet me.

JJ put her arms around my neck. "Let them gossip," she said, nodding at the other office personnel. "I don't care. Where have you been forever?"

We kissed on both cheeks, and then she lightly pecked my lips. I hugged her. "Married, with two children. Actually, recently divorced."

"So, there's hope for me after all?" she whispered in my ear.

"Only if you act quickly."

"Justice of the peace, this afternoon, downtown DC, I'll buy. Quick enough?"

"Actually, no. I have to fly back to the city this afternoon."

She pulled away. "Ha! You cad. Standing me up again." She laughed lightly.

It had probably been a dozen or so years since I had last seen her. I held her at arm's length. "You're as beautiful as I remember."

JJ was striking. A central gray streak parted her coal-black hair that hung mid-back. Dark eyebrows spanned intense, deep hazel eyes that never relaxed and inflamed easily when they witnessed incompetence, which was often. A rounded nose was the only dissonant feature in an elegant, contemplative face. Tiny gold stud earrings were her only jewelry. JJ shunned other facial markings often worn by Indian women. She wore a red, green, and black sari and radiated a sense of grace that set her apart from her colleagues. One of her wonderful attributes, it seemed to me when we were in medical training together, was her ease with who she was and with all those around her. Nothing seemed to rattle her—not the exams, the professors, or me.

JJ and I had dated—well, a little more than just dating—in London during my first year at medical school, before I met Miriam. She had graduated the All India Institute of Medical Sciences in New Delhi, had three additional years of training at St. George's in London, and was teaching the first-year medical student pathology course I was taking. But a teacher-student relationship was frowned on, and my senior registrar suggested rather strongly I end the affair. I found out later that he was dating her as well and wanted no competition from me.

"Flattery won't help. I've crossed you off my list," JJ said, writing an imaginary X with her finger in the palm of her hand.

"As I remember the events, you were the one who jilted me for that guy, Edward somebody," I said.

"Let's say, it was by the mutual consent of both parties."

I smiled at her and touched her cheek. "It's so wonderful to see you again," I said. "How have you been? And whatever happened to Edward? I left school while you two were still dating."

"He married a very pretty pediatric nurse, and I married pathology. And, as far as I know, we've both remained faithful."

"No other loves in your life?"

She looked serious for a moment and then shook her head. "Actually, no. This work, especially the forensics part, is a fulltime commitment."

"But you're happy?"

She took my hand and led me into her office. "I am. I date another pathologist in the department on occasion, and that's enough for me. At least for now."

She sat behind her desk and I sat across from her in a black and brown slatted wooden chair with an ASIP decal on the backrest, the kind of chair somebody important gets after years of exemplary service. There was a black cushion on the seat, also with the ASIP logo, to soften the wooden bottom. She looked the part as head of the ASIP cardiology branch.

"So, tell me about your family."

I settled into the chair. "I have two wonderful children, Joseph, who is three, and Rachel, five going on fifteen, as all little girls seem to do. Miriam and I split over a number of things, but mainly because I wasn't home enough."

"And that's it?" She rolled her eyes and grimaced. "You're not getting away that easy. Are the children in school?"

"Rachel's in kindergarten. Joseph's still at home."

"Tell me about Miriam."

"What can I say? Mim's a wonderful mom, great cook."

"And?"

"An interior designer. Works out of the home. Not enough to live on, but it helps."

"Picture?"

I reached for my billfold and took out our wedding photo. "It's an old one," I said, handing it to her across the desk.

JJ studied the faded print, crinkly from years in my wallet.

"She's very pretty."

"Thanks. I love her eyes. Soft, gentle eyes. But they frighten easily."

"How so?"

"She's great if everything's routine, but curveballs throw her into a panic."

JJ pointed to Miriam's hands holding a bouquet of flowers. "Long, tapered fingers."

"Very observant, Doctor . She plays the piano, classical stuff, not quite concert level but good enough for me. Now she teaches some. Rachel's already learning to play."

"Finally, we're getting somewhere. Where did you meet?"

"In England when I left school." I stopped. "Enough."

JJ uncrossed her arms and sat up straight. "I guess that's all I'm going to get. So, let's talk about how I can help you."

I handed her the autopsy reports and reviewed the three murders I had called her about. It had taken the New York mayor's intercession, but I had finally gotten Hunter to agree to this reexamination of Driver's autopsy.

"Take your time reading," I said.

JJ picked up the reports, turned pages slowly, and then went back a second time.

After about twenty minutes, she finally spoke. "Each pathologist emphasizes different details, but found one common feature: the chest slashing."

"I agree."

"And that occurred after the victim was already dead. Hunter stresses in his report the cuts were always superficial and never entered the chest cavity. Billroth notes it also. By the way, I trained him. Good pathologist and a nice man. I see him at meetings from time to time."

She laughed when I told her what Billroth had said about putting him on her autopsy table when he called her JJ. "I've taught a lot of them over the years," she said, pushing her hair back.

I handed her three boxes of microscopic slides the medical examiners had taken from each case. They were thin glass plates about an inch wide and three inches long. An ultra-thin slice of stained tissue was mounted on each one. Each slide sat in a partitioned slot in a clear plastic box, about a dozen slides for each case. JJ swiveled her chair to the L segment of her desk, on which stood a very large black and silver binocular microscope.

"Come, sit here and look at the tissue with me." She motioned to a chair across from the L. "I'm sure you remember your first year med school histology."

We sat opposite each other with the microscope between us. It had twin heads, so I could watch the same piece of tissue as JJ studied it. She took out a slide, placed it on the viewing mount of the microscope, and we peered at the first tissue sample, our heads inches apart. The smell of her perfume brought back memories of the lovely evenings we'd spent together. I gazed at her over the top of the microscope. Her eyes were locked into the eyepieces as she twiddled the focus dials, her forehead furrowed in contemplation.

She didn't look up when she spoke.

"Zach, concentrate on the tissue. Everything else is past history. See the scar where I have the pointer? That's an old myocardial infarction. So, Driver had a previous heart attack."

I went back to the scope.

She changed slides. "Zimmerman also has scars in his, but from a viral infection. See all the inflammatory cells." She manipulated the pointer.

Finally we looked at Hanson. "Heart is normal, but she has early cirrhosis of her liver."

"So what do you conclude?" I asked.

"Not enough data," she said. "None of the autopsies included samples of the slashed skin, so I can't compare the microscopics of the cuts to prove the same instrument caused them. Also, I don't know about the angles of the cuts to determine whether the killer was right or left handed. A right-handed person tends to slash in a downward left-to-right direction, like you would cut a piece of meat. Do you know if each pathologist saved the hearts?"

"I'm pretty sure they did. I do remember Hunter putting it into some sort of a jar."

"That'd be helpful. But I need to study the actual bodies as well."

"That'll require a court order to exhume," I said.

"And no one likes that, including me. The smell is awful. But I really see no other way to get answers."

"Okay. I'll work on that when I get home. Meantime, take a look at these pictures, and tell me what you think."

I showed her the photographs the crime photographer had taken at each murder and pointed out the strange stain, that round imprint with a tail in the photos of Driver's murder. It was not in any of the pictures of Hanson, nor was there even a suggestion of it on the gray rug next to Zimmerman's body.

She looked at it carefully and held it up to the light. "I don't know what it is, Zach."

"Take a look at this blow-up print of the stain alone."

"It can't be a body part—that much is clear to me," she said. "The edges are much too sharp, and there's no organ with a tail like that. None of the autopsy reports mentioned any body parts missing.

Were you thinking of people being killed and their organs stolen for transplant?"

"JJ, I'm groping for anything to explain the murders and slashings."

"Well, this picture doesn't fit anything I know."

"So, you need to study the hearts and the bodies of the vics?"

"I think that's where we are."

"How about I get the court order, fly you to the city, and you'll be able to analyze both at the same time?"

"Sounds like a plan. When?"

I rose to leave. "As soon as I can get the order. Hopefully, less than a week."

She stood and came around her desk. "It was good to see you again. I remember some wonderful times we spent together."

She put her hands on my shoulders, and I gave her a hug. "Better to have loved and lost … didn't somebody say something like that?"

She looked in my eyes. "By the way, I don't think you ever knew I did the autopsy on that young girl who died while you were a medical student."

"Thanks for putting it so delicately."

JJ smiled ever so briefly. "The girl had very critical mitral stenosis, and a greatly thinned left ventricle. Almost no heart muscle left. I doubt she would have survived surgery, and without it, she had less than six months to live."

"I appreciate your telling me, JJ. Thanks for that." I gave her another hug and turned to go. "I'll be in touch."

Chapter Twenty-Six

A week later I met JJ beneath the four-faced brass clock at New York's Grand Central Station. We drove straight to the Manhattan morgue.

"So you must be the famous JJ," John Hunter said, tossing his paperback onto his desk, "so-called biggest name in cardiac pathology." Arms crossed on his chest and feet on the desk, he did not extend his hand or get up.

JJ and I stood in front of Hunter's desk, since there were no additional chairs in the cramped space. We practically filled the entire office.

"They warned me you were coming, but I guess it slipped my mind. I was actually on my way out to another meeting after finishing this Cornwell book." He waved it at us. "Take Kay Scarpetta. Now, *there's* a pathologist worth her salt." The corners of his mouth turned down in a smirk.

JJ smiled a bright greeting. "Good afternoon, Dr. Hunter. I'm Jayanti Joshi. I'm very glad to meet you and would like to compliment you on the very thorough autopsy you performed on Mrs. Driver. One of the best I've ever seen. I couldn't have done any better." She reached across his desk, hand extended.

The transformation was instantaneous. A pleased look washed away his smirk, and he stood and walked around the desk, taking her hand in both of his. "Thanks."

"I'm so sorry you have to go to another meeting. I had hoped you would be around to help me review your findings. You know the body better than I do."

He shuffled his feet and bit his lower lip. "I did have an appointment, but if you want, I'll cancel it and help you with whatever you need."

I smiled to myself. Thirty seconds. She hadn't lost her touch. "That would be great. I mainly want to examine the hearts and take a skin biopsy of the slashes. Your job was so complete, I certainly don't need to do anything more than only look at Driver."

This time his smile practically lit up the room as he led us to the autopsy suite. I lagged behind the two of them. JJ turned. "You sure you want to see this?"

"No, but I'm coming anyway. John, got a bottle of Vicks?"

Hunter shook his head. "Don't believe in babying cops. You tough it out or you leave. Your choice. I don't much care one way or the other." He looked me over. "It's usually big guys like you who keel over. Ladies rarely do. Besides, the menthol vapor under your nose only helps temporarily. Your clothes and hair will carry the death stench after you leave. And I don't want any strange aromas like menthol screwing up my own ability to smell. I need that. I can smell the odor of bitter almonds from cyanide poisoning. Only 50 percent of pathologists can do that. Good genes." He stood taller when he said that and glanced at JJ. She smiled.

So much for Vicks.

Hunter began opening the containers I'd had shipped by overnight mail. Each heart was packed in a clear plastic bottle filled with the preservative formalin and sealed with rolls of Saran Wrap. To the uninitiated, the jugs could have contained takeout chicken soup from the local deli.

Except for the smell. When the lid came off and he extracted the organs, the formaldehyde bouquet filled the room as a pungent, nose punishing, acrid stink.

JJ donned thick plastic gloves to protect her skin. She picked up Driver's heart, rubbery and gray from the fixative, and held it in her hands, slowly turning it under the bright illumination of the dissecting microscope light. A cuff of the superior vena cava was still connected to the right atrium. She studied it through the 12X magnifying glass.

"Well, well," she said, "What *do* we have here?"

Hunter and I both moved closer. "What?" I asked.

"These little scars along the lateral wall of the right atrial endocardium. See, right here?" She pointed, and I could see whitish streaks in the muscle.

"If we trace the paths, we see the trail of fibrosis crosses the tricuspid valve—you can see some fibrinous strands right here—and snakes to the tip of the right ventricle. See here?" Again, she pointed. "I suspect the microscopics will show additional local scarring and probably some bleeding in the apex of the heart where the lead has been yanked out."

"What lead? What are you talking about?" Hunter asked, an edge to his voice.

"Let's look at Zimmerman's heart next," JJ said in a soothing tone, "and see if it has the same changes. Then, I'll explain all and be able to tell you what caused that bloodstain."

Zimmerman's heart held the same scars, despite the absence of the round bloodstain in the crime scene photos. Hanson's heart was normal.

"Now, let's look at the bodies. I think the chest slashings in two of the three victims will obscure the evidence. That was their intent."

Hunter opened the steel refrigerated container and activated the creaky overhead pulley. Driver's body slid onto the autopsy table. Despite the cold storage and our face masks, the smell was horrible, and we all stopped breathing for as long as we could hold a breath.

After putting on gloves and a gown, JJ went to work quickly. She seemed to know exactly what to look for. Taking a pair of forceps in one hand and a probe in the other, she delicately pulled back skin beneath the left collarbone that had been slashed by the assassin and was now adhered to the chest wall. In moments she stopped with a satisfied, "There it is."

Hunter and I stood on each side of her, peering intently over her shoulder. We stared where she was pointing and then looked at each other with raised eyebrows.

Hunter finally broke the silence. "There *what* is?"

I was starting to get an idea where she was going.

She didn't turn around but raised the skin flaps out of the way. "See," she said, pointing with the probe, "a round space under her skin. Some old sutures tied there."

My breath was raspy through the mask, my face close to her right ear. "Holy shit," I said. "A pacemaker pocket."

"Exactly. This woman had a pacemaker beneath her skin when she died. The murderer took it out, along with the lead that ran to the heart. He then laid the pacemaker and lead down on the carpet next to her after he removed it."

I felt my face crease into a smile. "The round bloodstain with a tail."

"Exactly. I don't know why Zimmerman's photos didn't show the same thing, since I bet he'll have this pacemaker pocket also."

"Maybe the killer didn't set that pacemaker down. He didn't want to make that mistake a second time," I said.

"I didn't have that picture when I did the autopsy," Hunter said with crushed eyebrows and a defensive whine. "I only saw the skin lacerations."

JJ patted his gloved hand with her own, a mother reassuring her child. "Of course you didn't see it. That was the whole point of the skin slashings—to throw you off and make sure you didn't find the empty pacemaker pocket. The pathologist who autopsied Zimmerman missed it also. At least there's no mention of it in his report. I'm sure we'll find it when we study his body."

"And Hanson?" I asked.

"Nope. No pacemaker and no heart trouble."

I started coughing. The smell was awful. "Finished, JJ?"

"As soon as I biopsy several slash marks. The cuts make me think the killer was right handed."

"Mmm," I said.

She looked at me. "Go wait in John's office, Zach. I'll be real quick with the other two autopsies."

****

Molly brought us coffee as we sat in my office reviewing the facts of each case. "How can I help?" she asked.

"Thanks, Molly," I said. "I don't know yet."

"Do you mind if I listen in?"

"Of course not. We can use a fresh mind. Sit down next to JJ."

"Sorry I missed the autopsies," Harry said, joining us. He then grinned. "That's a lie. I'm glad I did."

JJ smiled back. "You get used to them."

"But I find it hard to believe two people were murdered for their pacemakers. They cost what, five, six thousand dollars new? And what the hell would you do with one after you got it? Sell it to a hospital cut rate?" Harry said.

"You can't legally reuse pacemakers in the U.S.," said JJ. "And the foreign market is nonexistent. Used pacemakers in the U.S. are actually donated to Third World countries."

"And that doesn't explain Hanson," I said.

"Nor does it really explain why any of them was murdered," JJ said. She looked at her watch. "It's been a full day for me, gentlemen, and I've still got a four-hour train ride back to the seat of government."

"Can I call you a cab, Doctor, or would you like one of our officers to take you to Grand Central?" Molly asked.

"A cab would do fine, Molly, thank you," JJ said, looking quickly at me and then away.

We were all silent as Molly left the room. But a question hung in the air.

Why in hell kill someone for a pacemaker?

Then my mind jumped to another thought. What about my own daughter and her pacemaker? If someone was killing people for their pacemakers, *could she be a target?*

JJ interrupted my thoughts. "What're the next steps, Zach?"

"Frankly, JJ, I'm not sure. I think I need to read up about pacemakers and try to get a lead on why someone would want to steal them. I'll call you with any developments."

We both stood. "You've been great, JJ. This is the first solid lead we've had, and all that goes to you," I said.

We kissed on the cheek. "It was wonderful to see you again, Zach. Even under these circumstances. Don't wait for the next murder to call me."

*****

When I was alone again, I dialed a phone number in Israel that scrambled the call. I did this every several months as Jake, now General Hertzog, and I had agreed when I moved to New York. He picked up on the first ring. I explained what had happened.

"Certainly more than just some local murders," he said.

"I agree, and so does my captain. We've been able to keep the slashings out of the papers so as not to alarm the public. Captain wants to retain control of the investigation for now. He's afraid bringing in outside help might tip off the killer and drive him underground. If we play it cool, he'll eventually make a slip and give himself away."

"Maybe. Obviously, you run the risk of more murders. Do you have any idea how the murders tie into something bigger?"

"No, you?"

"We *are* seeing an increase in communication traffic between Middle Eastern operatives in Syria and Jordan and some hidden cells in the U.S. We've not been able to locate them, but activity is stepping up. I think something's being planned, but I can't imagine it's related to your murders."

"Anything more you think I should be doing?" Some things don't change. He was always the guy I turned to growing up.

"Catch the murderers."

"That's helpful."

"Only joking. There may be something I can do. If your captain agrees, there's a guy in the FBI named Mac McBride. He's my U.S. counterpart in terrorist surveillance. I might give him a call to see if he has any ideas—not dragging in the FBI, only tapping his brain. "

Chapter Twenty-Seven

Frankie waited for the third ring before she went to the door. She was wearing a white lace cami, her bra clearly outlined beneath. Her tight black skirt sat low on her hips, hugging her shapely legs mid-thigh. A wide silver belt draped beneath her bare midriff. She stood tall in three-inch black platform shoes. Her hair, scented with lavender, was a crown of golden spikes. After his phone call, she had searched Bergdorf's and Saks until she found exactly what she wanted.

She greeted Harry with a kiss on the cheek. Ignoring his fumbling handshake, she leaned forward into his extended hand, which accidentally brushed her breast. He breathed in sharply.

"Wow," he said, standing there, unmoving, staring at her.

Frankie pirouetted and said, "I guess that means you like my outfit." From the front of her cami she slowly pulled out his handkerchief, newly cleaned and scented with her perfume. "I've kept it warm for you."

Her eyes twinkled as his face turned scarlet.

"You look pretty cool, too," she said, looking him over. He was wearing Zegna black slacks with an oyster shell Malo cashmere turtleneck pullover and a gray striped Brioni sports coat. Black Bruno Magli loafers, with deep claret colored socks, and a cream silk handkerchief in his jacket pocket completed the ensemble.

Frankie took him by the hand and led him to the couch. "Have a seat while I open some wine."

"Whoa. This is purely a professional visit. Or at least it's supposed to be. You're still suspect number one."

"Yeah, right. You don't drink on duty?"

"Okay, maybe just a glass."

Frankie felt his eyes on her as she walked to the kitchen, hips swaying. She pulled a bottle of Rombauer Chardonnay from the refrigerator, popped the cork, and filled two glasses. She carried them back, placing his on the coffee table in front of the couch and sipping from hers as she sat down next to him. She crossed her legs and her skirt inched high on her thighs. *Piece of cake,* she thought. No different from any of the others.

"Okay, what do you want to know?" she asked.

"Whatever you haven't told us yet."

"You know everything I know."

"Let's start with your relationship with the Hansons."

"I already went through that with you and Zach. They raised me. We had problems. I loved and hated them, and I left. Many years later, I went back to get my yearbook and try and make amends. I couldn't, so I left again. That's it."

"And when did you drop your earring?

"Oh, c'mon. I was wearing the pearl ones. I have no idea how the Swarovski rose got there."

"Frankie, that's the most damning evidence we have. You're looking at a murder one charge."

"Maybe it wasn't mine."

"Your DNA checks."

She inhaled sharply. "When did you get that?"

"Two days ago. Symanski sent us the earring and we ran the lab check against the swab you gave us. It's yours. No doubt about it."

Frankie spotted his empty wine glass. "Want a refill?"

"No, I don't think I'd better."

"I won't tell." She refilled his but sipped hers slowly.

"Maybe *you* could tell *me* some things I don't know," she said.

"Police interviews don't work that way."

"Usually they don't, but maybe this one'll be special."

He swirled his wine glass, sipped, crossed and uncrossed his legs. Then he sat still and studied her. She smiled at him. "Like what?" he asked.

"Are there other murders?"

"Frankie, I can't tell you that."

"Oh, so there are."

He remained quiet.

"How many?"

"Let's change the subject."

They sat side by side, thighs touching. She topped off his glass again.

"How do you like working with Zach on this case? He seems pretty intense."

"Zach's a great guy. He taught me a lot, and I'm proud to be his partner. Usually he's pretty gentle, especially with women, but sometimes he can play rough. Actually, he was pretty nice with you."

His tongue was starting to loosen. A good sign.

"You didn't say much during the interviews."

"I know. Zach pretty well told me to butt out and he would handle it. He likes to do the interviewing alone. He's my boss; I listen to what he says. Sometimes he lets me take the lead in the interview as the tough bastard …"

He stopped, and she smiled. He went on. "It's usually with lowlifes. And then he chimes in as Mr. Nice Guy. But beneath that he's one hard cop, especially with us at work. He doesn't like losing at anything. Still, he's a straight shooter. Only wants the scientific evidence and never caves, regardless of the political heat. He can run a single clue until a whole case falls into place."

After the long answer, he sat quietly, fingers fidgeting on his knees. She thought maybe he had used up all his words.

"Do you like my pearl earrings?" She turned her head from side to side, posing, teasing.

He didn't answer at first, only stared at her with a pained expression. "Pretty."

She looked at him, glass in one hand and rested the other on his knee to still the agitated motion. "Am I still a suspect to you?"

His eyes dilated briefly at her touch. "Kind of, but not really."

She moved closer to him. "What does that mean?"

"Zach won't drop the fact that he found your earring in her room, but I'm not sure he really thinks you had anything to do with the murder." He sipped again, his words running together a little. She hoped the three quick glasses were starting to have an effect. She slowly nursed her first.

"But you don't think I killed her, do you?" Another smile.

"I did in the beginning. But not now."

"What changed your mind?"

He took a breath, collecting words like widely scattered flowers, and spoke hesitantly. "I guess just getting to know you. Though, like I said, we still don't know how your earring got in Melinda's bedroom and don't have a clue why she was murdered. She didn't have a pacemaker."

"A pacemaker!" Her brow shot up. "What does that have to do with Melinda's murder?"

Harry's cheeks flushed, and his eyes got big. She saw clearly he had slipped.

He remained silent. Her hand slowly stroked his knee. "C'mon, tell me," she said in a soft voice. She poured the rest of the Chardonnay into his glass. "The other murdered vics had pacemakers, too?" She was swirling her wine glass in an agitated fashion, still sipping the first pouring.

He nodded and tentatively put his hand on hers to control the glass. "Careful you don't spill. Even white wine stain is hard to remove." She wasn't sure if he was worried about his Zegna pants, the rug, or whether it was simply an excuse to touch her hand. Probably all three, she concluded.

"Why would anyone murder somebody for a pacemaker?" she asked.

A buzzer from the kitchen interrupted her. She looked at her watch and then the oven. She flashed a tiny smile. "That's dinner."

He raised his eyebrows. "I really can't stay."

She stood in front of him, hands on hips, knowing the backlight from the kitchen silhouetted her figure. Her lace cami shimmered in the early evening sunlight. She watched him watch her, a serene look on her face. "If you want to leave, fine. I'll eat the lasagna tomorrow … alone."

He finished his wine with a laugh. "I love homemade lasagna." She held out a hand to guide him to the kitchen.

****

Harry drank most of the second bottle, this one a Cakebread cabernet she took from a small oak wine rack over the sink, with little help from

145

Frankie. After the last bite of lasagna, she kicked off her shoes, cleared the dishes, and brought the salad. "Like in Italy," she explained, placing the salad bowl on the table.

He sighed. "Great dinner. The only time I ate like this was when Zach used to have me over before his divorce. Miriam is an excellent cook."

"Glad you liked it. The lasagna recipe was in a box of my real mom's stuff. Nothing special but it is good."

"Are you Italian?"

"My mom was but my dad was English. What is Scarpia?"

"My father's Italian and my mother Spanish."

"Nice blend." She smiled at him, but he looked away.

"Can I help you with the dishes?" he asked, pushing back from the table.

She washed and he dried standing side by side at the small kitchen sink. Their hips touched, sending an electric shock through both of them, and he moved closer. The melancholy arias from the third act of *La Boheme* played softly in the background. That and the two-bottle wine buzz stilled conversation. She hummed softly, following the music.

When he had dried the last dish, she took the dishtowel from him, wiped her hands, and dabbed at a wet spot on his lapel. She stood on her toes, her five foot seven inches reaching his chin, put her arms around his neck, and planted a gentle kiss on his lips. Then she took his hands, let them slide down her chest, and said, "Help me open the bed. You shouldn't drive home after all that wine. We don't want New York's finest to get a DUI, now do we?"

Chapter Twenty-Eight

"Zach, what's going on?" Miriam stood in the hall waiting for me when I let myself in.

"Daddy's here! Daddy's here!" Rachel and Joseph barreled through, tackling my legs. I kissed Miriam on the cheek, dangled Joey from my ankle, and picked up Rachel. Joey fell off, laughing. I picked him up also. He pulled at my beard, while Rachel hugged my neck and kissed my cheek. Their hands rummaged in my pockets to ferret out the butterscotch candy.

"Daddy, can we go see a movie?" Rachel asked.

"Too late for that, honey. When I come back this weekend, we will. What do you want to see?"

"*Shrek.*"

I groaned. "You've seen it three times already."

"Okay. *Lion King.*"

"We've been twice. And besides, I don't think they're playing anymore. We'll find a new one you like. Go watch TV for a little while so I can talk with Mommy. Then, I'll read you a story before you go to bed."

They ran off, Rachel in the lead.

Miriam and I sat down at the kitchen table.

"Coffee?"

"A beer if you have it."

"Zach, what's going on?" she repeated.

I told her all I knew.

Her face turned pale and her eyes widened. "Rachel's in danger! First your car accident, and now this. We're all in danger."

"Maybe, but I honestly don't know, Mim. My gut is that this has nothing to do with you. Someone tried to kill me, but I think it was to delay my investigation of these pacemaker murders."

"You think, but you don't know that."

"They've only targeted adults. Like I said on the phone, maybe the pacemaker she has is too small or something."

"But you don't know for sure."

I wanted to reassure her, but I was scared for my family, too. I touched her cheek. "Mim, I think you should take the kids and go to Israel. It's safer there."

"I don't want to go back to Israel, and I especially don't want to stay with your mom. I want to go to London."

"No protection there. If you're going to leave the U.S., it should be to Israel."

Her lips set in a stubborn line.

"Okay, let's compromise. I'll find out more about Rachel's pacemaker. If it's not a target, then we sit tight. Otherwise, you take the kids to Israel, but we'll rent a different place."

She grimaced and reluctantly nodded. "And in the meantime?"

"Keep Rachel home a day or two. I'll have a black and white in the driveway during the night until I figure out what's happening."

"Will you stay here tonight?"

"That's my plan."

Teary eyed, she took my hand and put it to her lips.

****

At work the next day, pipe clenched in my teeth and clean doodle pad on my desk, I wrestled with the autopsy findings. Anger made Frankie the top candidate for Hanson's murder, but assuming the same killer of all three, I needed to come up with a motive why she'd target people with pacemakers. And given the hundreds of thousands of patients all over the world with pacemakers implanted, why these two? Who might be next?

Harry came in. "Zach, I'm starting to wonder if the pacemakers are a red herring. Maybe Driver and Zimmerman were murdered for a different reason? After all, Hanson didn't have one."

"Sure that's possible. But consider this. If those two were just in the wrong place at the wrong time, they would've been killed but not have their pacemakers ripped out. It has to be the pacemakers. We need to figure out why."

To do that, I researched about them in the medical textbook I still had from St George's. While that of course was out of date, it did tell me there was no such thing as a pediatric pacemaker. Kids got the same kind as adults. That meant Rachel could be a target.

Then I went online, but after an hour or two, I wasn't any closer to figuring out why someone would kill for one. Basically, they were small battery-powered devices connected by a wire to the heart, which was called a lead, to control the heartbeat. The engineering design of the integrated circuits and components was all very costly to develop, but the actual guts of the device couldn't be worth much, at most a couple of hundred bucks for a thin film of gold, lithium for the battery, stuff like that. The most expensive part was probably the platinum for the electrodes on the end of the lead that went into the heart. Also, the pacemaker can was hermitically sealed, like two halves of a pocket watch lasered together. So they would have to be cut apart to get at the insides. Snipping off the platinum electrode at the end of the lead would be easier than opening up the can.

Finally, I called Rachel's pediatric cardiologist, who had implanted her pacemaker. He was an electrophysiologist, a specialist in heart rhythm problems. I probably should have spoken with him earlier.

"Are all pacemakers the same or are some brands different?" I asked.

"Some have different bells and whistles, but basically they're all pretty much the same today."

That started me thinking. "You said, 'today.' What about five or ten years ago?"

"Obviously, like electronics in other areas, there have been major developments in the components, manufacturing processes, batteries, and so forth. And today's pacemakers are miniatures compared to the hockey pucks they were years ago," he said.

"How long do they last?"

"Depends on the battery. For example, early batteries were made of mercury-zinc and only lasted a couple of years. Their big problem was when they wore out, they did so precipitously, and a patient could go from having a normally functioning pacemaker to having a dead battery in hours. Not too good if your life depended on the pacemaker. You had a blackout spell if you were lucky. If not, you died. Then, for a while, some of the batteries were made of nickel-cadmium, so patients could recharge them. But that didn't go over well, since patients didn't like the idea of wearing a recharging jacket plugged into a socket for an hour or more each week. Now, they're made of lithium iodide, which lasts six or eight years, and pacemaker end-of-life happens gradually and can be monitored quite closely."

"That's the kind my daughter has?"

"Yes, it's pretty much one size fits all. So she has the same kind adults have."

Shit. Sounded like I'd better call Jake to find an apartment in Jerusalem.

Chapter Twenty-Nine

James Adair was a fourth-generation cop. His great grandfather came to the United States during the Irish famine in the 1850s, when a million people died at home and two million immigrated to other countries, especially the northeastern United States. But he had too much wanderlust to remain east and eventually moved his family west through a succession of cities, finally making a partial U-turn in Oklahoma and ending up as chief of police in Petoskey, Michigan, a quiet lake resort town of six thousand two hundred and twenty-seven people. The biggest news was an occasional tourist skipping out on a hotel bill. Now, one hundred and fifty years later, his great grandson ran the same police force, and still not much happened. The force had increased from three to thirteen officers to keep pace with the summer population growth and was as modern as the city fathers would pay for.

There were twelve men and Amanda Pallone. Mandy took no shit from the guys and could shoot the heart out of a standup target at thirty yards as well as any of them. She ran three miles four mornings a week and did pushups and sit ups the other three. She didn't smoke or drink, but she did have one weakness: men like Jim—tall, handsome, dark haired, and T-shirt muscled. For that she had paid with a marriage lasting three years that produced two daughters, four and six years old, an ex-husband constantly in arrears for child support, and a recent affair with a tourist that petered out after a few months.

Despite all her attempts to the contrary, Jim treated her as one of the guys. This was good for working but bad for living. He didn't date, or at least no one locally, and didn't seem influenced by Mandy's long brown hair, green eyes, and stacked chest. Mandy had cajoled the old desk cop who had lost a leg in a car chase to pair her with Jim as much as possible. She was convinced that, one, Jim was not gay, two, he was young and had to have circulating hormones affected by a half opened blouse with no bra, and three, if he saw enough of her, literally and figuratively, he would eventually yield to her charms. Her daughters needed a father.

Jim didn't know it, but she had plans for him that Thursday night after they made the sweep of the homes near the lake. Her house was only three blocks inland, and she had dropped the girls off with her mother. She had recently bought creamy white satin sheets and a snowy white down duvet. It had cost her a sizable chunk of her week's salary, but she considered it an investment.

At one in the morning, the call about a suspected breaking and entering interrupted those plans.

The house in question was in the upscale neighborhood of Riverdale, occupied by a retired professor of music and his wife. It sat at the end of a U-shaped cul-de-sac flanked by two houses on either side of the stone entrance. Tall red maples lined the street, and each house had a well-groomed lawn surrounded by dense boxwood shrubs pruned to window level.

Jim and Mandy pulled up slowly in their unmarked police car with lights off. They parked in front of a white Victorian with green shutters and a sweeping veranda, the first on the right as they entered the cul-de-sac. They got out and stood beside their car for a moment, scanning the area. Nothing seemed amiss in the quiet neighborhood. Softly they knocked on the door where the woman lived who had called in the B and E. After they flashed their shields in the window of the front door, she let them into the foyer. A muscular Doberman stood at her side, warily looking at their faces.

"Hank, heel," she commanded. Hank moved next to her left side, leaning his sleek black body protectively against her leg. "I named him after my husband," she explained. "I like the Doberman a lot more. He's better looking and minds me."

She beckoned to them and they followed her into the living room, with its bay window facing the road, and sat on the couch. "I saw this black car—I don't know what kind—drive by slowly three times earlier this evening. You see, I don't sleep well, and Hank and I sit by the front

window a lot watching TV. I notice things that happen around here."
She stopped to see if they understood.

"Go on," Jim said.

"Then, about half hour ago, the car came back. You can see it from
here. It's parked in the driveway beneath the trees of the first house
on the other side of the cul-de-sac. See it over there, right across from
us?" She pointed out the window at the dim shape of an automobile
sitting at the foot of the opposite driveway. The black outline was barely
perceptible in the darkness. It was parked facing the road.

"You're sure that car doesn't belong to anyone living in that house?"
Mandy asked.

"Positive. If you look real closely you can see a 'for sale' sign on the
lawn. The Greens moved out last month and are selling. They retired
to Boca Raton in Florida, so no one's home."

"Did you see anyone get out of the car after it was parked?"

"Yes. I think it was a man."

"Are you sure?" Mandy asked.

"No. Whoever it was had on dark clothes and a cap pulled
low, walked fast toward the house at the end of the cul-de-sac, and
disappeared around the side. You see the left side with the big tree and
all those bushes? Where it's dark?" Again she pointed. "He or she went
back there and I haven't seen anybody since."

"That was how long ago?"

She checked her watch. "About twenty-five minutes."

"And you're sure no one's come out?"

"No one and the car's still there. So I would guess he or she's still
inside."

Jim looked at Mandy, and she acknowledged his unspoken question
with a slight tip of her head. They both stood.

"Before you go, you might like this." Smiling, she held up a key
ring with a house key dangling. "The key to their front door. The
professor gave it to me so I can get into their house if I need to when
they're away."

"Thanks very much, Mrs. Cassin," said Mandy, taking the key.
"We'll go have a look." Mandy scanned the room. "It might be best if
you moved away from this front window. We don't know what might
happen, and you'll be safer in a back room."

Olivia Cassin ignored the warning; this was the most exciting adventure that had happened to her since she moved to Riverdale twelve years ago, right after her husband died, and she wasn't going to miss a minute of it. She'd even turn off the TV so as not to be distracted.

Jim and Mandy left the house and conferred briefly on the veranda. "Should we call for back up before we go in?" whispered Mandy.

"Probably a good idea," said Jim, "but the guy may be gone before they get here. We can't wait for backup. But call it in anyway."

"Maybe the professor and his wife are away."

"Possibly, but it doesn't really change anything for us. It's still a B and E we have to investigate."

Mandy talked softly into the microphone on her shoulder that transmitted to the dispatcher at headquarters. She told the desk to send available backups immediately, but that the two of them were going in now.

They crossed the street. Jim put his hand on the hood of the parked car. "Still warm," he whispered. They hugged the shadows of the bushes as they approached the professor's house. Nothing stirred in the dark night. Only a dim sliver of moonlight helped penetrate the blackness.

When they reached the lawn, Jim tapped Mandy's shoulder, pointed at the front door, then at her, and then gestured a key opening a lock. She sunk low into a half squat and ran silently toward the house, key ring in her hand.

He unholstered his .38 semiautomatic and crept around to the right, careful to stay in the shadows and beneath the window sills, taking a quick peek in each window as he passed. When he reached the rear of the house he tried the door. Locked. He looked to his right and saw the outline of an open window in the darkness, only apparent by the drapes billowing out over the window sill. He hesitated, considering whether he should get Mandy as his backup since this was most likely the B and E site. The perp had left the window open for a quick escape.

Mandy tried the front door, but it was locked. Quietly she slipped the key in the lock and slowly opened the door. It moved smoothly on its hinges as it swung wide. She stood for a moment, letting her eyes adjust to the pitch black interior. Her heart pounded in her ears. Suddenly she heard a muffled cry and raced in its direction. She ran into a large back bedroom, tripped over the leg of a chair, and fell with a loud thud, crashing her head into the corner of a table. Momentarily stunned, she looked into the room, blinking her eyes, trying to focus.

Before she could get to her feet, someone kicked the gun from her hand, grabbed her hair, and pulled her head back, cutting off her scream. Mandy felt the sharp edge of a blade at her throat as she was yanked to her feet.

She saw the professor in a chair, hands and feet bound, his eyes dilated in fear and his head shaking uncontrollably from side to side. Incoherent animal sounds filtered through the cloth stuffed in his mouth. His wife lay on the floor, bleeding from a gunshot wound in the head and multiple chest slashes. Blood was everywhere.

Jim also heard the gurgled cry and ran to the open window. He could barely make out a human shape standing with its back to him. He vaulted through the window. As his feet hit the floor, gun drawn, he saw the person holding Mandy and shouted, "Drop the knife or I'll shoot!"

The killer spun Mandy around and looked at Jim over Mandy's shoulder. The sudden move loosened the cap and long black hair tumbled out.

A woman!

"*Now!* Do it now or you're dead!"

The killer tightened her grip on Mandy's hair. She stared at Jim through the slits in her mask. With her knife hand pressing the blade into Mandy's throat and beginning to draw a trickle of blood, she screamed into her ear, "Don't move, woman." Then she let go of her hair, reached to her waist with her free hand, and shouted, "*Allahu Akbar.*"

A moment later a blinding flash of red and yellow lit up the sky as a gigantic explosion ripped apart the house and its occupants. Olivia Cassin, watching from the front window, had a fraction of a second to register the brilliance before the powerful wave leaped the distance and incinerated the front of her home along with most of the cul-de-sac.

Chapter Thirty

The pacemaker, still stained red with Zimmerman's blood, dangled from Sarah's arthritic fingers. "It is a fine gift," she said. "Thank you."

"I'm glad you like it," Wahad said, seated at a table in the hidden room in back of the bookstore. Ruth was in front of a computer screen, completing an e-mail. She reread her message before sending it.

Ruth put her hand on top of the computer screen and turned to Wahad. "With this e-mail I have ordered the equipment you asked for. Amir said the lab is being built to your specifications. At first, the director argued about blocking the path, but a little *bakshish* convinced him. So they have closed off the steps in the back—all nine hundred, as you asked—and the interior is being prepared. They hung a big canvas cover over the opening to keep out the weather and any curious visitors. A few tourists objected, but nothing serious. Amir says it is perfect and will work well. We have a nice, steady flow of new workers, and the scientists are in place."

"It should be ideal. I'm anxious to return, both to finish our project but also because it's a very beautiful, special place. I'm also waiting for our friend to send the final plans on how to protect all the workers and scientists," Wahad said.

Sarah wiped off the pacemaker and held it by the lead like a pendulum, swishing it back and forth. The pacemaker case glinted in the light, looking like an oversized glossy silver pocket watch.

"We are always pleased when you bring us presents like this one," Ruth said, pointing at the pacemaker. "But as you know, we do need more. Our friends are working hard, and all but six have been successful—at least once, and some twice. In fact, we now have more than one hundred pacemakers. And you should see the young people from the university dropping them off! So clean-cut. Nice jeans and short hair. They come in, go to the bookshelves, and drop off our little presents. No one would ever suspect them."

"Only eight hundred and some to go. Seems like a long ways off," Wahad said.

Sarah said, "It does, but think in the good fashion! We are more than one tenth of the way toward finishing this part of the operation. We are actually ahead of schedule. The doubters said, 'A thousand. It can't happen. You can't do it.'"

"It will be more difficult once the newspapers pick up the story," Wahad said.

"That is to be expected. But the murders in America and Europe will go unconnected as long as the agencies are not sharing information," Ruth said. "And it turns out we will need less than we thought."

"True. That does help. I'll continue doing the best I can, but I'm afraid I'll have to be even more careful."

"Because of Michigan?" Ruth asked.

"Yes, that was too close. If I'm caught, I'm afraid the whole operation will blow up with me," Wahad said.

"We cannot take that chance," Sarah said.

"How near is Dayan?" Ruth asked.

"He knows about the pacemakers and he's very tenacious. So we need to be more cautious, while at the same time stepping up the process," Wahad said.

"It is too bad your attempt at eliminating him was not successful. But you've got something else planned I'm sure, yes?" Ruth asked.

"I do, and it has to be soon. But for that I will need your help. If my plan succeeds, it will eliminate him permanently."

Ruth put her arm around Wahad's waist. "You know we're prepared to do anything to serve this mission. We have worked and waited a long time for this day. All you have to do is ask us."

"It will be very soon."

Chapter Thirty-One

"Triacetone piperoxide triggered by PETN," said Daniel McBride, Special Agent in Charge of the FBI's Explosives Unit–Bomb Data Center, talking to the Petoskey police force. "Same stuff that British guy, Richard Briton, tried to detonate in his shoe on that Paris-to-Miami flight in 2001. Hamas and al-Qaeda routinely use it for their suicide bombers."

They sat around the small police station after the funeral. The coffins had been buried empty, since not even fragments of the bodies were found, even though the FBI experts had meticulously sifted through the rubble within six hours of the bomb blast. McBride, an FBI lifer working toward his twenty-year recognition pin, headed the team.

He was an improbable looking special agent. Skinny to the point of being gaunt, with floppy ears, a pointed nose that matched a pointy chin, and small brown eyes framed by thick-lensed granny glasses, he resembled the school nerd more than a gun-packing spy. But his electrical engineering degree from Purdue University and law degree from Yale, plus a year's tour in Iraq as the FBI liaison, made him an expert in improvised explosive devices.

"The professor's house took the maximum effect of the blast, so we have to assume that house was the target. Any reason to suspect the guy of terrorist activities?" McBride asked.

"None at all," said the chief, shaking his head. "He was a retired music professor, living there with his wife. Played piano and I think wrote some music. Someone else had to have planted the bomb. Probably the B and E guy."

"Okay, let's start there," said McBride.

"Based on what my people called in, and witnessed by that Mrs. Cassin, we can assume it's a B and E. So maybe a simple robbery attempt gone sour. My cops catch the guy, who blows himself up, along with the professor and his wife," said the chief.

"And half the neighborhood? Pretty drastic response to avoid a little jail time, don't you think?" said McBride. "Guy would have to carry the IED with him, or strapped on him, and be prepared to die for a simple B and E. And that's as big an IED as I ever saw in Iraq."

The room was silent. The cops looked at their hands, the floor, anywhere but at McBride.

"But suppose it wasn't a simple B and E," McBride said, standing and pacing the floor. "Suppose the professor had something the perp wanted real bad. But being identified was so unacceptable that he had to get rid of all evidence, including himself."

"That could work," said the chief, "if you tell me what the professor had that was so important."

The room fell silent again.

"Anything with his music? Maybe an original manuscript or something like that?" McBride said.

"Yeah, right, he found a signed long lost Mozart opera in the attic. Not in this little burg."

"You know, we keep focusing on the professor," McBride said. "What about his wife? Maybe she was the target."

"Okay, but same question like you asked. What could she have the perp wanted? The usual jewels and stuff? Cash at home? Or maybe the bad guy was part of a crime syndicate that didn't want to be IDd?" the chief asked.

"Whatever, it's still a pretty drastic response. That's the answer, seems to me. A disproportionate response to being taken in for a routine bungled burglary," McBride said, sitting again.

"You know, the other thing is this bomb stuff. If it's what suicide guys use in the Middle East, where'd the B and E guy get it?" the chief asked.

"That's the easy part," said McBride. "TATP's made from drain cleaner, bleach, and acetone you can buy almost anywhere, and usually gets past bomb detector equipment and sniffer dogs. Could've built it right under your noses here in Petoskey. Assembly directions available all over the place. In fact, our guys even found instructions in an al-Qaeda safe house after the fall of Kabul in 2001. Problem is TATP's unstable, and many bomb makers accidentally blow themselves up or lose fingers if they're not careful," McBride said.

"And the PETN, or whatever you called it?"

"Other name's pentrite. Also easy to make, mixing sulfuric and nitric acids and pentaerythritol. You can find a blow-by-blow description, complete with pictures, on the Internet. You just have to be careful," McBride said.

"Might be a good idea to check local stores to see if anyone's purchased any of the ingredients," said the chief.

"I agree, though I doubt you'll find anything. More than likely the stuff was bought elsewhere and brought in. Still, you don't know if you don't look. You've checked out the professor?"

"We've gone over all of his activities as best we could, since all his records went up in smoke. But nothing unusual with the phone company, bank, or credit cards. Owned his home and car. Bank checks to Goodwill and Salvation Army but nothing to any suspicious charities. His car was totally incinerated, liquefied to a metal puddle. We've found Mrs. Cassin's car and a car that must've been parked near the house across from her that we've traced to Petoskey Hertz, paid for in cash with a forged driver's license."

"Man or woman?" McBride asked.

"Both, according to the Hertz agent. A guy rented it but had a woman with him. We showed the agent pictures of possibles, but no ID. He's working with a police artist now, trying to put a likeness together. So the car's our only lead so far."

"But a big one," said McBride. "If okay with you, we'll tow it to our garage and go over it with a magnifying glass."

"We've talked to the neighbors and no one reports any suspicious activity. Mrs. Cassin was a benign busybody, well liked, and people in the house opposite had moved to Boca, so their house was empty," the chief said.

"And nothing suspicious around town? No groups of people going in and out of one house? Local gangs? We have to be careful about ethnic profiling, but no one of Middle Eastern characteristics around?

Or, as funny as it sounds, anybody with missing fingers or a missing hand?" McBride asked.

The cops looked at each other, shaking their heads.

"Could be whoever planned this hoped that their activity might go unnoticed in a small tourist town. I would guess they didn't plan on having to use the bomb," McBride said.

"Let's go back to the professor. Enemies?" he asked, looking over his glasses. "There are plenty of weirdo musicians out there. Maybe somebody broke in to settle a grudge?"

"None known. He lived on retirement income and rarely left the place over the last few years. Was at least seventy-five years old, and married over fifty years. I remember," the chief said, "because the neighbors threw them a fiftieth wedding anniversary party several years back. You guys remember?" he asked his squad.

There was widespread murmuring and nodding.

"His wife had been ill prior to that," the chief continued. "High drama for our little town. The husband found her unconscious on the kitchen floor and called 911. We were there first, CPRd her and kept her heart pumping till we reached the hospital, where the docs put in a pacemaker. They lived a quiet life since then because she was afraid to travel."

"So, I assume no one with a personal agenda for blowing them up?" McBride said.

The chief looked around the room at the rest of his force. All were shaking their heads. "None. No unusual travel, no funky friends, and no family we know of."

McBride stared hard at every face in the totally silent room. "Think carefully, each one of you. Think back to any interactions with the professor or his wife. Anything. Even if you don't think it's important."

All shook their heads.

"What's next?" asked the chief, breaking the silence.

"I don't know what else to tell you except to be super vigilant and contact the FBI with anything suspicious." McBride continued. "It may not be related, but my counterpart in Israel tells me there's increased communication traffic by Hamas to the U.S. Jordan, usually our buddy, has lots. We're working on deciphering the messages, but so far, nothing useful."

"Sounds too international for us," said the chief. "Why the hell would a terrorist want to blow up a bomb in our little burg?"

"You never know," said McBride. "This reminds me of just before 911—a few isolated pieces of a jigsaw puzzle, but nothing fit because too many pieces were still missing. I don't know what to tell you except be suspicious and look for an overall picture, any patterns, even here in Petoskey. It'll happen; patterns develop to connect the dots."

McBride stood. "I think we're done. Once again, my condolences to all of you, and to the families of the two police officers."

****

Back in Washington the next day, McBride's scrambled phone line rang.

"Hey, Mac. Heard you had an explosion in Michigan."

"Good morning, Jake. I guess, good afternoon in Jerusalem. Didn't take you long, did it?"

"Got to stay ahead of the bad guys. So, what gives?"

"I just got back from Petoskey. Small tourist town. Nothing ever happens there, and all of a sudden they have a bomb explode from stuff I'd expect to find in your neighborhood."

"That's why I called. Worried me you might've had a suicide bomber."

"Worried me too, which is why I went out personally when the bomb guys told me it was TATP and PETN."

"Find anything useful?"

"Unfortunately, no, although we're tearing apart the rental car the perp used. Nothing else left standing."

"Heard the bomb went off in a residential neighborhood."

"It did. House of an elderly couple, retired, living a quiet life after she got sick a while back, and got a pacemaker implanted."

The line went silent.

"What did you say?" Jake asked.

"Elderly couple, retired."

"No, the part about a pacemaker."

Chapter Thirty-Two

My secure phone rang.

"Hi, Zach. Jake here. Got a minute?"

I was surprised. Jake rarely called me from Israel, unless it was an emergency. Something was up.

"I'd like to patch through to the FBI guy I told you about," he said. "He basically does for them what I do here, though the title's a bit different. Name's Daniel McBride. He's the special agent in charge for the Explosives Unit–Bomb Data Center and the National Center for the Analysis of Violent Crimes. I think you'll find the conversation interesting."

"Sure, Jake. Put him through. Do you mind if my partner, Harry Scarpia, sits in?"

"Not a problem." I had Molly call Harry to come in.

"Mac," Jake said a moment later, after a couple of phone clicks, "I want to introduce you to my childhood friend, Zach Dayan. He's an ex-Israeli cop we transplanted to the NYPD."

"Transplanted?" the FBI agent asked.

"Yeah, we do that. They give us a guy and we give them one. Keeps both sides informed. We started Zach as a beat cop to get a feel for the city, so most think he's an ordinary detective, but he's an expert in Middle Eastern affairs and Israeli-Arab relations, so he helps us and the U.S."

"If you vouch for him, Jake, that's good enough for me. Hi, Zach."

"And good morning to you, Agent McBride."

"That was my father. Mac will do."

Harry poked his head in my office, saw I was on the phone, and started to back out. I waved him in. "My partner, Harry Scarpia, is here. Can I put you on the speaker phone?"

"Sure, as long as your office is secure." I motioned Molly to close my door.

"All set," I said.

"Good morning again," McBride said. "Jake tells me you've had several pacemaker murders and you're concerned about your daughter."

Harry looked at me with raised eyebrows.

"Yes, two, with a third murder that had identical MO to throw us off."

"Any clues?"

"A possible suspect, but otherwise nothing." I filled him in about the murders. Molly came in and set a fresh cup of coffee on my desk. She closed the door after she left.

"Let me tell you what happened two days ago in Petoskey, Michigan, and get your reaction," McBride said. He described the bombing. "What do you think?"

I saw surprise on Harry's face.

"Very interesting," I said. "Could've been an attempt at a pacemaker murder, and if it was, this thing's much larger than I thought. It fits with someone trying to kill me. Harry, what do you think?"

"Maybe. But we're still left with no reason for stealing pacemakers, if that's really what's happening," Harry said. "I still have my doubts."

"So there are at least two issues. First, do we have something on a national scale rather than some local murders?" I asked.

"We can help on that score," McBride said. "We can check for similar crimes. That's what NCAVC does."

"That would be helpful. But the second issue, equally important, is *why*? Why are people being killed for their pacemakers?" I asked.

"My problem, exactly," said Harry. "What's so important about them? I still think it may be chance."

"Zach, you went to medical school. You tell us," said Jake.

"I've been trying to do just that. I researched the textbooks and online and came up dry. The guts of a pacemaker aren't worth more than a couple hundred bucks. And the pacemaker itself has no resale value."

"Then, these people having pacemakers is only coincidental, like your partner is saying?" McBride asked.

I looked at Harry. "He's been trying to convince me of that, but it doesn't float for me. Too many coincidences, and why extract them if it's just chance? Doesn't figure."

We talked about fifteen minutes when Molly burst into my office. She dropped a handwritten note on my desk and stood back, hands crossed on her chest, a triumphant look on her face. I read the note, stopped talking, and just looked at her.

"You were saying?" said McBride.

"*Holy shit!* Forget what I was saying. I now know why the pacemakers are being stolen, and you're not going to like this. Not one bit."

****

"How did you figure it out?" I asked Molly after the phone call.

"As I've always said, Detective , you look but you don't see."

"So?"

"So, I went online to read about them, starting after JJ was here."

"So did I. And?"

"And you just didn't go back far enough. You only read about the modern ones."

She was right. "Okay. Go on."

"Well, I found this book, *History of the Modern Pacemaker,* and saw that some of the older pacemakers were different."

"Rachel's doctor never mentioned them."

Molly smiled and poked a finger through a curl. "He doesn't have enough gray hair to remember."

Chapter Thirty-Three

Miriam showed me a card the pediatrician had given her describing Rachel's pacemaker. Apparently, every patient got one at the time of surgery. It listed the kind of pacemaker implanted, when it was put in, type of leads, and so on. After reading it, I called off security. She would not be a target.

That night, Molly's revelation so stunned me, I couldn't sleep. After two hours of losing a wrestling match with the pillow, I went into my small den, lit up a bowl, and watched a smoke ring float to the ceiling.

I Googled Cardioelectrics, the company that made the pacemaker I was interested in. The company's Web site flashed in bold red, white, and blue. They were big: thirty-eight thousand employees worldwide, thirteen billion dollars annual sales, main office in Milwaukee and twelve factories scattered across the United States, Puerto Rico, Europe, and Japan. They sold six different kinds of pacemakers.

It was 5:00 a.m., 4:00 in Milwaukee. Obviously I couldn't call anyone at the company at this hour, but I could grab the first flight out and personally talk with someone at the company.

I drove to LaGuardia and flew out on a 6:00 a.m. Delta flight to Milwaukee. By 10:00 a.m., a cab deposited me in front of the World Headquarters of Cardioelectrics, Cardiac Rhythm Management branch. It was a brisk fall day with a metal sky and a chilling breeze. I had a friend living in Milwaukee who told me the weather was either winter or road repair. I guess they were just finishing road repair before the first snow.

The receptionist, a petite elderly woman with gray hair piled on her head in braided circles like a coiled snake, sat behind a desk in an open reception area. The walls around her were covered with enlarged photos of smiling patients brimming with health after receiving a Cardioelectrics product. A huge glass enclosed cabinet held an array of Cardioelectrics devices. Shiny silver pacemakers, connected to wires implanted in red plastic hearts, blinked on and off. A brass sign on the wall near the cabinet read, "A Cardioelectrics product improves the life of someone around the world every 8.7 seconds."

"May I help you?" She spoke with the nasal As of a native Midwesterner.

"I'd like to talk with someone about a pacemaker."

"Do you have the name?"

"If I did, I would have said so."

I guess that was a bit too sharp and her face closed up. "You have lovely gray eyes," I said. Usually works with waitresses when I've complained about the meal.

She smiled and her body relaxed. "Let me see what I can find out."

After several phone calls she said, "I think you want Dr. Elizabeth Burke, chief medical officer of Cardioelectrics."

"Fine, thanks."

She pulled a visitor's badge from a pile on her desk, wrote my name on it, and stamped the date. She entered the badge number in a ledger and handed me a pen. "Would you sign in next to the number, please, and put the time and date?"

After I did she said, "Please wear the badge at all times. Now would you walk through the security check?" She pointed to a metal detector guarding the entrance to the hallway.

Tougher security than airports. I debated and said *screw it*. Wrong decision. The alarm clanged and red lights flashed before I got halfway through. I should have removed the .38. I did now and laid it on the counter.

"We don't allow firearms on the premises."

"Would you hold it for me?" I handed her the gun, but she recoiled.

"My God, no! I've never even touched one of those things."

"Then maybe I'll keep it."

"No, you can't enter the building with that … gun."

"How about giving Dr. Burke a call?"

"Just escort him to my office," was Burke's response. "I doubt he's going to steal a pacemaker or shoot anyone."

Dr. Burke had short dark hair, big eyes, and a big office. She dressed in a dark suit and wore a dark expression that said, "Tell me why you're here and get on with it." I didn't think I would enjoy working under her. "Can I help you, Detective?"

I got on with it. "Your company sold nuclear pacemakers, but I can't find any information about them. They're not listed on your Web site."

"Model N350 incorporated a nuclear battery manufactured for us in France by a company called Alcabel. We stopped making them years ago."

"Why?"

"Several reasons. Lithium iodide batteries are a lot cheaper, easier to handle, and don't require adherence to the Atomic Energy Commission restrictions. Also, the nuclear batteries last too long, and patients should get replacement implants every six to eight years to benefit from other improvements in the pacemaker."

"Can you tell me anything about the nuclear pacemaker? How much plutonium it had, in what form, stuff like that?"

"No. I started with the company when the decision was made to discontinue the nuke. I could get you the technical manual, but it's on microfilm and you wouldn't understand it anyway. The one who knows most about it, Chester Goodpasture, is ... he left the company about a year ago."

"Why?"

"He's a senior engineer. In fact, very senior, close to eighty. He was the one who designed the nuclear battery in the 1970s. When the company stopped production, he got angry and told us we'd made a huge mistake. He hung around after that doing other projects but finally retired."

"Can I talk with him?"

"Why?"

"Police business."

"You can try." She clicked her computer and wrote out the address that flashed on the screen. "He doesn't talk to many people, particularly on this topic." She handed me the paper and was back typing at her computer before I left the room.

Chapter Thirty-Four

A thirty-minute cab ride north on US 43 took me to an apartment building in Glendale. An old man answered the door. His white, unkempt mane and matching cottony beard framed a wrinkled leathery face and rheumy eyes. "What do you want?" he said.

I told him, and he slammed the door in my face. I rang the bell again but got no response. After I pounded for five minutes, the door opened. This time I flashed my badge.

"We can talk here or downtown at headquarters." Of course I had no jurisdiction, but Goodpasture didn't know that. Leaning heavily on a dark oak cane, he limped toward a coffee table, and I followed his shuffling slippers. He sat down with a groan, motioning me with his cane to sit. Once we got started, he warmed to the topic, if not to me.

"It works from heat produced by a plutonium-fueled thermoelectric generator that has a little more than three grams of weapon's grade plutonium-238 oxide. The plutonium creates a temperature differential that triggers an electrical voltage from a Seebeck effect—"

I interrupted him. "What's that?"

He looked at me as if I was mentally challenged and tugged at his beard, fingers lost in the cotton. "I'll make it simple enough, even for a cop," he said. "The heat conversion generates a small pulse of electricity that paces the heart. Okay?"

"Isn't there a risk of nuclear contamination to the patient?"

I got the look again. "I designed this. Don't you think I would take that into consideration? The plutonium's triply encapsulated and then hermetically sealed by two titanium containers to eliminate any radiation leak. No leak whatsoever. You can hold a nuclear detector right next to the can and get no response."

"How long will it last?"

"Plutonium's half life's about eighty-five years, and the pacemaker would lose less than 1 percent of its capacity per year. So, expected battery life span is unknown, but it's well in excess of thirty or forty years. Even fifty years. That's what upper management didn't like. They couldn't sell replacements every five or six years like they do now. They'd lose a lot of sales."

But that's why the nuclear pacemakers were targeted, I thought. With no radiation leak, they could be transported anywhere without detection. Governments now used satellite technology to discover even tiny amounts of emitted radiation. And if the pacemakers lasted forever, all patients who had them would be targets, regardless of the pacemaker's age.

"Where do you store the plutonium?" I asked, worried about a factory break-in.

"We don't."

"What do you mean?"

"We stopped stocking when the idiots running Cardioelectrics decided to stop making the pacemakers."

Another puzzle piece fell in place. That's precisely why *patients* were being attacked and not Cardioelectrics factories. The pacemaker itself was the only source of plutonium.

I wrote in my notebook, *Need patient list. How many?* And if there were thousands, would all be in danger, and how could we protect them? *Should we go public?* What a panic that would set off! Anyone with a pacemaker would be frightened to death, hiring body guards or requesting police protection. Or they would even want the nuclear pacemaker replaced with different batteries. Doctors' phones would be ringing off the hook. But how could we not go public with the information we had?

"What're you writing?" he asked.

"Nothing important. Who keeps the list of patients?"

"Why do you want to know?"

"Answer the damn question."

"It's closely guarded in the Data Warehousing and Analytics System of Cardioelectrics."

"Why the security?"

"This is called Protected Health Information, because you can identify patients' personal stuff. Only a handful of people have clearance to the PHI in DWAS."

"Do you, or did you?"

"I did, because I took personal interest in the patients who got my invention. I would call them to see how they were doing."

"And did you turn in that list when you retired?"

"No. I still follow them."

"Anybody else have access to it?"

He shook his head. "I keep it on my computer."

"Could you tell if anyone other than you used it?"

"Can't happen. I'm always here, and besides, no one else knows my access code."

I thought about that for a bit. There was no real need for him to get the list, since I figured the patients were followed by their own doctors. But if Cardioelectrics let him have the list, who else might they have given access? And was his computer really that secure?

"Were there ever any factory break-ins when you were still in production?"

"Not that I know of, but there are other sources of plutonium if you're looking to make a nuclear pacemaker—or a nuclear bomb." He squinted at me. "You a terrorist?"

"No, but I may be trying to catch one. Like where?"

"Like all over. Almost two thousand tons of purified plutonium—enough for thirty or forty thousand bombs—are stored at research facilities, weapons depots, and other storage sites in over twenty countries. The former Soviet Union had three hundred tons, and they've had break-ins with stuff stolen. Ukraine, Belarus, and Kazakhstan still have stockpiles of weapons-grade uranium and plutonium. Our own country has seven to ten thousand nuclear war heads, half a dozen nuclear bomb facilities—some called "plutonium pits"—and more than one hundred power plants. There are terrorist opportunities galore."

But if it was that easy to get, why take chances with all those murders? He was probably talking pre-911. I'd have to check with McBride.

"You know the airplane, the *Enola Gay*? It dropped a uranium bomb made of U-235 over Hiroshima and three days later, the plane

Bockscar bombed Nagasaki with Pu-239 plutonium. That ended the war with Japan."

"Is the bomb hard to make?"

"Once the plutonium's obtained any skilled machinist—even a cop—could assemble a bomb small enough to fit in the back of an average truck or small plane, yet be as destructive as those dropped on Japan."

"How do you build one?"

"Google it. They list detailed instructions. Pictures, too."

"Give me a summary."

He sighed and stroked his beard. "Plutonium and uranium are unstable elements, ready to fly apart if given a nudge. You know that, right?"

I didn't. "Right."

"Well, an explosive charge like TNT squashes the radioactive material together, creating a dense critical mass that then flies apart, releasing huge amounts of destructive energy. For plutonium, the element is often arranged as a hollow shell, with explosives on the outside to compress the shell into that critical mass to set it off."

"Would that influence the shape of the bomb?" Maybe that would help spot it.

"Of course."

"How much plutonium do you need?"

"Depends on how big a bomb you want, but three kilograms would do for a start. Six and a half pounds."

I did the math in my notebook, but he beat me to it.

"About one thousand pacemakers."

Impossible for a single killer. Maybe there weren't even that many people alive with these pacemakers. Most likely many had died natural deaths and were buried. Cremation was not an option unless the device was removed. I breathed a sigh of relief and my heart rate slowed.

Goodpasture changed my mind. "Ever hear of a dirty bomb?" Before I could answer, he went on. "Package dynamite or explosive plastics with radioactive material. The bomb kills or injures through its initial blast but scatters the nuclear debris, which is then dispersed by airborne radiation. That way you don't need much plutonium to get a big radiation effect," he said over his shoulder as he stood and retrieved his cane. "Got to take a leak. Be right back."

The old man started me thinking again. Where could a terrorist achieve maximum effect with such a bomb? Obviously, the amount of killing would be minimal, so radioactive contamination and panic would be the goals. The White House or the Capitol in Washington DC were first in my mind, but probably any major U.S. or European city had select sites where such an explosion would be devastating. A bomb on Wall Street would paralyze the city more than the Twin Towers devastation, and for an even longer time, costing billions of dollars a day.

"Lots of juicy targets. Reservoirs, power plants, or food factories, to name a few," he said, returning. "All nicely unguarded."

And all accessible by sleeper operatives already in the United States, acting alone or with sympathetic extremist groups. I remembered JJ talking about no security lines riding the train from DC to New York. Another perfect target.

The old man went on. "If there's enough exposure, radiation sickness will follow, and then radiation-induced cancers and leukemias, like after the 1986 Chernobyl meltdown outside Kiev."

"Tell me, how could somebody steal the list of patients with nuclear pacemakers?"

"I already told you, from the DWAS."

"I know, but how could they gain entry? Where's DWAS located?"

"Computer floor, main building."

"How do you access it?"

"How the hell do I know? I designed the pacemaker and built it. I wasn't in charge of recordkeeping. Why don't you ask that bitch, Elizabeth Burke? She's in charge of everything—or thinks she is."

"Why don't you like her?"

He snorted. "She ruined my life's work. And then fired me."

"She said you retired."

"What the hell was I supposed to do after she stopped production on my pacemaker, took away my lab, my technicians, and said, 'Have a nice day'?"

"Why?"

"She'd just started with the company, said we'd been losing money on the nuclears, and the bitch wanted to impress the CEO. So, she killed the program and me along with it."

****

On the flight back to New York, I thought a lot about what Goodpasture had told me. I wondered whether what he *didn't* tell me was equally important. I suspected I would have to return to Cardioelectrics in the near future to find out.

Chapter Thirty-Five

I spoke with McBride the day after I got back from Milwaukee.

"Zach, like I said, the FBI has the National Center for the Analysis of Violent Crimes here in Washington. NCAVC provides operational support to investigate particularly vicious and repetitive violent crimes like what you described. It's part of the George Bush Strategic Information and Operations Center at the J. Edgar Hoover Building in Washington."

"How do you get people to report the crimes? The FBI doesn't have the greatest reputation for sharing intelligence or working with local cops."

"I agree, but 911 changed that attitude. FBI policy now is to 'catch and pass on as soon as possible' all intelligence, and share it among our own intelligence community as well as the locals in the trenches. In fact, the Intelligence Reform and Terrorism Prevention Act that created a director of national security also mandated that change in 2004."

"So, you have any similar murders reported?"

"I checked the records in the system before I called you," McBride said.

"And?"

"You've hit pay dirt. Five murders with chest slashings similar to what you described, in Oklahoma, Florida, Kentucky, Ohio, and Colorado. There're probably more, since, as you pointed out, reporting is voluntary and some locals may not have called them in."

"We need to get the word to law enforcement offices throughout the U.S. to be on the lookout for similar cases," I said.

"We can do that through the Law Enforcement National Data Exchange. LENDE allows us to contact law-enforcement agencies at any level—local, state, or federal—and coordinate activities. Even at a tribal level, if you can believe that."

"What about Europe or the rest of the world?"

"Whoa. Slow down before we go international. We need proof this is an international thing and not some sort of cult murders."

"Cult murders for chest slashings maybe, but stealing pacemakers? Doesn't make sense. And what about the explosives in Michigan?" I said.

"Maybe. If it is, we can use Interpol. They have a special agency for international terrorism and almost two hundred country members. We've got our FBI field agents in many foreign countries."

"I'd like to fly in and go over what we have."

"Good idea. We may want to involve the National Joint Terrorism Task Force. They coordinate terrorism acts between the FBI and local enforcement agencies."

"Homeland Security, also?" I asked.

"You bet, if it is terrorism."

"When can I come?"

"Tomorrow too soon? You could fly in tonight."

"Will do, as soon as I clear it with the chief."

****

I took the eight o'clock shuttle to Washington that night. It was dark and cold waiting on a long taxi line at Reagan International, and I regretted not taking the train. Finally a cab pulled up with two guys in the front seat, a little guy driving and a big guy sitting alongside. I gave the driver my address, and he asked if it was okay for his friend to ride with us. The guy was learning the streets before taking his taxi driver's test. I said fine. He put my carry-on in the trunk and we sped off.

When we hit the George Washington Memorial Parkway, the driver looked at me in the rear view mirror. "You tired?"

"I am."

"How about I turn off the radio and you lean back and sleep until we get to your hotel?"

"Great," I said. I closed my eyes and began to doze. After a few minutes, I felt the cab slow and I bolted awake.

"The battery indicator light is flashing," the driver said, pointing to a flickering light on the dash board. "I'll have to stop."

"Bullshit! Keep driving as long as the motor is running. Key Bridge to downtown DC is right ahead."

He ignored me and turned off into a dark road that expanded into an alcove of trees with a small parking lot alongside the Potomac River. Moonlight glinted silvery off the water's surface.

I was wide awake now. Instinctively I reached for my gun. *Shit!* I had packed the damn thing along with my phone in my carry-on for the security check.

The driver stopped the cab, flicked the headlights on and off twice, and blew the horn. So much for a dead battery. Then he got out of the cab, opened the hood, and I saw a shower of sparks when he disconnected the battery cable. He got back into the car, turned the ignition key, and the car motor was silent.

"See," he said, "battery's dead, like I told you. Sit back and relax until roadside assistance comes." *Sure,* I thought, *wait for your buddies to show up.* The big guy in front got out and scanned the dark foliage surrounding the empty lot, looking for his friends to help. He looked to be an inch or two taller than me, and heavier. I didn't want to fight him if I could avoid it.

I scrambled out of the back and flashed my badge. "I am a New York police officer. Open the trunk!" I pounded on it. "You both are under arrest."

The big guy came around the car holding a long object that flashed in the moonlight—an aluminum baseball bat. "You can shove that badge up your ass, pal. You want to live to get back home, hand over your wallet and watch." He tapped the business end of the bat on the car's roof.

I glanced around. The driver had disappeared, probably looking for his buddies.

I reached into my jacket pocket and took out my wallet.

"Put it on the ground, along with your watch."

I did as ordered. "Now back away from it."

I took two steps back and he bent down, keeping his eyes on me. Suddenly noises from the brush got his attention, and he glanced sideways for an instant. That was enough. I kicked at his head like a winning sixty-yard field goal attempt. Except for the crunch as his jaw disintegrated, he went down without a sound. I ran to the driver's side and reached for the keys. None! I groped beneath the dashboard for the trunk release latch, found it, and popped the lid. I grabbed my carry-on, fumbled with the zipper, and snatched my Smith and Wesson .38.

"Boris, you there?" The driver and a clone of the guy on the ground emerged from the shadows.

"Boris?" the driver asked again.

I stepped from behind the car. "Boris is taking a nap. Hands up where I can see them and turn around. You're under arrest."

They bolted for the bushes. I got off a shot apiece but heard no groans, so I figured I missed them both. I then dialed 911.

Chapter Thirty-Six

I was in McBride's office in Washington by 8:30 the next morning.

"Heard you had a welcoming party last night. Sorry for that. DC is usually a bit more hospitable. We've had a rash of similar muggings in the past month."

"They picked the wrong guy this time."

"And do they know it. The cops arrested the driver early this morning from his ID in the cab. His buddy showed up at GW Hospital emergency with a gunshot to his left hip, so you winged him. The guy you kayoed won't be talking for a week until the swelling goes down and they wire his jaw back together. So I think you put a big dent in their operation."

"A pleasure to help the city cops. That little encounter did teach me never get into a DC cab without my weapon and cell phone."

"Good policy in any city, not only here."

I laid out my casebook, and McBride studied the evidence log, photos, and the statements by the witnesses and relatives.

After ten minutes he looked up. "Zach, I agree about the lady, Frankie. She's your number-one suspect. The DNA fingers her."

"She fits, except why kill Hanson? No pacemaker. And she had an alibi of sorts the night Zimmerman was killed."

"She knocked off her adoptive mother with a lookalike murder, and the Zimmerman alibi is easily rigged."

"But what's she doing with the pacemakers, if that's her motive?"

"Terrorist ties is what I'd look for. Either directly or through acquaintances. What's your partner think?"

"Initially Harry was more aggressive about pursuing Frankie as a suspect, but now he defends her innocence. She's very manipulative and could've fed him the poisoned apple. Put his head to sleep—at least his big head."

McBride smiled. "What about Zimmerman's murder?"

"He's the only hope so far. We found one casing from a .45 semiautomatic under the bed, probably kicked there during a fight with the killer. Must've picked up the other one. That casing and a single bloody footprint are the only mistakes he's made so far—or she. The killer probably looked for the casing and got careless."

"You ran it down?"

"Your guys did it for me. Analysis from the FBI Shoe Prints Database shows it's a right foot, size ten Nike Dart VII running shoe, found in any sporting goods store. Men's. But of course that doesn't rule out a woman wearing it."

"True. Frankie have a pair?"

"Runs in them, but a woman's size eight."

"She could've worn a different pair for the murder. Stuffed the toes."

"Of course. But we'd need a search warrant to look for them."

"What about the bullet in Driver?"

"It was pretty badly damaged, a .38 slug."

"So maybe Frankie bought a .45 to do Zimmerman?"

"Could be. She threatened to buy a bigger gun if I took Boom Boom."

"Boom Boom? What kind of an idiot names her gun?"

I gave him a palms-up.

"Could Frankie have whipped Zimmerman in a fight?" McBride asked.

"Certainly possible. She's in great physical shape, and Zimmerman was no match for even a hundred-pound kid, his heart was so bad."

McBride snorted. "So maybe you have your suspect?"

"She's high on the list."

"She belong to any extremist groups? Cults?"

"Not that we've found out, though the one who might know would be Scarpia."

"Maybe an avenue worth exploring?"

"I'm on it. Someone's got to be coordinating all of this, collecting the pacemakers. And of course, once the pacemakers are opened, they need to know how to handle it."

"That takes it pretty close to the end. And suppose the extraction's in some foreign country like Iran or Syria? Sure'd be nice to stop them before they get that far," McBride said.

"Exactly. And that's why you need to go live with this to every police department in the U.S."

"I'll use national data exchange to do just that."

Chapter Thirty-Seven

I sat in my office, pipe clamped in my teeth and doodle pad working as I searched the patient list for the next likely victim. I needed a court order to subpoena the names from Cardioelectrics because of the patient confidentiality law, known as HIPAA. I now knew the names of the twelve thousand five hundred people in the United States and Europe implanted with an N350 nuclear pacemaker. Molly pared the list by twenty percent by removing names on the National Death Index. We'd probably have to warn the people still alive, but pandemonium was sure to break loose, which would play directly into the hands of the terrorists. Fear was an important part of what they were trying to accomplish.

As I thought about all those people on the NDI who had died despite getting the life-saving pacemaker, I remembered what Chester Goodpasture said about its expected lifespan.

"Molly," I shouted through the open door. "Please come in right now."

"Okay, okay," she said entering my office. "No need to shout. I'm right here. What's the excitement?" She had my coffee and set the mug on my desk.

"Molly, those names you were eliminating."

"The dead people?"

"Yes. I want you to call each family, find out where the dead were buried, and then call the cemetery to see if any graves were disturbed in the past few weeks."

She scowled for a minute. "How am I going to find time to …" Then she smiled. "Not bad for somebody who can't find his magnifying glass. You finally found something important. Grave robbers stealing pacemakers?"

"You got it," I said, leaning back in my chair.

"Good job, Detective!" A rare compliment from Molly.

I put my feet on my desk, puffed on my pipe, and doodled cemetery headstones. My teeth chewed the stem as my mind worked the ideas. Grave robbing couldn't be that easy, or the terrorists would have done only that and avoided the killings. But it sure would decrease the number of murders needed.

A few minutes later Molly burst into my office. "California and Nevada!"

"Tell me."

"Graves robbed. Two of my first four calls. An Abbott and an Ackerman, right on the top of my list! Abbott died in Los Angeles eighteen months ago and Ackerman in Reno two years ago. I spoke with both spouses, and they told me the graves had been dug up in the last two weeks and the bodies slashed. From their descriptions, like Driver's."

"Add those to the explosion in Michigan and we must be dealing with killers all over the U.S. I bet there'll be a lot more grave robbings than murders. Much less risk."

Harry was at the door. "What's the excitement?"

I waved him in and briefed him where we were. "Now do you think the murders were for the pacemakers?"

"You win," he said, looking glum. I guess he didn't like being wrong any more than I did.

Over the next two hours, Molly found another twelve grave robbings in multiple states. I had Patricia O'Malley help with the calls. She'd been riding a desk since her vomiting episode at Driver's murder, but she seemed eager to get back in the field.

"Can you believe this lunacy?" Molly asked as she came back in the office. "Most of the morticians said families asked them to remove the pacemaker before burial, because they had the crazy notion the pacemaker might keep the heart beating in their dead relative."

"What did they do with pacemakers?" Harry asked.

"Just threw them away," Molly said.

"That explains why the terrorists had to be killing people, not only robbing graves," I said.

"And, surprisingly, not all of the graves can be found," Molly said, "even after accounting for those cremated."

"I wonder how many of those robbed graves were restored after the pacemakers were stolen so there'd be no trace. The terrorists may be a lot closer to finishing than we figured."

"You've convinced me," Harry said. "So, what's our next move?"

"You know, McBride thinks Frankie's the top suspect." I waited several moments for Harry to answer, but he was quiet. Molly slipped out of the room.

"Are you dating her?"

"Why?"

"That's a dumb question. I could can your ass right now if you are."

Harry concentrated on finger pressing the already perfect crease in his pants before he answered.

"She's just fun to be with. It's not going anywhere."

"Have you slept with her?"

"With all due respect, Zach, that's none of your damn business."

"I'll take that as a 'yes.' Do you have any idea the risk you're running? You're out of your goddamn head getting this involved with our prime murder suspect. If Internal Affairs found out you'd be gone in a second—if they didn't lock you up first."

"It started as part of this investigation. Now, I see her off hours, not on police time."

"There's no difference."

He sat there looking at his shoes. I filled my pipe, lit up a bowl, and inhaled the smoke.

"Could she kill?"

Harry shook his head no. "We've been here before, you know? She handles a gun like a pro, she likes excitement, and she has a new toy. Bam Bam she calls it, if you can believe that. But I don't think she's the one."

"You did before."

"Well, she changed my ... I've changed my mind."

I let the slip go. "What kind of gun?"

"Smith and Wesson .45. An SW99 automatic."

"Lot of gun for a little lady."

"Yeah, but she handles it well."

"How would you know? Joe's Guns?"

A sheepish grin gave me the answer.

"Look, Harry. We have no leads except for Frankie. I agree with McBride she's our only bet so far, but nothing concrete enough to arrest her. We have the casing from Zimmerman being processed by the DRUGFIRE screen. You need to get hold of her new gun … is it really Bam Bam, for Christ's sake?"

"Yes," Harry said.

"Well, we need to check it out. Zimmerman's was a .45."

"It's brand new. She just bought it."

"Before or after Zimmerman was killed?"

"Before."

"So it's still a possible?"

"I suppose. But not likely."

"Well, get it in and run a ballistics check. We can try a match against the casing we have and enter it into the DRUGFIRE database for the future. You can give Boom Boom back, since the ballistics didn't match the bullet in Driver's head."

"Will do."

"She knows about the pacemakers, right?"

"I already told you that."

"What about the list of patients?"

"She knows we got it."

"Jesus Christ, what else have you told her?"

"What do you think I am? A spy for her?"

"I don't give a shit what you are. No, that's not true. If I thought you were, I'd arrest your ass along with hers. I want to prevent another pacemaker murder."

Harry stared at his shoes in silence.

"She ever talks about any groups, like Hamas or al-Qaeda?"

"Not a thing. I spent a lot of time finding out about her life. She's not a member of any club and doesn't go to meetings. Nothing suspicious at all."

"No? Only murder her adoptive mother! And she had good reason to do that." Harry didn't answer me. "Harry, I know you like this lady, but we've got zilch so far. Somebody killed her adoptive mother and she's our best bet."

"Yeah, I thought like that in the beginning, but since I've gotten to know her, I don't see it anymore."

"What a surprise. I suppose I wouldn't either if I was schtupping her."

In a second Harry was in my face, fists clenched at his sides. "Watch it, Zach. I'm being the cop like you trained me."

That was the angle I needed for Internal Affairs, so I backed off, defusing the confrontation. He'd be my plant. He could continue seeing her if he reported anything useful. "Easy, guy. Seems to me I remember you were hot on Frankie as the killer right after Driver's murder."

"That was before I got to know her."

"Maybe true, but it still doesn't change the facts."

"The facts are she's not the killing type."

"Why, because she's a woman?"

"I guess so. At least partly."

"Well, let me educate you, my friend. In Israel, we had female suicide bombers as young as fourteen strapped with bombs to look like they were pregnant. And you know about those Chechnya women? The ones involved with the Moscow Dubrovka movie house, the Russian plane crashes, and the school hostage thing in North Ossetia? They're called the Black Widows because they murder to avenge the deaths of their male relatives. Read the newspapers if you think mothers won't kill! Suicide bombers, just like the men, and just as ruthless."

I could see him opening and closing his fists as I went on. I had clearly struck a raw nerve with Frankie. I had to turn that to my advantage.

"Okay, okay. Let's cool it and go back to what we do know. We're dealing with people who're not afraid to die. In fact, who may *want* to die, and that's screwing us up. It's like trying to catch a house full of bees by hand. If you're lucky enough to get one, you get stung for your troubles. Like bin Laden said, the Western world loves life and his people love death."

"So what do we do?"

"Somebody out there's got to have a clue about a suspicious character, a house with late-night visitors, somebody buying explosives, something, for Christ's sake! We need inside information, or we're only reacting to them and not preempting, and we're going to have more murders."

"I agree."

"You're in so sweet with her. Try and find out. She's the one who's going to lead us to whoever is behind this, and you've got to find a way to get her to tell you."

Chapter Thirty-Eight

They walked slowly arm-in-arm from the movie house at Times Square. "Did you like it?" Frankie asked.

Harry hesitated before answering. "I thought the acting was great, but honestly, two guys kissing each other turned my stomach. I almost puked my popcorn."

She chuckled. "What if it'd been two girls?"

"I wouldn't like it either, but it would have been better than two men."

"Why is that different?"

"I don't know, but it just is."

"Typical male chauvinism."

"May be so, but it still disgusts me. I was in training once, when I was eighteen or nineteen. We slept about thirty guys to a room. Two in each bed. And one night I woke up, maybe three in the morning, feeling some sort of a pressure on my chest. The guy I was sleeping next to had tossed his arm across me. He was sound asleep, but his open hand was cupping my breast. Maybe he was dreaming about being home with his wife. I can't tell you the revulsion I felt."

"What did you do?" Frankie laughed.

"I picked up his hand between my thumb and forefinger," he showed her a delicate pincer movement with his hand and a disgusted look on his face, "and gently lifted it off my chest and put it back on his side of the bed. Then I poked him in the ribs with my elbow and made him roll away. He never even woke up. Ugh." The noise was a retch coming from the pit of his stomach. "For the rest of the night I squeezed so far over on my side I almost fell off the bed. I stared at the ceiling until he woke up the next morning."

She giggled and leaned into him. "Good thing you don't mind when I do that."

He drew her close, shortening his steps to synch with hers, hips rubbing. He bent down and kissed her lips, then her nose. He slipped his hand inside her coat and caressed her breast, shielding her with his body so no one could see. "If you did it with another woman I might."

"You just said it was okay."

"No, I said I wouldn't like it, but it'd be better than two men. But that's in the movies. We're talking about you."

"I have."

He recoiled. "You have what?"

"Done it with another woman."

He dropped his arm, stopped walking, spun her toward him, and looked in her face. "Don't tease me."

"I'm not."

Hands gripping her shoulders he asked, "Okay then. What have you done with another woman?"

"Made love."

"Bullshit."

"No bullshit. I have. More than once."

"When?"

"A long time ago."

He stared into her eyes. Neither blinked.

"You're serious, aren't you?"

"Absolutely."

"Why?"

"Why not?"

"No, c'mon. Why'd you do it?"

"Why not? There's no law against it, and it's a lot safer than with guys."

"Maybe not a legal law, but it's against … well, it's against religion. A moral law."

"Maybe your religion, not mine. By the way, what is yours?"

"I believe in God."

"But where does God say two women can't make love?"

"It's unnatural."

"Back to what you said earlier, bullshit."

Harry ran a hand through his hair. His face was flushed. His eyes narrowed and brows furrowed. "Frankie, don't do this to us. *To me.*"

"What the hell am I doing to you? I'm only being honest. I wanted to explore how it was with another woman, with someone my own age who I liked. So I tried it. In college, not since. Something different. For fun. Not a big deal."

They resumed walking, two people together but separated, and came to a late night coffee shop on the corner of Sixth Avenue and Fifty-fourth Street. He kept his hands in his coat pockets, and she hugged her purse with both arms, as other strollers passed between them. His face was tight, the tenseness emphasizing all the lines around his eyes and mouth.

"Want a cup of coffee?" he asked, his voice gravelly with the effort of speaking.

She gave a nonchalant shrug. He walked to the outdoor patio of the café and she followed, lagging two steps behind. They took seats on opposite sides of the small table. Overhead, two large silver heaters stacked on tall poles glowed red, radiating heat down onto their necks.

He ordered two decaf cappuccinos without asking her. They both looked in silence at late night New Yorkers walking by, avoiding each other's eyes.

After the coffee had sat long enough to get cold, he swung his body around to face her. "Frankie, this is very important to me. You can't imagine how important. Exactly what did you do with other women? And how many were there?"

She stared at him, a bemused look on her face. "What's with you? Why is this any of your business? You have no right to judge me."

"I'm not judging. I just want to know what you did."

"Why? Why do you want to know?" she taunted. "Does it turn you on?"

Rage ignited in his narrowed eyes, and his mouth tightened into a white line. He stood, towering over her, almost as tall as the heaters. He was shaking, his neck muscles bulging and jaw clenched. He looked down at her through the slits his eyes had become and raised his right hand, fist balled.

She looked up, seemingly unafraid, but the bemused look was now forced. She dropped her shaking hands beneath the table, fumbled with the clasp of her handbag, and fingered the newly returned Boom Boom. She slipped her right hand around the handle, her forefinger alongside the trigger guard, and pointed the barrel straight ahead at his gut, not taking it out of her purse.

Then he stopped, hand in mid-air. He stood still as a statue, staring at her with a confused expression. After a moment he shivered and slowly sat down, letting his arm drift back to his side. He put both hands on the table, intertwining his fingers and repeatedly squeezing them together to control the spasm. His face relaxed a little as he fought to regain his composure. He separated his hands but clenched and unclenched his fists, still breathing fast. "That's not it at all, and you know it."

She tried to conceal her fright, her shaking right hand still cradling Boom Boom. "Then what is it with you? You know I'm hardly a virgin. I've had other men before you. Quite a few actually. Why doesn't that bother you? Why is sex with another woman, with several women, so upsetting?"

"Because one act is natural and the other isn't."

"According to whom?"

"According to my religion."

"Which is?"

He sat down and stared at her, his eyes meeting hers. Then he looked out at the street, into the night, a worried expression on his face. He hesitated.

She asked the question again.

"Which religion?"

"Muslim."

Her eyebrows raised and her mouth opened. "You told me you were Italian and Spanish."

He was silent.

"You don't act like a Muslim. You drink wine, wear expensive clothes, and hang out with me. And I thought you were Italian. Italian and Spanish, you said."

"I'm flexible."

She gave a short *ha*. "So, basically, you adhere to Islam when it's convenient."

They were silent for a few moments. She tried to rescue the situation. "Well, it's not like *you* did it with a man. You only fuck women, don't you?"

He grimaced. "I have ... known only women. And very few at that. But you ..."

"But me, what?"

He grabbed her upper arm and squeezed it hard. "You have done those things and now I've been with you." His face was dark, eyebrows drawn together.

"Let go of my arm. You're hurting me."

He dropped his hand as she wrenched free.

"So? So you've been with me. Big deal. What's that supposed to mean? Are you now contaminated? It's not like I gave you herpes."

"Let's drop it, okay? It's late. I'll find you a cab."

"No, I don't want to drop it. I'll tell you. We were four roommates in our freshman year, away from home and on our own for the first time. We got drunk one night and watched a sex flick. It looked like fun, so we started kissing each other, then touching each others' breasts. My girlfriend Angie was the leader. She took off her shirt and bra, and asked me to kiss her nipple. I did and then we all started doing that. Our pants went next and—"

"Enough! Enough! I don't want to hear any more." He stood again, scowled at her, turned, and disappeared into the dark.

Chapter Thirty-Nine

I crouched over the body, squatting on the balls of my feet. I studied the chest slashes, comparing them in my mind with the previous murders. JJ had taught me how to search for the pacemaker pocket in the upper left chest and not be deceived by the mutilation. It was so obvious if you knew where to look and what to look for. I called Harry and Patricia over.

"Look here," I said. "Pacemaker pocket. Exactly like the others."

We were in Franconia Residence Hall at East Tenth Street, one of the New York University dorms for freshmen students. The victim was a nineteen-year-old girl who had received a pacemaker three years ago for an erratic heartbeat. Her roommate found her dead. I had passed her parents sobbing outside in the hallway when I came in. Stupidly, the mother had been allowed to see her daughter. She had fainted and was now laid out on a couch crying hysterically. I chewed out the cop who had given permission.

Harry and Patricia both sank down beside me, studying the corpse. Harry took a cotton-tipped stick from his pocket and gently pried away the skin tatters that had already adhered to the chest with the blood coagulum. He called the crime scene photographer to take pictures of it. Patricia was breathing hard, a hand pressed against her mouth.

I left them both still crouched next to the corpse and walked around the room, visualizing the killer's moves to get into the dorm. He would have had to climb the fire escape to the second floor of a building in which public safety service officers were on duty twenty-four seven and enter through a locked window. Obviously, he had been successful. But that was a big risk to take. My guess was the grave robbing was not going that well.

I looked back at Harry and Patricia studying the body. The girl's chest was slashed multiple times, but something struck me as odd. What was it? Harry was dressed in his usual impeccable Italian suit, polished shoes, and silk handkerchief, all his trademark accoutrements. Patricia crouched next to him. Although a skinny girl, she was unmistakably a woman. Once, in what I thought was a friendly gesture, I called her Pat. She told me in no uncertain terms her father, a second-generation Irish cop, had wanted a son named Patrick, and she had spent her childhood proving she could replace that son in his eyes. But, by damn, she would do it as a girl and would be called by a girl's name, Patricia, thank you very much.

I saw Harry looking at the body closely, jotting notes in a pad. But something was different. Or was I noticing it for the first time? I couldn't be sure, but I sensed something ... something way out at the periphery of conscious thought. My gut was talking to me.

At that moment, Harry looked up and our eyes locked briefly like two magnets. He half smiled, a troubled smile, it seemed to me. He rose from his squat and walked over.

"Pretty much the same as all the others," Harry said, shaking his head, hands crossed over his chest. His body language conveyed futility, a sense of frustration with what he was doing. "Damn shame."

I put my arm over his shoulders. "It's okay, Harry. We'll get him. By the way, how the hell do you sit back on your heels like that? I can't crouch down unless I'm on my toes, like Patricia." I pointed at her still crouched next to the body.

"Years of practice," he said

Patricia was still staring intently at the body when she jumped up. "I think there's something different about this corpse," she said, as if reading my mind. "But I can't figure out what it is."

Harry glanced at the body, then at Patricia, and finally at me. "I don't see anything."

"The slashes! That's it ... the slashes," Patricia said. "They're not as deep or extensive as the Driver killing. It's almost as if the killer was in a hurry, or maybe he didn't care about trying to trick us anymore and only hacked things up a bit for the sake of appearances."

She was right. That's what I had seen but it hadn't registered.

"You think?" Harry said.

"We can get JJ to take a look and compare the depth and number, but I'd bet the ranch she's right," I said. "Get some good photos," I told the crime photographer, "especially of the slashes." I took out my notebook. "Okay, let's go over what we've got."

"Four murders—if you include Hanson—who didn't have a pacemaker. So that's three pacemakers," Harry said.

"And the guard at Driver's murder," Patricia added.

"That totals nine grams of plutonium from our area. I spoke with McBride this morning. He said reports are rolling in from almost every state and half dozen countries in Europe ... either a killing or multiple grave robbings. Seems like a three- or four-to-one ratio of grave robbings versus murders, maybe even five-to-one in some places. Put it all together and I'd bet the terrorists have captured at least several hundred pacemakers. Maybe even a lot more. It's hard to estimate."

"How many do they need?" Patricia asked.

"A thousand to build a nuclear bomb," I said. "Less for a dirty bomb."

"So, a goal of maybe eight hundred grave robbings and two hundred murders total?" Patricia said.

"Seems like a lot of murders," Harry said.

"I agree, but spread out over the U.S. and Europe with a small army of terrorists, definitely doable. Maybe a hundred of them, ten pacemakers apiece. Two or three killings in each state, and a similar number in Europe, and they've got their two hundred murders. Even after the FBI warned as many patients as they could locate and the media finally publicized the murders, the two hundred is easy. We can't protect them all. But the more successful the terrorists are with the grave robbings, the fewer murders they'll need."

McBride told me the bad guys had lost a few: one in Petoskey, another in Miami, a third in Milan, and a fourth in Istanbul, all ending with explosions like in Petoskey. Six U.S. cops, three Italians, and two Turkish police were dead because of it. He had conferred with Jake Hertzog to find out how Israeli police captured suicide bombers, but the FBI had decided it was too dangerous to try to take them alive and warned police forces throughout the world to shoot to kill on sight before the terrorist had a chance to detonate a bomb belt. He also told me the stuff Goodpasture had said about how easy it was to get hold of plutonium was all pre 9/11, as I suspected. All those sites were now supposed to be air tight, which had to be why the terrorists were targeting the pacemakers.

"Nothing new from Frankie?" I asked Harry.

He looked at me with a pained expression.

"What's the matter?" I asked.

"We had a fight. I don't think I'll be seeing her anymore."

I guess my face registered surprise. "What happened?"

"Personal. Sorry, Zach, but you'll have to take her over," Harry said. "I'm done here."

****

Back at the office, my secure phone rang. It was McBride.

"Zach, the number of murders and grave robbings are escalating. We've told all patients with nuclear pacemakers not to leave their homes. We can't protect them all. The terrorists seem to know their whereabouts. Not only who has the pacemakers, but where they're going during the day, what they're doing, and so forth."

"Like what?"

"We had a guy in Naples, Florida, who was warned specifically by the local FBI agency not to leave his apartment, let his wife do the shopping, keep the doors locked, and so on. He agrees, then he's found all slashed up dead on the beach two miles from his house, near Old Naples. Wife says he got a phone call, left the house, and that's the last time she saw him alive."

"How many like that?"

"At least half dozen."

"How's that possible? How could the terrorists get such information?"

"That's what I was going to ask you," McBride said. "Anybody with connections to them?"

I thought for a moment. "I have an idea. Give me twenty-four hours."

Chapter Forty

My unique position at NYPD gave me the flexibility to respond quickly. I caught the next flight to Milwaukee and four hours later I was knocking on Goodpasture's door. He looked more disheveled than I remembered, the white hair and beard both needing a wash and comb. He was wearing samples of his lunch or dinner on a plaid shirt.

"You again? Didn't you get enough information the first time? Or maybe you forgot what I told you."

"You were very helpful, Mr. Goodpasture, but I have a few more questions."

"Well, make them quick. I've got better things to do than talk to you."

I pushed myself into his house. "Like what? Calling patients?"

"What's that supposed to mean?"

"I think you know."

"I told you the last time, I keep tabs on the patients who got my pacemaker. So, yeah, I call them from time to time."

"And what else?"

"You tell me."

"Who did you give the patient list to?"

"I told you. No one has access to my computer."

"That wasn't my question. I believe that. But the bad guys somehow got the list of patients with nuclear pacemakers and now seem to know their activities. I want to know who you sent information to and why. Pissed off at your boss, Elizabeth Burke, and maybe Cardioelectrics? Maybe you're looking to get even, or maybe even make some extra retirement cash?"

"I don't know what you're talking about."

"I think you do. I think you're calling these patients and these calls are getting them killed—that's what I think. Your phone records will show that."

"You're full of shit. Get the hell out of my house. Right now. Leave."

"Where's your computer?"

"None of your goddamned business. You want it, show me your search warrant." The old guy's hands were quivering, and his tongue was working dry lips. His breathing increased. A positive lie detector test in the field.

"Where is it? You have an office in here?"

I tried to walk around him, but he blocked my way. We were still standing in the entry way to his condo. He pulled a revolver from the drawer of the table next to him and pointed it at me. His eyes were widely dilated. "I'm protecting my home from an intruder. Leave or I'll shoot you. And don't think I wouldn't."

"I'll tell you what, old man. I'm not going to give you the chance. I'll be back in two or three hours with a search warrant. You had better be here with that computer. If not, you'll be in even bigger trouble than you are now."

"I don't scare easily, Detective. You think because I let you talk to me the last time when you pulled that phony jurisdiction bullshit with your NYPD badge, I'm going to listen to you again? Out of my house and don't come back."

I left and called McBride. He'd follow up with the Milwaukee FBI office, who would work with the locals to get the search warrant. I suspected Goodpasture's computer would be clean, however. He was too sharp to have left a trail. Or if he did, he'd erase it now. But at least I may have put a stop to the patient phone calls. And maybe under questioning, the FBI would be able to get a lead on who Goodpasture was talking to.

Chapter Forty-One

Wahad sat in the back room of the book shop in Chappaqua, reviewing the operations with the two ladies.

"How many pacemakers do you have?" Wahad asked.

"Seven hundred and ninety-five. We expect seventeen more tonight," Ruth said. "We will keep the store open until they are delivered."

"So we're awfully close."

"Only a few more days. A week at most. Then we are done, at least with this stage. They are just putting the finishes on the lab. As you predicted, paying off the tour guides was all we had to do. Not even one problem with the government so far."

"Has the mount cutter assembly arrived to open the pacemakers? We'll need it with the mill spindle. That will be the tricky part. The spindle speed is five thousand revolutions per minute, so it has to be securely bolted down."

"It is scheduled for delivery at the port tomorrow," said Ruth, "and will be at the lab four hours later. I will check to be sure when we make contact with Amir. They said they could bolt it to the rock floor."

"Perfect. This has been the hardest part. The date has been set. It will be 10:00 AM in exactly twenty-one days. That gives us a week to complete the thousand, nine days to build the bomb, and five days for transportation."

"And the site?" asked Ruth.

"Exactly as we suspected. Eleven Wall Street in lower Manhattan."

"Access?"

"All in place, as we discussed. The time has come to get rid of Dayan permanently."

"*Allahu akbar!* I knew if I waited long enough I would see my men avenged. What can we do?" Ruth asked. Sarah flexed her twisted fingers.

"Listen closely," Wahad said. "Dayan's family has a small house on Long Island ..."

Chapter Forty-Two

I drove to Frankie's apartment, pipe clenched in my teeth, and thought about the Hanson murder. The earring was first on my list of questions. And then her alibi. She'd been pretty casual about seeing a movie alone with no ticket stub.

But something else was niggling at me. Something I had put in the back of my mind but now was ready to jump out. That's the way it was with me. Random thoughts always like this one seemed to coalesce in my brain, like pieces of a jigsaw puzzle coming together, especially when I was smoking my pipe. Then they'd surface after bonding into an idea. What the hell was it? Something that had to do with the last murder.

I drove on, concentrating on Garrison Keeler's *Lake Woebegone* radio program, knowing if I tried to think about it directly, I would never remember. It was like looking at an object in dim light. You could see it more clearly if you looked alongside the object rather than directly at it. That had something to do with where the rods and cones were located in your eyeball. I didn't know whether there was a similar set up in the brain, but I knew if I waited it would come.

Suddenly it hit me. The minimal chest slashings of the last victim that Patricia noted and JJ confirmed via photos I sent. It was as if the killer wasn't concerned about hiding the pacemaker pocket anymore; it was as if *he* knew *we* knew. *But how?* Information about the pacemakers had not been released to the press before the NYU student was killed, so the killer could not know we were on to the motive. But Frankie must have known, thanks to Harry. Still, the murders were so widespread, I suppose the leak could have come from anywhere.

McBride thought Frankie was the killer, but my gut no longer agreed. Harry didn't think so either, and he knew her well, certainly much better than I did. But his last words, "I'm done here," stayed with me. Was he really leaving the case? If so, why?

In reality, what did I have on her? The earring, of course, the fact that her adoptive mom was murdered, and a flimsy alibi. All circumstantial evidence. No gun, no motive for killing the pacemaker victims. Not a lot to base a murder-one charge on. But the thought lingered: did she have a friend or friends who *could* kill and mutilate? Harry didn't think so, but could I trust his judgment?

Frankie let me into her apartment at the first ring.

"Thanks for seeing me."

"Did I have a choice?"

"We need to talk."

"Where's Harry?"

"Better you and I talk without him this time."

She looked at me with a querulous expression on her face, eyebrows wrinkled. "Well, okay, c'mon in. Coffee?"

"Sure."

I sat at the kitchen table while Frankie busied herself making a pot. I pulled out my pipe.

She glanced at me. "This is a no smoking building."

"I won't light it. Fiddling with it helps me think." I took out a packet of pipe cleaners and began cleaning.

She turned to make the coffee and I talked to her back. "Frankie, I'm going to cut to the chase. You are still my only suspect for the murder of Melinda Hanson. Your friend Harry,"—I saw her shoulders hunch forward when I mentioned his name—"has been your major supporter. He thinks you're not even close to the profile we got from BSU, and I agree. But there're some issues we need to clarify."

"Like what?" she asked over her shoulder.

"For starters, did you kill your adoptive mother?"

She turned around and ran her fingers through her hair. Then she sat opposite me while the coffee dripped through a filter. "I don't know what a BSU is, but thanks for that, I guess. I thought we already talked about Melinda."

"We did. But I want to do it again. We still have no suspect and haven't explained finding your earring in her bedroom."

She fingered the pearl in her right ear. "I didn't kill her."

"I'm going to come back to that but before I do, would you do me a favor?"

"Maybe. Depends on what it is. Last guy I did a favor for tied my hands and feet to the bed. With gossamer lace ribbons of course. Pink and blue."

I couldn't help but smile. "Would you squat down like you're looking for something under the table? Just for a minute."

"Whoa. That's a new one. I hate to disappoint you, but I have on both a bra and panties today. No stockings though." She stuck out a leg and ran her hand over her smooth shin.

I laughed. "None of the above. Just do it. Humor me … please?" I did notice she had nice legs.

She squatted on the balls of her feet. "Anything while I'm down here? Foot massage, calf stroking?"

"No thanks. Maybe another time. Can you rock back and sit on your heels?"

She tried, lost her balance, and fell back on her butt. We both burst out laughing.

I reached for her arm and helped her up. "Sorry about that."

Stifling her laugh, she winced at my touch.

"What's the matter? Did I hurt you?"

"It's okay. I bumped my arm this morning in the shower. Still a little sore."

"I'm sorry."

"Not a problem. So what the hell were the acrobatics all about?"

I ignored her question.

"We need to talk about your alibi."

"I told you I was at the movies."

"It was pretty weak when you first told me and still is. As is your phone call to your friend on the West Coast."

"Maybe so, but it's the truth. Want me to make up another one?"

"What about the earring?"

"I also told you I don't know how it got there. I wasn't wearing those rose earrings when I visited them and haven't for a long time.

And I didn't go into her bedroom either." She gently massaged her arm.

"So you said. And you know, for some strange reason I buy that. But to think it was in the rug from the time you lived there, like you suggested, is bullshit."

"I agree. I was only groping for an answer."

"So let's be hypothetical. Say the killer got your earring, and maybe planted it there. How could he have gotten it?"

She shrugged.

"You always lock your apartment door when you leave?"

"Triple locks."

"And obviously no evidence of any forced entry or anything else missing?"

"Zip."

"And no strangers visiting, salesmen, telephone repair guys, plumbers?"

"None. You guys. You're the only ones I've let in. Not even the janitor's been in for at least six months."

"No cleaning people?"

"Who can afford it? I do my own—as you can see." She swept her arm over the messy one-room apartment.

"Boyfriends sleeping over?"

She shifted in her chair. "Getting a bit personal, aren't you?"

"You want to stay out of jail?"

"Harry, but that only started after Melinda's murder."

She screwed up her face and shut her eyes. Her lips mouthed "fuck."

"What is it?"

"Nothing."

"Frankie, don't bullshit me. I'm here trying to keep you out of jail. You can help me do that, or you can continue to be a wise guy and end up with a life sentence for first-degree murder. Because honestly, the next step is I arrest you and take you cuffed down to the station house, where you'll be arraigned, and then you go straight to jail. You don't seem to really understand what that means."

"I'll make bail."

"This isn't Monopoly, where you get out of jail for fifty bucks."

"I'll make bail," she repeated.

"You've been reading too many detective novels. First, on a murder-one charge, you'll be lucky if the court grants it, and if it does, it'll be at least half a million bucks. And unless you've got that much change hanging around, you'll need a bail bondsman who will charge you ten percent to put up the half million. You got a spare fifty grand cooling somewhere?"

She shook her head.

"I didn't think so. Second, unless you've got lots of cash stashed away to pay some hotshot lawyer five hundred or more an hour, you're going to get a public defender fresh out of law school who doesn't know jack shit and can't even find the courthouse bathroom."

Her head sagged on her chest, tears cresting in the corners of her eyes. The bravado was gone. She looked so vulnerable and I was the only one who could help her. I was holding the baby animal in my hands and was damn sure not going to drop it.

I reached over, cupped my hand under her chin, and raised her head. I gave her one of those little-kid-sitting-on-my-lap smiles. "Frankie, like I said, I don't think you did it, and I am trying to help you. Believe me."

She burst into tears. Between sobs she said, "I didn't do it. I swear to God I didn't. Really." Her fists pounded the table.

I took out my white cotton handkerchief, the monogrammed one Miriam had given me, and dabbed her eyes. "I've got to start carrying my own handkerchiefs around you guys," she said, forcing a smile through the tears.

The white linen came away smeared with black mascara, but I put it back into my pocket. "It's about Harry, isn't it?"

She nodded, trying to catch her breath.

"You care for him a lot?"

Her answer was barely audible. "I did."

"Did?"

A smaller nod. "Until last night."

"What happened?"

She told me. "He looked like a complete stranger. He *was* a complete stranger. He was so angry, and his face was so scary, I wouldn't have recognized him." Frankie rolled up her sleeve and showed me the black and blue bruises on her upper arm, an almost perfect outline of four fingers and a thumb encircling her biceps. She started sobbing again.

I took out my handkerchief and this time gave it to her. "Would you have shot him?"

"I lay awake almost all last night thinking that very thing. I don't know. He's the guy you were talking about before, isn't he? The one who crouched back on his heels?"

"That's not a typical Western trait, as you found out. Westerners usually squat with their weight forward on the balls of their feet, heels off the ground, not sitting back on the entire length of their foot. I watched him do that when he was studying the body of the last victim."

"Why's that so important?" she asked.

"You see that in Africa, the Middle East, and the Far East. Do you know where Harry grew up?"

"He told me Chicago."

"Did he ever introduce you to someone from his past who verified that? Parents, friends, relatives?"

She shook her head no.

"That's why it's so important. I went back through his application. Apparently the NYPD ran a routine check on him when he joined, but it was pretty superficial. All they did was go over his application and talk to a few of his friends, ones he had recommended. So I think he's been passing himself off as a native-born American."

"You know, he's Muslim."

I was stunned. "When did you find out?"

"During our fight. I don't think he wanted to tell me. It kind of came out."

"With that wardrobe?"

She didn't answer. "Are you ready to tell me what you thought of earlier?"

She was silent and swiped at a tear. She took a deep breath, let out a long, ragged sigh and began. "Remember the first time you guys were here?"

"Yes. So?"

"Remember how Harry wandered around my apartment and I teased him about looking into my underwear drawers and how embarrassed he got?"

I grinned, remembering. "I do."

"Well, the earrings were in that jewelry case on my dresser, the music box, and he could have opened it and taken one out."

I made a face. "Doesn't work. The box played 'Claire de Lune' when you opened it. I remember, because Debussy was one of my mother's favorites. We would have heard it if he had opened it."

She jumped up shaking her head. "No! No! That's just it. That's what hit me before, that I didn't want to tell you. *The box was broken then and didn't play.* I had knocked it off the dresser during one of my rare cleaning manias the week before and had it repaired *after* your first visit. Remember when you were here the second time? I dropped it again and bitched that I just had it repaired for fifty dollars, and now I'd gone ahead and broken it a second time."

I racked my brain trying to remember. She was right.

"You think Harry took the earring then?"

"Of course I don't know for sure, but it was an opportunity. And there was no one else who had the chance."

"You're sure?"

"Absolutely."

"So, if I believe you, that lets you off the hook and puts my partner of two years at the scene of the murder. I don't know if I can handle that." I thought, this was the guy who was my friend, who had dinner at my house, who babysat my kids, and who covered my back. I'd have to do some serious checking before the next dark alley.

"Maybe your partner, but my lover. He wasn't one of those priests I was banging for sport." She couldn't go on and cried softly into the handkerchief.

I didn't know what to do and just sat there letting her cry. After a while she said, "Harry and I, we had a very nice thing happening. Not that I think it was going very far, but I did care for him. And I think he liked me. At least until last night. That may have ended it for both of us."

"If he does like you, then why do you think he would kill Hanson and plant the earring?"

She sat down again. "You know as well as I do: to put the blame on me. Set me up to slow down your investigation or derail it entirely. He knew who my adoptive parents were and where they lived from his initial investigation. Don't you think he was the guy who ran you off the road?"

"And you're saying he fell in love with you *after* he murdered Melinda, that's why he changed his mind and tried to convince me you didn't do it?"

"'Fell in love' may be a bit too strong, but he certainly cared a lot. But he'd already planted the earring. He couldn't undo that without exposure."

She was right. That would explain some other things also, like how the killer always seemed to be a step ahead of the investigation and why he had killed Zimmerman with a .45, knowing Frankie had bought one. And why the bloody imprint of the pacemaker on the rug alongside Driver's head was not seen in the subsequent murders. But the most damning was the earring—assuming she was telling me the truth.

"What do you know about him?" I asked.

"While you and I have been talking, I have been racking my brain trying to think about that. And the answer is, very little of any substance. I know he dresses well and buys his clothes from Milano Men, a pretty expensive men's store on Fifth Avenue. I know he has some sort of family abroad, but I don't know where. And I'm pretty sure that's where his money comes from. Says he visits them during his vacation and that they like him to dress nice. And I know he likes good wine."

"Not a very observant Muslim."

"I agree. And he's pretty good in bed."

"I wasn't going to go there."

"But I will, because it may be important. He's good, like I said, but very modest. Careful about disrobing, lights out, no oral sex, gentle but in command. He had a hissy fit when he first saw the tattoo I have—on a very intimate body part." She gave a little snort. "I suppose that description could fit most any man, but I thought I'd throw it out."

"And you think your fight last night would fit with that description of his character?"

"In spades. I mean, he damn near came unglued when he heard about my messing around with a few girls in school."

"And he said that was because he was a Muslim?"

"Yes."

"Any inkling where he's from in Chicago?"

"No."

"Ever been to his place in New York?"

"We always meet here."

"What do you talk about?"

"Work mostly. His."

"About this case?"

"He tried to avoid it, but it came out by accident, about the pacemaker patients and stuff. By the way, he says he thinks the world of you, especially that you helped him pass the detective exam."

Yeah, he likes me so much he tried to kill me with his Hummer. "How many dates have you had with him?"

"Maybe eight or ten."

"Next one?"

"None scheduled after last night and I haven't heard from him since." She glanced at the telephone. The message light was dark.

She smelled it first and got up to retrieve the coffee pot. "I forgot the damn coffee. I hate it when it's been sitting. You still want it?"

"Sure. If I was as fussy I'd never drink a drop."

I added sugar and sipped. "Frankie, I am going to ask you to do something, but it may be dangerous, so I understand if you refuse."

Her eyes widened. "What?"

"Do you know what a wire is?"

"Now that's a stupid question."

"Sorry. What I was thinking was to fit you with a wire so we could listen to the conversation. We need more incriminating evidence. Any evidence. I don't have a thing to tie him to the pacemaker murders. If he's involved, he's got to be part of a group. We'd supply you a script of questions to ask and tail you wherever you went."

"Suppose we're screwing? Even I can't do that knowing you guys are listening."

"Do all of your dates with him end up in bed? Sorry for being so blunt."

She grinned. "So far they have."

"Well, you said he was pretty careful about getting undressed. I took that to mean you would talk first and then you'd have the chance to go to the bathroom and take off the wire before getting into bed."

"Won't work. We do fool around before we jump into the sack and he'd feel the wire. I assume it's on my chest somewhere?"

"How about we plant a bug in your apartment? I wanted to use the wire so we could listen if you went out. But we could sacrifice that and just listen here. With a bug you'd be on the air all the time, all your conversations, but only at home. Would that be a problem?"

"I've got nothing to hide. But you don't really have a lot to go on about Harry. How a guy sits on his haunches, the earring, and stuff. That's about it."

"And maybe lying about where he grew up. That's why we need to bug you. It's a tiny thing, even smaller than a real bug, that'll stick to any surface and transmit over very long distances. Frankie, you know you may be in danger if Harry is the killer."

She clenched her lips tight.

"You'd need to play along with him exactly as you are doing so you don't arouse any suspicions. But you'd need to pay attention to any details that might help us."

"And what're you going to do?"

"Well, at this point, the evidence incriminating Harry is pretty meager, like you said. But my gut tells me this is the right path. I could start with dumpster diving."

"What in hell's that?"

"Search his garbage for clues. But it'd take too long. I'm going to try to get a search warrant for his apartment. If I find something, then I'll go forward. If not, I'll have to do a lot of apologizing to my partner."

"You know, the biggest obstacle may be that he's not coming back," she said.

"Then we strike out, with no risk to you."

"I suppose I could call him to come over."

"Have you ever done that before?"

"No."

"Then don't."

"It's a little scary," Frankie said.

"True, but if I'm wrong, there'd be no danger, and if I'm right, we'd be here to help you."

"Yeah, like the IRS." She stared into the distance, obviously struggling with her decision. "Okay, do it."

Chapter Forty-Three

Harry parked his police car in front of Zach's house, a two-story brick residence in Bethpage, a hamlet in Nassau County on Long Island. The house was in a quiet residential neighborhood about a mile from town. Lawns were small but neat, with Fords and Chevys parked in the driveways. Miriam answered the first knock.

"Why, Harry. What a pleasant surprise. What are you doing here? And all dressed out in uniform?"

He gave her a hug and a cheek kiss. "Hi, Miriam. Zach asked me to meet him here. Is he in?"

"No, I didn't know he was coming. I would have prepared some lunch."

"It was a last-minute thing. He said he wanted to go over some case material about the stuff we've been working on."

Miriam's face pinched into a question mark. "That's strange. He moved all that stuff to his apartment in the city. But come on in and I'll call him that you're here. The kids will be excited to see their daddy."

Harry could hear noises coming from the kitchen as he entered the small foyer.

"Can I get you something to drink? Or make you a sandwich? I'm afraid we didn't save much from lunch. We're just finishing."

"Thanks, Miriam, a cup of coffee would be great."

"Let me call Zach first."

"Why don't you wait on the call? I'm sure he's on the way."

Miriam hesitated a moment, fixed Harry with her eyes, but then led the way into the kitchen.

"Rachel, Joey, Uncle Harry's here."

"Hi kids," said Harry, bending down to kiss the tops of their heads. "How's lunch?"

Three-year-old Joseph mumbled something and dribbled apple sauce down his chin. Rachel, a precocious five-year-old with red spaghetti sauce on lips and both cheeks, said, "Uncle Harry, did you bring me anything?"

"I'm sorry, honey, not this time. I will next time, though."

"My daddy always gives us butterscotch candy because he loves us. He carries it in his pocket. He said my grandpa always gave him candy when he was little like us," Rachel said with a pout.

"Your daddy's coming home today," said Miriam. "Won't that be nice to see him again so soon?"

"Yeah, Daddy's coming, Daddy's coming," Joey sang, apple sauce flying as he banged the table with his spoon.

"Okay, calm down," said Miriam, "and I'll give you some ice cream for dessert."

Harry smiled.

"How about you, Harry? Some ice cream with your coffee?"

"Sounds good. Maybe you'll join me? And then, if Zach's still not here, you can call him."

"Ice cream! Ice cream!" shouted Rachel, running to the freezer. Joseph followed, and Miriam chased after them both.

"Wait, wait, let me help you with that," Miriam said as the kids wrestled a gallon container of Ben and Jerry's Butter Pecan from the freezer.

"Let me! Let me!" screamed Joey as small hands tussled for the cardboard carton, which ended up on the kitchen floor.

"Uh oh. See what you did, Joey," said Rachel.

"Now, that's enough from both of you," Miriam said, her voice stern as she sponged up the mess. "Sit quietly or you don't get any."

They did as ordered and Miriam spooned out dollops of ice cream into a bowl for each child and one for Harry.

"And one for you?" Harry asked. She spooned one for herself and turned to pour the coffee. She and the children didn't notice the white powder Harry sprinkled on their ice cream.

Fifteen minutes later, Harry made a phone call.

"Leave the shopping center now. You're only a mile away. Follow the driveway around to the back of the house. I unlocked the French doors off the living room. They open into the back yard surrounded by a tall wooden privacy fence. Shouldn't be a problem."

Chapter Forty-Four

I called McBride and briefed him on my meeting with Frankie. He liked the idea about planting a bug but wanted the FBI to do it so he could have direct access to the information. Also, since he thought this was linked to the bombings, he considered this FBI territory. In return, he promised to use FBI influence to get me a search warrant for Harry's apartment. I thought that was a fair deal, if he'd let Patricia participate. I wanted to get her back in the field and I also wanted some insurance that the FBI would share everything they found, as promised. We struck the deal, and three hours later I had the warrant.

I parked in an underground lot near 131 Madison Avenue. Harry's building was an old fifteen-story high-rise on the corner of Madison and East Thirty-first Street, sporting a newly remodeled entrance of shining steel, a vestibule of black and white marble, and a crystal chandelier. While the neighborhood wasn't the greatest, the building still had a well-dressed doorman who wanted to take me upstairs but couldn't shake a tenacious tenant arguing about who would pay for repair of a leaking faucet. The doorman told me to wait, but I said I couldn't. He wouldn't let me enter Harry's apartment alone, so he called over the janitor, a surly guy angry at having interrupted his chat with a pretty young thing showing a lot of skin. He rode the elevator with me.

"Normally I'd have my partner with me," I said to him, making conversation. "But since I'm alone, I'd appreciate it if you would stay with me while I search the apartment to verify what I've taken, if anything. You okay with that?"

The man, a sullen, swarthy fellow with a metal name tag on his chest saying Rodriguez, glared at me. "What you paying?"

"Sorry. Nothing for this. Consider it your civic duty."

The man's dark face darkened further. "I don't do civic shit. I got other things to do."

"It won't take long."

Rodriguez unlocked the door to apartment 6E. I looked around as I crossed the threshold into a short hallway that had a coat closet on the right and a mirror hanging opposite. The closet held the usual assortment of coats and hats. I picked up a pair of black slipover rubbers for a size-ten shoe. I flipped through the pockets of the coats and found nothing but lint. The walls were all solid, as was the ceiling and floor. No hidden trapdoors. Rodriguez leaned his hip against the wall and watched with disinterest.

He followed me down the hallway into the bedroom. I tore through the dresser drawers, bed linen, and closet. Nothing again except expensive Italian shoes, suits, ties, and shirts. Next to the bed, a night table contained a packet of Sudafed tablets, a bottle of aspirin, and a strip of Trojans. Two left from a six-pack.

The living room, large by New York standards, was across from the bedroom with corner bay windows facing south and west onto Madison Avenue that let in loads of late-afternoon sun. But again I struck out. Next, the kitchen and bathroom. Nothing.

"Thanks for all your help, Rodriguez." He led the way out of the apartment, ignoring or failing to hear my sarcasm. We rode the elevator down in silence, Rodriguez staring at numbers cycling above the door. I was jotting in my spiral notebook when a thought struck me. "Wait a minute," I said as we exited the elevator on the first floor. "Do you know if Scarpia travels any?"

Rodriguez put his hands on his hips. "You want more information, you pay for it. I don't give a shit you a cop. Nothing about that in your search warrant. And it sure ain't my civic duty."

I took out a ten-dollar bill.

"What you think, I'm stupid?"

I gave him another ten.

"Yeah. He travels out of the country two or three times a year. So?"

"So, I didn't see any suitcases in the apartment."

"Because he stores them in a wire bin in the basement. Every apartment has its own. How come a smart New York cop don't know to ask about that?"

I ignored the jibe. "Show me."

"Your search warrant cover that or just the apartment?"

"You know, I'm getting tired of you busting my balls. You want, I'll be happy to arrest you right now for taking a bribe from a New York cop a minute ago. Lock your ass up so tight you won't crap for a week. Now you can show me the bins or go to jail. Your choice."

Rodriguez slouched back against the wall, taking his time to decide.

"I don't have all day." I looked at my watch. "You got ten seconds to make up your mind. Your basement or mine. Choose."

Rodriguez pushed himself off the wall and sauntered to a door off the foyer. I followed.

We descended a poorly lit staircase to a dark basement. Rodriguez flipped the light switch, and dim florescent lighting cast dense shadows along the concrete walls. Lining both sides were rows of floor-to-ceiling wire cages, storage bins for each apartment. I quickly found 6E.

"Open it."

Rodriguez unclipped the round metal ring from his belt, chose a key, and unlocked the door. Two shelves lined the back stone wall. On each was an assortment of Louis Vuitton luggage. There was a large steamer trunk occupying most of the top shelf, several smaller trunks with wheels, and a carry-on taking up the bottom shelf. Except for a dirty cardboard box on the floor, the cage was empty. I moved the steamer to the floor. Locked.

"You got keys for any of this?"

Rodriguez shook his head.

I took out my Swiss Army knife—the Hercules, with ten attachments and a razor sharp blade—and tried to pry open the lock. No dice. I slashed through the leather top and peeled it back. Empty. I tapped the bottom of the trunk and got a hollow ring, then sliced into the false bottom, but the hidden compartment was also empty. Frustrated, I pulled the other trunks off the shelf and cut open each one. All empty.

Rodriguez was standing back with a bemused look on his face. "This guy Scarpia got something you want?"

"No. I'm only jerking around here because I've got nothing better to do."

"You got another twenty? Make it two."

"You have something more to say?"

Rodriguez crossed his arms on his chest and shrugged. "Maybe."

I peeled off two bills and handed them to him. "Better be good."

"I heard a lot of scraping awhile ago and seen him carry out loads of dust and shit in that cardboard box." He motioned to the box on the floor. The top was open and it looked empty. "Didn't want my help when I offered. Cheap bastard wouldn't part with a few measly bucks."

"Get me a flashlight."

Rodriguez went into a back room of the basement, where a fire extinguisher and flashlight were mounted on the wall. He brought back the light. I shined the beam across the walls and floor of 6E. The floor was spotless except for the Vuitton rubbish and the cardboard box. Angrily I kicked a hole in the damn box. A tiny corner of cinderblock flew out. I retrieved it and saw it matched the walls.

I went to the back of the cage, shining the light more carefully at the wall and floor. This time I noticed a miniature pile of dust that had accumulated underneath the lower shelf. I bent down close to the floor and saw that the edges of four cinderblocks had different color caulking, some sort of a gray clay compound molded in place to look like caulking. I touched it. Still sticky. Using my knife, I peeled it back and then wedged the blade between two cinderblocks. Carefully I pried one loose. One by one, four blocks came out, revealing a two-by-three-foot hole in the wall.

Pushed to the back was a black knapsack with a plastic clip holding the flap shut. I slipped on a pair of Latex gloves, pulled the sack out, and undid the clasp. In it I found a scalpel handle, a pack of #10 Bard Parker surgical blades still in their protective jackets, a .45 semiautomatic, and a .38 revolver. I flashed the light into the hole. Tucked against the back wall was a pair of running shoes. I took them out and read the label. Nike Dart VII, size ten.

Son of a bitch! It *was* Harry all along.

"I hope you're pleased with your discovery, Detective. Turn around, but very slowly."

Chapter Forty-Five

I turned and saw the doorman pointing a gun at my chest. Rodriguez, full of bravado before, now cowered on the floor in the corner.

"I have been expecting you for several days now, Detective Dayan. Wahad warned me you were getting close."

"Who's Wahad?"

"You know him as Harry. Wahad is his operative name. It means 'first' in Arabic, as he is the leader in this project. His Jordanian name is Hrayr."

"And who are you?"

"Only a doorman helping with the cause. We knew sooner or later you were going to search here. If not for my friend," he gave Rodriguez a kick in the side, "I would have been the one to escort you to Wahad's apartment, where you would have met with a quiet 'accident.' Unfortunately, Rodriguez has complicated things a bit."

"He's an innocent bystander."

"True, but civilian casualties are common in war, aren't they? And this indeed is war, Detective. Your own country dismisses them as 'collateral damage,' I think the phrase is. Women and children are expendable. *Yours, for example.*"

"What in hell are you talking about? What's my family got to do with this?"

"Consider it a preview of what's to come—like in the movies. Perhaps you can think about that before your own exit, Detective."

"Stop talking in riddles and tell me what the fuck is going on." I had to make a move, but the guy had the gun aimed directly at me. He couldn't watch both of us at once, but it didn't look like Rodriguez was going to be any help, so the doorman ignored him.

"Detective, take your gun with your left hand and toss it on the floor."

I had no choice.

"Now, kick it toward me."

I kicked it hard, trying to get it past him to Rodriguez, but he stopped it with his foot.

The doorman surveyed the ripped suitcases. "Now, the knife."

I tossed Hercules at his feet.

"What about my kids and my wife?" My mind raced with possibilities, none pleasant.

"We have a special plan for them."

I could feel panic starting in my gut. "What?"

"Not for me to say. Rodriguez, stop quaking like an idiot and stand up. Take this tape and tie the detective's hands behind his back." He held out a roll of black tape.

I had to move now, even though I knew it could cost Rodriguez his life. But if I didn't, we'd both be dead. As Rodriguez walked in front of me, blocking the guy from view for a split second, I dropped my shoulder and shoved him hard toward the gun while falling away and drawing my 9 mm from my ankle holster.

The doorman fired at the target coming at him. By that time I had my automatic out and pumped four shots into him. The doorman squeezed off another bullet, which hit the ceiling as he fell to the ground. Rodriguez writhed on the floor with a slug in his chest, spouting a red geyser. I took off my shirt and plugged the hole as best I could and dialed 911 from my cell phone. Then I called Miriam but got no answer. I dialed headquarters and told them to send a black and white with flashers and sirens to my old house: *Miriam and my kids might be in danger*. I sat back and held Rodriguez's head in my lap until help arrived. "Shit, shit, shit!" was all I could say.

Chapter Forty-Six

Harry parked his black and white at the curb in front of Sixty-fourth and Lex, got out, and checked the tools hanging from his Sam Browne belt cinched tight around his waist. He rode the elevator to the fourth floor and pushed the buzzer to Frankie's apartment. He saw the security hole flash for a moment and he knew Frankie was looking at him. She opened the door, and he walked in.

Having just finished her shower, she wore a loosely fitting black silk kimono with pink flamingos flying over a tranquil Japanese garden. The chill made her nipples press out from the silk.

Harry took no notice. She played with the neck of the robe, let it slide open, but his eyes remained glued to her face.

"What's wrong, Harry? Why are you dressed in a cop's uniform?"

"Because I'm a cop."

"But I've never seen you wear that before. You always had on a suit."

"Today is different. I want to take you for a ride."

"You're not still mad, are you?" She forced a smile, but her hands were moist and she rubbed her palms on the sides of her kimono. She started to walk toward him but his look stopped her.

"Get dressed. I'll tell you on the way."

"I'd like to Harry, but I can't today. I have an appointment with … my college roommate, Jill. We're going to the Plaza for tea."

"What roommate? You never mentioned her before. And you drink coffee."

"Actually I met her jogging in Central Park the other day, and we planned this little get together."

"Fine. I'll drive you."

"I'm sure you have other things to do. I can take a cab."

"Get some clothes on. I'll wait here." He stared at her through narrowed eyes. She remembered that look.

"I'll change in the bathroom. Make yourself comfortable. You know where the bras are," she said with a light laugh.

His expression didn't change.

After she left, Harry slowly walked around the apartment, picking up and discarding a playbill from the Met where they had seen *Otello* in orchestra seats for scalper prices of three hundred bucks each, a Starbucks cup with teeth marks and lipstick on the rim, and a taxi receipt crumpled in an ashtray. He checked the date—the night of their fight. He opened the jewelry box and listened to "Claire de Lune" while flipping his finger through the contents. The single rose earring lay at the bottom. His face softened for a moment. He picked it up and broke off the petals, one by one, dropping them into the box.

Harry turned back to the kitchen and his glance caught a glimmer of white sticking out from the garbage bag. He walked over and extracted a long, fuzzy pipe cleaner, its end browned from tobacco stains. His face contorted, becoming dark and angry. He grabbed the jewelry box and hurled it at the mirror over the sofa. Both exploded into fragments, like a bomb, and shards of glass along with earrings, bracelets, and necklaces scattered all over the living room sofa and rug.

Frankie came running from the bathroom still buttoning her blouse. "What the hell are you doing? Are you nuts?"

"Was Zach here?" he demanded.

"Fuck you." She picked up the jewelry box now missing its cover. "Look what've you done to my things," she said, her voice trembling.

"Was Zach here?" he repeated. His tone was dark and threatening.

"If he was, it's none of your goddamn business."

She got down on her hands and knees, retrieving glass and jewelry from the rug. Her hands were shaking and she cut her finger. She removed a glass splinter and licked the cut.

He watched her.

She stood up and tossed the jewelry onto the couch, squared her shoulders, and faced him.

"Harry, I've decided to walk after all. I need the exercise. So you needn't bother driving me."

He shook his head. "No."

She paused a moment, looking at him. "I have to wash out this cut." She walked to the kitchen and turned sideways so that her body blocked one hand from his view. She fumbled briefly beneath the table edge and quickly slipped her hand into the pocket of her denim skirt. Then she went to the faucet to wash her finger, dried it, and picked up her jogging pack.

"I want you to come with me. Now," he said.

"I already told you, I don't want to."

He leaned to grab her, but she backed out of his reach. She pushed a kitchen chair in front of her and pulled Boom Boom from her back pack.

Act, don't react!

"Good move. I should have seen it coming. So, now you're going to shoot me?" His laugh was ugly.

"Harry, I don't know who or what you've become, but it's not something I like or want to be with. Just go away."

"Frankie, put the gun down. Give it to me." He reached to take it.

She took a step back and aimed Boom Boom at his chest, both hands holding the gun steady. "Harry, I want you out of here. Out of my life. I don't know who you are anymore, and I don't care. We're done. Leave, or I'll call the real cops. If you don't, so help me, I'll blow you away." A loud click resonated in the still apartment as she cocked the gun.

"I *am* a real cop. You mean you'll call Zach?" He tossed the pipe cleaner at her, a sneer on his face. She brushed it aside and let it lie where it fell.

"Yes."

Harry glanced at his watch. "He's busy with his own problems now."

"What do you mean?"

He ignored her question. "You know, I once liked you. I liked you a lot. But doing that stuff with other women ... I couldn't handle that. You really shouldn't have messed with them and then been with me. It made me ... feel dirty. *You* made me dirty."

"That's your problem." She kept the gun pointed at his chest. "A bath might help."

He locked eyes with her, testing her resolve. "Put the gun down. Now!"

She didn't move.

Five seconds later, he said, "Okay. I'm leaving." He turned and walked toward the door, his back to her, his hands concealed. She followed him at a distance.

Watch the bad guy's hands at all times!

He whirled, simultaneously pulling the trigger of the Taser gun he had drawn from his belt. Before she could react, the darts struck her in the chest and fifty thousand volts electrified her entire body. Boom Boom spun from her hand and she crashed, writhing on the rug in an epileptic seizure, arms and legs whirling in uncontrollable spasms and her face distorted in a rigid snarl.

"I have good moves too, Frankie," he said to her unconscious form. "*You* should have seen it coming."

****

Frankie fought through the fog of unconsciousness. Her lips were wet from drool, and her tongue hurt where her teeth had clamped down and lacerated a corner. She could taste the blood in her mouth. She shook her head, trying to unscramble her thinking and focus her eyes. She attempted unsuccessfully to massage the large, painful knot on her forehead where her bucking had rammed her head into the kitchen cabinet, but her trembling hands were cuffed behind her. Her hair was still standing on end from the electricity.

"Sorry to do that, Frankie, but you need to come with me, like I said."

She struggled to sit up on the floor. She pulled against the metal cuffs, scraping her wrists on the sharp edges.

"What the hell do you think you're doing?" she screamed, her voice scratchy and tremulous, her vocal muscles not yet fully recovered.

"Quiet." He took her by the elbows and helped her stand. "I told you. You're coming with me."

"Where?"

"You're going to meet my mother. Shouldn't a guy introduce his mother to the girl he's been dating?"

"Your mother! You never told me your mother was in the U.S."

"Well now you know. She's been here for ten years."

"Where does she live?"

"You'll find out soon enough. It's a nice quiet place for what we want to do. Enough talk. Let's go."

"Take the cuffs off. I swear I won't try anything."

"Maybe once we're in the car. Be happy I haven't gagged you. But that'll be next if you make any noise." He opened the apartment door and shoved her through. She took two paces across the hall and fell heavily against the door of the opposite apartment, banging her shoulder as hard as she could near the peephole. Immediately the door opened and the hairy shrew looked out.

"Help me, Mrs. Orlovsky! Please! He's kidnapping me! Call the police."

With one hand holding Frankie's handcuffs, Harry used the other to flash his shield. "I *am* the police Mrs. ... Orlovsky. Detective Harry Scarpia, NYPD. This woman's under arrest for the murder of her mother. Please close the door and go about your own business."

"Don't listen to him!" Frankie screamed. "That's not true. Call the police ... call Detective Dayan. He's kidnapping me!"

Harry yanked up on her handcuffs and slapped her hard across the face. "Frankie, shut up or I'll tase you again."

Her eyes dilated in fear as she shook her head and began sobbing. "Mrs. Orlovsky, please help me ... please." She planted her feet on the rug and lurched back against Harry, trying to throw him off balance. As Harry released his hold of her cuffs to keep his balance, Frankie bolted.

She traveled only two steps before Harry pulled the Taser trigger again. The darts, still stuck in her clothes, did their job, and Frankie collapsed in a writhing heap. When her seizures and retching stopped, he lifted her upright, heaved her over his shoulder, and walked toward the elevators.

Mrs. Orlovsky watched and then closed her apartment door with a slight smile on her face.

Chapter Forty-Seven

Two cops from my department were waiting outside my old home.

"Zach, we've searched the house. Empty. No signs of a struggle. Neighbors saw nothing. Doors unlocked."

"Send the crime unit over to work the house," I said as I rushed in through the garage. "I want it done immediately."

Miriam's car was parked where it always was, keys still dangling from the ignition where she always left them. The hood was cold. I walked through the kitchen. Three plates with remains of spaghetti and apple sauce sat on the kitchen table, along with a carton of Ben and Jerry's ice cream melting in its round cardboard container. Two coffee cups and four dessert bowls with spoons were arranged neatly in the dishwasher. I picked up a plate. Cool, probably sitting several hours at least. But why wash the coffee cups and dessert plates but not the lunch dishes? A pair of Joseph's soiled Pull-Ups was in the wastebasket, but a new bag had been torn open with a handful missing and some scattered on the floor. Somebody was in a hurry. I felt panic rising, and I struggled to think like a cop.

The cleaned dishes fit the description of two adults drinking coffee and then maybe eating ice cream with the kids. That would mean it was someone Miriam knew, or at least felt comfortable enough to invite in. But why leave the ice cream out to melt? It was not like Miriam to do that. No signs of a struggle, meaning she agreed to go—or worse, she was not capable of resisting.

I stood there fighting the sickening dread building in my gut. The telephone ring startled me, and I dropped the dish I had been holding.

****

Harry shoved Frankie into the back seat of his squad car. "I'm going to free up one of your hands, Frankie. But I'm going to cuff the other to the door."

"Fuck you," she said, scanning the back seat to see if she could open the opposite door and wrench the handcuffs free.

He slid behind the wheel. She heard a click and saw the lock snap shut. With her free hand, she tried to grab a handful of his hair, but he leaned away, hit a button, and a perforated metal screen rose to separate the front and back seats.

"Patrol cars are made for transporting prisoners. Sit back and enjoy the ride."

"Go to hell." She fell silent, fighting tears and fear, her bravado dissolving. She sat back on the seat and drew her knees under her. She shivered, even though it wasn't cold.

After a while she said, "Where are we going?"

He didn't answer at first and then glanced at her over his shoulder. "Chappaqua."

"Where the hell is Chappaqua?"

"Stop shouting. I can hear you through the screen. In Westchester."

"Why are you doing this to me, Harry?" Her voice trembled. She felt helpless, like the little girl Melinda put in the closet.

"You made me commit terrible things." His lips, drawn tight, seemed to make the words fight to get out.

"I didn't *make* you do anything. As I remember, you enjoyed yourself."

He looked at her in the rear view mirror. "I liked you a lot."

"And I liked you, Harry, I really did."

"Until I found out about you—and what you did with other women. You have brought shame to me and my family." He shook his head slowly from side to side.

"No one knows but you and me."

"That doesn't matter."

Frankie remembered sitting in the closet: after sitting in the dark awhile, her eyes accommodated to the blackness and her courage returned to face Melinda. "Then tough shit, Harry. What's done is done."

"Not really. I can atone for the disgrace."

"How?"

"An honor killing by stoning."

"Yeah, right."

He caught her eyes in the rear view mirror. "Exactly, right."

****

Ruth steered the Hummer off the Saw Mill River Parkway at exit 32 to Chappaqua. She drove several miles past their house to King Street and entered the spacious grounds of the national headquarters of *Reader's Digest* magazine. The area was crowded with subcontractors, trucks, and construction supplies, as the huge building complex that housed a once giant publication was downsizing to a third its original size. The main building was being sectioned to lease as individual business units. The whirlwind of activity provided ideal cover for their plans. Chappaqua, a short drive from New York City, was a perfect place to hide a terrorist cell located less than two miles from an ex-president's home. *Keep your friends close but your enemies closer.*

No one noticed them as Ruth drove the Hummer to a separate building tucked in a wooded back lot. She had rented it because the structure, an ugly warehouse that had once been used for paper storage, was hidden from the road and faced an empty lot accessible only by a curving dirt driveway off the main parking area. They had a clear view of anyone approaching.

"Electronic publishing eliminated its need," the realtor told them, and the entire building, almost half a city block, was empty. But what appealed most was the underground steel-reinforced room, built in 1948 as a bomb shelter for DeWitt and Lila Atcheson Wallace, founders of *Reader's Digest*. It had never been occupied and would be perfect for what they planned.

Miriam and the children began to stir as Ruth pulled the Hummer in front of the warehouse door.

Quickly, Sarah got out, punched in a code, and the door opened. Ruth drove the Hummer inside and the overhead garage door closed behind them. She hobbled out, stifling a groan as she swung her left leg down, her hip stiff from the ride. She took out a key ring and clicked open the heavy Yale lock on the trap door in the floor leading to the underground room. They guided Miriam, still groggy, down the stairs and into the pit. Then each carried a child down.

The underground room was 15 by 17 feet, equipped with a ventilation system that, if not provoked, still worked sufficiently to make the air breathable. There was a bed, a desk and two chairs, a bathroom, and a small kitchen. Two bottles of water stood on the sink. However, the toilet didn't flush, and there was no running water. Ruth had hired one of the college kids to clean the room of years of dust and cobwebs so it was reasonably inhabitable. There was even a mildewed replica of one of Van Gogh's sunflower paintings hanging on the wall, a favorite of Lila Wallace.

They helped the dazed Miriam to the bed, placed a child on each side, and climbed the stairs. The climb hurt Ruth's hip and she ascended slowly. When she reached the top, she lowered the trap door and snapped the Yale lock in place.

Sarah smiled at Ruth and they hugged. Then Sarah handed her the phone. Ruth dialed.

"*Payback at last*," she said, her eyes glittering. "*Allahu akbar.*"

Chapter Forty-Eight

I grabbed my cell from my pocket before the first ring stopped and listened a moment, but I only heard heavy breathing.

"Hello, who is this?" I could barely decipher the garbled voice. "I can't understand what you're saying." It sounded like someone talking through water. "Speak more clearly."

"Your children are pretty."

A woman's voice! "Goddamn it, who is this?"

"If you want to see them again pretty like that, listen carefully and do exactly what I tell you."

"Where are they? Let me talk to Miriam."

"She cannot come to the phone right now." There was a peculiar flatness to the speech.

"Put her on the line!" I couldn't place the foreign accent. I needed her to talk more.

"Stop the questions. Do as I tell you. And come alone."

I scribbled instructions into my pad. "What do you want? Money? What?"

"Just you."

I was fighting fear and not thinking clearly. "Listen, I'll pay you whatever you want. Just don't harm my family. I'll give you—"

The phone went dead.

A million thoughts crashed through my head. The cop-like ideas flickered briefly, like a dying light bulb, but reality chased them away. This was *my* family the lady was talking about! *They* had been kidnapped, not some anonymous person at the police station who I'd be placating with best-case scenarios.

I paced the room. My heart was racing, my face wet with sweat, and there was an empty feeling in my gut, like when I had to pack my bags after the divorce. Leaving my kids that time broke my heart, and this was the same. My first urge was to call the station house, but I sat down to review what I knew. I had to calm down, get a grip. I had to think and not panic! Somehow I had to save them.

This woman on the phone said she just wanted me. So the kidnapping was not for money. My family was the bait to get me because of the pacemaker murders. Harry. It had to be him.

Gradually my heart rate slowed and my thinking became more rational. The caller had given me only four hours to meet. I had three options, none of them great. I could go it alone as the kidnappers demanded. The upside was it would get me to the kids and Miriam, and maybe a chance to set them free. The downside was obvious, no backup, which was why they wanted me to come alone.

I could call in the NYPD SWAT team and storm the place. They were trained for hostage rescue. But I first would have to know exactly where they were and take the big risk that during the assault, one of the kids or Miriam would be hurt. I knew SWAT would start with the ear-splitting stun bomb, called a "flash bang" or percussion grenade, which would blow out eardrums and give the ear-muffled and Kevlar-protected police precious seconds of surprise. Then they'd rush in with guns blazing, making microsecond decisions about whom to shoot. I worried especially over the kids, who might panic and not hit the floor as ordered. SWAT's actions were too fast for logical thought processes. Instinct and reflexes controlled nervous trigger fingers, which could get my family shot.

Or, I could call in the FBI, which had its own SWAT team but also had experienced hostage rescue negotiators. That might be the best option, through Mac McBride, if they could mobilize quickly.

But none of these approaches was a guarantee I would ever see my kids or Miriam alive again.

My cell phone rattled alive. "Who is this?" I shouted into the receiver.

"Easy Zach, Mac McBride here."

"Sorry, Mac. What've you got?"

"I had my guys plant the bug in Frankie's apartment early this morning."

"And?"

"I'm in the monitoring truck outside her apartment building. Patricia O'Malley's with me, like we agreed."

"Okay."

"We got into position about half an hour ago and started picking up fragments of Frankie's conversation. It was not very clear and was fading. Sounded like the bug was someplace where something was rubbing its surface. Certainly not under the kitchen table, where my guys put it."

I was only half listening. "Like where?"

"Could be in her clothes. Maybe in a pocket or handbag."

"So you think she took it with her?"

"It sure as hell isn't in her kitchen anymore."

"What was she saying?"

"That's the thing—it wasn't only her. Harry was with her."

That got my attention.

"Smart lady." A thought began to tug in the corner of my mind. I told him about my family. "Where do you think Frankie and Harry are?"

"The transmission was poor but was better when she talked, so the bug was probably on her, like I said. There was a lot of static, and they were moving away from us. We spent the better part of the last hour trying to triangulate its position. The sound was moving quickly, so they were probably in a car. We finally lost them completely going north out of the city. What kind of car does Harry drive?"

"Give me a minute."

I put him on hold and dialed headquarters. The desk sergeant told me Harry had signed out my old squad car, #111. I reconnected and told McBride.

"I can have the FBI send out an APB for the car," he said.

"Won't need to."

"Why not?"

"After my crash, all black and whites got a GPS locator installed beneath the engine mount to be able to find a cop in trouble. I doubt

Harry even knows about it, since they were just put in. Did he say where he was going?"

"The place sounded something like Chappaquiddick. I know that's ridiculous. So, maybe Chappaqua."

That was it! That's where my family was!

"I'll verify with headquarters. They can track him like a mouse in a maze."

"We have the same gear in the truck they do," McBride said.

"Where are you, Mac?"

"We circled back to her apartment to see if she returned. Sixty-fourth and Lex. Patricia's driving."

"I'll meet you there as soon as I can."

"Roger. In the meantime, I'll let myself into her apartment for a little look."

That call decided it for me. Go with Mac McBride and Patricia. The worst thing was having no direction.

I had it now.

Chapter Forty-Nine

Miriam gradually regained consciousness and sat up in the bed. Rachel and Joseph were still asleep on each side of her. She tried to lick her lips, but they were taped shut. Her wrists were bound together in front of her, so she was able to peel the tape from her mouth. She looked around, trying to remember where she was, how she got here, but it was all hazy. She remembered eating ice cream with Harry … Harry! That was it. He had been acting strange, said he was waiting for Zach.

A door creaked above and footsteps on the stairs interrupted her thoughts. Her heart jumped in her chest when she saw two old women climb down the stairs. She tried to gather her children to her but couldn't because of the tape.

"Who are you?"

Sarah approached and ripped the tape from Rachel and Joseph. They woke with a start and began to cry. "Stop or I will put back the tape," she threatened, raising an open palm to slap them.

Miriam tried to pull the children close to her. "It's okay, children, it's okay. Close your eyes and go back to sleep." Their cries faded to whimpers, but their eyes stayed wide open.

"Who are you? What do you want with us? Please let us go. We didn't do anything to you." Miriam sobbed, and the children began to cry again.

Sarah paced in front of them with an AK-47 assault rifle cradled in her arms, her right forefinger constantly flexed alongside the trigger guard. She aimed the rifle at the ceiling and let loose a burst of gun fire. The noise in the small room was deafening. Bullets ricocheted off the walls and plaster flew like snowflakes. Hysterical, Miriam and the children fell back on the bed, clutching at each other in a tangle of arms and legs. The gunpowder made their noses burn.

"Well? Are you going to shut up or should I do this again?" Sarah demanded.

Ruth removed a rubber plug from the bottom of her cane and pointed the barrel at the family. Miriam cowered against the wall and the children burrowed into her side until Ruth took the cane-gun away, aiming it at the ceiling.

"Why are you doing this to us? What do you want? Please let us go. You're frightening us." She started to cry.

"You should be frightened. This is your destiny. *Our* destiny," Sarah said.

"But why? What did we ever do to you?"

"Tell her," Sarah said to Ruth. "Tell her what happened."

"Your husband killed my men, my husband and son," Ruth said, her voice flat and heavy.

"Zach? That can't be true."

Initially calm, Ruth's anger caught fire. "Wrong! You are very wrong. My men lie side by side, forever sleeping in Palestinian graves because of your husband. Today is the ten-year anniversary of their murder."

"No, you must be mistaken."

"I have no need to lie. He killed them," said Ruth, eyes dilated and breathing fast. She stood tall in front of the bed, her stance wide, looking down at them. The pitch of her voice rose. "It was after a bombing in a market called Mahaneh Yehuda in Jerusalem. He came into my house and attacked my men with a squad of policemen. They killed my father-in-law. Your husband shot my husband and hit my son in the head with his rifle, killing them both. I saw it all." Ruth was now yelling, waving the cane-gun over her head.

"Then it was an accident."

"Not by an accident. Do you hear me? Are you even listening to me?" Her face was red, sweaty, eyes bulging. She pointed the cane-gun just over their heads and fired into the wall behind them. The whole room shook. "Your husband killed them. The blood of my men was on the floor, on the ceiling and the walls, all over me. Even in my mouth, my hair! My younger boy Hrayr fled out the window or they would have killed him too. It has taken a long time, but now your husband will pay for what happened." Then she slapped Miriam across the face. The children screamed.

"And not only him," shouted Sarah, pacing up and down rapidly, waving her automatic. "Your son also will die. Yes, this little one." She pointed at Joseph, who buried his head in his mother's lap. "A fair trade. *Inshallah!* Two males each. But you and your daughter will die also." She waved the rifle at them. "That can be the ten-year interest on the debt. As a Jew, surely you have not forgotten your Old Testament? An eye for an eye? *Allahu akbar,*" Sarah said.

"You must be out of your mind! What kind of a person kills innocent children?" She tried to hug her babies closer to her.

"It is justice," said Sarah, pointing the rifle first at Rachel and then at Joseph. "I have lost my family, and that was not fair either." She mimed the gun's actions. "*Rat-a-tat-tat,* the gun went in a movie I saw." The children recoiled against their mother, eyes scrunched closed, sobbing hysterically. "After my family was murdered in Afghanistan, I wanted to kill the Russians, but we had no way. We give thanks to my Chechnya sisters. They started the Black Widows to seek revenge. We are members and will pay you back."

"But these children are innocents." She had finally freed her wrists and squeezed the children to her. "How can you harm them if the Russians killed your family?" Miriam said.

"Russians, Americans. It is all the same. I want revenge," Sarah screamed. "I lost my whole family! My whole life was taken from me! *Do you hear me!*"

Ruth said, "Are you the only one with innocent children? Was not my child innocent too? He was only twenty when your husband killed him."

She dropped the cane-gun and wrenched Joseph from Miriam. The little boy was kicking and screaming, fighting to get back to his mother. Ruth held him by one arm and one leg high over her head, almost touching the ceiling. A manic grin distorted her face.

"Now!" shouted Sarah. "Do it now, Ruth." Miriam lurched forward to save her son, but Sarah pushed her back onto the bed.

The little boy writhed in Ruth's grip, hysterical. Ruth threw him at Miriam, who caught him just before he hit the floor.

"As soon as Hrayr gets here, with Allah's help, your man will die! And your little children," said Sarah, calming down and flicking her finger under the chin of first Rachel and then Joseph. "Sugar and spice and all things nice? I read a story about that once in a children's nursery rhyme book. Is that what you think about the children? All sugar and spice? Well let me tell you a little secret, lady. *The sugar is sweet, we say, but the spice will rule the day.* Soon enough," said Sarah with a sneer. "Our revenge will be ... enormous. And the last thing your husband will hear on this earth will be the screams of his children."

Chapter Fifty

"How much further? I've got to pee."

"Almost there," Harry said.

"I'm going to pee in your car."

"You won't be the first."

Harry stopped directly in front of the overhead door of the warehouse and beeped twice. The curtain in a window parted briefly and the garage door rolled up. He drove in, parked alongside the Hummer, and the door came down again.

"Out!" Harry said. He turned off the motor, slipped from behind the wheel, and opened the back door. He uncuffed the hand attached to the door but then re-cuffed both behind her.

"Where are we?"

"This is your first stop."

She looked around at the empty warehouse. *And maybe my last.*

Ruth and Sarah opened the door and came out of the large office into the warehouse. "*Salaam,* Hrayr. It is good to see you—"

His mother interrupted Sarah's greeting. She pointed the cane at Frankie. "What is this? Who is she?"

"*Salaam,* Mother, Auntie. This," he said, looking at Frankie, "is a woman I have been seeing." He then switched to Arabic, but he spoke so fast Frankie had trouble following. His expression told her he was explaining a lot, and when his eyes narrowed to slits, fear enveloped her like a dark cloud.

"What are you talking about? Let me go, now," Frankie said.

The two older women frowned at each other. Sarah stepped forward and slapped Frankie across the face. "Shut up, you stupid woman. You are filth!" Frankie blinked back tears and fell silent.

Ruth spoke rapidly in Arabic. Her tone showed she was clearly displeased with her son. "Do you know why you are here?" she said to Frankie in English.

"Mother, I'll handle it. Let's put her down there with the others first."

"What others? What are you talking about?" Frankie asked.

He pushed her toward the trap door. "Down there." Harry opened it. He took off her handcuffs, pushed her down into the room, and closed the trap door.

Frankie sank onto the stairs and reached into the pocket of her skirt. "Zach, I hope to God you can hear me."

Chapter Fifty-One

C'mon Frankie, I pleaded in silence. Talk to me some more. The "down there with the others" had to be Miriam and the kids. I paced the back of the van, keeping my head bent to avoid the ceiling, until I got a stiff neck and had to sit down again. I wasn't made for stakeouts. It would drive me nuts to watch when you could imagine what was happening inside.

We were parked alongside the main building of the *Reader's Digest*. A small pond separated us from the warehouse. I sucked the pipe stem of my Meerschaum, not wanting to light up in the van. Before we drove in, we had changed the side paneling of the truck so that we were now UPS Delivery. The difference in the truck's appearance allowed us to blend in with the on-site construction. On the way, McBride briefed me. He had found the shattered mirror and jewelry box, and the neighbor across the hall told him about a cop shocking Frankie with some strange gun and carrying her off in handcuffs. Apparently, this had all taken place just before they started monitoring.

I studied O'Malley and McBride, trying to gauge what kind of support I could count on from them. I had to get into the building, specifically "down there," wherever that was.

Frankie's voice crackled on the transmitter and I stood up too fast, cracking my head on the ceiling. "I *can* hear you, Frankie," I said.

"She can't hear you," Mac said.

"I know."

I heard Frankie's voice again. "Who are you?" she said. *She must be talking to Miriam.*

"I'm Miriam Dayan. And these are my children, Joseph and Rachel. Who are you?"

"Frankie Walters. I know your husband from a case he's working on."

One of the children sniffled. "Mommy, why are we here? I want to go home." It was Rachel.

"Some bad people are mad at Daddy," said Miriam.

"I thought it had to do with stealing pacemakers," said Frankie.

"The tall woman said Zach killed her husband and son ten years ago. She wants revenge. But why are you here?" Miriam asked.

"Because of Harry. It's a long story."

I heard Miriam start to cry. "Harry Scarpia? I thought he was our friend, but I don't know what to think anymore. What are we going to do? My children! What will happen to them? To all of us? Where is Zach? We need him now." Broken sobs obscured the rest of the transmission.

My gut was in knots and my vision was blurred with tears. They were "down there" because of me, facing possible execution. *Collateral damage*, the doorman said. And there was no way to let them know I was trying to get them out.

I heard Frankie's voice again. "Miriam, I think—I hope—the FBI and Zach can hear us." There was a lot of static, and I guessed she was taking the bug from her pocket.

"Oh, I hope so. Zach, please hurry," Miriam said.

"Zach, if you can hear me, Harry said we are in an old building of the *Reader's Digest*. His mother and aunt are the only others I saw. There's a trap door in the floor that leads to an underground room. No windows. I'm here with Miriam and the two kids. We're all fine so far."

To find a way in, I needed to know more this underground room—where it was and the layout of the building.

"Mac, can you locate a copy of the building's construction plans?" I said to McBride. "I need a layout of the building and location of that underground room."

"I'll see what I can find." McBride went out the back of the van, blended in with the construction workers, and hurried through the main entrance of the *Reader's Digest*.

I checked my watch. Half an hour until my rendezvous with Harry. Not much time. I re-read the notes I had scribbled during the phone call. The faceoff was about two miles away, on Pleasantville Golf Course off Nannyhagen Road, wherever the hell that was. The golf course was closed today. Smart, I thought. By meeting me there, Harry could keep me from learning where my family was and deal with me alone. My instructions were to get a golf cart and drive to the first green, most likely buried deep in the woods. I was sure there'd be no exchange of my family, only an act of biblical revenge. Probably something slow and painful. And he'd leave my body there, maybe in a grave already dug.

I checked my weapons. The Smith and Wesson was strapped in my shoulder holster with extra ammunition in my dump pouch. And the 9 mm semiautomatic sat snug against my ankle with a full clip.

"Patricia, do you know if Mac kept any body armor in the van?" A Kevlar vest would be great.

"Not that I know of."

"What are you carrying?" I asked her.

"My 9 mm Glock."

Several minutes later I saw the garage door open and the Hummer back out. It looked like the same car that had run me off the road. I couldn't see who was driving because of the dark tinted windows, but I guessed it was Harry.

Two knocks, a pause, two knocks. Patricia opened the van door to McBride, who waved a sheath of papers in his hands. I spread them out on the floor of the van. After studying the drawings, we gathered in the back of the van.

"Harry's gone. I've got to get inside that building now."

"What about your meeting?" McBride asked.

"The best plan is to *not* show up. What I want is trapped here, not on the golf course."

"How about backup?" asked McBride.

"The only ones I'd trust are guys from my own squad, maybe from the FBI unit, and they're both at least an hour from here. No way am I going to use locals. Not with my family in there."

"The dirt road circles the building," said McBride, pointing out the front windshield of the van. "Suppose we drive around the warehouse by going around the pond, and give you a chance to look at the back. Get you onto the roof; maybe you can find a way to get in from there."

"According to the construction plans, a ventilation system was added about ten years after the building was built. It feeds an underground room built as a bomb shelter. I'd bet that's the 'down there' we heard. I'd need to get into the ventilation system from the roof. But judging from its dimensions, I'm too big," I said.

"Not me," Patricia said, her big eyes bright with anticipation. "I can do it. Hundred pounds with my clothes on! I'll shimmy through the ventilation shafts and save them."

"That might work, but these pipes are almost fifty years old. God knows what shape they're in and what weight they'll hold."

"But I could do it, maybe give you some information about the place they're in."

"Assuming you can get out the same way you get in."

"Why shouldn't I?"

"Okay, let's do the drive-by. Mac, get behind the wheel and drive at a steady pace. Don't look at the window in the front; just keep going, like maybe you're looking for a delivery sign or something. Are you packing?"

He looked at me and shook his head, arms akimbo. "Not much on this job. Just a Glock 27."

"It's okay." I handed him my 9 mm. "What kind of tools you got in this van?"

"An electronic lab. Practically anything you need."

"Can you rig me up with a receiver so I can hear Frankie's transmitter? And a transmitter to talk to Patricia?"

"No problem."

After McBride outfitted us, the van slowly pulled forward. We reached the back of the building and came to a dead end. There was a blank wall with one curtained window. It took McBride some maneuvering to turn the van around in the narrow dead end. Patricia and I jumped out.

Chapter Fifty-Two

Harry knew the exact location of Nannyhagen Road from his practice run days before, and he arrived at the golf course in ten minutes. He parked the Hummer in the parking lot of the deserted club house and snapped on a pair of surgical gloves. Two golf carts were waiting. Fifty bucks for the attendant was a cheap investment. He drove out, glancing at a map to remember the first hole, with a green hidden in a copse of trees.

As he approached, he took a sharp right onto a path leading into the woods and parked behind a deer blind he had built. He cradled the Browning 30.06 semi-automatic rifle on his lap and made sure he had a clear shot. The armor-piercing bullets had enough punch to get through any protection Zach might be wearing. Even if they didn't, they would stun him long enough for Harry to finish the job. But that was not his plan. He fingered the scalpel handle in his pocket. That was his plan. Afterward the newly dug grave was waiting fifty yards deeper in the woods. Revenge for his father and brother would be sweet, and he would also eliminate the biggest threat to their mission. Then he would tend to Frankie and the rest of the Dayan family.

Finally.

****

Patricia and I climbed up the downspout on the corner of the building and stood on the roof. I could see McBride returning to position.

It was easier than I thought. The bolts holding the ventilation mounting to the roof were rusted but easily removed after a drop of *Rust-Off*—McBride's foresight. I lifted off the cowling to expose a long, round tube that melted into darkness. It was like entering a black tunnel that stretched forever. For me, the sight triggered a claustrophobic shiver.

Heights and tight spaces. You couldn't pay me enough!

"You sure you're ready for this, Patricia?"

Patricia tested her flashlight. The beam drilled a bright hole in the darkness for a short distance but then was swallowed by the nothingness. "Turn me loose, Detective." She stuck her head in the hole. "I'll be talking to you," her voice echoed back.

"Wait, test communications first." The tiny radio transmitter and receiver McBride had fitted us with worked fine. "Talk to me on the way down."

Patricia slithered into the black hole like a snake into its den and vanished. The last I saw of her was her hands batting away cobwebs and her skinny butt wiggling in the shaft, inch-worming along, barely fitting, dragging a black canvas tool bag attached to her leg by a rope. *Bravery comes wrapped in lots of different sized packages*, I thought.

"Okay, Detective. I can't see shit in front of me. This pipe is filled with soot or dirt or some kind of dark crap. Loaded with so many cobwebs they're in my hair, my nose. I'm chewing on them like gum! There's a deep bend coming up, almost ninety degrees to the right. You got to be a contortionist to get around it. It must be heading in the direction of the underground room. This is going to be rough, even for skinny—"

Silence.

"Patricia. Talk to me, Patricia."

"Okay. I'm back. Just made the turn. Now headed straight for a few feet, like a walk on the beach." Pause. "Feels like it's angling down. Shit!"

She sounded like one of the guys. "What happened?"

"I tore my arm on some sort of screw or nail sticking out from a joint where the bend is. Bleeding like hell. Hurts. Wait a minute."

I heard a lot of rustling.

"Back on. McBride has everything in this tool bag. I had to hold the flashlight in my teeth but I found antiseptic, a bandage, and tape. Just remind me to get my tetanus booster later. Ready to go again. Now this pipe is really headed downhill. I got to brace myself on the sides here, because it must be straight down into the room. Slipping fast like on a rollercoaster. *Oof!*"

"What happened?" I asked.

"I rammed my head into a door or something. Looks like the wire mesh grating in the ceiling to the room. Hello in there. I'm Patricia O'Malley, New York police, come to get you out."

"Holy Christ! Where are you?" Frankie's voice came through loud and clear.

"Up here in the ceiling," said Patricia.

"Are you for real?" Frankie again.

"Oh, my God! Where's Zach?" I heard Miriam and then the kids screaming.

"Shhh. Keep it down or they'll hear you. I got to get this grate off. Wait a minute."

I heard metal scraping and a grunt from Patricia. A couple of snaps, which I figured must be the wire cutters.

"Catch this grate so it doesn't fall and clatter on the floor. Thanks. Now help me down. Good." Pause. "You want to talk to him? Wait a minute."

"Zach, Zach, where are you?" Miriam cried. "Are you here? I can't believe it. They want to kill us, Zach. You're going to get us out, right?" She started to sob, followed by the kids.

"I'm here, and we're going to get you all out safely. It's going to be okay. Listen to Patricia. She knows exactly what to do."

"Detective, there's no way we can climb back through that shaft. The last twenty feet were straight down. We're in a small room that must be under the floor of the warehouse. Trap door in the ceiling opens out, but it wouldn't budge when I pushed on it. Must be secured from above, probably in the floor of the warehouse. I can't find the emergency exit in the drawing. Probably plastered over years ago. Let's go with plan B."

"Fine. Mac, you on?" I asked.

"Ten four."

"Okay. Set watches. Plan B in five minutes starting ... now!"

Chapter Fifty-Three

Ruth watched the UPS van slowly return to its parking place alongside the main building next to the pond. "Sarah, what do you think?"

"I couldn't see the van after it passed the window, so I don't know what happened when it turned around. You don't really believe it's UPS, do you?"

"Of course not."

"So you think the police know where we are?"

"What else can it be?" Ruth said. "Somehow they followed Hrayr."

"Should we call him to come back?"

"He would be walking straight into a trap," said Ruth.

"But we still should warn him."

"You see that long antenna on the roof of the van?" said Ruth, pointing with her cane.

Sarah looked closely.

"They have got some sort of listening device in that truck and would be able to intercept the cell phone conversation. We would end up telling them where Hrayr is."

"But we need him here if they try to come into the warehouse."

"Yes we do, but we can't endanger him or the operation."

For a moment, Sarah locked eyes with Ruth. Then there was a glint of a smile. "I know what we can do." She walked quickly toward the trap door.

Ruth ran after her. "Good idea. They are perfect hostages. No one will dare come after us."

Sarah lifted the trap door and shouted down into the room below.

"Up the stairs, all of you. Hurry. Come up now or you will have more of my bullets," Sarah shouted.

Patricia hugged the back corner of the room, out of sight from above.

The women each carried a child up the stairs. When the trap door slammed again, Patricia said softly, "Detective, cancel plan B for now. Hostages taken upstairs. I don't know what they're planning, but I say wait for now."

"Roger that," said Zach. "You copy, Mac?"

"Ten four."

"Patricia, did Frankie keep the transmitter?"

"As far as I know."

"Okay. First sign of trouble, plan B goes into effect instantly. Patricia, they probably didn't lock the trap door, since all of them are topside."

Then I heard one of the women's voice. "Sit down on the floor over there and you won't get hurt."

"Children, do what the lady says. We'll be okay. C'mon, Rachel, you can sit on Frankie's lap, and Joseph can sit on mine," Miriam said.

"Patricia," I said, "can you lift the trap door a tiny bit to see what is happening?"

I heard could hear Patricia's feet on the steps. "Detective, there's a center post in the garage, near the door to an office. They've got them sitting on the floor next to it. It's maybe fifty feet from me. Harry's patrol car is parked nearby."

"Are they tied up?"

"I don't think so, but the two women are guarding them with guns. The short one's carrying an AK-47 and the tall one has something looking like a cane."

I heard one of the women speak again. "We know your husband is waiting outside in a van. You will be the live bait, like a small fish wiggling on a hook to get a bigger fish. He will come for you, we know that. When he does, you will die and he will die, and this part of our mission will be fulfilled."

There was a long silence, with only intermittent sobs from the children. I had no idea how much patience the two women had.

Probably not much. I felt a chill run up my spine. "Patricia, what are they doing?"

"The short one—that's Sarah—has been pacing up and down with the AK on her shoulder. She seems agitated, like she's deciding what to do. Now she's pointing it at the women and children." I heard the pitch of Patricia's voice rising. Something was going to happen. "Now she's talking to Ruth, the tall one," Patricia said.

I heard one of the women say, "I am tired, Ruth—so tired of my life, so very tired of all this." Her voice was flat and I could hear the futility in it. "I am tired of waiting. Over ten years. So now it is time. They must die."

"Let's wait until the husband comes and then we will kill him also," Ruth said.

"No. Enough waiting," Sarah said.

The AK rattled off a string of bullets, drowning out their voices.

I screamed, "Patricia, what the hell is happening?"

"Frankie threw something at Sarah and she let out a burst. I don't know if she hit anything, but I'm not waiting. *Initiating plan B, now! Plan B, now!*"

I heard the flash bang go off. Patricia must have thrown it through the trap door. The explosion was deafening.

The noise triggered our attack. I crashed through the window at the back of the warehouse and McBride rammed the van through the garage doors. I saw the short one—it must have been Sarah—on her hands and knees, holding her ears and shaking her head. The tall one—Ruth—was staggering but upright. She stood in front of my family, fumbling with her cane-gun, perhaps reloading. I got off three quick rounds. I was too far away to do any damage, but the noise made both women look at me. Sarah recovered first and began shooting her AK-47 wildly in my direction, spraying anything in sight.

I saw Patricia's head pop up from the trap door. "Stay down!" I screamed. She ignored me and came charging out of the hole, shooting while she ran toward Miriam and Frankie.

"Put your heads down and stay behind me," she yelled, shielding them as best she could. Patricia had just reached my family when she got off a shot that hit Ruth in the head. Ruth fell backward with her finger stuck on the cane-gun trigger. Patricia was in the direct line of fire as the cane-gun arched upward. She collapsed, blood spewing from her uniform.

The front of the van had torn through the garage doors, but the rest was stuck in the middle. The cab door jammed, but McBride wedged it open and squeezed out. I saw Sarah take aim at him and I yelled, "Hit the floor." A bullet caught him in the leg. It buckled, and he went down trying to shoot her with my ankle gun.

Sarah was about twenty feet from me, and the cloud from the flash bang obscured my vision. I dropped to one knee, braced, and fired at her until the chamber was empty. One of my shots caught her in the shoulder and she spun around, dropping the gun.

But she remained standing, her hands tugging at her waist. Blood from her shoulder dripped onto her hand, and her fumbling became more erratic. "

I screamed at Miriam and Frankie. "Get in the basement. *She's wired to explode!*" They bolted for the trap door, each carrying a child.

I ran to Patricia, but she was dead. McBride hobbled as best he could to the trap door but was never going to make it in time. I threw him over my shoulder and we dove into the hole in the floor.

As I slammed the door over our heads, I heard, *"Allahu Akbar!"*

Chapter Fifty-Four

A thundering explosion, followed by another one several seconds later, tore through the warehouse, and shockwaves sent all of us caroming off the furniture and walls. But the reinforced structure with its thick ceiling remained intact. The children, semiconscious, screamed and clung to Miriam, who sat on the floor in shock. Blood oozed from a gash in her lip and from her ear. Frankie lay spread eagle on the floor, groaning.

I was the first to move, wedged beneath the overturned bed. I pushed off the box spring and mattress and gingerly tested my arms and legs. Nothing seemed broken. I stood on wobbly knees and went to Miriam and the kids. I just hugged them. No words would come, and none were necessary.

McBride was mumbling something, just regaining consciousness. He was bleeding from his leg where the bullet had torn through his calf. I used my belt as a tourniquet, and the bleeding slowed and then stopped. Frankie was now sitting up, rubbing her eyes.

I surveyed the room. The plaster cracks on the walls looked like giant spider webs, but the damage seemed superficial and revealed the reinforced steel beneath. The steps leading to the trap door in the ceiling were littered with pieces of the wall, and I stumbled over plaster and glass, clearing the way with my shoe. When I reached the top, I pushed on the square door. It didn't move, so I put my shoulder to it. Not even a tremor. Figuring it must be covered with debris, piled high from the blast, I backed down the stairs.

The kids were already coughing, and the biggest danger now was the very ventilation system that had been the key to the rescue. It had sucked in smoke from the explosion and suddenly quit. No air was circulating. We would not last long without a fresh supply of oxygen, and I knew we had to find a way out quickly or die of smoke inhalation. Our survival depended on it. Catching Harry would have to wait.

****

Harry checked his watch. Zach was almost an hour late. It was not like him to be late for anything, particularly if his family was in danger. He opened and closed his cell phone, hesitating. His mother had said not to. But he dialed anyway. No answer.

Harry jumped in the golf cart and raced back to the club house. He started the Hummer, gunned it, and sped off. Halfway to the *Reader's Digest* he saw the plume of smoke and heard the wail of fire trucks screaming in the distance. As he approached the entrance, he could see the devastation, with hundreds of people running about in confusion. The warehouse no longer existed, only a rubble-covered slab of concrete on which it had stood. He shook his head in disbelief, drove past the entrance without slowing, and pointed the Hummer toward his mother's house. He knew what he had to do.

Chapter Fifty-Five

Gasping sounds, ragged and rapid, echoed in the small room. Rachel's and Joseph's lips had a dusky color. They sat on the floor, heads drooping and mouths open, struggling to breathe. I rammed a piece of wood from the side of the bed into the latch of the trap door, but it didn't budge. I pounded the door, and we all yelled.

I tried to remember the architect's drawings. I could see ribs of steel shining through the cracks in the pink plaster—on all sides but one. That side was cracked, and there was something beneath the plaster.

Where the hell was the bag Patricia had been dragging? I found it in the corner of the room, beneath the sink. I spilled the contents on the floor and grabbed a long file, the only thing I could find with a point on it. Seeing what I intended to do, Frankie yanked the cover off the bed and threw it at me. I tore off a piece, wrapped it around the flat, rough surface of the file, and plunged the point into the middle of the wall. The plaster crumbled easily, and I ripped away big chunks of dry wall to reveal a door that opened into a dark corridor stretching out in front.

"This must be the emergency exit. It may lead to the main building—or it may be a dead end. But we've got no choice. Let's go."

I picked up Joseph in one arm and clutched Miriam's hand with the other. Frankie grabbed Rachel, and we charged ahead into the black void, feeling our way along the walls like the blind, despite the weak beam from Patricia's flashlight. McBride hobbled after us. The air in the corridor was cleaner than in the room but the passageway rapidly collected smoke. We hurried, maybe two hundred feet or so, and came to a locked door. Dead end!

I pounded the door but got no response. I shined the light on the door handle and saw it was ordinary, not bolted like a protective door. That made sense, since the underground room was only an emergency bunker, not for hiding anything of value. I tested the door with my shoulder, but it didn't give, since it opened *toward* us.

"I've got to go back and get a tool to open this door," I told them. "Sit on the floor and take slow breaths. I won't be long."

"Don't leave us, Zach!" Miriam cried.

"Frankie and Mac will be here. I'll be back in a minute."

I started to run, but the air was too thick with smoke. I choked up, coughing, and my rasping breath doubled me over to my knees. When I could breathe again, I walked as fast as I could to the room, searched for the wire cutters, and went back into the dark corridor.

I saw willowy forms like shadows in the dim light. "I'm here, where are you?"

Rachel and Joseph were lying on the floor, practically lifeless. "Hurry, Zach! The smoke is hardest on them," Miriam said. I remembered from medical school that kids breathe faster than adults and will take in more smoke.

I put the mouth of the wire cutters on the neck of the door handle and crunched. The handle snapped off, and I pulled out the remaining guts of the lock. I slid my finger into the hole where the door latch had been and pulled the door open into what must have been the editor's office. The sudden transformation from the dark, dense, smoky corridor to the brightly lit, clean office was like emerging from a murky cave onto a bright Caribbean beach. I shoved them into the office and closed the door to keep out the smoke already crowding around us. The children looked terrible. Their lips were blue and they were barely breathing. I panicked. "Start mouth-to-mouth, both of you! I'm going to find help."

I ran out of the office door into what seemed to be a major corridor in the main building. It was empty. Everyone had gathered outside to watch the firefighters wrestle with the warehouse blaze. I shuddered, thinking, *We were just there, underneath all that!* I needed some big-time medical talent now. How the hell could I get their attention?

I pulled out my .38, raised it overhead, and squeezed off a round. The hollow click reminded me I had emptied the chamber in the warehouse. I reached for the ankle gun, forgetting I had given it to McBride. Fortunately, I always carried extra bullets in my dump pouch. I reloaded the Smith and Wesson and winged off two shots into the sky. That got everybody's attention. I waved them to follow me and ran back into the building. I'm sure the cops thought I was one of the bad guys, because the first one in the building was a uniform with a drawn revolver. He radioed for help and two EMTs arrived in a couple of minutes. One look at the kids and he said, "Asphyxiation arrest. Keep up the mouth-to-mouth while I hook in oxygen and put on the AED!"

Chapter Fifty-Six

Harry parked the Hummer in front of his mother's house and unlocked the front door with a key on a chain around his neck. He bolted the door behind him, then drew the blinds before turning on the lights. He sat down and for the first time, absorbed the full weight of what had happened. Mother and Auntie were certainly dead, blown up as martyrs and now in Paradise. He had promised them retribution and failed. He hoped the explosion took the others as well, but he had no way of knowing. He now had to finish the mission they all had started.

Harry walked into the dining room and sat down at the table covered by the red checkered tablecloth. He used the edge of a quarter to press the beak of the eagle. The drawer opened. He reached in for the piece of paper, memorized the phone number, and tore the paper into shreds, flushing it down the toilet. He dialed, and a man answered on the first ring. "I have some packages to deliver. We're a few short, but close. I need a plane. *Immediately.*"

****

The EMT applied patches from the automated external defibrillator to Joseph's chest and read the EKG it transmitted.

"Heart's fine. Keep breathing for him," he told Frankie. "He'll come around. Take it off him and hook up the girl," he said to the other EMT.

He put the leads on Rachel. "The kid's in ventricular fibrillation! Smoke inhalation has caused full cardiac arrest! Stand back for a shock." He pushed a red button.

Whoomp!

He looked at the EKG. "Hit the girl again. She's still in VF!"

Whoomp!

"Try it again, with max AED output!"

"But she's only a kid! You'll fry her heart."

"Maybe, but it won't matter if we don't stop the fibrillation."

Whoomp!

Miriam's face was buried in my shoulder. Her fists pounded my chest, and she screamed, "No, no, no!" But there was nothing I could do except watch. Frankie was doing a great job getting Joseph to breathe, and all I could do was hold Miriam to keep her from collapsing. I prayed silently for Rachel to fight on.

"Inject adrenalin directly into her heart and try again. If this doesn't do it, we've got nothing else."

Miriam shrieked hearing that. I wanted to wring the bastard's neck.

One of the EMTs took out a syringe with a long needle and positioned himself to drive it into Rachel's chest.

"Wait!" I yelled, grabbing his arm. "The defibrillator pads are wrong! You've got them placed for an adult, not a little girl!" I adjusted them front-to-back on her chest. "Now try it!"

Whoomp!

"That did it! Sinus rhythm. Breathe for her a little while longer, but she'll come to in a minute," the EMT said.

Frankie stopped doing mouth-to-mouth on Joseph, who was pushing her hands away and calling for Miriam. She ran to him and hugged him to her chest. He squiggled around and saw me. "Daddy, do you have any candy for me?"

I searched my torn pockets. With sadness, I shook my head. "Not this time, Joey. But when we get out of here, I will get you some—as much as you want."

Given all the trauma he'd endured, my not having candy must have been too much for him, and he became hysterical.

I groped again in my pockets. Both were ripped open and empty, but I felt a slight bulge in the lining of my jacket. My fingers worked through a hole in the pocket, and I fished out a lone butterscotch candy, peeled it open, and popped it into Joey's open mouth. He stopped crying, smiled, and laid his head back against Miriam, eyes closed and lips moving rhythmically.

I saw Frankie stand and look around, taking in the pain wracking my family.

"You fucking son of a bitch," I heard her say under her breath. "*Harry, you'll pay.*"

Chapter Fifty-Seven

The FBI televised a description I gave them of the ladies, and almost immediately a young man named Jimmy at the local Safeway called in. He supplied us their names and address, and we had the house in less than three hours. Armed with a search warrant, we literally tore the place apart, board by board. We found hollow flooring in the dining room where the pacemakers must have been stored. There wasn't even a trace of radioactivity. The dining room lamp, a blue Colonial with an eagle on its base, had been wiped clean of fingerprints, but I could see the false bottom drawer. The bookstore was a bust. We found the back room but no equipment or useful information. Harry had sanitized it well.

The Hummer was gone. I put out an APB but with no luck. He probably dropped it off at a chop house in the city and the car was now in a thousand untraceable pieces. I knew Harry would not remain in the United States, but none of the commercial airports had any listing of a passenger resembling him. I finally called McBride's office at the FBI. "How's the leg?"

"Crutches, but I'm walking. Couple of stitches after they cleaned it out. Still had a piece of lead in the muscle. Could've been a lot worse. Thanks for saving my ass. Literally."

"Pleasure. I need help."

"Pleasure. Name it."

"Harry's vanished with the pacemakers. He's most likely skipped out of the U.S., maybe to the Middle East, and I need international help to catch him before they build that bomb." Fortunately my role with the Israel Defense Force and NYPD gave me international status.

"Way ahead of you. You think because I was almost killed I don't do my job? I had the bomb guys from the Explosives Unit–Bomb Data Center team up with the Terrorist Explosive Device Analytical Center to analyze the IED used in the warehouse explosion. Same guts as in Petoskey. We've already issued a worldwide alert and we're working with Interpol. We've notified public and private airport security, international shipping, and border guards throughout Europe, the Middle East, and South America. More people have a picture of Harry Scarpia than of Ben Franklin in their wallet. We've listed him as a wanted terrorist, armed and dangerous. There's also a two-million-dollar reward, dead or alive. You want more?"

"That's a good start. But whether you got it in place before he flew is the question."

"Better late than never."

"True. What's happened with the killings?"

"None in the twenty-four hours since Harry's skipped. Grave robbings stopped too."

"How many?"

"Over one hundred and fifty murders in eighteen countries, including forty-one of fifty states in the U.S., and more than five hundred grave robbings or thefts from morticians. But these are probably low estimates. We figure a number of murders were not linked to the terrorist operation and went unreported. Same for the grave robbings. I'd guess they've got their thousand or close to it," McBride said.

"Do you have contacts here or in the Middle East who would know about building a bomb on this scale? The pile of one thousand pacemakers is easily hidden, but I would think that the plutonium extraction and the actual building of a nuclear device would require a fair amount of sophisticated engineering, scientists, and stuff."

"We're checking various sources now. I should know in the next day or two. How're Miriam and the kids?"

"The kids are fine, but Miriam won't talk about what happened. Just sits around most of the day staring out the window. Barely eating enough to keep alive. Her sister's staying with her."

"Tough. So what are your next moves?"

"I plan to talk with Frankie again. I'm thinking maybe she knows something about Harry she doesn't know she knows."

"Happens all the time. In the meantime we'll continue to check Scarpia's exit moves."

"Thanks, Mac. Keep in touch."

****

The next day, after the children were released from the hospital, no worse for almost dying, we all attended funeral services for Patricia O'Malley. Her casket sat on a table to the side of the pulpit.

I looked out at the formally dressed NYPD corps, with color guard at attention, flags at half mast, and leadership shining in their gold epaulets. The captain gave a short eulogy and handed the Legion of Honor Award posthumously to Patricia's parents. He brought tears to my eyes when he said, "Grief is the pain we all pay for love, and there is not much the NYPD can do to relieve that for you. It can, though, recognize the great courage of your daughter, through this award. Thank you from the NYPD."

Tears streamed down Frankie's face, but Miriam sat mute, staring straight ahead, unable to come to grips with what had happened. I hoped the police's grief counselor could help her handle the post-traumatic stress.

Chapter Fifty-Eight

I sat at the kitchen table while Frankie made coffee. We weren't quite like an old married couple, but it was becoming a comfortable ritual for us. We'd been through a lot together in a brief time, and that kind of experience is binding. I've seen that happen with couples who have shared a tragedy, like a child kidnapping. Of course, watching her tight blouse made it even more appealing and reminded me I hadn't been with a woman in a long time. But more importantly, I was starting to like her—a lot.

"Let's go over things one more time."

"We already have—three times."

"Patience. Hear me out. Sometimes you remember a small thing when you go over it again in your mind. Close your eyes."

She looked at me wide eyed. "You're serious, aren't you?"

"Absolutely. Close your eyes."

"Why, so you can put me through that squat stuff again?"

I laughed. "This time it might have different consequences."

"Hmm," she said. "I can't think with my eyes closed."

"Okay, just concentrate. What happened after he threw the jewelry box at the mirror?"

She ran her fingers through her hair. "He was really pissed. I pulled Boom Boom on him, but he tasered me. Twice. Oh, and that bitch across the hall, Mrs. Orlovsky, saw the second one and did nothing. Watched him drag me off. If she thinks I've been a pain in the ass in the past, wait, just wait. I'm going to give her husband cardiac arrest before I'm through!"

"Whoa. Slow down. Back to Harry. Go on."

Frankie took a few deep breaths. "Then, in the car he told me he was going to atone by stoning me to death." Her face showed pain.

"In Chappaqua?"

"That's what he said. You think they still do that?"

"You tell me. You're the Middle East scholar."

"Yeah, but you were raised in Israel."

She was right, of course. I spoke Arabic and likely knew more about Muslims by growing up among them.

"To tell you the truth, I don't know," I said. "Muslim attitudes toward women are based on ancient traditions, so I guess it's still possible. Their attitude toward rape, for example, has not changed for centuries."

"I think there has to be something like four male witnesses before charges can be brought against the man. And then the woman is shamed forever, guilty or not," Frankie said.

"Back to the stoning. Aside from fitting with Muslim tradition, does it help us nail down a specific country where Harry might have come from or gone to?" I asked.

"No, they all do it." She sipped her coffee and slowly shook her head.

"What? The expression on your face …"

"Nothing."

"Yeah, like remembering the broken music box was nothing. I know that look. What?"

"Well, I just thought about a conversation with Miriam. We were locked in the basement room before Patricia arrived, and she was telling me what the women told her about wanting revenge. She repeated something strange."

"Which was?"

"Apparently Sarah was mouthing off about the Black Widows organization."

"We know all about them. But we couldn't link them with any other group. These two were part of a decentralized independent terrorist cell. They've cropped up all over the place since we attacked al-Qaeda."

"Miriam said Sarah quoted a nursery rhyme verse when they were talking about the kids. The one that goes, 'Sugar and spice and all things nice.'"

"So?"

"So, first of all it was way out of context, considering where they were."

"I'll buy that."

"But even more important, Sarah said something—*The spice will rule the day,*' something like that—and Ruth got all pissed off and told her she had a big mouth. Then Sarah laughed."

"That is strange. But I don't know what to make of it."

"Me neither. But I thought I'd tell you."

"'The spice will rule the day.' Some kind of poison maybe?"

She shrugged.

My cell phone went off.

I checked the caller ID. "Hey, Mac. Got something?" I listened to McBride for several minutes. "Can I put you on the speaker phone? I'm here with Frankie, and I want her to listen also." I thought about how Molly had come up with the pacemaker explanation. Maybe Frankie could help. I hit the speaker button.

"No problem. Here's what we got. Seven private jets left the New York City area for international destinations on the night of the explosion. They all filed their mandatory flight plans. No way could they take off without that. We've done due diligence on each and narrowed the list to two possibles. One was a Lear that went to Bogotá, Columbia, with two men aboard. But they had no luggage, so unless they shipped the pacemakers separately, no dice. They got off and melted into the city. I suspect that was drug related, but we're following it up. The other was a Gulfstream V SP. The plane left from a small airport near Kennedy with a final destination of Gatwick, England. Cruising speed five hundred sixty miles per hour and a non-refueling distance over seven thousand miles. Leased from a company called OwnYourJet Inc. and paid for in cash. Big plane—seats twelve to fifteen—but only one guy got on carrying a single briefcase."

"Luggage?"

"No personal luggage. But he also brought along almost two hundred and fifty pounds of 'electrical supplies' stored in three wooden crates. The guy called himself Antonio Agostino with an Italian passport that fit. We tracked it through the Investigative Data Warehouse and it's legit. He offloaded and went through security without an alarm. Airport people faxed me the X-ray pictures, and the crates contained a lot of little round metal things that sure could've been the pacemakers you're tracking. Since that wasn't his final destination, no customs issues."

"Can you count them?"

"Picture's not clear enough for that. Anyway, the guy gets on another private jet to Istanbul. Same thing through security, although now it's a Turkish passport that says Beral Iskender. Finally boards a third plane that takes off from Turkey without a flight plan. But our contacts there leaned on a few people and found out the destination was Amman, Jordan. Officials at all three airports got his picture an hour ago, and a guy in Gatwick has made a 'maybe' ID."

"Sure sounds like Scarpia."

"I agree," said Mac.

"Did you find a black Hummer parked in the airplane lot?" Frankie asked.

"Didn't look for it. Sorry. We'll do that now." I heard Mac give the order to someone.

"Don't worry if you don't find it," I said. "It's probably in pieces by now. What are the next steps?"

"We go after Scarpia and the pacemakers."

"Who's the 'we'?"

"Unless you've got international contacts, it's us, the FBI, working with Interpol in Jordan."

"You know I have international contacts. How about this idea?" I looked at Frankie. I was sure she'd go along with it. "You make Frankie an FBI agent."

"Are you nuts? I can't do that."

"Bullshit. Of course you can. One phone call from you to the FBI director is all it would take."

"And why would I want to make that phone call? We've got a lot at stake here."

"I'll tell you. First, she knows the Middle East, and the language— she majored in it in school—so she fits the needs of the agency for experts in that area. Second, she's a pro with a firearm, she's in great physical shape, she's bright, and she's pissed off at Scarpia. And last, and most important, you know I'm going, and I want her to come with me. What more do you need?"

"Assuming I went along with this crazy idea, what would she do?"

"She and I would go to Jordan, under cover as a married tourist couple. It's a beautiful country, friendly toward the U.S. and Israel—or reasonably so. We do the tourist bit and see what we can find out. My upbringing and Frankie's formal knowledge of the Middle East and Islam make us a perfect pair. If we get into trouble, or if we get hot on the trail, we give you a buzz, and old mother ship bails us out."

I watched Frankie's face as I said that. Her smile rippled from ear to ear, her eyes sparkled, and she mouthed, "Yes! Yes!" while pumping her fist in the air. I guess she wanted to go.

There was a pause on the phone, and I heard a muffled conversation. "Zach, the director would bust my balls if he knew I was letting you run the operation at this point. And besides, new agents train for seventeen weeks at Quantico. That's six hundred fifty hours acquiring academic, firearm, and operational skills."

"She has the firearm skills, and she'd be with me, so she wouldn't need the others for this single operation. Plus, we'd get backup from Jake Hertzog, so it's not like we'd be going in blind."

We could hear more mumbling in the background. "Suppose she was to tag along with you. Nothing I can do to stop that."

"Maybe so, but it makes packing a weapon in a foreign country more difficult. And, on the remote chance I wasn't around to help her, if she was an agent, she'd have the full cooperation of your guys abroad."

"Zach, we're looking at a potential nuclear assault and you want me to deputize a civilian? You're bonkers."

"She's no ordinary citizen. And I'll be working with Jake Hertzog and the IDF. Besides, you have a better plan?"

"Yes, go through the usual command. Use the FBI resources in the Middle East."

"It'll take time to get them up to speed, and time is what we don't have. The two of us could leave right now." I looked at Frankie, and she nodded.

I heard more discussion in the background.

"Zach, I can't do it. What you say is true, and you two would probably be great in the field. That's not it. Think of the political implications. If you screwed up, it wouldn't be only my neck, but the whole FBI would be blamed, which could lead to an international incident. I can't take that chance."

"Tell you what," I said. "Give us a few days in the field—maybe three. If we don't come up with something in that time, we come home, and the FBI takes over. No harm in that."

"Sorry, my friend. No can do. The FBI will have to go through regular channels. But who knows, maybe something else will open up for you."

"What do you mean?"

"Just stick around," he said, and then he hung up.

Ten minutes later, my phone rang. It was Jake Hertzog calling from Jerusalem.

"Zach, I need your help to chase some bad guys."

My eyebrows rose and I looked at Frankie. "Can I put you on the speakerphone? I'm here with a woman who—"

"I know. Sure, go ahead."

"Jake, let me introduce you to Francine Walters, a.k.a. Frankie."

"Hi, Frankie. Welcome to the IDF."

"What do you mean?" I asked.

"Zach, we're cooperating with the FBI on this terrorist operation, and I want your help. I'd like you to take a brief leave of absence from the NYPD. Since I'm paying your salary, that shouldn't be a problem. I want you to take a short term commission with us at the IDF. Frankie, too. Come to Israel and help us find Harry before he builds a nuke."

Frankie had a big grin on her face. "Yes."

"But you'll keep in close touch with us and let us handle any rough stuff. No Rambo shit," Jake said.

"You got it. How do we get there?"

"This action has claimed top priority in your country. My office has been working with Homeland Security, so you'll fly courtesy of the Israel Defense Force, but Homeland will arrange it."

"Nice of them."

"We've got an informer in Amman who says the bad guys are planning something big in New York."

"When? That's going to take a lot of work for them to get the nuclear material ready and into the U.S."

"Not sure when, but he thinks in the next two weeks."

"So when do we leave?"

A pause and mumbling in the background. "Three hours suit you?"

I checked with Frankie. "I'll have to pack a few things, Frankie too. But three hours should do it. I'll also need to be sure Miriam's sister can stay a while longer."

Three and one half hours later we were in a private hanger on the tarmac at Kennedy International. The plane was the same kind Harry took, rented from OwnYourJet Inc. Some irony here.

"So you're going to Amman?" the pilot asked.

"Eventually. To Tel Aviv first. Need to talk with some friends."

"Okay. I'll have to file the flight plan for that, and then we're off."

Chapter Fifty-Nine

We landed on a private runway in a restricted section at Ben Gurion Airport in Tel Aviv, Israel, at 6:30 the next afternoon, in time to view the fading remains of a bright Mediterranean day. A black sedan with a red light whirling cut in front of the plane after it turned off the runway and led us to a distant hangar. Two airport police officers stepped out of the car when Frankie and I descended from the plane. They had M16s slung over their shoulders.

I lit my pipe and inhaled—the first in many hours—as the officer addressed me in Hebrew. "Are you Zachariah Dayan?"

I nodded.

"ID please."

I flashed my badge.

"Passport also."

He studied it and looked up, matching the picture with the face. He then beckoned at Frankie.

"Who's she?"

"My assistant, Francine Walters."

The cop addressed Frankie in Hebrew, as he had done me. She looked quizzically at me.

"He wants to see your ID and passport."

The officer switched to English. "You don't speak Hebrew?"

She shook her head. "No."

"Look, all this has been cleared through General Hertzog's office. Check with him."

The officer gave me a hard stare and continued talking with Frankie. He rattled off a series of questions, barely giving her a chance to answer. "Why are you visiting Israel? Are you married? Any family in Israel?

Have you been here before? How long do you plan to stay? Where are you going?"

It was the usual stuff. He knew all the answers already from the information sent by the NYPD. He just wanted to see how she responded. These airport cops were pros at reading body language. People profiling, illegal in the U.S., was what they did best.

"What languages do you speak?"

"English and Arabic."

His eyebrows shot up and he addressed her in Arabic. "Where did you learn that?"

"Princeton. It's a university in New Jersey."

"I know where it is. I went to school at Columbia. Why Arabic?"

"I was interested in religion and majored in Middle East history and culture."

"What religion are you?"

"Christian, but not practicing. Agnostic, I guess."

He apparently was satisfied. "Please get in the back of the car, and I'll take you to the General's office.

****

"Welcome, Zach. It's good to see you again. How's the family?"

We had entered a nondescript white two-story building that had no identification, off Jabotinsky Street in central Tel Aviv. The office was small, not much bigger than a walk-in closet in the States, with a table for a desk, a chair behind it, and two brown wicker chairs in front. The flag of Israel was mounted in a stand behind the desk.

I shook hands with my childhood friend, Jacob Hertzog, ex-tank commander. His blond hair was rimmed by gray and showed more forehead than I remembered, but he was just as lean and muscular. I pointed to the stars on his shoulders. "Not bad for a kid from the bad side of town." I hadn't seen him since I left the Israel Defense Force, despite our regular phone calls.

"Well, some of us stay to do cleanup work; some of us leave to have fun elsewhere. It's all the same when you boil it down. The world divides into good guys and bad guys, whether you're here or there. The battle is a never-ending cycle. Sometimes we win, sometimes they do. But both sides will enjoy job security in perpetuity."

"Wow! What happened to the fearless avenger of years ago?"

"Replaced by the cynicism of old age that has witnessed too many rounds of killing and destruction, rebuilding on top of the ashes, and then killing and destruction all over again—the history of the Middle East since before recorded time. And sadly, the rest of the world as well. Enough of this bullshit. You know it only too well. Introduce me to the lovely lady, who is about to become a member of the IDF and who is watching two old farts show their age."

"Francine Walters, General Jacob Hertzog of the Israel Defense Force, once my childhood playmate and older brother substitute, then my commanding officer in military police training, and a tiger in the IDF. Now ... I don't know what."

"A realist, maybe? My pleasure, General," Frankie said.

He took her hand. "Please, call me Jake. Now sit down and we shall have some tea. It's one of the few British customs I admire. So civilized. Let's talk about your trip to Israel. Our mutual friend McBride has told me you would like to visit Jordan. A beautiful country. Let's discuss your plans and how I can help."

****

Three hours later we boarded a commercial *El Al* flight to Eilat, Israel's southernmost city, adjacent to the Egyptian city of Taba and the Jordanian port city of Aqaba. This picturesque seaside resort on the Red Sea was a popular tourist attraction, but its location also made it a critical port city for Israel's access to East African and Southeast Asian markets.

We were met at the airport by our tourist guide, a swarthy, muscular fellow named Yoel who held the rank of captain in the IDF and who Jake had assigned to guard our butts. He had a beer gut that hung over his belt and a three-day beard, but the size of his muscular chest and arms and the way he carried himself convinced me he would be a good guy to cover our backs.

As Yoel drove to the hotel he said, "Here's the scoop," sounding as American as he could get. He had graduated from Dartmouth College and Dartmouth's Tuck Business School. "You act exactly like tourists, with me as your guide. We'll spend tonight here in Eilat, have a leisurely dinner in a restaurant overlooking the Red Sea, and set out early tomorrow morning. That's when we cross into Jordan, spend a day in a little side excursion walking through a desert called Wadi Ram." He turned to look at both of us expectantly.

Frankie responded. "That's where Lawrence of Arabia fought during World War I."

"Right on," he said with a smile. "From there we'll go to Petra." He stopped again, this time looking at Frankie.

"Capital of the Nabataean Arabs around the sixth century BC, and center of the spice trade," she said.

I was watching her face as she spoke, and I saw that same enlightened, almost astonished, "broken-jewelry-box" look. Her hands flew to her mouth as if the words had physically emerged and she could capture them and hold them up to study.

Sugar and spice and all things nice, but spice will rule the day.

"Petra!" we said together.

"Do you think that's what Sarah meant?" Frankie asked, excited.

"Certainly possible, but now the big question is, should we go to Amman to try to pick up Harry's trail or head directly to Petra?"

"What am I missing?" Yoel asked.

I explained, and he thought for a moment. "How about we do this? Let's keep the schedule I outlined. Reason is that my guess is some people are watching us, even as we are driving along, talking. I like to think I am undercover IDF, but the other side has its spies also and could know who I am." Involuntarily I looked out the window but saw nothing unusual. "So, changing plans now will send a message I don't think we want to send."

"But we're tracking a terrorist building a nuclear bomb."

"True, but we don't want to scare the quarry into hiding or maybe close down operations too soon. The IDF has already made contacts with our friends in Amman who will keep us informed. If they have something hot, we can always change our plans and go straight there. Otherwise, we continue a tourist's pace from here to Amman, stopping at the usual sites as we go. Sound okay?"

I considered that for a moment, weighing the urgency of finding Harry and the pacemakers against some excellent common sense. Saving a few days versus blowing the mission entirely. Still, playing tourist when we could be going after Harry didn't sit quite right.

"What's the real reason?"

Yoel smiled. "You have good instincts. The real reason is these guys need equipment and scientists to build the nuclear bomb, even if they have the atomic pacemakers, right? They've got to open each one, take out the plutonium, make a pile of it somehow, and then put it into a bomb."

I nodded.

"If they have been preparing to receive the pacemakers, that means they have had to import a lot of people and stuff from someplace. Maybe Syria or Iran. Or even Russia, who knows? Amman as the capital is closely guarded, so coming in there would be risky. However, Aqaba is as porous as Swiss cheese, so that would be the likely entry site. And if they came in there, they would have to travel along the Desert Highway, which happens to be exactly the route we'll be taking. And we have some friends along the way who might have seen increased activity. Make sense now?"

"Good by me," I said.

Chapter Sixty

Yoel had booked us adjoining rooms. I took the small room with a pull-out sofa bed and closed the door to the larger room where Frankie slept. We rose at sunup, had a light breakfast, and loaded food and water, luggage, and ourselves into Yoel's car. In the bright light of morning I could see the car more clearly than yesterday: a beat-up four-wheel Jeep SUV that had witnessed a lot of desert years.

"Don't be deceived," Yoel said, reading my thoughts. "Beneath this rusted exterior … is a rusted interior!" We laughed. "Seriously, this buggy can catch—or outrun—most anything around. Not to worry."

We drove to the Jordanian border. While passport control checked our identities and collected shekels for a ten-day visa, Jordanian border guards changed the car's license plate from Israeli to Jordanian. "We'll switch back when we exit."

I had a questioning look on my face.

"Routine precautions," Yoel explained. "They do it with all tourists from Israel. Young Jordanian men are unpredictable, especially after a little hashish. Best not to advertise you're an Israeli or an American if you can avoid it."

Yoel drove north on the Desert Highway connecting Aqaba to Amman. After several hours, he turned left into a small Bedouin town and we drove through on the dirt road, attracting eyes from behind curtained windows and rug-covered doors. Naked or scantily clad children played in the sand alongside "Main Street." We passed dozens of tent houses with yards filled with goats and sheep, then left "civilization" behind.

"Welcome to Wadi Ram," Yoel said. "This is a giant valley of desert in southern Jordan."

I looked around. Huge granite and sandstone cliffs reared like monoliths from the desert floor.

"This desert is so forbidding yet so magnificent; we call it the 'Valley of the Moon.'"

The vast open area of red sand and stillness apparently affected him because he promptly got us lost and then stuck in a sand dune! We piled out to help push, but sand trapped the car half way up the tires and all four spun uselessly.

"Why don't you let some air out," Frankie said, "for more traction?"

Yoel gave her an admiring look. "Mind reader," he said. "Keep her around," he said to me, smiling.

"I just might."

Yoel half-flattened the four tires and after another push, we were off again. We stopped in the shade of a small grove of bushes growing by a tiny spring and got out to stretch. Yoel spread a map on top of the engine hood and studied it before we took off again. I didn't know whether he was being very sly or whether all this was all accidental, but I didn't think anyone would need more convincing evidence we really were tourists.

Finally we arrived at Gabel Burda deep into Wadi Ram. A group of Bedouins were camped at the base of the mountain, where the only sounds were a gurgling spring and bleating goats. A single-humped camel with a bit in his mouth and a dirty blanket and saddle on his back rested on legs bent beneath him, eyes closed in repose and fat lipped jaw munching mechanically. He was tied to a tree, which seemed like an unnecessary safeguard. Two tents pitched nearby were held up by thick round poles stuck in the sand. In front of the tents two women hunched over a large squat charcoal brazier, cooking meat on skewers. The aroma wafted through the open car windows, making my stomach growl. Yoel parked in the shade of the only other tree in sight. He approached the Bedouins and spoke for some ten minutes to two men. I saw money change hands. Yoel then waved us over. "We're invited to tea. It would be rude not to accept."

We lowered our heads to enter the tent, a surprisingly spacious area covered by several layers of multicolored rugs on the sand, making it feel quite soft underfoot. We sat cross-legged on the floor in front of the two men. They wore the typical Arab clothing of a *shmagg*, the red and white checked scarf-like head covering held in place by the *ogal*, a black band around the head, and the *dishdashah*, a long sleeved one piece dress covering the entire body. Frankie and Yoel conversed with them in Arabic and I sat silent, listening. I wasn't in the mood to talk about the weather or the price of goats.

Two little kids, maybe four and five, stood in the background. I motioned them to come to me. Cautiously they approached. I reached into my pocket and gave them each a candy. They looked questioningly at one of the Arab men, who shook his head yes. The kids ripped off the paper wrapping and popped the candy in their mouths. From the smiles that lit up their faces, I guessed it must have been the very first butterscotch they ever tasted.

Finally the two women brought in a small silver tray with five glasses and a silver pot with a wooden handle and set it in front of the Arab men. Both wore the *abayah*, a long black garment covering them from shoulders to feet. From the corner of their eyes they kept glancing at Frankie, clearly an unusual guest. One of the men poured each of us a glass of tea, and we sipped the hot brew. The conversation continued until the glasses were empty, when they were promptly refilled. After another ten minutes we said our good-byes, shook hands, and left.

As we walked back to the car, Yoel said, "They wanted us to stay and share their lunch, but they were only being polite and it would have been ill-mannered to accept. Meat is very scarce and expensive."

"What did they tell you before we sat down?"

"I was coming to that. The Bedouins in the town we just drove through have been paid to watch for tourists like us traveling along the Desert Highway and into Wadi Ram. No doubt they are informers, but for who is the question. Could be for the Jordanian government, but it also could be for Iran or Syria. Regardless, it's important to show them we really are tourists. So we continue our walk in the desert. Also, I need to get to someplace high. Gabel Burda—*gabel* means mountain—is actually only a big hill, an easy climb to a neat rock bridge on top, maybe fifteen hundred meters. From there we can see for miles. It's a pretty good place to spot anything unusual. We'll go up there, have tea and a light lunch, come back to the car, and be on our way. We should arrive at the outskirts of Petra by evening. A very nice hotel there—the Sofitel in Taybeh Wadi Mousa only nine kilometers from Petra—has a great Turkish bath and restaurant."

"You make this sound like a touristy romp through Jordan."

Yoel smiled. "Trust me. Appearances can be deceiving. These friends," he looked at the encamped Bedouins, "are eyes and ears on the IDF payroll. They'll watch the car and anything else that comes along while we are gone. Oh, and by the way," he added, almost as an afterthought, "they have seen lots of trucks traveling from the port in Aqaba to Petra in the last month."

"So something's going on?"

"Not just a ... what did you say, 'touristy romp'? Ready for Gabel Burda?" I looked up at what he called a big hill and got weak kneed, visions of terrorists dissolving before the size of what we were going to climb. "Nothing dangerous about forty-five hundred feet?"

"A simple walk in the desert. The trail is well marked—you see that little pile of stones?" He pointed through the brush to a collection of brown and black flat rocks peaking with smaller ones on top, like a tiny lighthouse. It sat at the beginning of a trail up the mountain. "Bedouin marked. They've used them as roadmaps for thousands of years. We follow the markers. Nothing to it."

"I hope you read them better than the map in the car."

"Not to worry," he said with a laugh.

So we set off, slowly hiking higher and higher. Initially we climbed from one large red rock to another and admired the scenery. The grandeur of the sandstone reminded me of an Ansel Adams photo, only in color. The bright sun bathed the rocks and cliffs, drenching them with slanting rays that created skyscrapers of burnished gold, deep amber, and undulating purples.

But then we came to a ledge about six inches wide with nothing but air below and the beauty, at least for me, vanished in a single footstep. Yoel and Frankie scooted across like mountain goats. "No way, José," I said, turning back. "I'll wait for you in the car."

"Don't be a wimp. Hold my hand and I'll lead you across." Yoel came back to get me and literally took me by the hand. "Don't look down," he said. "Just stare straight ahead into the side of the mountain. With your free hand, hold onto the rock jutting out. Kind of shuffle your feet along the ledge and try to put them where mine were. Keep your toes nudging the base of the mountain so your feet know where you are and you don't slip off the edge."

"Thanks a helluva lot. I'll do my best not to!"

Frankie pranced along, fifty yards ahead. "C'mon, scaredy-cat," she said. "Nothing to it."

And so we crept across this skinny ledge about twenty-five feet long, like crabs at the beach. I started breathing again when we reached the other side and planted my feet on big, wide rocks once more.

"I hope that's the end of six inch ledges," I said.

"Maybe one or two more," Yoel said.

I looked back at what I had just crossed. "I can't believe I did that."

"Outward Bound, courtesy of the Israel Defense Force. When this is over, heights will never frighten you again," Yoel said.

I wasn't so convinced.

Two hours later we arrived below the rock bridge. The approach was up a flat face of mountain so steep Yoel went first to check it out.

"Maybe we should put you in the harness, just in case," he said looking down from twenty-five feet overhead. He threw down a canvas jacket attached to a long rope that he secured around a jagged outcropping.

"Frankie, snug the straps across his chest and around his waist. Then, give him a boost." She did, pushed on my bottom, and up I went, not looking down, pulling myself hand-over-hand, feet braced against the mountain, hoping the rope was new.

"This is fantastic," Frankie said, on top in a twinkling and already crossing the rock bridge.

Inching along that narrow arch of stone spanning a thousand feet of nothing below was about the scariest thing in recent memory. But the view from the other side of the mountain was spectacular for miles around. The granite and sandstone faces seemed on fire. Yoel took out a pair of powerful binoculars from his backpack and scanned a very slow 360 degrees. He then walked to the highest point of the mountain and made a twenty-minute call on his cell phone. I suspect this may have been the major reason for the climb. At the lower altitudes, the mountains interfered with transmission.

"Our Bedouin friends were right," he said after the call. "Big time movements from Aqaba to Petra. People and equipment over the past month or so. Seems Scarpia slipped out of Amman and has vanished. He may be in Petra, but no one's had a visual, so it's a guess."

"Should we leave for Petra now?"

"I see no reason to change plans. We'll be in the outskirts of Petra tonight and will do our tourist thing in the morning. Let's eat. And ignore the tail we seemed to have picked up."

Startled, I looked around. "Where?"

"Behind the large bolder, directly over your left shoulder. Below the arch. Big guy, swarthy complexion."

I spun to my left but saw no one. "How do you know he's not another climber?"

"My Bedouin friends spotted him. Let's eat."

"Here?" I asked, looking down. "So close to the edge? With a possible enemy within shooting distance?"

"Sure. Prop your back against the side of the mountain, and remember not to look down. Frankie can make the sandwiches." He took off his backpack and removed an Uzi.

I pointed at the submachine gun.

"In case our big friend gets too nosy," he said, propping it against a small shrub. "I'll boil water for tea."

"Boil water?" Yoel's cool was unnerving. "And how do you plan to do that?"

"With this." Yoel removed a small kerosene stove from his backpack, lit it, and put on a kettle filled with bottled water. We drank fresh tea at forty-five hundred feet.

And so, feeling a little jittery over the height and uninvited company, I ate lunch, drank hot tea, and took a leak while Frankie turned her head. I returned her the favor. Then we went back down—very carefully. It didn't get less scary. A six-inch ledge was six inches in both directions.

Whoever was tailing us kept out of sight—or at least I didn't see him. When we reached bottom, I thanked Yoel for making me do things I couldn't believe I'd ever do, and certainly would never do again.

"Yoel, I'm not gay, but I've never enjoyed holding another man's hand as much as I did holding yours today!"

"Next time try mine," Frankie said with a fleeting smile.

On the ride to Petra, I thought about just that.

Chapter Sixty-One

We arrived at the Sofitel hotel late that afternoon in time to watch a golden sunset blanket the desert sands. The hotel was a welcome surprise, a lush four-star Bedouin-styled resort in the middle of nowhere. An expansive veranda wrapped around the main entrance. It had a secluded section where ten hookah pipes stood on a ruby red rug like little silver soldiers guarding a table, waiting for after dinner smokers. In the back of the hotel, a huge swimming pool beckoned from the middle of an expanse of purple tiles. Private rooms were in air-conditioned stone guest houses complete with satellite television and direct-dial telephones. The hotel even sported an Arab souk where local pottery, woven baskets, and other crafts produced on site were sold.

"Okay, guys," Yoel said. "I have a lot of paperwork to do, so I am going to get room service and spend the night working. I highly recommend the Turkish steam bath and massage on the ground floor before dinner. I'm sure you've got a few sore muscles from our little walk." He smiled at me. "It'll get you in shape for tomorrow."

"Another leisurely trek in the desert?" I asked.

"No telling, but I'm sure it will be a pleasant surprise," he said as he got his bag to go to his room. "Petra lies in Wada Araba, a valley running from the Dead Sea to the Aqaba Gulf, a sort of basin at the foot of the mountains. So you may have the opportunity to show your newly acquired climbing skills."

"Great," Frankie said. "Don't forget to re-inflate the tires."

"Already done. Enjoy your evening. See you bright and early in the morning."

I put a hand on his arm. "I don't want to seem impatient or anything, but we *are* chasing a terrorist making a nuclear bomb."

"Zach, we have to sleep somewhere tonight. The Sofitel is the best around and close to Petra. We're not going to rush into Petra on white horses and say, 'Stick 'em up' like in one of your cowboy movies. Stop with the guilt. It's okay to enjoy the evening. Scarpia will be there in the morning. Judging from the trucks and supplies going in, we have a few more days. My people are watching."

"I guess Israeli cops are different," I said to Frankie after Yoel left. "But he's right about sore muscles," I said, rubbing my chest. "I don't know about you, but I must have knocked against the side of Gabel Burda a dozen times. A steam room and massage sounds great. What do you think?"

"I've never had one before. What do you do?"

"I'm sure there's a robe hanging in the closet of your room. Put it on and meet me in the basement in a few minutes."

"What do I wear under the robe?"

"Your imagination."

So we met in the steam room, our white robes in the fog transforming us into ghosts. The room was a blue-tiled square box big enough for four people to sit on wooden benches along two walls. A red-hot fire hissed and crackled, boiling a huge pot of water into heavy wet steam that made taking a deep breath seem like work. Through the mist I could barely see Frankie sitting next to me.

An ethereal voice broke the stillness. "Good evening. I am Dmitry, your attendant. Please to adjust how much steam you want by opening or closing this little curtain," said Dmitry as he walked in and pushed back the cloth covering the entry.

"Good evening. Your accent—it's not Middle Eastern," said Frankie.

"I am from Moscow. I have worked all the Sofitel hotels around Europe, sometimes like waiter, sometimes like bartender. For here, I am to be a Turkish masseur. I like this job the best," he said, flexing large hands with sausage fingers.

"Why?" Frankie asked.

"I get to know my guests very well after a massage. People who have no clothes cannot hide anything."

Frankie gave a little gasp.

"I will come for you one at a time when the steam has loosened your muscles. This is the meat tenderizing stage."

I leaned back against the cushion and sighed, letting my body succumb to the soporific waves of wet heat. "Man, I didn't know I hurt in so many places. My legs look like someone has been kicking me in the shins all day." I stuck one out from under the robe for Frankie to see, but she couldn't because of the dense steam. Instead, she ran a light hand over my shin, tracing the bumps. It felt like a soft breeze riffling my skin.

"I can feel them," she said. "You need more practice as a rock climber. You've got to stay close to the surface of the mountain, but not that close."

"Thanks a lot. Now you tell me." But her gentle touch raised a different issue and I pulled the robe tighter.

Dmitry saved the day. "Medium-rare time. Who would like to be the first one for me to go to work?"

"I'll go," I said, perhaps a bit too quickly. "Okay, Frankie?"

"I'm fine here," she mumbled in a sleepy voice. "Only don't forget to come back and get me before I'm well-done."

I followed Dmitry to an even smaller steam room down the hall that had a raised platform covered by a rug. "Please to take off the robe and lay down on stomach." I obeyed and then his hands did the rest, lathering on oil and playing my muscles as a talented concert pianist played the ivories.

I closed my eyes and let him work. I was transported into a dream-like state with the steam fogging my mind as well as my body. I drifted along, curled up safe in some sort of white cocoon, floating over a sunlit meadow of soft cotton. Wherever I was, I had never been there before and didn't want to leave. Unfortunately, Dmitry's hands stopped with a light pat on my shoulder and so did the spell. I woke with a bizarre thought—I don't know from where—that the bath and massage were like some sort of Roman gladiator ritual on the eve of a pitched battle. I remembered from high school Latin, "*Morituri te salutamus. We who are about to die salute you.*" Away went my dreamlike state and I plunged back down to earth-hard reality, hoping the phrase would prove wrong.

Frankie had her turn and we went back to our adjacent rooms to shower for dinner.

Dinner in the Sahtain Restaurant was excellent, as Yoel had promised, and we washed down lamb kabobs, rice, and grape leaves stuffed with ground beef and sweet onions with—I couldn't believe it—a bottle of 2004 David Bruce Pinot Noir from Sonoma Valley. After espressos we returned to our rooms.

I was gathering my courage to knock on Frankie's door when someone knocked on mine. *Can't be her,* I thought.

It wasn't. The concierge stood there with a bottle of Dom Perignon champagne nestled in an ice-filled silver bucket.

"Compliments from an admirer," he said. He placed the bucket on a table in my room and left.

I stewed for a millisecond about what to do and then knocked on Frankie's door. She answered wearing the terrycloth robe she had worn to the steam bath. "I was just getting ready for bed," she said.

I held up the bottle. "From Yoel."

Her eyes lit up. "Your room or mine?"

I glanced at her robe. "Depends on whether you're wearing your imagination under that."

Her smiled broadened and she swung her door open. "I guess you'll have to find out for yourself."

I followed her into the room, identical to mine, and set the bucket on a table next to the door. She turned to me, eyes twinkling. "I've never had a Jewish detective before."

"Do I have to sit up and beg?"

"Not if you're good." She put her hand on my cheek and stroked it. "A little rough." She stood on her toes, pressed her body against me, and her cheek on mine. She kissed my ear. "But not that rough."

Her hair smelled of coconut, the same shampoo in my shower. I put my arms around her and just held her tight. She burrowed her face into my neck. The warmth from her body made me realize how long I had been without a woman.

"You want the champagne now?" I whispered through her hair.

"Depends."

"On what?" I asked.

"On how thirsty you are."

Her hand dropped and her fingers danced along the front of my pants. "Something tells me you may not be thirsty, but you're very hungry."

I undid the cloth sash and slipped both hands under her robe, hugging her to me. She had on a bra and panties. I fumbled with the bra clasp until it opened. She shrugged out of her robe, and I pushed the bra straps from her shoulders. Her breasts were full and firm, nipples erect. "Hmm. Nice," I said.

"Your turn," she said, unbuttoning my shirt. When I slid it off, she said, "Hmm. Nice, yourself."

We kissed and she unfastened my belt and slacks. I stepped out of them and kicked them aside. We hugged again, her breasts tight against my bare chest. She slid her hands inside the back my shorts and I did the same to her, pulling her toward me.

"Good buns," we said simultaneously and laughed.

I picked her up and carried her to the bed. Her arms were linked around my neck when I lowered her to the mattress. She held tight and raised her hips as I slipped her panties off and then my shorts. We kissed, and she pulled me down on top of her.

Afterward, we fell asleep in each other's arms and that's how the sun found us the next morning to begin a day we'd never forget.

Chapter Sixty-Two

Yoel met us for breakfast. "Here's what I've been able to find out. Scarpia's definitely arrived in Petra. One of our guys got a clear visual with a telescopic lens. He likely came several days ago, with wooden crates on the back of two mules. Unknown to us or the Jordanian government, the back stairs in Petra have been closed off for the past month by a group of local Bedouins."

I was about to ask a question when Yoel answered it. "The back stairs is a climb of some nine hundred steps, chiseled into the mountainside that goes to *El Deir*, a huge, magnificent monastery carved into the face of the sandstone mountain. The tourist approach is to walk up the steps or be carried on the back of a donkey. The path, which is a pretty steep climb at times, weaves northwest through the surrounding cliffs to this enormous plateau in front of the monastery. Most people don't know there is another access to *El Deir* around the back. The plateau extends further to the north, past the monastery, and then literally plunges into a deep gorge, kind of like a mini Grand Canyon, called Wadi Marwan. With mules and experienced hikers, someone could carry all kinds of equipment through this back way and avoid detection. They could either come up through Wadi Marwan or maybe skirt along its rim, because the canyon ends at the plateau. Then, they could set up their lab or whatever is needed inside *El Deir* and do their stuff."

"That's where the operation is?"

"That's what we believe. Pretty clever now that I think of it. No one outside would know what they were doing for quite some time, right under tourists' noses. The weak link is how long they could keep closure of the steps from being reported to the central tourist agency or the government. If they bribed the appropriate Petra officials and some of the guides, I'm sure they could get away with a month or more, certainly long enough to take the pacemakers apart and build their bomb."

"So what's our plan?" I asked.

"Our problem is no one has seen what I've described up close, so it's hard to prove and therefore to plan anything. That's what we need to do—go as tourists and try to see as much of their operation as possible. Then we'll be able to devise an attack strategy and call in the troops."

****

"Petra is an ancient city of beauty that cannot be imagined," our guide Hassan said as we began our walk down the *Siq*, or gorge. Petra had its own tourist bureau, so we had to hire a local to show us around. Hassan had pushed to the front of the line to take us. "The entrance we are walking along is a crack in the sandstone cliffs that winds through the mountains." He pointed to both sides. "These mountains climb hundreds of meters on each side of us. People living here for many centuries could easily defend such a narrow path against invaders and stay safe."

I looked up from the russet road to the towering mountains and saw marbled whorls of whites, pinks, reds, and browns. Tombs cut into the striated rock looked like caves big enough to house the living rather than interments for the dead. Tourist carriages driven by drivers whipping donkeys passed us wherever the *Siq* broadened. An aqueduct system chiseled in the stone on one side of the *Siq* snaked along the base of the mountain just above the path.

"Yes, the Nabataeans were great engineers. Petra has a stream of fresh water all the year, but sometimes heavy rains made floods, or no rains made it go dry."

"A drought?" Frankie asked.

"Yes. A drought sometimes and floods other times. So the Arabs built what you call sluices and cisterns that catched the extra water and stored it to stop the flooding and to use for the drought. It was like the best Roman plumbing," Hassan said, "until they had an earthquake in the fourth century that destroyed some of the pipes and started Petra to go down the hill."

"Downhill?" Frankie asked.

"Yes."

Every several hundred yards or so I saw a group of two or three Bedouins who weren't moving with the tourist flow and seemed more interested in us than in the beauty of the place. Some had bulges beneath their robes. Yoel and I connected glances but neither said anything.

After twenty minutes of walking down the narrow gorge, sometimes only several meters wide and giving me twinges of claustrophobia as the soaring mountains blotted out the sky, the *Siq* abruptly opened into "downtown city central."

"Oh, it's awesome," Frankie exclaimed, and I heard a sharp intake of breath. It was like coming to a crack in a sheer rock wall, barely large enough to squeeze through, saying *Open Sesame*, and crossing into another world beyond.

"*Al Khazneh*," Frankie said, pointing. "The treasury. I can't believe I'm actually standing in front of it. That picture is on the front page of so many travel brochures. It's as famous as the one of Machu Picchu."

I stared at this magnificent building, a rose-colored edifice forty meters high with two floors of elaborate Corinthian columns, topped by lintels and pediments and crowned by a gigantic urn, all intricately sculpted into the sandstone cliff. Frankie's gasp was quite appropriate.

Hassan continued. "They thought *Al Khazneh* maybe was to hide treasure, but who knows—maybe it was a temple or a tomb. Look at this square room in its base." He pointed. "Very plain insides and beautiful outsides, like for all the buildings in Petra. The people, they enjoyed the outsides to look nicer than the insides." We walked in. The room was smooth walled, simple, with no ornaments at all, a rectangle cut into the side of the cliff. "*El Deir*, the monastery, is like this with a very large plain room in its base. You go in by a doorway about eight meters high. Its front is bigger than *Al Khazneh*, about fifty meters wide and forty-five tall, but the wind wore down its edges so *El Deir* is not as pretty as *Al Khazneh*."

I thought if *El Deir* had a room similar to this but larger, it would be perfect for Harry's purpose. Block off the entrance and you had a great laboratory. "When do we see *El Deir*?" I asked.

"I'm afraid we cannot. The authorities have closed the steps to it off," Hassan said. Yoel gave me a slight confirmatory nod.

So we wandered Petra, stopping to walk through the eight-thousand-seat amphitheater cleaved in the mountainside, the many tombs, and the High Place of Sacrifice where animals were killed. We watched an artist create a nomadic scene inside a small glass bottle using different colored sands, and we bought handmade jewelry from a Bedouin mother guarding her brood playing in the sand. She observed *hijab*, or modesty in dress, by wearing a *chador*, the big black baggy cloth women wore to cover their bodies and faces. I passed out candy to her squealing kids. We couldn't look or act more like tourists, but I noticed the same groups of Bedouins following us along at a distance.

Gradually our walk took us to the base of the nine hundred steps. As we approached, we saw a sign in English and Arabic: *Steps unsafe and closed for repair. El Deir cannot be seen this day.* Two large Bedouins stood on either side of the first step. I could see the grip of a gun, probably the butt of an AK-47, peek out of the robe of the bigger guy.

Hassan said we couldn't go there.

"That's too bad. I was looking forward to the climb to the monastery," said Yoel. "When will the steps be opened again?" he asked the Bedouin, who put his hand on the gun butt. Clearly something about Yoel made him nervous.

"I do not know. We have been ordered to make sure no one tries to walk up the steps because it is so dangerous. You could fall off the mountain. Come again another time. Maybe in a week or two, after it is repaired."

"I'm a licensed guide as you can see." Yoel flashed his plastic ID hanging from a cord around his neck. "We weren't told of such a problem."

"I cannot help that," the guard replied. "We have our orders what I told you."

"Will this change the orders?" Yoel took out a new two hundred-shekel note, worth about fifty dollars.

The guard snatched and pocketed it. "No. You still cannot go up."

"Then give me back my money."

"What money? Ghazi, did you see any money?" he asked the other guard.

Ghazi shook his head, laughing. "No, Amir, none."

Yoel brushed it off. "Amir, is it? Suppose we try the climb ourselves and take our own chances with the danger. We'll tell anyone Amir warned us, and if anything happens it was not your fault. How would that be?" As he said this, Yoel started up the lower steps.

"No! Stop!" the guard shouted, grabbing Yoel's arm and spinning him around. Yoel had to clutch my shoulder to keep from falling. "I said no one is to pass, and that means for you. You do not try that again or bad things will happen." He opened his robe slightly to show the AK-47.

Two groups of Bedouins approached us. "Okay, sorry. We won't," Yoel said, backing away from the step with his hands raised, palms forward. "But I will report this to the Bureau of Tourists."

Amir shrugged. "You do what you want as long as you do not try to go up those stairs again."

We strolled away at a nonchalant pace. I paid off Hassan and told him we'd like to do the rest of the tour on our own. He gave me a funny look but took the money and walked away.

"What do you think?" Yoel asked me when we were well out of earshot.

"I think they mean business. No way are they going to let us up those stairs. We could take the two of them. Both Frankie and I are packing, not the heavy equipment he has, but we'd have the element of surprise."

"Yeah, and his buddies would be on us like a pack of wolves," Yoel said.

"I could show a little leg," Frankie said with a smile.

"Not here. This isn't New York. I think there's a better way, but I doubt you're going to like it," Yoel said.

"And that is?"

"There's a small road from Petra to a place called Gabel Abu-Swera that's on the other side of Wadi Marwan."

"What's that?" Frankie asked.

"*Wadi* means gorge or canyon. Wadi Marwan is like Jordan's Grand Canyon, as I told you. It abuts the end of the plateau outside *El Deir* and flows into Wadi Musa that goes from Petra towards the Araba Valley. We would drive around it, placing the canyon between us and the monastery. This would give us a way to get close to *El Deir* without being spotted."

"How? It can't be a simple walk, judging by the look on your face. You're not suggesting we climb down one side and up the other, like going from Grand Canyon's north to south rim?" I asked.

He shook his head. "The canyon ends here. We could stroll around the rim from Gabel Abu-Swera and come to *El Deir*."

"Sounds good to me," I said.

"And get shot doing it. You see, the rim is totally unprotected and we'd be spotted in an instant."

"I don't think I'm going to like your next suggestion," I said.

Yoel smiled in agreement. "Or we can walk down from the rim maybe ten meters into Wadi Marwan, find a Bedouin trail and follow it around until we get to the other side, climb out, and we're at the plateau in front of *El Deir*."

"Whoa. You're talking about walking along a path *in the side of the canyon*, not on the top?"

"Something like that. There's this ledge—"

"I think this plan sucks," I said.

"Why?"

"Because what's to prevent us—well, maybe not *us*, *me*—from falling off that ledge or whatever you think we're going to walk around on, down to the fucking bottom of the canyon?"

"You're a pro now. It won't be any worse than Gabel Burda—well, not much worse. Besides, have you got any better ideas?"

"Frankie, what do you think?"

"It's doable. How about this? Zach, you walk between us attached by a rope front and back. That way we can guide you without holding your hand and maybe catch you if you fall."

"Yeah, right. Your one hundred twenty pounds is going to prevent my two hundred and twenty pounds from plummeting to the bottom of the canyon! Good luck. You'll both end up going with me. How about we just call for the troops?"

"Like I said before, we've been asked to reconnoiter, give them the information, and then they'll come," Yoel said.

We continued our stroll through Petra, walking out the *Siq* as we had come in, along with hundreds of other tourists. When we got to the car, Yoel said, "This is the tricky part. We need to drive like we're leaving, double back on the trail in the desert to the other side of the canyon, and then hide the car. Once we're in the canyon I doubt we'll be spotted. Now would be a good time to check weapons. I'll take my Uzi and several extra clips. What have you two got?"

Frankie took out a .45 from her backpack and I showed him the Smith and Wesson .38 beneath my arm and my 9-millimeter semiautomatic on my ankle. "Kind of lightweight for this action, but they'll do," Yoel said. "Let's go."

Chapter Sixty-Three

Yoel drove out of Petra at a leisurely pace, made some false turns as if he were a lost tourist, and finally got onto the trail to Gabel Abu-Swera in the desert. He parked the car behind a large, round sand dune. "Pay attention to where we are, in case we get separated." He glanced at me with a look that implied one of us might not be coming back. "I'll lock the car and leave the keys in this magnetic case attached to the inside of the front bumper." He bent over the bumper. "Right here." I heard the metallic click as the magnet fastened.

We walked a short distance to the canyon. The sun beat down on us in early afternoon, and I was glad we had extra water in our backpacks. As we came to the trail down Wadi Marwan, I picked up a rock and threw it into the void. It took forever before the stone bounced off a boulder at the bottom. I looked at Frankie's face. She was excited, actually looking forward to this.

I followed the two of them, half sliding down the first twenty feet into the gorge, grabbing onto whatever I could to stop my fall. Yoel gave me a shoulder block like an open field tackle to keep me from overshooting the ledge. Not a great start.

I walked between them, untied, trying to copy Yoel's moves. The beginning of the trail was reasonably wide—at least two feet—so we moved quickly. Then came the first six-inch ledge spanning the void below. Yoel strolled across as if he were shopping at a mall and waited impatiently on the other side. Frankie was behind me with her hands lightly on my waist, trying to offer stability, both moral and physical. My heart pounded as I looked into the chasm and then at six inches of bumpy sandstone. I really was frozen, a totally new experience for me.

"You can do it," Frankie whispered in my ear. "Remember what we told you and how you did it at Gabel Burda. Don't think about the ledge. Double the width in your mind."

So I told myself it was twelve inches wide. That was still too narrow, so I made it twenty-four. What bullshit, I thought, knowing the head game wouldn't work for me. Anyway, I had to go. I stared at the mountain, averting my gaze from the rocks below, grabbed at outcroppings in the wall, shuffled my feet as Yoel did, and fought some of my fear.

Fuck it, I finally said to myself. *If I fall, I fall, but I've got to get across.* I crossed that ledge and about ten more, trembling before each one. Then I finally made it across, sighing with relief. I'd have rather faced an armed killer in a dark alley any day. Finally we turned the curve at the end of the canyon and came up under the plateau. The path to the top of the rim was almost straight up, and I had to literally pull myself along on my hands and knees.

Maybe that was what kept me from getting shot.

Yoel, walking ahead, was nearing the canyon rim when I heard the *ping* of a high-powered rifle, and he fell back toward me. I grabbed at him with one arm, holding onto the trunk of a skinny tree with the other. The tree slowed us but gradually uprooted and we began to tumble toward the gorge. Frankie somehow threw her one hundred twenty pounds at me, dug her heels in the ground and her back against the mountain, and stopped our freefall, halting us inches short of a plunge to the bottom.

I rolled Yoel onto his back and looked at his wound. It was a high chest shot that shattered his right clavicle and probably collapsed his lung. I could see both entry and exit sites. The bullet had nicked the subclavian artery, which was pulsing in angry red spurts. His eyes were starting to glaze as he tried to say something but couldn't.

"Frankie, check his backpack for first aid stuff!" I took the phone off his belt and tried to dial. All I got was static. We were too deep in the gorge.

She found bandages that I stuffed into the hole in his chest. I took off my belt and cinched it around his shoulder, compressing the binding into his wound. The bleeding slowed to a trickle.

"Did you see where the shot came from?"

She shook her head.

"Neither did I, but I think there's someone standing on the rim. See that shadow near the tree?" I pointed. We both drew weapons and fired. The shadow disappeared out of sight. "That must have been it, but I don't think I got a hit."

"Me neither. These pea shooters work better at Joe's Guns."

"I'm going to try to get Yoel's." He had dropped his Uzi when he got shot, and it was about ten feet from me, caught in a shrub. "Cover me." While she got off a stream of shots from her .45, I snaked my way over to the bush, grabbed the submachine gun, turned, and sprayed the rim where the shadow had been. Then I crawled back to her.

"You need to get out of here. I can hold them off with this for a few minutes. No way are they coming after you over those ledges, and the undergrowth will protect you from the guys on the rim. Get back to the car and get the hell out." I handed her the phone. "Call Hertzog. I think we've got enough for him to come."

She shook her head. "I'm not leaving you."

"Brave sentiments but not realistic. One of us has to get out alive."

She shook her head again, tears welling up, her mouth set in a stubborn line.

I glanced around. We were reasonably well protected by the underbrush, but we were also pinned down by open space on either side. Going up was out of the question and down was the bottom of the canyon, a sheer drop. We could hold them off as long as our ammo lasted and maybe escape when darkness fell, although we'd have to find another way back. Six inch ledges in the dark? Forget it. I didn't even know if we had packed a flashlight.

The problem was Yoel. Blood had soaked through the bandage, and if he had any chance to survive, we'd have to get him medical attention soon. There was no way we could carry him back the way we came.

"Frankie, the guy on top's got us boxed in unless we make a break for it. I'm going to try to take him out. Cover me." I poked my head from around the bush, ready for a run to the top. The whine of the bullet missing me by inches changed my mind in a hurry. Automatic fire from several other sites on the rim followed.

Then a voice above yelled, "Your situation is without hope. We have more than five guns pointed at you. If you want to get out alive, put your hands on top of your head and walk to the top."

I looked at Frankie and checked Yoel. He was not moving and was barely conscious. I could feel a faint pulse in his neck, so he still had a chance. "We've got to try to save him," I said. She agreed with a nod.

"You shot my friend. I can't leave him or he'll die," I yelled back. "Will you let me carry him to the top so we can get a doctor?" I knew there wasn't much I could do about it, whatever they said. But I had to give Yoel a chance to survive.

"Leave him there and we will come and get him after you come up."

"No, I'll bring him up."

A warning shot ricocheted off the bark of the tree next to me.

"Leave him."

"I can't do that. So, if you want us, it'll have to be with him."

"Stand with your hands on top of your head. The lady too." We both did.

"Now come up the path very slowly."

"I can't and still keep my hands on my head."

"Look up here."

I squinted into the sun and saw three more men with guns trained on us move to where the shadow had been.

"Use your hands to climb, but make no mistake as you come up. It will be your last."

Frankie helped me put Yoel over my shoulder and we frog-climbed twenty feet to the rim, hauling ourselves along by pulling at the underbrush. I barely made it. At the top, I laid Yoel on the ground. The climb had opened his wound and the bandage looked like a red sponge. I doubted he'd make it.

They were on us in an instant, and I recognized faces that had followed our tour.

"You must think we are stupid," Amir said, shaking his head. "You are not like the typical Petra tourist. Fortunately for you there were so many real tourists around, or you would not have made it this far." He gave a look to Ghazi and another man and they patted me down, taking my guns. Ghazi bound my hands behind my back with plastic cuff restraints, very professionally. The guards searched Frankie's body a lot more slowly than they did mine, but she stared them in the eye without flinching. Ghazi took her .45.

"You have come such a long way, I am sure you want to see Hrayr and his pacemakers," Amir said.

"Can you get a doctor for our friend first?" I asked.

Amir glanced at Yoel lying unmoving on the ground and then pointed at two burly guys. They lifted Yoel and held him up between them. Amir nodded at Ghazi standing behind Yoel. Ghazi moved close to Yoel and said in his ear, "I hope you enjoyed your tea on the mountain, Captain." Before I could move, he fired Frankie's .45 into the back of Yoel's head. The two men supporting Yoel let him go and he tumbled down into the ravine.

"Sorry about that," Amir said. "The gun must have misfired."

"You son of a bitch," I shouted. "He did nothing to you." I struggled and lunged at Ghazi, but Amir and another guy held me tight. Frankie gasped and then sobbed. "He was a good man," she said.

They pushed us across the plateau to *El Deir*. It was a giant monolith sculpted into the stone like *Al Khazneh*, some fifteen to twenty stories high. The monastery had a huge front room, also like *Al Khazneh*, but much bigger. They had fashioned a protective canvas to cover the entrance, shutting it off from the world and the environment, without damaging the stone. They obviously were not worried about break-ins, since they had secured this entire area. Ghazi shouted something in Arabic as we approached, and a door in the canvas opened to let us enter.

Inside, the transformation was incredible, and I had to remind myself I was standing in a city twenty-five hundred years old and not in the most cutting-edge laboratory of the Atomic Energy Commission in the middle of downtown Manhattan. Fluorescent lights hung from the high ceiling, making the dark room as bright as it was outside. Sleek countertops of stainless steel were divided into individual work stations with scientists hunched over microscopes and whirling centrifuges. Metal vents over some of the counters connected to long tin shafts that funneled noxious vapors outside. Men on Segways were busy picking up and delivering between scientists. I heard the high-pitched whirr of cutter blades opening the welded seams of the pacemakers. An emergency chemical shower hung from the ceiling near the lead-proof glass enclosure where the plutonium was being collected.

"Hello, Zach," Harry said as he walked up to us. "Nice to see you again. And you too, Frankie. Thanks for giving me a second chance."

"Oh, my God," Frankie said, leaning against me.

I fought the handcuffs but it was useless. They just bit my wrists. "You know, Harry, even after all the evidence, I still had trouble believing it was you," I said, "that my friend could commit such brutal murders."

He laughed. "You really are a very naive man, Zach. I expect that in Americans, but you are an Israeli, so it surprises me. You call me your friend? Hardly." He laughed again. "We come from such ancient traditions, you and I, where time is measured in centuries. Grievances are passed from one family member to another until they are settled. Ten years is yesterday. We have been planning this operation ever since I saw you kill my father and brother."

"You had plenty of chances for revenge."

"Oh, indeed I did, but killing you during the course of police work would have been too easy. I liked saving your life so I could be the one to end it. And to do that while killing the leaders of the United States and its allies made it even better."

"What happens now?" I asked.

"It would be very easy to have you join your friend, and I have considered doing just that. But you might be more useful alive for the moment. You see, we have a much better way of dealing with non-believers and murderers."

Frankie's response was a whisper. "*Stoning*."

Chapter Sixty-Four

"Indeed. But this one will be a major event for all of our supporters to watch. Unlike the crude videos on the Internet, this stoning will be a professional event. We will invite CNN to cover it. My friends will cheer as each takes a turn with a rock, from the youngest boys to the old men, many of whom knew my father and brother."

"You're fucking crazy," Frankie said.

"Crazy? No, I don't think so. Stoning is an ancient and revered capital punishment in Islam." I watched his face carefully. His look was demonic, eyes wide and excited. "It is said that the prophet Mohammed pronounced stoning as punishment for a pair of adulterers, so I am merely following tradition. You both know what to expect, don't you?

"Your faces are blank. Let me explain so it is perfectly clear. Your hands will be tied behind your backs and you will be put in a cloth sack, white linen so the bleeding shows through. Then you are buried in a hole, women to their shoulders and men to their necks, recognizing the different strengths of the sexes and their ability to escape."

Frankie started to cry again, but Harry ignored her.

"The crowd, restrained to a certain distance by a circle drawn around you, will throw palm-sized stones—neither too small, as a pebble that does no harm, nor too large to kill you instantly—until you are dead or you escape and cross the line of the circle. Of course, the latter will be impossible with your tied hands and your bodies buried in the hole, but we try to make it a little sporting."

"One like this?" Amir, excited, handed Harry a stone.

Harry flipped the stone over in his hand, testing its heft. "Perfect, Amir. Thanks. You can be the first to throw this at my *friend*." He sneered the word, looking at me.

"That's what you have to look forward to. Now, I have to oversee the final stages of the bomb preparation. We are very close. We've collected nine hundred and ninety-three pacemakers and have extracted the plutonium from just about all of them." He swept his arm over the expanse of the room. "It will be a shame to turn this modern scientific laboratory back into a stop-off attraction for gawking tourists, but that was my agreement with the locals. They do need the income and *El Deir* is a big draw. So, if you'll excuse me, I have much to do. We have to meet a very special deadline very precisely."

He turned to go but then came back. "You will be my guests for one or two more days. Amir, you and Ghazi know where to put my *friends* to make them comfortable, don't you?" Harry climbed on a Segway and sped off to the other side of the room.

Amir grabbed my arm and Ghazi took Frankie's and they led us to the back of the room, where a hole dug in the floor at least twenty feet deep was littered with thin shiny metal containers looking like flattened tennis ball halves. They must have been the opened casings of the pacemakers.

"Our storage pit," Amir said. "It is deep enough to keep any radiation from leaking out. We will fill it back in when we are finished. It will be interesting when archeologists a hundred years from now explore Petra and find modern pacemakers in this pit. They will think, 'What an advanced society lived here.'" He laughed.

"I am sorry we do not offer four star accommodations," said Ghazi, dragging over a ladder. "No blankets, but later we will give you a nice white sheet to wear."

Climbing down the ladder was tough with our hands cuffed in the back. We backed down, leaning forward as far as possible and stepping on each rung carefully to keep from falling. Amir watched us closely, his automatic ready, and there was no chance to escape. Frankie went down without mishap. I was only halfway when the ladder jerked and I fell the last ten feet, landing on one hand and my butt. I heard laughter above as they withdrew the ladder.

"Your hand's bleeding," Frankie said.

"Quiet," I whispered. "Wait until they leave."

The bottom was damp, and I figured we must have been close to the underground water level. The air was chilly out of the sun, and we huddled together to stay warm. After another hour or so, the work above gradually slowed and then stopped. The major overhead lights went black as the scientists left for the night.

Harry appeared out of the gloom. "I've made my plans about the stoning, and I wanted to let you know. Zach, you will debut in the amphitheater below the nine hundred steps—perhaps you saw it during your tour? We'll invite CNN and the world, because the bomb will be in the U.S. by then and the stoning will provide a nice distraction. Petra is impregnable by foot, but is easily attacked by helicopters landing on the plain right outside *El Deir*. So a public stoning before the bomb left for the U.S. would invite an attack prematurely. Therefore, the first stoning will be only for you Frankie, tomorrow morning in front of *El Deir*, as a kind of thank-you to my staff before the final push. But it will have to be a private affair with only us and the workers present. I wanted you to have the night to think about it. Now I'm leaving for a lovely meal and a little wine. Start with Dom Perignon and then a nice David Bruce from Sonoma. Good night." The room went black and I could hear him chuckling as he walked away.

"Frankie, are you okay?"

"If you call being scared out of my mind okay, then I guess I am. What are we going to do?"

"The edges of the pacemaker halves are sharp. That's what cut me when I fell."

"You think that'll work?"

"Grab a pacemaker half. Then turn back-to-back with me and see if you can saw through the plastic handcuffs."

Frankie cut for thirty or forty minutes, discarding the can for a new one every several minutes after the edges quickly dulled.

"My hands are cramping." She rested and then worked for another hour without success. With my fingertip I could feel the groove in the hard plastic, but it was very shallow. "It's difficult holding the half in my hands."

"Let me try to get yours off." I sawed at hers until my hands cramped also. After three hours I finally cut through, and Frankie was freed! Now with both hands functioning she went back to work on mine. In an hour she did it. It was now early morning and we still had to get out. The work had warmed us, but we were thirsty and tired, and our hands were sore with lots of little cuts.

"We can't stop now. Climb on my shoulders and see if you can scale the wall." I lifted her up and she stood on her toes as I held her ankles.

"I can't," she said. I heard the frustration in her voice. "I can't reach the top, and the wall is so smooth I can't get a grip on anything." I let her down.

"Let's try this." I linked my fingers to make a cradle. "Put your foot in my palms and I'll slingshot you to the top." I bent low, lifted her by the foot, and flipped as hard as I could, while she kicked forward to propel herself to the top. She fell back each time. The wall was too high. She sat with her back propped against the wall, hands over her eyes.

"Frankie, we're not quitting. If we can't go up, we'll go down. You see how damp the floor is? I think we're just above water. Maybe we can dig down into an underground stream or something. Remember how the guide said there was a great aqueduct system?"

We converted the pacemaker halves from knives to shovels and began scooping out handfuls of dirt. A few feet down, we hit something hard that had a rounded shape and the consistency of clay. Before I could dig further, a light spread above us and I could hear conversations. The workday had begun. I checked my watch but stared at an empty wrist. Amir had it. I heard him and Ghazi talking as they approached. Frankie's face blanched.

"It is now time for doing the show," Amir said to Ghazi. "Hrayr will be here soon, and we want to have everything ready for him." His head peered down at us. I stood over the hole, which I had quickly filled in with dirt, hoping he would not notice.

"Oh, we have some busy guests, Ghazi. They have managed to remove the handcuffs. Good work for the two of you, but it will not matter."

I heard Ghazi drag something and the ladder slowly slid into the hole. Just before I was ready to jump for it, Amir let loose a volley from his AK-47. The bullets ricocheted off the pacemaker cans and splattered into the dirt. "That is a warning for you, Dayan. Move to the back of the hole. Woman, walk up the ladder."

She burst into tears and ran to me, holding on tightly.

Another burst of bullets hit the ground near us. "If I have to come down to get you, I promise it will end up to be very bad for both of you. *Climb the ladder now!*"

Her hands dropped from me and she turned her face to the top. "I'm coming," she said in a small voice. Then she stepped onto the rungs. Halfway to the top she turned. It was a look of desperation and sadness I'll never forget. A sob broke loose and she almost fell back into the pit. She grabbed the ladder to steady herself, gave me a little wave, barely moving her fingers, and was lost over the top, leaving me feeling empty, like when my family was kidnapped. The last I saw of her was Ghazi binding her arms behind her back and leading her off.

Chapter Sixty-Five

I had to get out. Scaling the top was impossible, so I turned back to my digging. I was sure everyone would be busy preparing for the stoning, and I would be left unwatched. I uncovered the top of the rounded structure quickly and figured it must be a segment of one of the ancient sluices the Nabataeans used to transport water. The clay was old and brittle, held together for twenty-five hundred years by the dirt over it. I took off my shirt, bunched two halves of a pacemaker can together in a wad of clothing, and struck the pipe. The muffled noise drew no attention, so I increased my efforts.

Finally I saw a crack appear, like an egg shell opening. My patience exhausted, I stomped on the clay. The opening widened. Now I jumped with both feet and it broke apart, sending me down five or six feet into a moving stream of water that came up mid-waist. The current was cold and swift. The light from overhead illuminated a big round pipe half-filled with water. The sides were overgrown with a slippery substance, some kind of moss that grew without light. The smell was dank and old, like a damp basement. The flow of the stream seemed to be down toward the center of Petra, which made sense with water collected high on this plateau and distributed to the town below. I shivered, not sure whether it was from the cold water or my claustrophobia. But if Patricia could do it, so could I. I dove in.

I swam with the current and quickly was swept into a turbulent, twisting downward spiral. In less than three minutes the current slowed dramatically, and I could no longer stand or touch the sides of the sluice. Sounds echoed, and I figured I had reached the underground cistern. It had to have stairs to climb in and out, because people would enter to fill water buckets. So I moved to one side and began a circular swim, touching the walls as I went. I got that mossy stuff all over my hands, but after half a minute I hit a protruding object that felt like a stair or rung. I pulled myself up about fifteen steps until I came to the ceiling. I figured there had to be some sort of a release mechanism for the Nabataeans to get out, so I groped around. Finally I touched something like a handle. I wrenched it first one direction and then the other, but it wouldn't budge. I pounded it with my fist to loosen, but it remained stuck. Then I filled my mouth with water from the stream, spit it onto the handle, and pulled at it again. I felt a little give. I sprayed water several more times and yanked. Finally, bracing my feet against the stairs, I strained with all my might, and the handle unlocked with a groan.

I pushed the door open into the small square room of *Al Khazneh*. Maybe that's why it was called the treasury—because it housed the water supply. The crowd of tourists gave a startled, "Oh, my God, what is that? *Who* is that?" and backed away from me. I must have looked like an apparition as I rose dripping wet from the trap door in the floor and ran from the room.

I had to get back to *El Deir* as quickly as possible, but I was sure the steps would be guarded. I doubted they knew I escaped, but if they did, they would be doubly cautious. I had to catch them off guard.

I remembered during our tourist walk passing a shop that sold *chadors*. I found the store, bought a black one, extra large, and draped it over me as I ran to the foot of the nine hundred steps. When I got close I could see Amir and Ghazi chatting with one of the other Bedouins. Two AK-47s were propped against the first stair.

I now moved slowly toward them. I had no idea what state Frankie might be in, so I had to get up those stairs. At least twenty minutes had passed since they took her, but they had to bury her in the ground and wait for Harry to arrive.

I probably looked like a walking black mountain as I kept my head bent and hunched over. They were busy in conversation and didn't notice me until I was almost under their noses.

These guys were in *my* world now. No six inch ledges to worry about.

When I grabbed for the AKs, the *chador* loosened and the hood fell from my face. Amir saw it first and lunged. I sidestepped and chopped the back of his neck as his momentum carried him past me. He went down, but I hadn't hit him hard enough to cause any lasting damage. Ghazi lowered his head and came at me, arms wide, looking like an open-field tackler. I put both fists together and sledge-hammered his skull into my knee. I heard his nose crack, and he folded. The third Bedouin was now running down an alley, no doubt to get help.

Amir was back on his feet with a six-inch knife in his hand. We circled each other, keeping our distance.

"So, American, now you will die by the knife instead of the stone." Amir slashed at me, missing my chest by a fraction and slicing a rent in the *chador*. He handled the knife like a pro, feinting first one direction and then another. I looked for a stick, anything, but the ground was barren.

"Hrayr will not be happy. He has big plans for the stoning with CNN coming in," I said.

The thought struck home and for an instant Amir glanced up the steps. That was all I needed. I yanked the *chador* off my shoulders and threw it at him as he attacked. He swung his knife hand to ward off the cloth and I hit him with a roundhouse right that stove in his left cheek bone. I grabbed his knife and drove the blade deep into his gut, sawing sideways to slice his abdominal aorta. He collapsed to his knees and then fell face down in the dirt.

I ran my hands through their clothes. Amir had my .38 and Ghazi Frankie's .45. Ghazi was starting to regain consciousness. I debated putting a slug in his head but didn't. Instead, I pulled the knife from Amir's belly, and when Ghazi's eyes focused on me, I said, "For my friend, Yoel," and then I cut his throat.

After slinging both AK-47s over my shoulder, I ran up the nine hundred steps. I only hoped I was not too late.

Chapter Sixty-Six

A nine-hundred-step run is agonizing. I know people race each year climbing almost two thousand steps to the top of the Empire State Building in New York City, but in Petra, the stairs were uneven and twisted in, out, and around the mountainside, and the sun was already hot. After a couple of minutes my calves bunched into knots, my breath was raspy and rapid, and my heart rate too fast to count. My body told me to stop and rest while my head said, *Keep going—she may still be alive.*

I won't let her die today!

Finally I reached the last step, wheezing like an asthmatic. It opened onto the plateau in front of *El Deir*. A circle of people stood around a white robed statue, buried to the shoulders in a hole. The sheet was tied with a string at the top like a sack of laundry. But the sheet was clean.

No blood stains—yet!

Harry stood before a pile of stones talking to the crowd. He flipped a large rock up and down in his hand and seemed to be reaching the climax of his speech. He was at least a hundred yards away, but the wind changed and carried his Arabic words to me.

"Our al-Qaeda, which shifts and flows with the times, molded like desert sand under the wind, with Allah's grace is proud to have formed this alliance with Hamas, Hezbollah, and Islamic Jihad," he said as he gestured to groups of people standing together, "for the first time aligning Iraqi and Palestinian interests in Osama bin Laden's declaration of jihad against the United States and its allies."

The crowd cheered and two of them shot guns into the air.

"In five days we will launch a preemptive strike with a nuclear bomb that will destroy the leaders of eight countries and the U.S. financial center."

The crowd went wild. Harry pumped his arms in the air and skipped like a prize fighter winning a title bout. The crowd quieted as he raised his arm overhead to throw the first stone. He took his time and scanned the throng, building up the tension. I ran toward him, but I was still too far away. He hurled the rock, hitting its target. A red stain spread across the top of the sheet. The strike triggered a fusillade of stones.

Frankie's head slumped sideways and twitched twice. She must have lost consciousness. I ran toward her, my screams drowned by the noise of my gun spraying the crowd.

People in the circle ran in all directions, and I kept firing at anything that moved. I quickly nailed the two who had shot guns off. The AK finally jammed, and I threw it away and switched to the second one. Bodies fell, and I didn't care who I shot. There was no resistance, so I assumed most of them were the scientists and workers. The big muscle was probably still at the bottom of the stairs. I remembered the fleeing Arab, and knew I had only a few minutes to get Frankie and move the hell out.

Harry vanished. I didn't know where he went, and at this point I didn't have time to find out.

I ran to Frankie, quickly untied the sheet, and pulled it off her head down to her shoulders. She was unconscious and bleeding a lot from her head wounds. She also had purpling bruises on one cheek and her neck.

The dirt, piled to her shoulders, had actually had protected her from many of the stones. I started scooping it from her body as fast as I could. They had packed her in solid, like a burial. Suddenly a second pair of hands worked alongside mine. "Who the hell are you?" I asked a young man who had come to help. Then I recognized him. Hassan, our guide.

"I came up the back way. I will help you. These are bad people."

Together we lifted her out of the hole, and I pulled off the sheet and untied her hands. I took out the gag so she could breathe more easily, and she opened her eyes! Thank God, she must have only been stunned from a mild concussion.

"Am I dead?" was the first thing she said. "My head hurts."

"Can you walk? We've got to get out of here now."

"If you help me. I'm woozy." She looked about, dazed.

"We need to get to the car. It's in Gabel Abu-Swera, but I don't remember how to get there," I said.

"I do," Hassan said. "I have been here a guide for three years and I know everything about Petra," he said with a proud look. "Follow me."

I saw the first Bedouin head poke up in the distance. "Move it! Now!"

Chapter Sixty-Seven

We ran along the plateau carrying Frankie between us, her feet half-dragging on the ground and her head wounds dripping blood. I pulled a handkerchief from my pocket, put it in her hand, and placed her hand on her head. "Press tight."

Shots behind us were a good incentive to keep up the pace. Hassan guided us along the rim of the canyon to where we had parked the car. It was still hidden behind the dune. I groped for the keys beneath the bumper and couldn't find them. *Shit!* Someone had taken them.

I fell to my knees and searched the bumper. Nothing! Maybe Amir or Ghazi had found the car. Frankie said, "Let me look," the spacey expression now gone

"It won't help. The keys are gone." I could see the first two Bedouins coming closer, and I crouched to make a stand.

Frankie knelt in the sand alongside me. In a couple of seconds she stood and dangled the keys on her finger. "Is this what you're looking for?"

I grabbed them from her and started the motor as bullets hit the sand around us. One went through the back window of the car, exploding the glass. "Hassan, which way to the Sofitel?" I floored the accelerator. Yoel was right about the car.

We tore around the dune, wheels spraying up clouds of sand. Two men stood in the middle of the road aiming their AKs at us. "Get down," I yelled at Frankie and Hassan. I stomped the gas pedal and barreled directly at them. One managed to dive into the sand, narrowly missing my tires. I plowed into the other and bones crunched on the car fender a second before he became airborne. I glanced in the rearview mirror to see one man bending over the still form of the other.

Halfway to the Sofitel, Hassan asked me to let him out. "You saved my life a long time ago after we moved to the U.S. from Nablus."

My Legion of Honor Award!

"We moved back to Palestine after that. I recognized you when you came into the tourist office. I can no longer be a Petra guide and will go back to Nablus. Allah be with you." He ran off.

We arrived at the Sofitel in ten minutes and parked in a far corner of the lot. The car didn't look too good, with a shattered rear window and a dented right front bumper. I couldn't be sure whether we were followed, but I didn't think so. We walked toward the entrance, trying to assume an unhurried pace. I didn't know who was foe or friend, and I wanted to melt in with the crowd. Loud, dissonant music assailed our ears before we reached the veranda, which was crowded with people in the middle of a wedding. The bride and groom sat at a long table surrounded by milling people drinking and eating, all seeming to talk at once. At one end of the veranda eight or ten men sat at a table smoking hookah pipes. One of them saw us and stood.

"Hey, Americans! Over here." It was Dmitry, our masseur. He was waving his arms, and heads turned toward him and then to us, exactly the kind of attention I wanted to avoid. Frankie's head had stopped bleeding, but her face and shirt were covered with blood and dirt. I didn't look much better.

I told her to stand still and I walked over to say hello. One of the men at the table, a big guy about my size, stood as we approached. "Americans." He spit on my shoes. "What you are doing at a Jordanian wedding? We do not want you to be here. Go home where you belong!"

This was what Yoel had warned us about. The guy was high on hashish, ready for a fight. He stood chest-to-chest with me, eyes locked with mine, breathing garlic in my face. He looked over at Frankie and his eyes narrowed. "Can you fight a man as good as you beat up a woman?"

I had to extinguish this quickly and quietly. I reached down, seized his nuts, and squeezed—*hard*. His face blanched, and his eyes bulged. He stood there open mouthed, arms glued to his sides and knees buckling. Squeezing even harder, I used my other hand to gently push him in the chest toward his chair, sat him down, and slowly released my grip. He sat with a vacant look, ashen and sweaty.

The table grew quiet until Dmitry spoke. "These are nice people, nice Americans. I could tell when I massaged them." He sucked on his hookah.

"Bye, Dmitry. Good to see you again." I tipped my head at him, and we entered the hotel.

The guy behind the concierge desk recognized us. "Another room for the night?" He stared at Frankie. "A doctor, maybe?"

"Not this time. Where is Harry Scarpia?"

"Who?"

"You heard me. Or maybe you know him as Hrayr Najar."

"I do not know him."

I reached across the counter and grabbed the guy's shirt. "Look, my friend, this can be easy or it can be hard. You choose. The man is a terrorist, and you have been letting him stay in your hotel. He sent the Dom Perignon you brought to my room last night. I don't know what he's paid you, but it won't be enough to keep your ass out of jail once I tell your government what you've done. Now where is he?"

The guy paled and became quite verbal. "Presidential suite. He ran in here ten minutes before. He said he had to get some papers and a computer from his room and then was checking out."

"I'm going to talk with him. You won't be calling to let him know I'm on the way, now will you?"

He shook his head with enough force that I believed him.

"Which way?" He told me and we sped off.

Presidential Suite, printed in gold letters, identified the room. I looked at the door. Not too substantial, and it opened *in* on the room. Both good. A hard shoulder would do it if he didn't have the security chain on. And I'd bet he was in such a hurry packing that it wouldn't be.

I whispered to Frankie as I removed the .38 from my pocket and handed her the .45. "Wait outside."

"You've got to be joking. After what he's done to me?" She rubbed her head.

"Then follow behind me."

I backed up and ran into the door, throwing my shoulder against the thin wood. It splintered with a crunch, and we almost fell into the sitting room of the suite. Harry was standing in the next room, a bedroom, bare-chested and in boxer shorts. Some sort of uniform with a lot of gold was laid out neatly on the bed, shined boots waiting on the floor.

His .357 Magnum revolver sat on a table near us in the sitting room. *Big mistake.* A calm look replaced his startled expression.

"My, my. Look who's escaped. Don't shoot. As you can see, I am unarmed." He put his hands high over his head and walked slowly toward us, a slight smile on his face.

"Stay in the bedroom, Harry. Down on the floor. Now!" I commanded.

He stopped, turned, and reached for the uniform. "Harry, you do that and you're dead," I said.

He moved back to face me. "I have no weapon," he said. He kept walking, hands over his head, the smile frozen in place.

"Stop, Harry, now! *Get down on the floor!*"

As he reached the transom between the bedroom and the sitting room, his hands jerked upward in a lightning move and he grabbed a gun concealed overhead. Two blasts echoed in rapid succession, and I felt the sting of a bullet ripping my bicep. Harry's smile transformed into a frown, and then he bit his lower lip as a bright red stain widened in the middle of his chest. He tried to say something, but the words wouldn't come, and he crumpled to the floor.

I looked at Frankie, both hands gripping the .45 in front of her, the barrel still smoking.

"I was a dead man," I said, clutching my bleeding arm. "I didn't even have time to get my finger on the trigger."

She nodded. "I've been here before."

"When?"

"FBI tryouts. A while ago."

"How did it go?"

"I flunked."

"Not this time."

Chapter Sixty-Eight

We sat in Jake Hertzog's cramped office the next morning sipping tea. My arm was in a sling, but it was unbroken. The bullet had gone straight through the muscle, and the sutures would come out in two weeks. Frankie's head had two silver dollar-sized shaved spots covered by five butterfly adhesive strips. She sported a black-and-blue shiner in her left eye and two Band-Aids on her neck.

"Close call," Jake said.

"Frankie saved my life. We're so sorry about Yoel. He was a brave man."

"Yes, he was. We pulled his body from the canyon. I visited his wife late last night. That's the hardest part of this job."

"Mine, too," I said. Frankie had tears in her eyes.

"So, your guys cleaned them out?" I asked.

"As soon as I got your phone call, and with the help of Jordanian helicopters. This was a joint effort. *El Deir* will reopen in several weeks to a month. The nuclear bomb was this close," he held thumb and forefinger a fraction apart, "from being finished and transported to the U.S. We found Harry's computer with all the information about him, the Black Widows, and their plans. They were going to smuggle the bomb into the U.S. through a drug tunnel connecting Tijuana and San Diego and then truck it to New York. His computer had all the e-mail traffic about the next meeting of the G8."

"That's the—" I started to say, but Jake interrupted.

"Group of Seven and Russia. The annual meeting of the heads of the eight major free-world governments was scheduled for the New York Stock Exchange, at 11 Wall Street. The United States was hosting the meeting this year, and planned to hold it there to show they were the financial leaders of the world. Bad choice, because the building itself was very porous and couldn't be adequately protected. The Black Widows obviously knew all this. Your FBI has already arrested the building supervisor, a Muslim collaborating with them."

"Oh, my God," Frankie said. "They were going to wipe out all those leaders at one time."

"Yes, and they were very close to succeeding. By the way, your friend McBride called to say congratulations."

I smiled. "Nice."

"He also said Frankie should apply to be an FBI agent, and you would know what that meant."

Frankie looked at me and we grinned. I said to Jake, "What now?"

Jake sighed. "Now we wait for the next lunatic to surface and be prepared to handle whatever shit comes down. Like I said, it's always the good guys against the bad, the same cycles of build and destroy—job security for both sides forever."

"Pretty depressing," I said.

"Reality often is. And it will remain that way until someone, somewhere, with enough charisma and creativity comes along to produce a major paradigm shift for mankind."

"A messiah to change the world?"

"Call it what you like, Zach. But, yeah, that two-thousand-year-old concept may still be our best chance to save man from himself."

THE END